THE GLASS TOWER

THE GLASS TOWER

J.B. HUGHES

Cerebral Books
Registered in Switzerland
cerebral.books@bluewin.ch
www.glass-tower.com

ISBN 978 0956862 006

British Library Cataloguing in Publication Data.
A catalogue record for this book is available from the British Library.

Typeset in 11pt Aldine401 BT Roman by Troubador Publishing Ltd, Leicester, UK

Printed and bound in the UK by TJ International, Padstow, Cornwall

For Greta and Anja

CONTENTS

CHAPTER 1

Sino

Sino walked along the wall, staring out of the windows. Actually, he was staring out of the walls, because the building was made of glass. On one side, the tatty towers of Kowloon stretched into the distance; on the other, boats and ferries cut their way through the grey-blue water of Hong Kong harbour. In the middle was Hong Kong Island itself – a beach of skyscrapers framed by tree-topped hills. It was an impressive view. It was what the rest of China was starting to look like.

Sino was in no hurry to sit down. He liked to sit in the front row, and the front row was always the last to fill up. He usually waited until there were almost no seats left before taking his. That way, no-one would know whether he was sitting in the front row because he wanted to or because he had to.

Sino had been looking forward to this meeting. He wanted to see the CEO in the flesh, to size him up, to get the measure of a man who commanded a company of this size. He liked to see things in real life; it helped him to imagine himself in those roles and situations. It was something he'd been told to do as a boy, by his grandfather.

"To make something possible, you must first imagine it in your mind," the old man had told Sino repeatedly throughout his childhood. "You must imagine it over and over until you can experience it with all your senses; until the experience becomes so natural and normal that it cannot but become real."

For years, Sino hadn't believed it. How could you imagine something into existence? Until the day he imagined himself falling. All he had to do was walk along a wall; a narrow wall. The other boys had already done it. They were waiting for him on the other side. But when he put out his foot to take his first step, he suddenly saw himself falling; saw himself losing his footing and crashing to the ground. The image was so powerful that he was unable to move. He stood there for a long time, trying to conjure up a different picture in his mind, one of him crossing the wall safely. But the image just wouldn't materialise. All he could see was himself falling. In the end, he'd crawled along the wall on his hands and knees – and still fallen off!

"What did you expect!" his grandfather exclaimed, when he told the old man about it. "You imagined you would fall. You succeeded in falling!"

Sino found his seat. He wasn't sure he wanted to be the CEO of a big company like this one. But he was determined to be able to imagine it.

There was a dull hum in the room from the rows behind him. In the front row, no-one was saying anything. They were all looking at the CEO, who had just arrived. He was standing near a screen in the front of the room with a woman who was doing something on a laptop.

Sino looked around, wondering why the others were there. He'd met a few of them, but not that guy in the back row. He stuck out. He was black, for a start, and he was sitting as far away from the front as it was possible to be. Also, he was wearing a jacket and trousers rather than a suit. Sino supposed he must be good at something, otherwise he wouldn't be here. But he looked out of place. Everyone wore suits – dark suits – to this kind of meeting.

The people in the room were the newest batch of 'potentials' to have joined the company's leadership programme. Most of them were around 30. This trip was the start of a rigorous, managed career path of three years that would have them work in at least two countries and expose them to the main areas of the business.

The CEO moved into position in front of them, his hands behind his back. The core of the building, with the lifts and presumably the stairs, was behind him. The room was vast, taking up the entire side of the 87th floor. There must have been 50 people present. The CEO was looking across all of them but Sino knew that once he got started, he would be more focused on those in the front. That was always what happened.

The CEO seemed very relaxed, as if he had all the time in the world. He was smiling and his body language was very friendly. Most of him was visible to everyone. He greeted the potentials warmly and introduced himself as 'Chris' – as if they didn't know who he was. Then he fell silent, and surveyed the room. The potentials stared back. The CEO smiled cryptically but still said nothing. As the seconds ticked by, the relaxed atmosphere started to dissipate. A few people chuckled nervously. Everyone, including Sino, was wondering what was going to happen next.

The CEO lifted his arms into the air and allowed them to fall to his sides. It was a highly exaggerated gesture, one you couldn't fail to notice. Then he shook his arms a little, as if to get the blood flowing.

Sino watched the man as he watched them. He was now turning his head from side to side, like a spectator at a tennis match. He kept it up until everyone was following his eyes, until he could control exactly what everyone was looking at simply by looking at it himself. Suddenly, abruptly, the man looked down at his right hand, which was lying limply at his side. Instantly, every eye in the room followed his. Then he flipped the hand upwards so it was at a right angle to his body, about as high as his waist.

"This is the level of good," he said, waving the hand slightly, and looking down at it affectionately as if it was a dog at his side. "This is good." His eyes crossed the audience. He took his time, making sure his gaze took in everyone.

"'Good' is no good," he said, shaking his head. The expression on his face started to change, as if a nasty taste was appearing in his mouth. "Good is lousy."

The CEO took a few steps forward. The chairs were arranged in a giant horseshoe, so he was now standing almost among those in the front. His arms were still at his sides. Suddenly, he lifted his right arm and brought his hand to the height of his eyes in a horizontal salute.

"This is excellent!" he exclaimed.

He smiled and, pulling an expressive face, pointed near his hip – where 'good' had been – and his hovering hand, where 'excellent' was.

He paused and considered his hovering hand for a second. "'Excellent' is good," he nodded approvingly. "Excellent is okay. There's nothing wrong with excellent!" As he spoke, his eyebrows were moving up and down and he had a slightly silly grin on his face.

The CEO took a step back. "Today, pretty much everyone is excellent. Excellent is normal. Excellent is the standard."

He slowly lifted his right hand a few inches higher, until it was just out of his field of vision, about as high as the top of his head. He swayed it back and forth gently. "This is outstanding," he said, in a loud whisper. He stared hard at them, his eyes moving from one person to the next. There was total silence.

The CEO looked up at his hand. "You'll have noticed that the difference between excellent and outstanding is rather small." He suddenly cupped his hand so that his thumb and fingers were less than an inch apart. "That's the difference," he said, stretching out his arm and moving his clawed hand slowly across their field of vision. "It's small."

As he spoke, he started opening and closing his hand, like a ventriloquist manipulating a hand puppet.

"Sometimes it's tiny," he went on. "Sometimes it's imperceptible. Sometimes you need help to see it."

He paused, and then in a loud voice: "But it's there. It's real. It's what counts!"

The CEO turned away and left the horseshoe. Now he was in front of them, pacing in a slightly distracted manner, his hands behind his back. "Every tennis player you'll see at Wimbledon is excellent," he said, lifting his right hand and pointing his index finger at the ceiling. He stopped and turned back to them. "But only one in a decade is outstanding!"

Pacing again and alternating his glance between his audience and nothing in particular, he went on: "In an Olympic sprint, the difference between excellent and outstanding can be a…" – he paused very briefly and then over-emphasised the next word – "millisecond!"

His voice dropped again. "That's all that separates gold and silver: a millisecond! Sometimes we can't see the difference.

Sometimes we need a camera to reveal it. But there is a difference – and that difference is the most important thing in the world. It's the difference between coming first and coming nowhere; between a new world record – a moment that changes history – and just another race."

He spun around and stared piercingly at them. "This is not about winning," he declared. "It's very important that you understand that – I'm not talking about winning."

He shrugged. "What is winning anyway?"

He stopped. It hadn't sounded like a real question, but no-one was entirely sure.

Suddenly, he was back in the middle of the horseshoe, turning as he spoke. "Some of you might have come to hear about winning. Some of you might be surprised that I'm not talking about winning."

When he said the word 'winning', his tone was haughty and contemptuous, as if winning was something sordid; something you did with a prostitute. The fact that he was English with a public-school accent heightened the effect.

"Don't get me wrong," the CEO continued. "There's nothing wrong with winning. There's enough room and profit in the market, if you're excellent. We don't need to be outstanding to take home our bonuses. If we're excellent, we might even get lucky and come first occasionally. We might even take gold..." – he paused in mid-sentence and slowed down his delivery – "...provided no-one else is outstanding."

The CEO walked back to the front of the room, talking to his audience over his shoulder. "Excellent is what delivers success. Excellent is what makes you rich and powerful and admired. Excellent is great!"

He turned to face them. "Excellent is enough. Isn't it?"

This seemed to be a real question. They all knew the answer. It was obvious: excellent wasn't enough. The CEO had said it wasn't. But you couldn't simply agree with him. If you were going to comment, you had to know why it wasn't enough, and the only thing you could be sure of was that it didn't have anything to do with winning.

"Don't feel you have to say it isn't," the CEO said, waving a dismissive hand at them. "Excellent can be more than enough. Excellent is good. Excellent is fine. Excellent is what the world expects of you. Excellent will get you your bonus."

No-one said a word.

The CEO looked them over in a slightly disapproving manner. "I don't think excellent is enough," he said slowly, shaking his head. His face took on an appealing smugness. "If I did, I wouldn't be here!"

He looked expectantly around the room. This was an important question to be able to answer. How could you be on the fast-track to leadership greatness if you didn't know why it was important to be outstanding?

Some people shuffled in their seats. Speaking out was risky; there was no cover here. A few braced themselves. If no-one said anything, the whole group would look stupid. If no-one said anything, someone might be singled out to give an answer.

The CEO looked around. After a few seconds, his eyes settled on Sino. Sino stared back, a respectful look on his face. He had no intention of trying to answer the question. He'd learned at business school that there was no point in trying to answer these types of questions. They were asked only to engage the audience. Most of the time you got the answer wrong – or at least not quite right – and even if you got it right, there was no reward for doing so.

The CEO looked around again. "No ideas?" he said. He sounded disappointed, as if he might afterwards go back to his office and cross their names off a list.

"Because we want to be the best?" ventured a brave soul from somewhere at the back.

The CEO's head spun in the direction of the voice. "You want to be the best?" The question shot out like friendly artillery fire.

"Yes," the brave one nodded, eagerly.

The CEO smiled at him. "Why?"

The brave one hesitated, swallowed, and then took a chance: "What else is there?"

"There's excellent," said the CEO, in a surprised voice. "What's wrong with excellent?"

"Everyone is excellent," the brave one tried again. But he'd blown it. The CEO moved on.

"Why do we want to be outstanding?" he demanded. But now no-one dared risk an answer.

The CEO stepped back out of the horseshoe and his tone turned rhetorical. "Let's go back to winning. What is winning?"

This obviously wasn't a real question. People started to relax. "Winning is how you find out who's the best!" the CEO continued. "Or am I wrong?"

Of course he wasn't wrong. He couldn't be wrong.

As he spoke, he smiled engagingly and held out his hands in an inviting manner. "And how do you win?"

This question, too, was obviously rhetorical. His tone was slightly patronising. But that was fair enough. They hadn't been able to answer the first one. Some people leaned back in their seats.

"You win by learning how the game works," the CEO went on, "by understanding the rules, by mastering it so you can play it better than anyone else!"

The CEO looked around expectantly. "So far, so clear?" he asked, still smiling.

Some people nodded.

The CEO stared hard at all of them. Suddenly, his smile disappeared. "The world has changed," he said slowly.

Now his tone was deadly earnest. His face bore not a trace of the mirth or the amicableness of earlier.

"The world has changed," he repeated, almost pausing between each word.

His audience began to sit up straight. Things were getting serious again.

"You're all young," said the CEO, who couldn't have been more than 45 himself. "You're young, but even for you this world is not the one you grew up in. Things are changing fast – very fast."

He was speaking slowly and clearly, moving his head from side to side to take everyone in. "Maybe you haven't noticed. Maybe it still seems the same – but it's not. What you are hearing are echoes, what you are seeing is a picture – once bright and clear – that has left an imprint on the lenses of your eyes."

He paused and looked around. "What I'm saying is: what you see is no longer there."

The CEO took a step back. He was still in the horseshoe, but only just. "Today there are no rules; nothing is clear. The future is an embryo. It is forming, taking shape. But no-one knows what it will look like or who it will belong to."

The CEO started to walk around the outer ring of chairs. It was the first time he'd gone behind them; the first time they'd not been able to see him.

"What you have to do today is more difficult than it has ever been," he said solemnly. "The leaders who came before you only had to win. They had a rule book and they were playing the same game their fathers played. In that world, it was good enough to be good. If you were excellent, you were special."

He was walking slowly. He was passing by so closely to those in the back row that he was almost touching some of them. Some of the potentials were keeping their eyes on him, even if it meant craning their necks or moving their bodies. Others were simply staring ahead, waiting for him to reappear in their line of sight. Some were holding their breath as he passed by.

"In the past, you could win by working harder, or by breaking the odd rule," he continued. "In the past, you could get ahead by cutting costs. You could win by focusing on your core business, by moving your production from expensive Europe to cheap China."

Now he was back in front of them, standing squarely between the two jaws of the horseshoe. "Today, all that is irrelevant!" he barked. He looked serious and a little angry, as if he might become threatening again.

The CEO lifted his head and stared at them with a sneer on his face. His voice was full of contempt. "Ask anyone and they'll tell you: it's all about winning, finding new markets and efficiencies, cutting waste."

He looked disgusted. "Don't kid yourselves. We've always had to do those things. There's always been waste to cut, efficiencies to be made. Don't be fooled. That isn't going to make the difference."

The CEO moved back into the middle of the horseshoe. "Why am I telling you this?"

Everyone was looking at him now; some had to lean slightly to one side; others tilted their heads to see him. Sino stared straight ahead; the CEO was standing directly in front of him.

"At the moment," the CEO said, "the future is writing itself. We're all so busy, so preoccupied, so bogged down with day-to-day stuff that we're not noticing the future arrive. It's here!"

The CEO stared at them with wide eyes: "The future is here." His lower lip was protruding slightly.

It seemed safe to relax again. Some of the potentials were already thinking about who to talk to at lunch.

"Can any of you see it?" the CEO asked. The question came out quietly, almost casually. But there was an unmistakable note of menace in his voice.

The potentials shuffled in their seats, hoping it might not be a real question.

"Well, can you?" the CEO asked.

This was definitely a real question – a question that should be answered, and answered in the resounding affirmative. But what would you say after that?

The CEO's eyes passed over the rows of people present. "No-one sees it?" His tone was one of disbelief. He was daring them to say nothing.

The potentials looked around. You had to have an answer. How could you be a leader, if you didn't have an answer? You weren't allowed to be in this room if you didn't have an answer. There was nothing for it. Someone was going to have to take a chance. Otherwise, they'd all be exposed as stowaways.

"I see it," said an American voice on the right.

"I see it," said another voice, of unclear origin.

A third, too, declared that he could see it.

More murmurs followed. Suddenly, the room was full of clairvoyants. Sino said nothing.

The CEO allowed his earnest face to soften; he turned in the direction of the first speaker.

"You see it?"

The speaker nodded. He looked like a man urgently needing to swallow.

The CEO waited. He had a wicked look in his eyes. "If you see it...," he paused, "...if you really see it – well, then, you might – just might – have the makings of a leader."

The American relaxed, exhaling happily.

The CEO glanced at his watch. "Excellent is what we call people and companies that have mastered the present..." – he paused and looked impatiently at his audience – "Outstanding is what we call those who have mastered the future."

The CEO moved to the front of the room and nodded at the woman who had been standing near the laptop throughout.

She activated the slide projector and the faces of several famous people appeared on the screen. The CEO picked up a pointer and, with a click of a button, stabbed a red dot of light at the screen. It landed on the forehead of Charles Darwin.

He turned back to his audience. "The world we are living in was invented by people like this; people who saw what nobody else saw."

He moved the pointer, mentioning names as he skipped across the faces of Einstein, Gandhi, someone nobody recognised, Bill Gates and the founders of Google.

"These people, in the past, invented what we call the present."

The pointer moved to the last image. Depicted was a silhouette – an outline of a head. It looked like a man's head.

The CEO looked at his audience. "Could that be you?"

Then he said goodbye and was gone.

Sino lingered in the room until most of the others had left. It was more comfortable waiting up here in the air-conditioned offices than it would be in the heat below. Anyway, there was no hurry – they had to descend scores of floors and find the bus. It would take a long time. The bus driver would wait. He had to wait.

The CEO's speech had been a disappointment. Sino had been expecting him to talk about the company's strategy and its future plans. But it had all been waffle, like the flowery sermons he'd had to listen to at business school. He shouldn't have expected anything else. For some reason, westerners could never admit that they were in it for the money. It always had to be about something else; something big and important, something with a moral purpose.

Once he'd been taken in, but not anymore. After years of being lied to in London, he was impervious to the bullshit.

Going down, Sino was surprised to end up in the same lift as the CEO. The man had left so quickly. He must have been in the men's room.

"Did you understand what I was telling you?" the CEO asked.

Sino nodded, along with the rest of the potentials who were there. The CEO started going on again. Sino glanced around the lift. The others were all listening intently, or at least pretending to.

Sino surreptitiously examined the man as they descended. He was the most powerful, influential person Sino had ever wittingly shared a lift with. Yet up close, he was remarkably unremarkable. Even with his height – he was almost a head taller than Sino – you could quite easily have forgotten that he was there. At this distance, he seemed as bland as cold water.

The lift came to a halt; it was the end of the line. They all got out. When the express shuttle arrived to take them to the ground floor, everyone stood back for the CEO.

He didn't move. "I need to get out first," he said, jovially.

The potentials scuttled into the lift. Sino stayed near the man, trying to salvage at least an impression of who he was. He was exceedingly difficult to read. He'd started his talk on the 87th floor as an approachable, friendly fellow. Then he'd been threatening and coercive, and after that wise and aloof. Now he was their friend again. It was all rather unconvincing. Sino had met plenty of westerners who had masks for every occasion, but they tended to be young and ambitious, willing to be anything they needed to be to get what they wanted. Surely this man could be himself. He was in charge. He was the boss. He didn't need to please anyone.

The lift arrived on the ground. The CEO shook a few hands and was gone. Sino and the other potentials boarded the bus. Next stop was lunch, somewhere on Hong Kong Island.

Sino stared out of the window. In the beginning, he'd been delighted – even honoured – to be invited to join the company's leadership programme. But the honour had been short-lived. As was usually the case with westerners, the problems started almost as soon as the handshakes were over.

"We have a problem," the HR manager told him, a few days after the agreement was signed. "You don't fulfil the qualification criteria."

The man's tone had been unmistakable. It was all Sino's fault. But how was he supposed to have known you needed a master's degree to join the programme?

"Didn't you check the criteria?" the HR manager said.

Sino looked at the floor. Of course he hadn't checked. Why would he have checked? They'd invited him to join. The HR manager had put the papers in front of him and showed him where to sign. He must have known Sino didn't have a master's degree. It was his job to know; he had everyone's CV.

Sino wondered whether the company was pulling a fast one to get more Chinese employees on to the programme. Or maybe the manager simply had a quota to meet. Maybe his bonus depended on it.

Whatever the reason, the man had been very helpful in finding a solution. The company would send Sino on a master's course. "That will solve your problem, and give you the theoretical grounding you need to make a career with us." As the HR manager spoke, Sino remembered him smiling and shaking his fist enthusiastically.

So Sino had picked up the pen to sign agreement number two. And, surprise, surprise, there'd been another little detail: the candidate had to pay a quarter of the cost of the course. Sino quickly calculated that this would use up all of his savings. Yes, it was a lot of money, the HR manager agreed. But the company would pay the lion's share, and it was important that Sino contribute. It was a demonstration of their shared commitment – their joint investment in his future.

"If you're committed, we're willing to invest in you," the HR manager nodded earnestly.

Sino remembered nodding back. In those days, he hadn't yet started to hate the man's guts.

"We're right behind you," the HR manager added. "And don't worry that you're a little older than the average candidate. We don't need to mention that."

The company would also 'support' Sino while he was studying

and working, the HR manager assured him. When his holiday leave was used up, the company would give him additional time off – on full pay – to attend the remaining classroom lessons that were part of the course.

"People are our greatest assets," the HR manager insisted. He knew those words could sound hollow because all companies said them. But here it was different. Here, it was understood that people really were the only long-term, sustainable source of value. "Our employees are our ambassadors," the manager said. It could not be stressed enough how important the people were.

After graduating, Sino would be expected to stay with the company for five years. That was normal; all companies had such policies. It was how they protected their investment. All it meant was that if Sino left before the five years were up, he would have to refund a diminishing part of the company's contribution. But the leadership programme lasted three years. It wasn't going to be an issue.

In the interests of fairness, Sino wouldn't officially be on the leadership programme until after he had graduated. But that was a matter of form rather than substance, because he could already start his first assignment while studying. Sino's boss was fully behind him – as were the rest of the management. He had an amazing career ahead of him.

Sino stared out the window of the bus. From the moment he'd started the master's course, he'd been doing his best not to feel taken advantage of.

"They're doing you a favour," a colleague told him. "If you want a future at this company, you have to be on the leadership programme. If you're not, you're not on the radar. It's as simple as that."

Sino knew the guy was right, but still he couldn't help feeling that the company owed him something – something for the 72 weekends, the 504 evenings, and the every waking hour that he had spent immersed in those books for 18 long months. He tried not to think about it. The important thing was that he had qualified and that he was finally ready to join the leadership programme. He'd been at the company for almost four years.

All the other potentials in the bus were newcomers. This trip was their induction programme. Sino was attending it years too late.

But that he could accept, almost; he hadn't had the qualifications.

What was really bugging him was the fact that the leadership programme had turned out to be open to anyone who'd been within eavesdropping distance of a master's course. Some people said they'd been pressured into joining. From the conversations in the office kitchen, one had the impression that HR people were prowling around the firm, press-ganging people into signing up.

Maybe that was why turnover on the programme was constant – why small, steady streams of potentials were regularly being dumped or dropping out. It was seldom clear why people left, because most of them also left the company immediately. Sino knew only two people who had dropped out of the programme and were still at the company. Both were women. They wanted children and, despite what the HR manager always said, the leadership programme could not in reality be combined with motherhood. At least there was no shame for them – it had been their decision. But the rule was clear. They'd blown it and would never be allowed back. Dimitri, the Russian, called it the 'American passport policy'. Sino had heard it whispered that the women were unreliable; slaves of their hormones. How could you be a leader if you couldn't control your hormones?

In truth, Sino had only joined the programme because he thought it would help him get home to China. After all those years in London, he was desperate to get home. Initially, he'd supposed it would be fairly easy – after all, he was Chinese, the company made most of its products in China and every western firm with operations there seemed to be desperate for people who understood the culture well enough to avoid being robbed or conned.

Sino's problem now was that he was supposed to go and work somewhere else – in some other country – before settling down, which made China seem even further away than before.

"It's just a matter of time," the HR manager had told him, when he'd mentioned relocating to China. But time was one thing Sino didn't have. The company thought he was 33, but actually he was 37, having knocked a few years off his age when he first arrived in London. Time was running out.

He had worked so hard to get here; it would be stupid to leave the company now. Going back to China without a job would mean starting from scratch and being hired on a local salary. Where would he be in five years if he left now?

But if he stayed at the company, where would he be going next? Virtually all the potentials Sino knew had been transferred to places where the company couldn't recruit people on the ground, and couldn't persuade a grown-up to go to. There was no shortage of these shitholes because the company's strategy was to have a presence everywhere.

"It gives them a head start as soon as the bullets stop flying," the Russian, Dimitri, used to say, before he finally told the HR manager to go to hell and went home to Moscow.

Matthew, an English colleague, had accepted a job in the Caracas office. Sino had pretended to be pleased for him and had even acted as if he was a little envious. There were plenty of openings in Africa. The HR manager had suggested Sino try the branch in Luanda, which was in Angola. "Lots of Chinese in Africa," the man had nodded enthusiastically.

Sino had almost walked out then and there, but if he left now, he'd have to pay back the rest of the course fees. He would be wiped out and in debt, and he'd have to turn to his family to help him start again in China. He would have failed his parents, who had spent everything they had to send him abroad to study. Sino kicked the seat in front of him. He should have gone back to China after he'd got his bachelor's degree all those years ago.

Sino knew he would succeed; he'd never had any reason to doubt himself, but he had underestimated how long it would take. Things always seemed to take so much longer than you expected. He wanted to get home and start his own business. He wanted to marry X'in and start a family. He hadn't seen X'in in years. He could picture her, with her long eyelashes and her pointy little nose. She'd been besotted with him. He'd only realised that he was in love with her once he left the village.

Why was it so difficult to get home? Why did everything have to be so difficult? He didn't know how much longer he could stand this.

CHAPTER 2

Gideon

Gideon was relieved it was over. He'd spent the whole meeting feeling uncomfortable. Why had he worn that jacket today of all days? He'd heard comments whispered about what he was wearing on the way in. He knew he should have worn a suit. It was Rosemary's fault; she'd told him how great he looked in that jacket. Why had he listened to her? She didn't have a clue what he should be wearing at work.

Gideon walked out of the meeting, listening to the mutterings around him. The CEO's speech had evidently gone down well. He wasn't surprised; the whites always made out that what they were doing was the most important thing in the world. Well, at least the speech had been more entertaining that the usual coma-inducing presentations that they tortured you with at this company. Gideon wondered if any of these suited sycophants believed a word the CEO had said. He supposed so; the company wouldn't be spending all that money if the indoctrination process didn't work.

You couldn't say things like that aloud, of course. Suggesting anything of the sort would either be met with total incomprehension or turn your name into shit. Gideon hadn't been at the company long, but long enough to know that they were scared of cynicism. Here, cynicism was like HIV – you did your best not to let it infect you, and if it did, you kept quiet about it. Gideon had been a cynic for as long as he could remember. How could you not be, working in a cash dispenser for fat, white bastards in America and Europe?

The screen in the lift lobby told Gideon to go to lift B. He joined a small group of potentials waiting to go down. He recognised some of them, but no-one made eye contact. That was nothing new. The few Asians he had encountered ignored him, and the whites were either overly friendly or avoided him.

Gideon didn't mind. He didn't want to talk to them anyway. He hadn't wanted to come to Hong Kong for this stupid conference; he knew he wasn't going to last at the company. He'd been working here for nine months and had hated every minute of it. He was only on the stupid career programme because of Rosemary – he only had the job because of Rosemary. He was pretty sure she couldn't care less if he stuck it out or not. But Sam cared. He was determined to turn Gideon into a robot, just like the rest of his pathetic employees. Catherine cared, too, but probably not that much.

Gideon wanted his old life back. Johannesburg might be a shambles but it was better than London or Hong Kong. At least Hong Kong was warm. But the people were distant and completely inscrutable. He wished he hadn't come. He still had days to go.

The lift arrived. It was full, but not crowded – the machine was evidently programmed to limit the numbers. But some floors down, when someone got out, lots of Chinese people suddenly flooded in. They probably weren't supposed to be using this lift; it seemed to be reserved for company employees. Suddenly, the potentials were being buffeted about in a sea of chattering Chinese. They seemed to be tourists. The whites were unhappy. Gideon wasn't surprised; whites were funny about space. They couldn't handle being too close to people – it made them panicky. Sometimes, when he felt like being nasty, Gideon would get too close to a white, just to make them uncomfortable.

Space had never been a problem for Gideon – he'd never had any of his own. But the whites were obsessed with it. They always had to keep everyone at arm's length. Gideon didn't know why they bothered, especially in London, which was one of the most crowded places he had ever seen. What was the point in worrying about it? His colleagues were continually trying to find bigger houses, and wanting bigger offices. Many lived in the country, in the middle of nowhere with huge tracts of space around them, and then spent hours every day sitting on crowded trains, commuting into crowded London. Gideon didn't mind the crowds. It was the weather he couldn't stand.

He was desperate to get out of London. He'd thought the

homesickness would wear off – or at least gradually lessen – and that he'd get used to the place. But the longer he was there, the more he yearned to leave. He liked some of the people; he'd even made a few friends. Occasionally, he even liked being there – the West End on a nice day was okay. The English could be racist, but they weren't as bad as the South Africans. It was the work he hated. God, he hated the work. He couldn't understand how people could spend every day of their lives doing such boring, meaningless shit.

The lift reached its lowest floor. Now they had to change. The Chinese tourists spilled out, literally dragging the rest of the occupants with them. The whites dusted themselves off, looking relieved and angry at the same time. The Chinese had already moved away, still chattering, still too close together.

On the ground, the bus was waiting to take the potentials to lunch. They had a full programme ahead – the afternoon and evening were fully booked, then it would be a short night before an early flight to Shanghai tomorrow.

At first, the idea of a trip to China had appealed to Gideon – everyone was always going on about how China was going to take over the world – but he should have realised it wasn't going to be any fun. Nothing to do with the company was ever fun. It was always just rush, rush, rush. The whole thing was ridiculous. Gideon opened his briefcase – another present from Rosemary – and took out the only thing in it: the itinerary. This pathetic piece of paper was ruling his life. That was what happened when you worked for white people. Everything was written down on little pieces of paper. God forbid you forgot something, changed your mind, or weren't able to do something – some white bastard was always there to pull out the paper and shove it into your face. Of course, it was fine for them to change the rules – then the paper suddenly became unimportant, a case of: "we have to be flexible".

Gideon looked at the paper for the hundredth time. In Shanghai, they had another packed day to look forward to, then another short night, before flying on to Beijing. The flight was at the crack of dawn. All the flights were at the crack of dawn. It was ridiculous. What was the point? After Beijing, they would be up again at sunrise to drive to a place called Tianjin. It was on the coast apparently, just like Hong Kong, but Gideon had a feeling they wouldn't be going to the beach. Finally, it would be back to Beijing for the return flight to Hong Kong. From there, they'd board a plane in the middle of the night for a 13-hour flight to London. Gideon was already exhausted. He hadn't slept a wink last night because of the time difference and he had no idea how he was going to get through the next few days. The whole thing was absolutely ridiculous.

He stared out the window of the bus. The person in the seat next to him was droning on to someone else across the aisle. The bus descended underground, under the water, back to Hong Kong Island. Hong Kong was strange – just tall buildings and the water. Gideon would have liked to go for a walk, just to get some air. He hadn't been outside since leaving London yesterday – or was it the day before? They were always rushing. Why did they have to cram so much in? What was the point? Everything was just a blur.

They came out of the tunnel. The traffic was heavy but moving. Gideon felt like a cigarette. There was a woman at the front of the bus explaining things. He had tried to listen at the beginning but had quickly given up; it was difficult to understand her accent and the sound was bad.

He suddenly missed Rosemary. This was a lonely trip. Hardly anyone talked to him and when someone did, that person moved away fairly quickly. Gideon assumed he must be saying the wrong things, but the conversations seemed to him completely normal. He was obviously missing something.

At lunch it was the same. He seemed to be the only person who didn't know anyone. Gideon walked up to a table and asked if the seat was free. He didn't get an answer, but no-one objected, so he sat down. All around him, people seemed to be engrossed in fascinating conversations. A Chinese-looking man, sitting on the other side of the woman next to Gideon, suddenly started talking to him. His name was David and he was from Hong Kong. Gideon decided to say as little as possible in case he said something wrong, so he just pretended he was interested. David obviously thought he was. He talked at Gideon the whole way through the first course over the woman between them. Gideon tried to pull her into the monologue a few times but she just smiled weakly at him. It was the most boring experience he could remember, all about how clever David was. Then – thank God – someone opposite recklessly said something to David. He never said another word to Gideon.

The woman was from Slovakia. She was tiny, plump and until then had not said a word. She turned out to be as loquacious as David. Gideon quite liked her. She was no beauty, but there was something appealing about her. He wondered if she fancied him; she was very friendly. She seemed not to notice he was African and seemed obsessed with the relationship between the Czechs and Slovaks. Gideon learned that every Czech understood Slovak and vice versa, even though they didn't normally speak each other's language, so everyone understood everyone else, which was probably why the two countries had separated peacefully and now lived in harmony as neighbours. This was the Slovak woman's theory. Gideon knew as much about the Czechs and the Slovaks as he did about particle physics and he cared about as much, too.

The woman talked until dessert arrived and then excused herself. Gideon spent the rest of the meal being talked at by a Frenchman who had been born in Cameroon. He seemed to think Gideon, as an African, would be interested. He might as well have been talking about Cambodia.

Over the next few days, Gideon saw David, the Slovak woman and the Frenchman regularly as the potentials were shuttled from place to place, but they hardly said another word to each other. Gideon gradually got to speak to some of the other potentials – or at least to be spoken at by them. Some then treated him like an old acquaintance whom you could acknowledge and then safely ignore. That was the Slovak woman. Others, like David, seemed not to be aware that they'd ever met. Gideon didn't mind. The thought of having to sit through another of his monologues was too much.

Most of the conversations were over meals – there was hardly time to talk otherwise – and the food got progressively worse as they moved deeper into China. Breakfasts were bland, western affairs at the hotel; lunches were inedible and taken quickly at the company's staff canteens, but it was dinners that Gideon would never forget. The potentials were broken up into groups and assigned private dining rooms, with Chinese hosts and interpreters. The meals consisted of continuous deliveries of mountains of unrecognisable food, most of which didn't taste of much and was difficult to swallow. The waste was shocking. Evidently, they were being spoiled. Wine was mentioned, but none appeared; it was just gallons of 'tea' – hot water with leaves in it – and not enough beer.

What Gideon did like was the set-up in the dining room – there was a wheel in the middle of the table and everyone helped themselves by spinning it. They didn't stand on ceremony here, but the potentials were expected to try everything. Duck was obviously the speciality, and every part of the duck at that. Worst were the duck feet. Gideon couldn't imagine why anyone would want to eat such a thing; it was like having a mixture of rubber and snot in your mouth that didn't dissolve, no matter how much you chewed. Even the Hong Kong Chinese, who until then had been indistinguishable from the mainland Chinese, were struggling to get the food down.

There was no time for tourism; in Beijing, they were given 20 minutes for a walk around Tiananmen Square in the dark. The guide told them that the government functioned like a parliamentary democracy.

Tianjin was unremarkable. They set off from Beijing early that morning on a two-hour drive to the city, which was supposed to be on the coast. They visited the company's offices, were lectured on the government's plans for the place, and then shoved back into the bus for another drive to the harbour itself. That was where the factories were, near the ships. Building was going on everywhere. The place was dusty and polluted; the roads chaotic. Gideon had never seen so much traffic. At one point, during a detour, they spent two hours stationary. Thousands of people trudged past them on foot. Further along, the problem became clear: the oncoming traffic had taken over both sides of road. Nothing was moving – it was total gridlock. They got through eventually because the driver, at the end of his patience, simply drove over the pavement and then across a field. They all had to hang on for dear life as the 50-seater bus skidded through the mud and grass, lurching dangerously from side to side. It was the most enjoyable part of the trip.

The factory tour was handled by an old Chinese man who had worked there for more than 20 years. His English was incomprehensible. It was the first time they'd been shown around by a man – all interactions with foreigners in China seemed to be through young Chinese women, who acted as interpreters and generally seemed to organise everything.

They marched around the enormous structure, gaping at things and occasionally stopping while the guide explained something. Gideon would have preferred to join the Chinese workmen who were drinking tea and smoking in a fenced-off area near one of the doors. The workmen were in the cage, but it was the potentials who were being gawked at. Some of the workers were grinning. It was difficult to tell whether they were being polite or laughing at the exotic animals being herded past.

An hour later, the party emerged from the factory and headed towards the canteen for lunch. Most of the site was covered with concrete but there were patches of grass and even the odd sad-looking tree. On the way, the potentials crossed a small bridge about three or four metres wide. The water below was completely black and motionless. At first, Gideon wasn't even sure it was water. He looked around for a stone or a stick to throw into it but there was nothing. He was used to brown, muddy rivers and ponds, with insects buzzing around. In Africa, you always wondered what might be living or lurking in the water. But there was obviously nothing in this water; not even a reflection.

Gideon looked around. The potentials were gone. The old Chinese man was waiting for him. "Don't fall in," he smiled, shaking his head. "Big pollution here."

The water in Hong Kong had been safe to drink, Gideon remembered. But when they arrived on the mainland, they were explicitly told: keep your mouth closed in the shower. Gideon hadn't believed it until he saw the bottles of mineral water in the hotel bathrooms for rinsing your mouth. The place was worse than Africa.

The potentials were led into the workers' canteen and taken through to a private dining area. The food arrived in black laminated boxes on black laminated trays. In one box were soggy green vegetables, another contained tiny shrimps and yet another had some sort of meat that was coated in a thick brown sauce. Everyone got a bowl of rice and a tin of Coke with a scratched glass. There was no water. The rice was glutinous and the veggies stringy. At least they would be easy to eat with chopsticks. Gideon was starving. He tried to shell a shrimp, but there was no point – they were so small that peeling them yielded nothing except a mess. The sauce wasn't that bad, but the meat – something like ribs – tasted strange. Gideon looked around to see how the others were handling the food. They were all watching their Chinese host, who worked there. He was eating only the rice. They all did the same, even though it was totally tasteless and in dire need of salt. At the end of the meal, everyone's plate looked the same: the rice was gone, the rest of the food untouched.

"How do you peel a microscopic shrimp with chopsticks?" someone asked as they left the room. Dinner was a long way off.

The afternoon was spent visiting more offices and factories around the port and enduring more presentations about China's export model. That night, they headed back to Tianjin, this time staying on the motorway. The Chinese were worse drivers than the Africans. It was already past nine o'clock at night and they still had dinner to get through before the two-hour drive back to Beijing. The flight to Hong Kong was leaving at 07:30 the following morning. Gideon felt like suggesting they skip dinner, even though he was starving.

He glanced at the man sitting next to him. Gideon had no recollection of having seen him before. He was a smallish man with spiky hair. He looked Chinese, but Gideon wasn't sure. Some Chinese people looked really Chinese, but this man next to him could have been from anywhere in Asia.

The man, sensing he was being watched, turned to Gideon. He leaned over with an outstretched hand. "Hi," he said. "I'm Sino."

Sino remembered Gideon from the CEO's presentation – the black man who hadn't worn a suit. They sat in silence for a while. Sino had expected Gideon to start talking – he was used to westerners droning on about themselves. But this man just sat there, saying nothing. Eventually he started talking.

Gideon seemed to be listening so Sino told him about his career plans and how he wanted to go back to China. After a while, he had the impression that the man was falling asleep. He thought about keeping quiet, but he was curious about how Gideon had got on to the career programme. He was the only African Sino had ever met.

"How long have you worked here?" he asked.

Gideon looked surprised at the question. "Nine months."

"Do you like it?"

Gideon shrugged and made a non-committal sound.

"Why did you join the career programme?"

"I didn't. They put me on it."

"What do you mean?" Sino asked.

Gideon shrugged. "They put me on it."

Sino smiled at him. "Well, it must have been your decision in the end."

Gideon stared out of the window. "They wanted me to do it."

Sino decided to change tack. "Where did you study?"

Gideon looked at the back of the seat in front of him. "Johannesburg."

Sino nodded. "Which university?"

Gideon didn't look at him. "It's called Wits," he lied.

"Is that where you got your master's degree?"

Gideon looked out of the window. "Yes."

Sino nodded. "I did mine while I was working – in London."

Gideon made a small noise.

"I've actually only just finished mine," said Sino. "I did an 'executive master's' – studying at home – because I was working."

Sino tried to continue the conversation for a while, but all he got were monosyllabic replies. He gave up.

Sino didn't have a particularly high opinion of Africans. He knew little about Africa, except that it was a backward place that had been ruined by western greed and African corruption and incompetence. Until now, the only black people he'd met were English and, apart from their colour, they were pretty much indistinguishable from the English themselves.

But this man, who wouldn't talk to him, must have something going for him. He obviously hadn't talked his way into the job.

Gideon, who'd never set foot in a university in his life, was glad the man had stopped asking questions. He dozed off.

Dinner was in a fancy restaurant in Tianjin, where famous people, including the Clintons – whose picture was on the wall – had once eaten. As before, the potentials were herded towards private dining rooms. Stuffed dumplings were the local speciality, and were prepared in a kind of lounge just outside the dining room. The potentials watched the elaborate preparations for a while before the meal started.

Gideon looked around for a place to sit and saw the Chinese man from the bus taking a seat nearby. He moved towards him. "Mind if I sit here?" he asked.

Sino was surprised. He nodded and pulled back the chair.

"You want a beer?" Sino asked. Gideon perked up considerably. It was the most animated Sino had seen him.

This meal was moving faster than usual – things were evidently being hurried along. They still had the drive back to Beijing.

"It's useful sitting next to someone who speaks the language," Gideon said, when the next round of beers arrived.

Sino was pleased. Maybe this African did like him.

The other potentials at the table weren't drinking.

By the time they got back to the bus, Gideon and Sino were about as drunk as each other, even though Gideon had polished off three times as much.

As the bus got on the road back to Beijing, Sino tried again. "So, what made you join the company?"

Gideon looked at him, amused. "You never stop thinking about work, do you?"

Sino smiled. "It's difficult not to on a trip like this."

"Are you from around here?" Gideon asked him.

Sino shook his head. "No, I come from a place called Hunan Province. It's quite a bit further south."

"When did you last go home?"

"About two years ago."

"Whew," Gideon responded. "But you're going home to see your family now?"

Sino look out of the window. "No, not on this trip."

"What?"

Sino shrugged. "There's no time."

Gideon shook his head. "Come on, man. You've flown halfway across the world. What's the problem?"

"The timing is no good," Sino said. "Anyway, I have no leave left this year."

Gideon shook his head and muttered something under his breath. Then he leaned forward and looked at Sino. "Did you even contact your family?"

Sino shook his head. "They would have been upset if they'd known I was in China."

"So when did you last have a holiday?" Gideon asked him.

"When I last came home, before the course. Just over two years ago."

Gideon mouthed something to himself and leaned back in his seat. He stretched his arms towards the ceiling, and exhaled.

Sino stared in front of him.

Gideon looked around and then, in a low voice, suddenly murmured, "Before we get on that plane to Hong Kong in the morning, why don't you suddenly find out that a close relative has just died?"

Sino looked at him in amazement.

Gideon grinned at him. "Why not? You don't think it really matters, do you? So you get back to London a few days later. Who cares? It's hardly going to change the world." He said 'change the world' in the same way that the CEO had said it during his presentation in Hong Kong.

Sino just looked at him.

"Don't tell me," said Gideon. "You're going straight to the office, after we land."

"Yes," said Sino.

Gideon shook his head. "Jesus." He looked away and then back at Sino. "Did you even ask your boss if you could stay for the weekend?"

Sino shook his head. "He wouldn't have agreed. I have to finish a project by next week. It's a big one and we have to present it to the management board on Monday. Four of us are doing it."

Sino looked like he wanted to talk about it.

But Gideon just laughed at him.

Sino said nothing.

Gideon turned away and settled down for a snooze, but he couldn't fall asleep. Paradoxically, the beer and the conversation had woken him up.

Sino had surprised him – not because he'd imagined the man would do what he suggested, but because he was obviously intelligent and educated, and yet he wasn't smart enough to see that the company was taking him for a ride.

He felt a bit sorry for Sino. This poor Chinese guy was so desperate to get ahead that he couldn't see through the corporate game. He obviously thought that if he did what he was told, and bust his balls, they'd allow him to become one of them. Poor deluded sod. For all his qualifications and big ambitions, he didn't have a clue. Maybe it was because China had never been colonised – they didn't understand the white mentality.

Gideon stared out into the blackness. This trip to China had turned out to be quite interesting. These people were really in a hurry; they didn't stop. Even in the short time he'd been there, Gideon could sense the frenetic activity and how hard they worked. China had surprised him.

Everyone was always going on about how successful the Chinese were; about how the rest of the poor world, particularly Africa, should be emulating the 'Chinese model'. Gideon assumed the Chinese had worked something out; that they'd come up with a Chinese way of doing things. But they hadn't – they were just copying the whites. It was business as usual, with a pagoda in the background. Actually, he hadn't seen a pagoda – not that he knew what one looked like, anyway. They'd all been torn down to make way for skyscrapers.

Having spent the past few days being shuttled around like a piece of livestock, Gideon had been surprised at how familiar it all was – the bosses were white and the workers were Chinese. It was just like South Africa.

In Hong Kong, it was different, but in the company's China headquarters in Shanghai, the similarities were unmistakable. As one went up floor by floor, the Chinese faces became fewer and the white ones more numerous. Even on the ground, where the managers were a mixture of white and Chinese, each one sat in a glass office around huge spaces full of Chinese workers caged in cubicles with low walls. When he'd first walked in, the room had seemed empty. Gideon had been amazed to realise that the cubicles were full of workers all keeping their heads down, literally. The Chinese spent every day like that – hiding from people who knew they were there. It was ridiculous.

Gideon adjusted his position to try and get comfortable. He glanced again at Sino, who was sitting upright in his seat. His eyes seemed to be closed. Gideon turned back to the window and curled up a bit more, into a semi-foetal position.

The CEO had been right about one thing; the winner was not the one who played the game best, it was the one who made the rules. White people were still making the rules and as long as it was their system, their capitalism, their ideas, the rest of the world didn't stand a chance. If the Chinese got too big for their boots, the whites would simply change the rules – tear up the paper. That was how they always operated.

The trick, Gideon knew, was the financial system. As long as white people controlled the financial system, everyone else was always going to be a slave. Back in his mother's village, they thought the whites' smartest invention had been guns. But they didn't know anything about how the outside world really worked. Their really clever invention had been money – paper money. Sometimes, Gideon couldn't believe how simple the whole thing was. Those pieces of paper decided the value of everything – what you grew, mined, made, sold, bought and killed; even what a human life was worth.

Gideon could picture them – old white men, with their grey heads and flabby bellies – sitting in their offices in New York, Washington, London, deciding how many pieces of paper a country was worth. It was unbelievable that the rest of the world was still falling for this bullshit. It was unbelievable that intelligent Chinese people, like this guy next to him, were busting their balls and ruining their country just to be part of the same scam that the whites had invented.

Gideon's father had done it; spent most of his life – and lost his life – in the gold mines of Johannesburg. His father had dug up enough gold to fill a vault and in return they'd given him nothing but pieces of paper. Over the years, his father had stashed away as many of those pieces of paper as he could. But at the end of his short life, when Gideon's mother opened the box, there wasn't even enough money to pay for a decent funeral. Somewhere along the line, some fat, white bastards sitting on the other side of the world had decided that the currency his father had sweated blood for wasn't worth shit. The bastards who ran the mining company had even tried to get out of contributing to the cost of the funeral.

Gideon glanced at his watch. It was nearly one o'clock in the morning. The bus was hurtling towards Beijing. Often, the driver would brake, rousing the potentials, before swerving – presumably to overtake something – then hitting the accelerator and charging forward again. The guy at the wheel was as bad as a Jo'burg taxi driver, and he was driving a bus the size of a building.

As a boy back in the 1980s, Gideon remembered an older cousin explaining how white people ran the world. "The system is designed so that you will fail, because you are black," his cousin told him. "They will tell you to work hard and stay out of trouble. But if you do that – if you do what you are told – you can look forward to being poor and exploited for the rest of your life."

Gideon hadn't believed it at the time; he'd believed his mother instead. She was always going on about how important it was to stay out of trouble and work hard. She'd been wrong all along. But then she didn't know anything. She was just a maid.

He remembered his cousin's last words to him before he disappeared. "Whatever you do," his cousin said, "you will always be nothing. Because you are black."

Gideon tried not to think too hard about these things. They just made him angry. His mother had always said everything was God's will, and for most of his life, Gideon had left things to God. Believing in God seemed enlightened, compared with the superstitions and fantasies that had ruled the lives of his grandparents, but he was pretty sure his mother was wrong about God, too. His cousin had told him God was white. Gideon had a feeling that God was just another of the whites' inventions – like

HIV, maybe. It was telling that white people had brought God to Africa. They seemed to have left Him there – Gideon hadn't seen much sign of Him in London.

It was two o'clock in the morning by the time they got to bed. They had to be up at six to catch the plane back to Hong Kong. The plane to London was leaving at midnight – another 18-hour day. Gideon was looking forward to that flight; he would sleep from the moment they took off till the moment they landed. The whole thing was ridiculous. He'd had enough. He was going to the office as soon as they landed, too. But not to work. He was going to tell his boss and the rest of them where they could stick their job, and then he was going home, to tell Rosemary that he was going back to South Africa – with or without her and the kids.

CHAPTER 3

The CEO

Chris walked up to the desk being used by his secretary. He grinned at her, leaned across and took a small bottle of mineral water she had just opened out of her hand. "So how was I?" he asked, before pouring most of the contents down his throat.

The woman made a small noise and resumed typing.

Chris walked past her to the glass wall of the building and stared out at Shanghai.

"Well?" he said. "How was my presentation for the potentials?"

She glanced at the side of his face. "Fine. Great."

"Do you think they bought it?"

"Bought it?"

"Believed it?" he said, turning to look at her. "Thought I was saying something meaningful? Or were they just pretending to be interested because I'm the CEO?"

His secretary took her hands off the keyboard. "I found it inspiring," she murmured, dropping her chin and looking at him over the top of her glasses.

Chris nodded. "Is he here?"

"Yes."

"Give me a few minutes."

Chris walked into the room that had been provided for him during his trip. It was awful; a multi-purpose space, one they obviously used for meetings and conferences – and for putting visitors in. They'd cleaned it up, made it look more like an office for him, but it still looked like shit. They'd taken out most of the furniture – he could see the indentation marks on the squares of turf that passed for a carpet – and arranged the remaining tables and chairs in a rectangle near the window, as if they were intended for meetings that he might want to hold. But the effect was not convincing. Another table was standing almost in the middle of the room; his secretary had already put his laptop on it. Someone had tried to make it look like a desk. There were a few pens in a plastic tray and a notepad, arranged in front of a single chair. The telephone was in the right place, but the cable connecting it to the wall socket was lying across the floor.

Chris sat down at the 'desk'. All around him was room: the space was far too large for an office for one. He would have preferred being squashed into a broom cupboard. He stood up and, suddenly angry, yanked the 'desk' towards him. It was lighter than it looked and he nearly toppled over backwards. He dragged the table closer to the wall behind him. The telephone crashed to the floor. The cable was snagged, but fortunately it was long enough. He dumped the phone back on the table, retrieved the chair and sat down. That was better; at least he had his back to the wall. The room looked ridiculous.

He pulled his laptop towards him and started checking his emails. The web connection was slow – infuriatingly so. Everything in China was a hassle. His secretary appeared at the door with the chairman's man.

Chris nodded and waved the man in the direction of the rectangle of tables. "Sit down," he said. "I'll be with you in a second."

The man nodded and walked to the far side of the rectangle of tables. He was the chairman's China advisor. Behind his back, he was known as the 'China Man' – with an appropriate pause between 'China' and 'Man'. When necessary, he worked with operational people, like Chris, who actually did the work, but most of the time, he inhabited a small, separate world of right-hand men whose job it was to take care of the chairman's business.

"How are you?" Chris smiled, approaching him with an extended hand.

The man had not sat down. "I'm fine," he said, with a polite smile, slowly extending his hand. He always looked awkward and uncomfortable, as if he'd been caught somewhere he wasn't supposed to be.

He was originally from Hong Kong but had lived in the States for years. Chris hardly knew him but had hated the man on sight.

From a distance, he looked okay, but the closer you got, the more repulsive he became. He wasn't fat, but everything about him seemed loose and saggy. His nostrils were too big and, when you got close, you could see the hairs sticking out of his nose. Sometimes, it looked like he needed to blow it. Chris couldn't smell him, but he was sure he stank.

The two men sat down facing each other, the table in between them. They were both looking down.

The China man flipped open a leather folder that he had been carrying, and began thumbing through some papers. His age was difficult to gauge – he could have been anything from mid-forties to mid-fifties. He dyed his hair and, despite the flab, was not really overweight. He began to speak, slowly, looking at the pages in front of him but not reading.

The two men discussed the content of the contract for about half an hour, with Chris making suggestions and occasionally insisting on an amendment, but more often allowing himself to be talked out of changing anything. As far as Chris knew, the man was simply presenting the chairman's ideas.

"You'll talk to Sam about coming to Shanghai," Chris said. From his tone, it could have been a question or an instruction.

"I'll talk to the chairman," the man said, nodding.

"Do you think he'll come?"

The China man shrugged, turning down the corners of his mouth in a non-committal way.

Chris could quite easily have hit him in the face. "Do you think it's necessary that he be there?"

The China man looked him in the eye for the first time. "No, I don't think it's necessary." He paused. "I don't think he should come."

Chris was slightly surprised.

"But he will come, won't he?"

"Probably," the man agreed.

"Thank you," Chris said. For once, he sort of meant it. The man left the room.

Chris looked out of the wall. He knew Sam would come; the old bastard couldn't leave anything important to anyone else.

This deal was yet another test for Sam – he was getting on. It was time he took a backseat. Sam had declared he was ready to do so, but no-one, not even his closest advisors – especially not them – believed him. He'd said it before. Earlier in the year he'd even taken a holiday, and delegated a few decisions, but he was still deciding what to delegate on a case-by-case basis. Christ, he wouldn't even allow Chris to be interviewed by the media.

Now they were about to conclude negotiations with a Chinese firm on a partnership arrangement. So far, Sam had mostly stayed in the background, but the end game was approaching. Chris could literally sense the old bastard chafing at the bit. There was no reason for Sam to be there. In fact, it would be better if he didn't come – the Chinese never sent the top man to negotiations – but Sam wasn't interested in cultural niceties. "Fuck 'em" was his usual response, when advised not to do something in another country. The sod was a typical insular American.

Well, there was no point in dwelling on it; maybe Sam would surprise them. Chris put the matter out of his head. It was time to do some bonding with the local management. He had a lunch appointment with the local managing director. He, at least, was Chinese. The Asia boss was a Yank, and in the finance department the westerners were still calling the shots. Chris put on his jacket and left the room. He hoped the restaurant would be Japanese.

There was a car waiting for him downstairs; the local MD would meet him at the restaurant. Chris stared out of the window. He'd never liked Shanghai; he much preferred Hong Kong. Hong Kong reminded him of London. He supposed it was what London would be like if it was invaded by the Chinese – once they'd taken over.

Sitting in the car watching the Chinese going about their business, Chris understood perfectly why the company was struggling in China. He found it hard to believe how much they'd done wrong. They'd quite literally fucked up everything from day one. The company's Chinese experience was a litany of disasters. Sam was still trying to run the firm like a western company, even though it was perfectly obvious they had to go native. The old fool couldn't seem to understand that building a business for the long term was not the way it worked in China. Things changed so fast that you had simply to grab whatever was going. The company's position in the market was a joke. It probably wasn't too late to turn the situation around, but they had to start thinking differently, and fast – and Sam was having none of it.

"Following the herd is not a strategy – it's a suicide pact," was the old fool's response whenever the issue came up.

The problem was that Sam never got angry in discussions about strategy. And a calm Sam was an immovable Sam. To have any chance of changing his mind, you had to wind him up.

Chris had stumbled upon Sam's 'flexible' side quite by accident, after one of those absurd meetings that he called periodically to put the world to rights. Until then, Sam had been relatively easy to get along with, but also impervious to persuasion.

"It's 'less', not 'fewer'," the fool suddenly interrupted, while Chris was talking.

Chris would never forget that moment; the instant when that moronic, ignorant, semi-literate, fucking Yank had had the nerve to correct his English! It would have been bad enough had the idiot at least been right, but the imbecile had corrected him incorrectly!

For a few moments, Chris said nothing. For a few moments, he'd almost been ready to let it go. But sitting there, surrounded by Sam and his circle of smiling sycophants, Chris' temper had got the better of him.

"I think you'll find that it *is* 'fewer'," he said, as pleasantly as possible.

Sam shook his big, thick head, still grinning. "It's 'less'!"

Chris smiled back. "We are talking about fewer things…"

"You mean 'less things'," Sam retorted. Everyone laughed on cue. It was pathetic.

"Why don't we look it up in the dictionary?" Chris suggested. He hadn't meant to go that far, but the old fool had made the whole thing very personal.

As soon as he said 'dictionary', Sam went berserk.

Chris just sat there watching him rant.

After a few more minutes of inarticulate abuse, Sam stormed out of the room.

Later, the director of communications sidled up to Chris. "Can I give you some advice?" he smiled, through his capped teeth. He didn't wait for an answer. "When the chairman makes the same point more than once, it's generally a good idea to drop the subject."

Chris had been tempted to take the man's advice. He'd known when he joined the company that indulging Sam was an unwritten part of the job description. Anyway, what was the point in arguing with an American about the English language?

But some time later, Chris noticed that Sam was using 'fewer' correctly. He must have checked it. Maybe it wasn't impossible for the bastard to accept he could be wrong? Maybe he could be persuaded? Maybe you could get through to him? – if you were prepared to endure a torrent of abuse and insults.

Over the months, Chris had realised that Sam was far more flexible in his opinions than he had originally given him credit for. He didn't change his mind often, but he certainly wasn't wedded to any particular ideas. The problem was that no-one pushed him hard enough.

It was ironic because Sam would frequently exhort them to challenge him. "Argue with me!", he would say. "Challenge me! I expect to be challenged."

And, of course, they did. Every inhabitant of Sam's world challenged him – usually very convincingly – right up until the 'moment', when every argument was instantly conceded. It was easy to see why. If you carried on, things could quickly get very unpleasant indeed, and few people were willing to endure that kind of abuse. It was much easier to capitulate, keep your job and have a quiet life.

The moment was easy to spot once you were initiated. It came when Sam suddenly introduced a new line of argument – usually an irrelevant one – or started insinuating that you were stupid or deficient in some way. Then you knew he'd run out of ideas; that an explosion wasn't far away.

Usually, it wasn't clear why Sam changed his mind. Of course, there was no question of him admitting that he'd done so – he'd never been wrong about anything. At most, he might acknowledge that circumstances had changed to the extent that a new course of action was unavoidable. He could maintain this farce because, up there on the executive floors, everyone was primed instantly to forget what Sam's position had been as soon as it changed.

In the beginning, Chris had found it quite spooky. He'd go into a meeting and hear the same 'facts' marshalled into an argument that completely contradicted a previous position of Sam's. You had to rehearse your thoughts carefully, in case you accidentally remembered the past as it was, as opposed to how it was now. What made it more difficult was that you had to remember the details, but forget the decisions, because Sam didn't like repeating himself.

Chris was getting the hang of it, but compared with the sycophants, he was still an amateur. In a way, you had to admire them – they were amazingly adept at the intellectual contortions needed not only to re-remember history, but also to communicate the new history to everyone else. Luckily, hardly anyone knew what the old history was, so they didn't notice.

On the bribery issue, the new reality had reached Chris in the men's room, courtesy of the communications director. Everyone knew that handing over brown envelopes to officials in the shitholes of the world was standard practice, but when some over-zealous technocrats in Europe busted a competitor and Sam saw the size of the fine, he decided that his company had always been a crusader against bribery and corruption.

"By the way," the communications chief said, as Chris was drying his hands, "did you hear about the fine?"

Chris hadn't. He'd not read a newspaper or checked the web that morning.

The man moved into position in front of the urinal and unzipped his trousers. "Yes, very embarrassing and expensive for our competitor."

The communications director started urinating audibly. "The chairman is concerned that our zero-tolerance policy on bribery is not being properly respected throughout the company," he continued, staring up at the ceiling.

"Oh, yes," Chris muttered cautiously, loitering near the door. He always made a point of not talking to people in the men's room, especially mid-flow.

The communications chief shook himself, zipped up his trousers, and walked to the taps. "So we will be focusing on getting the message across," he said, adjusting his trousers. "Legal will be enforcing compliance much more vigorously and we'll be communicating more often and in a more direct way."

He smiled at Chris. "We will also make sure that the policy is known about externally."

That was how it worked in Sam's world. From one day to the next, the company turned holier than thou, and everyone acted as if it had always been that way. Employees who wore suits had to sign a paper, promising never to bribe anyone, as a supplementary measure. That was typical of Sam. Get it on paper, get it signed. Everyone knew the bribes would still be paid. In most of the countries concerned, it was impossible to do business otherwise. You certainly couldn't meet your targets without paying off local officials. The people in the shitholes would just be more careful and get better at covering their tracks. Those unlucky enough to get caught would be made examples of. There would be no mercy, no amnesty, no allowance made for what was normal in the past. If you were caught, you were out, you were blacklisted, no reference, no bonus, no ticket home. Sam could have invented prohibition.

The communications director was usually the one who 'reminded' Chris about Sam's new decisions. He could get the message across with a straight face, even if it was totally contrary to a position that Sam might have argued for passionately in the past. Chris preferred hearing it from him because at least he was human, if a bit creepy. The other messenger – the chief financial officer – was a typical accountant, as hopeless with language as he was accomplished with numbers. He spoke like a flushing toilet; the information just poured out in a whirlpool of nauseating constructions. Also, being pretty much autistic, he was unable to tell whether you'd got the message, so he'd attempt to test you afterwards to see whether you'd understood. You couldn't even take the piss out of him – he took everything at face value, except the numbers.

For most people in the company, life was simple. Those in the know knew exactly what Sam's position was on any given subject at any given moment. Those who weren't were left to their own devices. It was only Chris and a few other top managers who were close enough to know what Sam's positions were on most things, but too far away to know when a change was coming. It didn't help to listen to him because, in public, Sam was very good at sounding decisive without actually articulating a position on anything.

Sometimes, if he got very defensive about something, a change might be imminent. But he could also cling aggressively to positions for years in the face of overwhelming evidence to the contrary.

In Sam's world, no-one helped you understand anything; you were expected to interpret and implement Sam's wishes. How you did it was largely up to you, but you had to be very careful about what you said and how your actions could be interpreted. Sam had moles all over the place – inside and outside the company – and could be positively tribal when it came to 'betrayal'. The company was always settling suits for unfair dismissal.

Chris's main problem at the moment was Sam's suggestion that he should relocate to Shanghai. "You're always telling us how much you know about China," Sam had said. "You should move there – show us what we've been doing wrong."

Sam was pulling a fast one – he hadn't mentioned China when he'd hired Chris a year ago – but the bastard had him by the balls. How could he refuse? The company made and bought almost everything in China and the country was its biggest growth market.

So Chris had moved on to the concessions he could wring out of Sam in exchange for moving. He'd already extracted a bigger bonus, a better car with a driver, luxury accommodation, school fees, and twice-yearly business class flights back to London for him and the family. But what could he get Sam to do for him on the ground in China? He hadn't been around long enough to know what he really needed.

A good start would be to dump the stupid American running the Asia operations. Sitting in his plush office in Shanghai, the Yank looked pretty convincing. But he'd been there for years, and no-one seemed to have noticed. Chris couldn't believe they'd appointed him. He had a sun-bed tan, wore designer suits and could charm the knickers off a lesbian. The problem was, he couldn't handle chopsticks, let alone a company full of Chinese. Based on Sam's defensive reaction, whenever the man's (non)performance was mentioned, Chris was pretty sure Sam was ready to dump him. However, at the moment, there was no-one else on the ground in China whom Sam trusted.

Chris had a guy at a competitor in his sights to take over from the American. He was Chinese and had spent enough time in Europe to know how to hold a knife and fork. He was also smart, dynamic and creative – for a Chinese manager. Chris was pretty sure he could lure him in – he'd heard the guy was answering head-hunters' calls – but Sam would have to be persuaded.

The problem was that Sam didn't know the man, and what he didn't know, he didn't trust. Also, he was paranoid about the Chinese – had been since the company had been shafted by a joint-venture partner back in the '90s. Sam always turned to the China man on questions about China, and the last thing the China man wanted was a competent Chinese around.

Time was running out. As soon as the Chinese guy appeared on the competition's radar, they would grab him. It was a long shot, but Chris had decided he would have to try and persuade Sam before he went back to the States.

The MD was waiting at the table when Chris arrived at the restaurant, which – thank God – was Japanese. The man was a typical Chinese manager: well-behaved, impenetrable and utterly uninspiring.

*

Sam didn't surprise anyone. He arrived in Shanghai just as Chris had expected, along with the CFO, the China man and the communications director. The meeting with the new Chinese partners was scheduled for 3pm, which would give them enough time to finalise the deal before dinner. The Chinese partners would have organised a huge, totally over-the-top feast to celebrate afterwards.

They spent the morning hammering out the final details. Sam was always a nightmare at this stage of the game, insisting on going over each point until every syllable of what was supposed to be said, and what not, was burnt into their brains. It was a waste of time, since he always did all the talking. The driver arrived to collect them at 2pm. They would be early – perhaps very early. No matter; they would drive around the area until a few minutes before 3pm, when the driver would drop them on the doorstep. They would announce themselves at 3pm precisely. If they weren't admitted instantly, they would leave. No deal. If they weren't seen by the partners within a maximum of ten minutes of being delivered to the room where the meeting would take place, they would leave. No deal. The first two minutes wouldn't count – Sam would make allowance for the fact that the partners' watches might not be entirely accurate – but every one of the remaining eight minutes would be taken as a measure of the partners' unreliability or, more likely, their desire to show who was boss. Sam would make them pay in cash and contrition for every minute they kept him waiting. If they weren't willing to pay to Sam's satisfaction – no deal. Sam and his men all wore Swiss watches. Needless to say, they were precise to the second. They had been checked that morning to make sure they were perfectly in synch with Shanghai time (just in case it wasn't exactly the same as Sam's time).

They wound up driving around the block for nearly 20 minutes in a six-seater vehicle. The CFO was next to the driver, Chris and the China man were in the row behind, and Sam and the communications chief were in the back. Sam was looking through a presentation on a laptop, vacillating about tiny details that no-one would notice. He didn't have a clue how to work a computer, so he was looking over the shoulder of the director of communications, telling him what to change. The communications chief said very little, but when he did speak, Sam appeared to listen.

Then it was five to three. The driver stopped and they went in. They were taken immediately to a large room on the top floor, which wasn't all that high, especially for Shanghai. The building was old and, despite having been recently renovated, looked like it belonged to a different era compared with all the shiny glass towers downtown. Their Chinese hosts were already in the room to welcome them. Chris could tell that Sam was delighted.

Chris was surprised. The top people were there: the business partner himself, accompanied by the government's man, who was actually a woman. She was ugly as sin, had a funny walk, and was as charming as only a communist can be. The softest thing about her was her teeth. Sam greeted his new business partners as if they were old friends.

The two parties faced each other across a large rectangular table. On one side, the boss and the woman each had a row of three people next to them, who they would confer with regularly. But the two in charge were the only people who spoke to the visitors. The man, who was called Zheng, did most of the talking. The woman, who was called Li, was obviously the one calling the shots. Both of them spoke enough English to make themselves understood, so the China man's interpreting skills were not needed. His job was to listen to the murmuring on the Chinese side and try to remember anything interesting.

As usual, Sam did all of the talking on his side of the table, although he would frequently refer to the communications chief or the CFO to seek confirmation about something or to clarify details. It was typical Sam. It gave the impression that he didn't concern himself with details and it allowed him to sound as if he was remembering facts rather than stating an opinion.

In spite of himself, Chris couldn't help feeling a grudging admiration for Sam at moments like these. As inarticulate and American as the man was, he could still charm the pants off any banker, businessman or government official. Even the woman was lapping it up; her hideous face contorting into what Chris imagined was her idea of a smile. Sam's capacity for bullshit had been honed over years of persuading suckers to buy the company's shares.

Throughout the meeting, a young woman kept reappearing with a pot of steaming tea to replenish the small cups in front of everyone. It was a bit like meeting the mafia.

The deal was closed successfully as expected. There was lots of gushing and lots of enthusiastic handshakes. Then the parties departed for dinner. It was going to be a meal to remember: shark fins, Shanghai lobsters, duck tongues – the lot.

"You know a smart, young Chinese guy who can handle a

partner like this?" Sam asked Chris on the way back to the hotel after dinner.

It was dark in the six-seater. Chris ran his tongue around his teeth – this was his chance. "I have a real star in mind," he said cautiously.

Sam made an inquisitive sound from the back.

"He knows the industry, he's very well-connected here, and he's got a record."

"Good," said Sam. "Who is he?"

"The thing is, he's not likely to jump ship just to look after a partner." Chris paused. "Even one as important as this."

Sam said nothing.

Chris waited a few seconds. "He's a real star performer, this guy."

Chris paused again, and then told Sam who the man was.

Sam grunted but otherwise didn't respond. They drove the rest of the way back to the hotel in silence.

As they were saying goodnight, Sam turned to Chris. "Call Scott," he said. "See if he's got a smart, young Chinese guy on that career programme of his. This would be a perfect assignment for one of them."

Scott was the company's HR director. There was no point in arguing. Chris nodded and went up to his room. He slammed the door and went to the mini bar. He needed a drink. All he'd had all evening was a lot of tea and a glass of shit wine.

He took two aeroplane bottles of whisky out of the minibar and emptied them into a glass, then he went and sat on the bed and turned on the TV.

"Fuck you, Sam," he said softly, raising his glass. The whisky made him feel better. He went back for a double gin with a splash of tonic.

Chris tried not to let it get to him. It had been a long shot; he'd been trying to appoint some of his own people since he joined the company, but so far with no luck. Sam approved all the key appointments and delegated the searching to Scott, who knew precisely what kind of people Sam liked. That was how he kept control. Each day Chris was at the company, he became more aware of how peripheral he really was.

He flicked through the channels on the TV. Usually, he didn't take things too seriously, but China was the big prize. If the company could crack China, his face would be all over the papers. He would have head-hunters bashing down his door.

He finished his drink. Why worry? As long as he was raking in the money, what did he care? He had a fat salary topped up with an even bigger bonus, which he could be almost certain of getting, and he had plenty of share options to unload once he'd had enough of Sam.

He was earning a lot more money than any of his old colleagues from the consulting firm. He had an apartment in London, a house in the country, a villa in the south of France, and he was running a global company with tens of thousands of employees. His old colleagues were green. What did the hell did he care what Sam did? As long as he got his money, why worry? Even if Sam really fucked things up, it would take a long time to run a company of this size into the ground. And he was way too risk-averse to make any major mistakes. The biggest danger was slow attrition; Chris would have jumped ship long before they started preparing the lifeboats.

Chris was pretty certain the company was heading into decline. The numbers were okay, but their Chinese rivals were getting better and better at producing just the kinds of products that the company depended on. Everyone pretended that they could keep ahead by innovating, but they weren't so much innovating as just finding ways to make the same products for less so that they could compete.

Then there was Sam. He was a shrewd old bugger and he'd bought some good companies, but he was crap at consolidation. He was way too much of a control freak to reconcile his world with anyone else's – he gave orders and expected them to be obeyed. If they weren't, he either came down on the culprit like a ton of bricks or, if that wasn't feasible, he simply ignored the situation and waited for it to go away. Chris had worked out that the company was less a global conglomerate than a bunch of disparate firms spread out across the world. The only thing they really had in common was that they bought their products from Sam's suppliers and sent the profits back to Sam. Sometimes, Chris had the feeling that the further away from Sam they were, the more successful they were.

Chris looked at the clock. It was past midnight. He'd better ring Scott. He pulled out his mobile and looked up the number. He hoped Scott wouldn't have a Chinese employee waiting in the wings. Then he would call Sarah, and tell her that they were moving to Shanghai. He would pretend he'd tried to talk Sam out of it – which was true. He had, before, but there was no point in bringing it up again. Sarah was going to freak. If she really got uppity, he'd stick her in a nice apartment in Hong Kong and commute down there for weekends. She'd be willing to live with that – at least when she saw what he was being paid.

CHAPTER 4

Sam

Sam woke up. He could tell it was early; his body clock was still screwed up by the jet lag. He turned his head on the pillow and glanced at the clock: 4:58. It was Saturday morning and he had a take-off slot at 11am that morning back to New York City.

He turned his head the other way and looked at Rosa. She was fast asleep on her side, facing away from him. The lights from outside faintly illuminated her back. He almost reached out to touch her, but he wasn't sure he wanted to wake her just yet. Her skin was like warm butter; her flesh was so soft that it felt like it might come off in his hand. In the dim light, he could clearly see the outlines of her shoulder blades and the snaking dent of her spine.

In this light, she was unbelievably desirable. It was a struggle not to touch her. It wasn't that she was perfect; up close, her features were a bit coarse. He didn't like her ears – they were a bit chunky – but normally they were covered by her hair. Her nostrils were slightly too big, and flared too much when she talked and breathed at the same time. There were some minute pockmarks on her cheeks that were normally covered with make-up but didn't look so great in the morning. Despite this, there was something delectable about her. The sight of her skin – any piece of it – almost made his mouth water. He always wanted to touch her with his mouth. It irritated her, but he couldn't help it. Her skin was like ice cream.

He continued staring at Rosa in the dim light. Her body looked like it was covered in a fine film of pink dust. He could easily live without her, he had no doubt about that, but sometimes he wondered what it would be like to wake up in the morning knowing he would never see her again. He'd get used to it; he'd given up cigars. Nothing lasted forever. The best moments were when they saw each other again after being apart for a while, like last night. He opened the door and there she was, almost jumping for joy. She was always so happy to see him. She seemed so fond of him that he had to keep reminding himself she was a hooker.

Being around Rosa was like that feeling you got after two flutes of champagne – when the muscles have started to relax and the bubbles are popping just below the brain. She never demanded anything. When they were together, she doted on him; seemed to be totally in love with him. He couldn't believe it was all an act. No-one could act like that, not long term.

Sam looked down at his exposed torso and belly. Under the long dark hairs that covered his stomach, his skin was grey, unreflective. His belly button looked like a hole in the mud – a place that might be home to something horrible. Sam was glad to be a man. Men didn't need to be young and good-looking for women to find them attractive. He turned his head again to look at Rosa's naked back. He couldn't resist – he reached out and gently stroked her spine. She stirred, sighed and rolled on to her back. The sight of her literally took his breath away. She lay there like an exquisite sculpture. She didn't wake up. He could almost have taken a bite out of her.

He didn't know much about Rosa, except that she was from Honduras. She had a brother somewhere in the States, who'd once been locked up for something. That was the only time Rosa had ever asked him for anything – if he could get her brother out of jail. She'd been so grateful, as if he'd risked life and limb. It had taken a phone call to his lawyer and a few thousand dollars. She'd wanted to pay him back, but he'd made her a present of it. He knew she had a few other clients. He even knew some of them – businessmen, Washington insiders and his old ally, George – but obviously she trusted him in a way that she didn't them. Their relationship had evolved into a bond with real affection. Sometimes, he had the impression she was falling in love with him. It sounded ridiculous to say that about a hooker, but when they were together, it felt like they were lovers.

As far as their arrangement was concerned, they saw each other three or four times a month. For that, the company paid her 500 dollars a week – a fixed item on the hospitality budget. Every now and then, Sam brought her a nice gift, usually jewellery. No money changed hands – had ever changed hands. When he was heading down to Washington, DC, he'd let her know in advance. Occasionally, when his wife Mary was out of town, he'd fly Rosa up to New York.

Despite the age difference, they got on very well. She was fascinated by his life and was always asking what he'd been doing since they last saw each other. In many ways, Rosa was the perfect woman: she always looked good, she was always happy to see him, never complained, was never bad tempered, never difficult. It was hard to believe they'd got off to such a bad start. Sure, it had been tactless to ask her to take an AIDS test, but he'd felt entitled to ask. It was fair question for a hooker that he planned to see on a regular basis.

She'd taken it badly, left the suite immediately and not come back. The next time they met – he usually booked her at least three days in advance – she'd produced a piece of paper. HIV-negative, it said. Then, as they were saying goodbye, she'd asked him if he'd take an HIV test.

"What for?" He'd been surprised.

"One thing I can promise you," she'd muttered, her voice dripping with acid, "is that I'm a damn shade cleaner than you are."

He couldn't understand why she took it so personally. VD and AIDS must be an occupational hazard for a hooker. He understood that – he was a businessman, for Christ's sake. Sometimes, he suspected that Rosa had trouble accepting she was a hooker.

It had taken him a while to get used to the idea that he was sleeping with a prostitute. Until Rosa, he'd only ever had affairs – until the last one. She'd turned out to be a real nut case; demanding he leave his wife and telling the whole world about their little fling. Eventually, he'd had to come clean with Mary. It had nearly destroyed his marriage. He'd even come under pressure from George, as if he was a politician or something.

That was when George had offered to introduce him to Rosa. Sam had been stunned. "I don't pay for sex," was his first reaction.

George laughed. "You're not paying for sex, Sam. You're paying her to go away afterwards – and to keep quiet about it."

George had a point. Who had time for affairs these days? And who actually wanted one? All he and George wanted was some good sex once a week with someone worth screwing.

"Women and men understand affairs differently," George had said. "Women have affairs because they are tired of their husbands; men have affairs because they are happy with their wives."

George liked to say clever things. He was a senator, retired.

In the meantime, Sam had discovered why he liked being with Rosa. She understood him; she accepted him for who he was. It sounded absurd, but she was the only person he could be himself with, who demanded nothing of him, who he felt really relaxed around. Sex with Rosa was like a massage, a game of golf and a workout in the gym all rolled into one. He always woke up the next morning feeling strong, vital and healthy. His arrangement with Rosa was also wonderfully convenient – she fitted perfectly into his schedule.

Until Rosa, Sam had pretty much given up on sex and women – on balance, it just wasn't worth it. All he'd ever wanted was a woman like him: one who had her own life and just wanted a bit of sex occasionally. Why did it always have to be so complicated? It always started well. In the beginning, women were charming, relaxed, easy to get along with, but as soon as you jumped into bed with them, it all changed. It even happened with the married ones. Even that Greek woman, who'd seemed so assured and so happily married, had turned into a pathetic sobbing wreck. Then, when he finally levelled with her, she'd turned into a real nasty bitch. Thank God she'd had her own marriage to worry about.

Just when he'd given up looking, just when he'd decided that it wasn't going to happen, that he was destined to spend the rest of his life celibate, he'd met Rosa. That was often how life worked.

Rosa had also cured him of his golf habit. Since she came along, he didn't miss golf anymore. He'd had to give up golf. These days, who had time to spend hours driving around a golf course? With Rosa around, who wanted to?

Sam knew he had George to thank for Rosa. He would never have dreamed of approaching a hooker had George not made it okay to do so. Truth be told, he would never have risked it. But the fact that George, a senator – a man whose career, whose life, depended more on his image than his ability – felt it was okay to consort with a hooker, made it safe. Politicians never ceased to surprise you. Sam would never have imagined that George would know a hooker.

"She's an escort," George had said in a very matter-of-fact tone, but with a twinkle in his eye. "We frequently have visitors to Washington, DC, who need escorts. What you do with her is strictly between the two of you." Someone from George's office had given him the number of the agency Rosa worked for.

He and George understood each other very well. George was on the board of Sam's company. He was expensive and tended to miss board meetings, but on balance Sam felt he got value for money. George was a fixture in DC. He didn't have to worry about being popular anymore now that he was retired. He was never going to be president.

In the course of his career, George had been on or connected to every important committee in DC. He knew everyone worth knowing. Of course, he could be stubborn, misguided and fickle – he was still a politician – but in the final analysis, you could count on George. He understood what was important. He understood what politicians were there for; he understood what it meant to be a public servant.

George was one of the few left who cared about the burden on business. He knew what had made America strong. He understood instinctively that entrepreneurs like Sam were the only people who created value. After a lifetime in DC, George understood better than anyone that government was a leech, a barren whore. He was determined to preserve America's pre-eminence in the world. Most of the other bastards in DC didn't give a damn about America. Most of them deserved to be taken out and shot.

The hill had always been full of whores, but now they had practically taken over. Sam knew enough about history to know that the biggest danger facing America came from within. Just like with Rome, the barbarians had always been at the gates. The only reason they eventually got in was because Rome had rotted away from inside. After centuries of conquering and civilising the world outside, the Romans had stopped listening to their generals and instead allowed those fat, lazy senators to intrigue and debate their way to oblivion. America had forgotten the lessons and it was going the same way.

Once America had been a place where work was rewarded, where wealth flowed to those who got off their ass to make a difference, where idleness was punished by want. But now these scumbags in DC had turned the world on its head, with their redistributive tax policies and rewards for the lazy and the useless. Not only was it unfair and absurd, it was bad for business. They were going to learn the hard way.

As of next year, most of Sam's remaining American companies would no longer be American. Only his holding company and a few local businesses would remain registered in Delaware – for the time being. Most of the other firms would be relocated to Switzerland. In this climate, even havens like the Cayman Islands and Panama were too exposed. Switzerland was a better bet. There, you had to pay tax, but the rates were reasonable and you knew what you were in for.

Sam's accountant had even recommended that he personally relocate to Switzerland. A part of him wanted to, just to spite the fucking whores, but Sam had been to the Swiss town where some of his firms had their headquarters – a place called Zug. He didn't relish the prospect of spending any more time in Zug than he absolutely had to, let alone moving there. The centrepiece of the town was a fucking aviary, for Christ's sake. The place looked quaint but had the atmosphere of an airport. You couldn't fault the Zug government, though. It knew how to look after its inhabitants. The tax rates were things of beauty.

The problem was that to be a resident of Zug, or any other Swiss town, Sam would have to spend six months a year in Switzerland. What would he do? He hated skiing. Presumably, Swiss hookers spoke English. If George and the few reliable ones left couldn't make the whores see sense on tax...

Sam quietly got out of bed and went to the bathroom. Left alone, Rosa would sleep for at least another two hours. For a few seconds before he got out of bed, he'd thought about waking her. It was a bit early. He wanted to have sex with her, but he also wanted to be alone. Usually, he was able to leave things behind when he was with Rosa.

Sam looked at his face in the bathroom mirror. He had bags under his eyes. He hadn't fallen asleep until the early hours of the morning. That was partly the jet lag, but it was also Catherine's fault; his stepmother was another problem to worry about. Life had become a succession of worries. Between Catherine, the company, the whores, and his health problems, he didn't know how much longer he could go on. The whole world had become very unreasonable very quickly.

Sam spat into the sink, rinsed his mouth and splashed water into his face. Then he put on a hotel bathrobe and went quietly into the lounge. He was hungry. There was a bowl of fruit on the table, but he wanted real food. For some reason, he didn't feel like turning on the lights; they would hurt his eyes. Anyway, there was enough light coming in through the open drapes. He turned on a lamp, called room service and ordered breakfast. After wandering aimlessly around the room for a few minutes, he went and stood at the window, looking out at the lights of the Capitol. 'The House of the Setting Sun', he called it.

Sam felt betrayed. He'd donated millions to both parties over the years and paid out even more for lobbyists, simply to try and make the bastards see sense, and they still acted against business.

Once, America had appreciated its entrepreneurs. Once, men like him, who built businesses, created jobs, and collectively made America the envy of the world, were listened to. Once, their contribution was valued. Those were the days when the real meaning of value creation was understood and appreciated. Men like him, who were able and willing, went out and turned nothing into something, went out and created jobs and prosperity for everyone. But that was then. Now it was becoming harder and harder to be an entrepreneur. Sam could imagine a time when entrepreneurs would no longer exist; when there would be no-one left who was willing to invest their time, money and effort into building a business – not with the restrictions that entrepreneurs were facing.

God, he hated DC. As a younger man, he hadn't minded coming

here so much, but the new generation of politicians thought they knew everything. Nowadays, coming here was like visiting a fucking ivy-league campus. These bastards didn't know shit about the real world. There was an idealism here that worried Sam. They were all out to change the world, like the business graduates who flooded Sam's companies every semester. They were so clueless that they didn't even know they didn't have a clue. His graduates were so clever that they didn't even notice when they were being fleeced by a Chinese peasant. Christ, some of them had even been caught paying bribes to the wrong people!

Sam reached out, grabbed a handful of the lace curtain and squeezed it as tightly as his muscles would allow. When he let go, the drape fell back into place without a crease. That was DC – nothing left a mark here. The streets were paved with Teflon; shit flew everywhere but stuck to nothing.

What really worried Sam was the speed at which the old guys in the firm were retiring. He'd seen the exodus coming, but even so, the pace was scary. Sam had never fallen for the bullshit idea that experience no longer counted. He didn't know who'd dreamed up that particular load of garbage, but he suspected it was an alibi created by downsizing consultants. It had never really gone away, and now it had permeated DC. The hill was full of academics, barely out of diapers. That was a recipe for disaster. Look at what they'd done with the banks.

Breakfast arrived. Sam didn't bother to sit down. He speared a rasher of bacon with his fork and stuffed it into his mouth. He shouldn't be eating this stuff, but he was starving. He should have ordered yoghurt and cereal but his body was militating against him. He'd been quite good about his diet recently but being hungry was not a distraction Sam needed at the moment. He wolfed down another rasher and wiped his mouth on the sleeve of the hotel's bathrobe.

He'd given up the booze long ago and cut out the cigars. Food was the only thing he had left. He patted his stomach. It wasn't that big, but his arteries were clogged up. He'd never thought about them. Until that day he felt his heart. It just happened – he'd felt it in his chest; suddenly become aware that this thing was there. It wasn't as if he was out of breath or anything. He just felt this thing inside him, somewhere in the chest area, and wondered what it was. Then he realised it was his heart.

"Didn't know I had one," he'd joked to his wife Mary that evening over dinner. As soon as he said it, she immediately got up and left the room. A little while later the doctor arrived. Mary had gone and called the quack without even mentioning it. Sam told him to go away, but she started making a scene. So Sam had allowed the doctor to inspect him in the lounge. He remembered sitting there, without a shirt on, while the quack tapped him and listened to his heart. He'd been making fun of Mary all the time, calling her a neurotic female, but neither she nor the doctor had paid the slightest attention to him. Then the doctor had recommended that he go to hospital for tests, right away, that night. He'd refused, but Mary had forced him to go. The woman had surprised him after all those years of marriage. He remembered her standing there with the telephone receiver. He was used to women being pathetic and neurotic, using tears and tantrums to get their way, but that night he'd seen another side to Mary. She'd stood there, phone in hand, and said in a totally calm, rational voice – just like a man – "We go now, Sam, or I call an ambulance."

The doctor at the hospital had been categorical. "A heart attack," the old guy had said. Sam protested that nothing had happened. He'd just felt his heart. That was all. Since then, doctors had become part of his life. Sam hated them.

Sam wondered if Mary knew about Rosa. She couldn't know – there was no way she could know. But sometimes women knew things. Catherine knew things, things she shouldn't have known. Women were like sieves; they leaked everything. You couldn't keep anything quiet when females were involved. They complicated everything. In the old days, life had been so much simpler.

Sam looked down at the unfinished breakfast sitting on the table. To hell with it! He sat down and started on the eggs. His marriage was another thing that had surprised him. Mary was 13 years younger than he was. After all those morose years with Cynthia, she had appeared like a young, sexy breath of fresh air. It was like he'd shed a decade himself. But she hadn't aged well. Her face was more lined than his. She was too thin – just skin and bone. Her buttocks, once plump and juicy, now looked like sacks hanging off her back. In her dressing gown, she looked like a scarecrow. They hadn't had sex for years. Sometimes, Sam thought about getting a divorce, but he knew he'd just wind up with another woman. He liked having a woman around. He and Mary were used to each other; she was easy to live with. She didn't spend much of his money and, provided he was home most Sundays for church, she didn't give a damn what he did for the rest of the week – as long as she knew where he was. Sam doubted that he would ever leave Mary. Women like her didn't grow on trees.

She also calmed him down. Like now. Just thinking about her made him calm again. It was because it was safe to explode around Mary. She wasn't afraid of him. She'd never been afraid of him, even in the early days when she'd been just a girl. He'd tried to scare her once or twice; behaved in a way that would have had the toughest bastards in the company crapping in their pants, but she'd just laughed at him. Mary wasn't the only woman who wasn't scared of him. His first wife hadn't been either. Nor was Catherine. For some reason, Sam had never been able to scare women. He didn't know why. Still, at least he could scare the shit out of men.

Sam polished off the last of the breakfast. He looked at his wrist. His watch was next to the bed. He got up and walked to the table where he had left his cell phone and looked at the screen. He never took his phone into the bedroom when he was with Rosa. It was nearly 6.30. He had some work to do. Should he do it now, or wait till after he'd said goodbye to Rosa? He bit his lower lip and stared out of the window for a few seconds, then he put down the phone, and headed for the bedroom. It was time for Rosa to wake up.

*

Six hours later, Sam was in the sky. It was a relief to be on his plane. While he was in the air, he could be alone, undisturbed. George had called again on the way to the airport with more questions about the deal in the Gulf. Sam had done his best to reassure him, but George was spooked. He probably should have told him about it before, but whenever George heard the word 'nuclear' and 'Arab' in the same sentence, he got the shakes. The deal was nothing out of the ordinary. It was just easier to have it handled from Europe. At least the company's client was a member of the Gulf state's ruling family. That should reassure George.

Sam made a mental note to have all the suppliers double-checked, and to have extra security arrangements put in place. In the Gulf, as in most places, a lot of material invariably went missing from construction sites. Most of the time it was just thievery, but with a nuclear power plant being built and Iran just across the water…

Sam looked at the clouds below. He liked flying in his plane. Sometimes, he would pretend his plane was an impregnable cylinder, hurtling through the sky. He could imagine his enemies shooting at him, could picture the missiles bouncing off the side of the plane like paper darts hitting a wall. He would wave at his enemies through the windows, laughing at their frustrated faces as they reloaded to fire the next harmless volley.

Somehow he had to de-fang Catherine. She was turning into a real problem. They'd had arguments before, but this time something was different. She was very upset about how things were going at the company, and he hadn't made any headway in getting through to her. It was too early to have an idea of the implications. But there would be implications.

When she joined the board, Sam had assumed she'd leave things to him, and for a long time, she had. Until now. At first, he'd been able to understand her attitude. He should have told her that the pension fund was making an investment in the Gulf. Her pension was part of that fund, too, and as a shareholder and board member, she had a right to be told.

But she didn't have a right to question the way he did business. Who the fuck did she think she was? Christ, she'd never set foot in the Gulf. What did she know about doing business there? As for her suggestion that she might have met the fucking partners – that really took the biscuit. It wasn't his fault the Arabs couldn't stand women. Bringing her would have been like taking your mother along on a stag night.

As usual, he'd tried to be reasonable, tried to explain how these things worked, but she'd obviously been looking for a fight, so he'd been careful not to provoke her further. Then the bitch had gone and brought up the deal in the board meeting in front of George, who had nearly freaked. Of course, George hadn't said anything at the time. But George didn't need to say anything.

What really got to Sam was that Catherine had the nerve to question his motives, when she – the cunning bitch – was no better than a grave robber. He still couldn't believe she could have been so scheming and unscrupulous. He could picture her now, holding his father's wrinkled old claw over the paper as he signed away everything he had.

God, had she ever taken them for a ride! After his father retired from the business because of ill health, he'd been worried sick about the old man, not even thinking about the implications of his death or dementia, while she – vulturous, leeching old bitch that she was – had all the time been conniving to snatch away everything the old man had. Sam was convinced the poor old fool had been conned. He had always trusted Catherine implicitly – he would have signed anything she put in front of him. There was no way he'd known that he was signing over control of the company.

As long as the profits were coming, Catherine was perfectly happy to leave him to bust his balls running the show, but now, when he needed a free hand more than ever, she had suddenly started interfering. Fuck the fact that she knew less about running a business than he did about open-heart surgery. Fuck the fact that their most profitable businesses hadn't existed until he had come along and set them up.

Sam still couldn't believe how badly she'd behaved during that board meeting, but he was more angry at himself for having underestimated her to such an extent. Christ, he thought she was coming as a spectator, for the thrill of attending a real board meeting. He'd even had Dick, his director of communications, explain to her how these meetings worked. It seemed she'd understood – for most of the meeting she hadn't said a word; they'd almost forgotten she was there. But then, towards the end, once they'd been through the agenda, she suddenly started asking questions about the pension-fund investment. It had been hugely embarrassing. She'd made him look like an idiot. Thank God the other directors were reasonable, experienced people, who understood how the world worked.

Afterwards, when he'd taken her aside to give her some advice, she'd behaved like a sulky child. He'd expected her to over-react but what really made him angry was that she had refused even to try and understand his position.

"People get nervous when you start asking these sorts of questions," he told her. "I've spent years getting the right people on this board. They are prestigious names and very influential people. I'm sure I don't need to explain to you how valuable such a board is for the company."

She said nothing, staring at him as if he was unbalanced.

"I'm not saying you shouldn't ask questions," he told her. "If you're concerned about something, of course you should ask questions. That's your right and – let's not forget – your obligation, as a director."

"Just not in board meetings!" she blurted out in a loud voice.

Even though he'd had better things to do, he'd taken the time to explain that board meetings were about strategy. "They are not the place to discuss operational business."

She said nothing again.

"We have very few board meetings," Sam explained. "They are our opportunity to get these people – highly influential, knowledgeable people – to let us know what they think about our strategy."

"They don't say much."

Sam shrugged. "They speak when they have something to contribute."

"What are you hoping they'll tell you?"

"They judge the strategy, and they help me understand how the economic, political and legislative environment is likely to affect the business."

"You don't have advisors who do that?"

He remembered Catherine's tone really getting on his nerves. Like Mary, she knew exactly how to irritate the hell out of him.

He kept his cool. "Advisors are like books. They are full of information, but you have to do the thinking if you want to get anything useful out of them."

He didn't have time for these ridiculous conversations. He remembered looking at his watch. "My directors know what information might be useful to me. They do their own thinking. You shouldn't underestimate their value as representatives of the company."

Then he lowered his voice. "You could argue that their real value is simply having them on our board. It's kind of an unofficial triple-A rating." He stood up and smiled at her. "They are highly exposed people – they have to be very careful of their reputations."

Before he left, he leaned down and kissed her cheek. "Just call me, or Dick, if you want to know anything. Don't hesitate. There's nothing to worry about."

He walked away then, hoping – but not hopeful – that she'd get the message.

She hadn't. She was the first woman he'd ever had on the board. He'd expected her to behave, to keep her emotions under control. Christ, she was older than he was. Now she was starting to ask questions about the future of the company – about the succession, as if he was about to drop dead. She'd even had the fucking nerve to question his decision to hire Chris.

"Are you sure the new CEO of the power division is up to the job?" she'd asked, just like that.

Sam kept his temper, but only just.

"What's the point in hiring him," she said, "if he's not able to take over from you?"

The bitch was as subtle as a curb-crawler. She'd then started on the regional bosses, demanding to know when the company was going to appoint someone Chinese to run Asia and a local to take care of South Africa. She knew they'd recently sent a limey to Johannesburg.

Eventually, he told her – in the nicest possible way – to mind her own fucking business.

He should have kept himself under control, but she was infuriating beyond belief. At the end, she just smiled, waved her index finger in his general direction, and said, "We need to find a successor, Sam. And you need to accept that you can't carry on forever."

He'd never come closer to strangling anyone in his life. Who the fuck was 'we'? It was his business. His! It had nothing to do with her.

He needed to calm down; Catherine was bad for his blood pressure. Maybe he should have taken her with him to the Gulf? He could have left her there with one of the sheikhs. Maybe with that old one who thought women were dirty.

Sam grinned to himself. He'd never bonded with an Arab before. It was a weird experience. Most people were like eggs: hard on the outside, but soft and runny when you broke them. The Arabs were the opposite. At first, they'd given him the creeps, with their long fingernails and their soft, cushiony exteriors. But inside – underneath the spongy layers – they were as hard as nails.

He'd thought of Catherine as soon as the old sheikh had started going on about women being 'unclean'. He would have a paid a lot of money to have had her in the room at that moment. By the end of the meal, Sam was convinced the Arabs were keeping their women covered up so they didn't get horny when they looked at them.

Still, the sheikh had a point about women using sex to manipulate men. Catherine had used it to very good effect to get his old father to the altar. Sam wondered whether he'd ever be able to forgive the cunt-struck old fool.

CHAPTER 5

Catherine

It was good to be back. Catherine had missed Zurich. It was one of the few places she had lived that she was always happy to come back to, even in autumn, when that grey damp mist descended on the city and hung over it for days, sometimes weeks, till one could forget what a blue sky looked like. Sometimes, it depressed her, but not today. She was relieved to be home. There, she'd thought it again: home. She supposed Zurich was home now – at least, it was more of a home than anywhere else.

Settling into her seat on the tram, Catherine really did feel in her element. She could relax here; let down her guard. That was why she liked Switzerland: you could be safe and alone at the same time, and anonymous and ignored. Particularly in Zurich, because here – on the tram – they were like Londoners. No-one looked at anyone else.

Despite the oppressive mist, she felt free. The days in New York had been a nightmare, especially that dreadful board meeting. Sam had managed to be pathetic and arrogant at the same time. Catherine didn't know what had happened to him – he was becoming quite impossible – but she'd made her point. She wished she could have left these things to him, but she didn't trust him anymore. She wished men weren't so competitive. Sam needed to calm down and act his age – or maybe that was the problem, maybe he *was* acting his age. She'd noticed he was less sure of himself these days. He wasn't growing old gracefully. Then there was the new mistress. It was ridiculous to be carrying on with other women at his age. He hadn't mentioned her, of course, but it was perfectly obvious that there was a new woman in his life. Men were so stupid. Sam was convinced his wife didn't know about his affairs; he couldn't seem to see that it was as clear as glass when he was seeing another woman. At least he'd learnt how to be discreet.

Catherine stared out of the window, getting glimpses of the river as the tram rattled along. Her mobile rang. It was probably Rosemary. She dug it out of her handbag. It wasn't – there was only a number on the screen. She wouldn't answer it now. She hated speaking on the phone in public, especially on the tram.

She adjusted herself on the seat. After ten hours on an aeroplane, she felt stiff and brittle, as if the moisture had been sucked out of her. The tram jolted slightly as it came to a halt. She watched people getting on, ready to look away if she saw someone she knew. She didn't want to bump into anyone, she just wanted to get home, make a pot of tea, and have a shower.

From the upper floor of her house, Catherine had a good view of Lake Zurich. It was a very desirable residence; not large, but well situated, and in a good old building – one that had been built in the days when things were still made properly. It was handsome and sturdy, and impervious to the climate: cool in summer and warm in the winter. She had bought it years ago when Joseph first got ill. They'd needed a place like this; a place where no-one knew who they were and cared even less; a place where Joseph could be away from everyone and everything.

Like most of the houses here, hers would have been perfect for a family with young children, but few families could afford to live here. Catherine had no idea where families actually did live. Perhaps in the countryside, or more likely in those hideous blocks of flats you saw through the windows of the train. That was one thing she didn't like about living here; everyone around her was old. Sometimes, it felt like she was living in a retirement village.

Catherine leaned forward and looked through the window at the house in front of hers. It was divided into flats and there was a couple with a little girl living on the ground floor. Catherine usually saw the girl leaving for school in the mornings. She looked a lonely little creature. The father obviously had a well-paid job because he was almost never at home and he bought her very expensive presents. Last summer, he'd bought her a trampoline for the garden. For a while, the garden had been full of excited children bouncing away. Then one of the neighbours had complained about the noise and the trampoline had been taken away. Catherine remembered the little girl sitting there with tears rolling down her cheeks while her father dismantled it.

After that, the garden was empty again, like a cemetery. Catherine knew who'd complained; it was that revolting lawyer on the top floor. He ran his office from the house and insisted that there be absolute silence all day. No-one could stand him. He had no business having a legal practice in a residential area, anyway. There were too many old, rich people around here – like her. That's why it was secure and safe. That's why it was like a morgue. Sometimes, Catherine thought that everyone over 65 should be put down and their assets distributed among the young people who were forced to live in those blocks of flats along the railway lines.

She went back downstairs to the kitchen. There wasn't much post – a few bills, the Sunday newspaper and the usual pile of junk. Nobody wrote to her these days, except her old friends, who still sent Christmas cards. She sifted through the junk. When she'd first moved here, she'd been surprised that the Swiss produced so much junk mail. She suspected it was because they had to do something with all the paper they recycled – old junk recycled to make new junk. Well, presumably it kept people in work and saved the odd tree. She kept meaning to get one of those stickers that said "no junk mail" to put on her letter box but never got around to it. Much of the junk mail was catalogues, which were not wholly unpleasant to page through, even though she hardly ever bought anything. She separated the junk into two piles – one for immediate recycling, the other for looking through – and then pulled the newspaper towards her. The front page put her off immediately. Normally she enjoyed reading the Sunday paper over breakfast, but after the flight she just didn't have the energy to tackle a German-language broadsheet.

She felt strange; vaguely light-headed – that odd, slightly empty feeling one has after returning home from another time zone. There were thoughts in her head that she didn't know what to do with. They needed to be filed in the correct places, but for that she would need sleep, and she couldn't sleep now. She felt alert but she knew her brain was not functioning properly. Only after a night's sleep would she start to feel normal again. It would take more nights to get rid of the jet lag.

After tea, Catherine wound up unpacking. She hadn't meant to. On the plane, she'd told herself it could wait. She would do it later, or even tomorrow. What was the hurry? There was absolutely no reason to unpack as soon as she got home, but she had to open her suitcase to get out her cosmetic bag, and then it was lying open on the bedroom floor, like a patient on the operating table.

Within an hour, everything was in its proper place, the washing machine on, as if she'd never been away. Now what was she going to do? The day stretched ahead of her like a desert. That was another thing she didn't like about living here – everything was closed on Sundays. She was irritated with herself for unpacking. She'd always had this problem – not being able to relax until everything was done. She sat down on the bed. Her shoulders were hurting. They always did when she was tense; she tended to hunch them without noticing and then they would start to ache. A hot bath would help. Usually, she took hot baths only in the evening because they left her completely drained of energy.

She stood up and looked out of the window. The lake lay before her. Through the mist, she could just make out the dim shapes of the buildings on the opposite bank. It was one of those days when you felt like closing the curtains and shutting out the world. She stared at the bleakness for a few minutes, unable to decide about the bath. Oh, to hell with it! She stripped, put on her robe and ran the bath. It was too late for breakfast and too early for lunch, so she ate a yoghurt that was right on its sell-by date and downed a glass of tap water.

Standing in front of the mirror in the bathroom, Catherine forced herself to look at her naked body. It was the arms she hated most – that had been a surprise. She'd always expected it would be the legs that would bother her. Even as a child, she'd noticed the cellulite that destroyed women's thighs, and dreaded the day when hers too would turn into cylinders of coagulated fat, but her legs actually weren't too bad. There was certainly cellulite, but not much of it, and it was behind her. That was one compensation of ageing – you couldn't stretch your neck around to see what was happening to the back of you.

What she hadn't bargained for were the saggy arms; the loose skin that hung down under her biceps. She stretched across with her right arm and tapped the flabby underarm flesh of her left. The skin swayed back and forth. She'd done everything to keep her arms firm: kept her weight down, exercised, even tried one of those muscle-toning machines that don't work. But still the skin hung. It wasn't bad, she'd seen far worse – the arms on some women of her age were only sag. At least hers had definition and the muscles still hardened when she tightened her arm. Gravity was a horrible thing.

Her breasts had held up pretty well, but they weren't large and she'd always been obsessive about wearing good bras. She took a step back and bent over, trying to touch her toes. As she lent forward, her belly button disappeared – really disappeared. For a second, she was slightly startled. Staring between her dangling breasts at her belly, there was no trace of it – she could see only small, wrinkly rolls of flesh. She'd never looked at her stomach from this angle before. It was horrible. And she wasn't even fat!

She straightened up and moved closer to the mirror. At this distance, and after all those hours on the plane, her thin face seemed to consist mainly of lines. It was only bearable to look at because it was framed by her dyed hair. Her jowls weren't too bad but the skin on her décolleté was as speckled and blotchy as a quail's egg. To the world, she was well and truly invisible now.

That had been difficult to get used to – becoming invisible. It didn't bother her anymore, but it had been a real shock at first. She'd never dreamt that such a thing would happen. No-one tells you that one day the world will simply stop seeing you. Since childhood, she'd been aware of being looked at, especially by men. As she'd turned into a woman, it had got better – or worse – depending on who was looking. And then during pregnancy, the men looked less, but the women more, and after pregnancy, the men looked again. As she got older, the ones looking were getting older still. But at least they were looking. Until one day, they stopped. Of course, it didn't happen overnight. It had been gradual, she supposed, but she'd been so preoccupied with Joseph and the hysterectomy and moving to Switzerland that she'd sort of forgotten about the rest of the world. When she finally started paying attention again, she'd noticed that somewhere along the line, she'd become invisible. Not entirely. She'd kept her figure – in clothes, anyway – and, with the dyed hair, men would occasionally notice her from behind.

From time to time, one of the old ones still gave her the eye, but these days, they were really old. At first she'd smiled back, assuming they were being polite, until one of them propositioned her. That was a shock. He was ancient, ready for the funeral parlour. It had been revolting and funny at the same time. Only the odd geriatric looked at her now, assuming his eyes were good enough. The men of her own age – the 60s brigade – were looking at the 40-somethings, or the even younger.

Catherine stepped into the bath and lowered herself carefully into the steaming water. It was hot – very hot – but not so painfully hot that she could be bothered to do anything about it. She squatted there, bouncing on her haunches, shrieking silently as the steaming water swirled around her nether regions, harmlessly scalding her sagging skin. After a while, it felt safe enough to sink in further. Eventually, she sat down and slowly slid into a horizontal position. Gradually, she let her muscles relax. This was always the best moment of a bath – the pain of entry was over, and the sweatiness and lethargy had yet to set in.

It was hard to believe that becoming invisible had bothered her so much. The hysterectomy hadn't helped. Perhaps it was the combination of losing her looks and having her reproductive organs ripped out at the same time; it was as though she'd woken up in a different world.

She remembered the day when she stopped caring. It was in the queue at the post office, when that cocksure young African behind her recklessly started chatting her up. She'd not looked around on purpose until he got really close. Then, when he was right there, she'd turned and given him a flirtatious wink. His face was such a picture that she'd fallen about laughing. She'd never seen a black man blush. Then he started laughing, too.

Sometimes, she still cared a little about being invisible, but on the whole not really. As long as she looked like this, she didn't want to be looked at. In any case, it was ridiculous for a woman of her age to be worrying about these things. What did it matter that men no longer wanted her? What did she want from them anyway? Company? Hardly. She'd rather have a good gossip with a woman any day. Sex? God, no. Truth be told, she'd never been particularly interested in sex. At her age, the thought of getting hot and bothered in bed with a wrinkly old man was too revolting for words.

Men were different – they never lost interest in sex. Catherine suspected that for men, getting old was easier. They didn't change. They did everything they'd always done, just more slowly. Usually, they died before their wives. For women, getting old was frightening, particularly if you were alone, and most women were, eventually.

The funny thing was that you noticed other people ageing but not yourself, even though the aches and pains and the mirrors confirmed it every day. Even now, Catherine had to remind herself that she was old and consequently utterly uninteresting. Sometimes, she would talk to a young person – in a queue or at a tram stop – without thinking. Small talk might ensue, but the young one was always only being polite. Really, she was talking to herself. The last thing a young person wanted to do was discuss the weather with a fossil.

Catherine had never imagined that getting old was such a physical thing. For most of her life, she'd assumed people were as old as their bodies. Her mother had been older than her body. But it wasn't like that. Once, hurrying past a shop window, she thought: "That old duck's not in bad shape. She just needs to update her look." Then, stunned, she'd realised she was looking at a reflection of herself.

For a while, she'd imagined she was in denial, then she'd started to wonder whether she was heading into the beginnings of senility. Now, with the scary seventies looming, she'd become convinced that ageing was – at its deepest level – a continual, accelerating breakdown in relations between the mind and the body. She had no idea whether this was a cause of ageing, or merely an outcome of it, but it was obvious that her mind was not ageing like her body. Her mind was changing but it wasn't collapsing. In her head, she felt young and full of life. She kept forgetting she was old. It was only when she looked down, or into the mirror, that she would be reminded of it. That could depress her. Sometimes, she felt like a girl trapped in an old woman's body.

It wasn't all bad. With every year, she became more detached from the physical world and more bound up in a world of meanings, nuances and ideas. Her old passions, desires and fears, once almost entirely physical, were now supremely uninteresting. She still enjoyed some sensual pleasures – a good meal or a glass of wine – but even these she consumed with waning interest. Reading and art she still liked, but it was the ways and workings of the world that interested her more.

With hindsight, it seemed logical that this would happen. Her body held no pleasures for her, or anyone else, and the senses were dulling, getting gradually weaker by the year. She had noticed her reflexes were slower, but her mind seemed not to be ageing. Perhaps it was remission – a last gasp of youth before senility really set in but for the first time in her life, she suddenly found she had ideas, plans and a sense of purpose. She had things to do. She was much more aware of the world now than she ever had been as a young woman. When she thought about her youth, it was as though she'd been walking around in a daze, as if she'd been permanently on pills. Now that she was awake and aware, she wanted to find out more, do more, to experience things she'd never dreamt were possible. But she had to be realistic. She was stuck in this body – an ugly, battered machine on its last legs, its best days long behind it. The world had moved on and there was no point in getting upset about it.

Lying in the bath, with steam rising around her, Catherine wondered about this disconnection between mind and body. She had the feeling people didn't appreciate just how separate the two things were. It sounded odd when you put it like that, but body and mind could be remarkably out of step with each other. She knew that from Joseph; his body and his reptilian brain were still functioning perfectly, but his mind was long gone.

She'd got used to that, too. In the early years, it had been a nightmare. When he first started to forget, she'd been warned it would get a lot worse. She couldn't have imagined how much worse. She'd looked after him for as long as she could, but once he forgot who she was, she had no choice but to move him into care.

The guilt had taken longer to get rid of. Eventually it had gone, too. The care cost a fortune, but they could afford it. Anyway, she didn't have a choice – she couldn't look after him at home. That had been another reality check; another case when a stranger – her husband's unpleasant Serbian nurse – had suddenly told her to put him into care and get on with her life. The nurse had said it, knowing that if Joseph wasn't there, there would be no job for her. "It wasn't him," the woman snapped, when Catherine eventually and apologetically let her go. "It was you! You and all your moaning – I couldn't stand it anymore." It was the only time she'd felt a hint of affection for the woman.

Alzheimer's was a dreadful disease. It killed people without taking their life away; it left you mourning a person you couldn't bury. Sometimes, she would forget her husband was no longer there. He looked like Joseph, sitting there in the garden of the care home with his sunglasses on. Sometimes, he would tilt his head and look at her in the way that he used to. For a short while, she could pretend that everything was the way it used to be; that he was still there, still in control, still the man she'd married – but the man in the care home wasn't Joseph. He was only a shell, a body. Well, that was going too far. There was some kind of person in there, but it wasn't Joseph. She hoped he wouldn't last much longer. There was no point in him being there.

Catherine stared at her toes. Her body felt heavy and her head was hot – sweat was dripping down her forehead. She pulled her legs towards her and let her abdomen slide deeper into the water, stopping when the water reached her chin. She lay there for some moments, feeling strange. For some reason, she had the urge to submerge her entire head.

She lay there, unsure, for a while longer, and then let her head sink further. As the water went into her ears, she panicked and quickly sat up. She realised she was breathing heavily. That was strange; she felt a little light-headed. Why had she done that? Then she heard something; the phone ringing.

Who was trying to reach her? It didn't matter. She knew

Rosemary and the children were fine – she'd spoken to her daughter from New York. There was no-one else in the world she cared about.

She hadn't planned it like this; would never have dreamt her life would turn out this way. For a long time after Joseph got ill, she'd wallowed in self-pity, convinced herself that it had all been foisted upon her, that life had dealt her all the worst cards. But there came a point when she accepted that she had to take some responsibility for herself. Once she'd got used to it, she realised she was actually not that bad at it.

That had been difficult to get used to – the fact that she was quite smart. She hadn't allowed herself to believe it for a long time, but gradually, and to her genuine amazement, she began to realise that she knew more about life and the world than most people did. With hindsight, it was inevitable that this would happen. It had nothing to do with being clever; it was simply because she'd been around for so bloody long.

It was just as well she had worked a few things out. With Joseph gone, it was all up to her. She'd assumed Sam would take over everything and that it would all carry on much as before, but Joseph had surprised her.

She had vivid memories of that conversation with her husband. She hadn't known it at the time, but it was to be one of those moments when she suddenly realised something about the world – about how it all worked – that she'd never been aware of before.

If she was honest with herself, it was the day she grew up; the day she first got an inkling of what the world might be like without her husband in it. She'd never thought about what would happen when Joseph was gone; it was too much to think about. He'd replaced her father as the rock of her life. She couldn't imagine life without him.

He'd seemed to understand that, but it hadn't stopped him. He'd trapped her – taken her by surprise – because whenever he'd brought up the subject before, she'd always run away.

"I need to talk to you," he said. It was a nice day. They were sitting in the morning room, after breakfast.

Catherine could tell something bad was coming. She stood up, muttered an excuse and walked hurriedly towards the door. But to get there, she had to pass him, and he was already on his feet, barring the way.

She tried to push past, but he was immovable. "We need to talk," he said, putting his hands on her shoulders, restraining her.

Catherine remembered staring at the floor, shaking her head, like a child refusing to listen.

"You will hear what I have to say!" he instructed. "You will listen to me, and then you can go and do what the hell you like!"

He was squeezing her shoulders, hard. He'd never done that before. She pulled away and glared up at him, ready to argue her way out, but there was something about the face that struck her. She peered more closely. Something about the eyes. Or in the eyes. It was like he was another person.

That was a long time ago. The memory was still so painful that she cried whenever she'd thought about it. She was crying now, in the bath; tears that were instantly swallowed by the hot water, leaving her with nothing but a slightly choked feeling in her throat. Now she was able to think about that conversation. That was progress – for years, she hadn't even been able to do that.

Joseph had sat down opposite her and, sounding like a lawyer, told her he'd been diagnosed with dementia, possibly Alzheimer's. To begin with, she'd been relieved. She'd thought he was going to tell her that he was going to die. She hadn't known then what Alzheimer's could mean. She desperately wanted him to live, but it would have been better…

"I have made all the preparations," he told her. "I intend to transfer all my assets to you – everything – and to give you my power of attorney."

She'd been surprised, confused, only able to stare blankly at him.

"Do you understand what I'm telling you?"

She shook her head.

"I'm giving you control of the company," he said.

She shook her head again. "Why? What about your will? What about Sam?"

Her husband leaned back in his chair and simply stared at her.

"Sam runs the thing," she persisted.

He still said nothing.

"Why?" she repeated. "Why me? I don't know anything. Sam runs the company. Give it to him."

"I should give it all to Sam?" her husband said.

"Yes. Well, the power of..." She hesitated.

He waited.

"I just don't understand why this is so urgent," she said, leaning to one side and shaking her head at the floor. "Why can't it wait? Why can't you put it all in your will? Why can't we sort it out later?"

She continued staring at the floor.

Her husband sat there in silence, waiting for her to look at him.

After a while, she glanced quickly at him. He immediately made eye contact. She looked away. He leaned forward and grasped her wrist in his right hand.

"It must be now," he said softly, looking over the top of his glasses at her. "We have to do this now. It must be made a *fait accompli.*"

He stopped again, and let her go. "I can feel my mind going. I've known for a while that something was wrong." His voice wobbled slightly.

She looked at him. He looked old, scared and helpless. She'd never seen him like this. She just managed to keep control of herself.

"Sam will ruin it all," her husband said. "He will destroy the company."

She stared at him in shock. "But he runs it. The two of you built it. It's a hugely successful company."

Her husband shook his head. "He can't do it. Not alone."

Catherine was stunned. "But he's been running the company for years. You put him there. He's turned it into a worldwide enterprise. It's been growing continuously. The share price..."

Her husband shook his head. "Things can change very quickly."

She protested again, insisting that Sam was on top of everything.

Her husband pursed his lips. "Sam is out of control, Catherine. He's a dinosaur who can't come to terms with his future. He's betrayed us; he's betrayed everything we stand for. If we leave him to it, he will run the company into the ground. We can't let that happen. We have to try and salvage it. We have to, for everyone's sake: the employees, the shareholders, for Rosemary – our daughter – and her children."

As soon as he said 'children', they both knew the matter was effectively settled. Nevertheless, she kept arguing. "I know nothing," she insisted.

"You have the right instincts," he countered. "And you are the only person capable of standing up to him."

"But you don't understand. I don't know the first thing about running a business. I have no idea how the company is doing. For Christ's sake – I don't even know how to find out."

Her husband waved a hand in the air. Then he seemed to lose interest in the discussion. He looked away, out of the window.

She repeated herself more forcefully.

"You can pay people to do those things," he said, still waving. "It's just a question of keeping an eye on Sam until someone else is ready to take over. Just stop him from doing too much damage. That's all."

She raised her voice. "Who's going to take over? Who?"

Her husband shook his head. "I don't know. Finding a successor was supposed to be his job."

"But who could do it?" she insisted.

Her husband shrugged. "I really don't know." He leaned back in his chair. "Don't worry about it too much. We can't control these things anyway. The best you can do is to keep the place strong, so that whoever does take over has a vested interest in building on what's there. What we don't want is for a new person to throw it all away and start again."

"What about the management?" she said. "We can hire someone to do it for us?"

Her husband shrugged but didn't look convinced. "Maybe."

His body had sunk slightly in his chair. He was looking very old.

"What happens if Sam walks when he finds out about this?"

Her husband growled. "Don't be absurd, Catherine!"

She had continued to press him, carried on demanding answers, but she got nothing more. The lawyers arrived the next day with the papers.

The speed with which her husband deteriorated shocked her. He had been right to act quickly. Living with him was terrible. Sometimes, she could literally see his mind unravelling. Worst was when he forgot who she was and started thinking she was his first wife, Winifred, or even at times one of his old mistresses. She tried so hard to remind him who she was, but it was like trying to put up a tent in a storm. Eventually, she just became Winny. It was easier that way, even when he commented on her changed habits, and talked about things she would rather have not known about.

In a way it became easier as his mind deteriorated because he was less depressed, but the periods when she was living with a stranger, who couldn't have cared less whether she lived or died, gradually lengthened. Once, stressed and exhausted, she cut herself badly, nearly sliced her index finger off, preparing his food. He sat there watching her bleed, like an ethnologist on a field visit.

She just left the company to Sam. Even after Joseph went into care, she just stayed out of it. She didn't have the strength, or the inclination, and she was afraid of igniting a conflict. Sam had taken the news of her 'inheritance' well, but only because she'd signed the paper appointing him Chairman in his father's place. Why not? Everything looked fine. All the charts were pointing in the right direction. The reports looked good; there was nothing in the newspapers. Sam was telling her nothing. There was nothing to tell, he said.

Looking back from the bathtub, it was obvious that she'd been afraid of taking it all. She'd lived up to everyone's worst expectations and gone further. Marrying her boss – an older man – had been bad enough, but getting his power of attorney, taking control of his money and his company and then putting him into care, made her look like the worst kind of money-grabbing bitch.

But what else could she have done? She owed it to Joseph, and she didn't doubt him for a moment, even if his mind was going. He'd always been right – that was why she'd married him. Everyone assumed it was for the money, but his wealth was incidental. When she first became his secretary, he'd seemed like a rock. People worshipped him. With him, she had nothing to fear. She was always safe and protected. He couldn't help it; he had to protect; like a guard dog. He went looking for danger – in times of calm, he was lost.

In the end, he'd turned out to be as weak and fragile as she was and he'd left her with a burden that had nearly destroyed her. At times, she almost hated him for it. At times, she'd sworn she wasn't going to do it. However, as the months passed, and the other burdens had fallen away, she'd found herself wondering what was really going on in that company; wondering what they were going to do with it, and who on earth they were going to get to run it. The questions were still unanswered – because she was scared of asking them. The money just kept rolling in.

Catherine sat up. The bathwater was cooling fast. For a moment, she considered adding more hot water, but decided against it. The skin on her fingertips looked like tiny alpine landscapes. 'Granny fingers', her mother had called them. She climbed out of the bath and put on her robe. Her body was totally drained, but her mind was as awake as before. She stepped off the bath mat and had to steady herself. She considered a cool shower, but decided instead to go and lie down. She walked cautiously to the bedroom and fell on to the bed.

Things had changed. She had changed. Sam was going to have to wake up to that. It was high time they brought in some fresh blood to run the business. It was obvious that the CEO – what was his name? Chris? – wasn't up to the job, which was precisely why Sam had hired him.

Catherine would take a closer look at Gideon. He was unpredictable and difficult, but at least he had a mind of his own. If he wasn't up to it, she'd start looking at some of the other younger people in the company – some of the people on the career programme. They could easily hire an employee to run the place until one of the grandchildren was ready to take over. Rosemary might still change her mind. Why shouldn't a woman run a company like theirs? The engineering business might be a man's world, but that was only because women weren't interested. Times were changing. Maybe, once the children were older, Rosemary might think again about joining the company.

Catherine sat up. It was time to see what Gideon was capable of. She picked up the phone. Sam should be at home now, with his wife.

CHAPTER 6

Leaving London

The plane moved forward on to the runway. They were about to take off with an hour's delay. Jane should have been almost home by now, but Sino had a feeling she was still at the airport. She'd insisted on coming, even though there was no point. It had been very difficult to say goodbye; she'd kept him back until he absolutely had to go through to the boarding gates. It was the longest, most drawn-out, painful goodbye he'd ever experienced. Why she couldn't have stayed at home, he didn't know. She could have spared both of them all that misery.

Through the window of his economy-class seat, Sino could see the airport buildings. He could imagine Jane standing in the lookout area, watching his plane.

The aircraft started to shudder as the pilot revved up the engines. For a few seconds, the plane remained stationary as it strained against its brakes. Then, slowly, it started to move. Sino kept his eyes fixed on the Tarmac. The painted marks on the runway began skipping past faster and faster. Soon they were darting, and then they became a solid, blurred line. The front of the plane pulled up into the air. It was about to happen. Sino sat dead still, waiting. Heavily, slowly, trembling, the aircraft dragged its back wheels off the ground.

Sino watched the airport shrinking away beneath them. From the way he was staring out of the window, it probably looked as if this was his first flight. For some reason, he wanted to experience every moment of this departure. He'd flown out of London many times before, but he'd always been coming back.

Soon, the ground was almost invisible. Sino stared at the scraps of it that were left until the clouds blocked it out completely. That was it, it was over; London was behind him. After all those years, it had ended so quickly – like a thunderstorm. He felt strange. He'd expected to be excited and happy, but all he felt was a weird mixture of relief and tension. Maybe it was the pain of saying goodbye to Jane; the sudden tearing up of everything.

After a while, he realised he still couldn't quite believe it was happening. In part, it was because it had taken so long, but it was also because it was simply too early to take it for granted. It was unlikely, but everything could still go wrong. They'd promised him that everything was arranged; that he was expected in Shanghai. There was supposed to be an office ready for him. He was supposed to be going to look after one of the company's Chinese partners. The HR boss had told him all these things, but he'd told Sino many things before.

It would probably be alright, but you never knew. In this company, you could never consider anything decided until it had actually happened. And even then – even after all was said and done – sometimes it could still all be undone. The company was inherently unreliable. For some reason, nothing ever happened in the way it was supposed to. In all those years in London, Sino could not recall one occasion when what had been promised, what had been agreed, what had been decided, had actually materialised in the way they'd said it would. Most of the time, things didn't materialise; at least, not on the strength of a promise or an agreement. Most of the time, commitments and promises and agreements just dissipated into nothing.

For anything to get done, things had to get ugly. Most of the time, you had to endure a pointless exchange of accusations and insults, followed by threats and dissembling and lies, before what was supposed to have been done had any chance of getting done. If it was done, it was done late, and hurriedly, and badly.

Sino tried to forget about it. He wanted to enjoy this flight; he'd been looking forward to it for years. He'd been imagining it for years: sitting in his seat, staring out at the clouds, planning his future. But now that he was finally here, all he could think about was the past. It was too soon to imagine the future; it could all so easily go wrong. He could land in another place he didn't want to be in. One unexpected change, one careless slip, one stupid decision by a clueless manager, and his whole future could come crashing down again.

Sino fiddled with the catch of the folding table in front of him. You couldn't take anything for granted when dealing with westerners. The criminals at the bank were a case in point. He'd made the mistake of believing them. All they'd had to do was transfer money to China. What the hell else was a bank there for? For months, he'd assumed they were sending the money home to his parents as instructed. That was what they'd agreed to do; that's what they were being paid to do. For months, he'd wondered why his parents hadn't said anything; hadn't thanked him. For months, they'd wondered why the money wasn't coming. Eventually, his mother had asked him. She'd had to because they'd needed the money – for his father's medical bills.

The people at the bank had cocked up everything. First, they had just not transferred the money. Sino still didn't know why. After he complained, they sent the money to the wrong place. Then they told him it was his problem because the money was somewhere in China and they couldn't get it back. Thank God he'd kept a record of everything, so he could prove that it was the bank and not him that had got everything wrong. What the hell was the point of a bank that couldn't handle money?

That was another thought he shouldn't have allowed into his head; now he was angry as well as tense. He hated the people at the bank. They had embarrassed him and humiliated his mother and made her sick with worry. At the end of it, after months of arguments and unpleasantness, they hadn't even had the decency to apologise. Instead, they'd simply sent him a letter which could have been written by a computer, confirming that the transfers had finally taken place. Sino could quite easily have strangled the man at the bank. He hated that man; he hated the bank. He hated all westerners who had anything to do with banks. He would do his utmost, for the rest of his life, never to have anything to do with a western bank again.

For a long time, he thought he'd been lucky. That was a laugh. How many Chinese got to study in England? His parents had worked day and night throughout his childhood to give him a 'proper' education; a western education. Neither they nor he had

had a clue how much it was going to end up costing them. All those years, all that money, all that separation, and he stuck in a place he didn't want to be, surrounded by people he didn't want to know, working for bosses he couldn't stand. At the end, what did he have to show for it? Two lousy pieces of paper. It was at the master's graduation ceremony that Sino finally realised what a scam it all was. "We've taught you everything we know," his old professor had grinned, tongue firmly in cheek. "Now you can call yourselves, 'Master'."

What a joke. Sino couldn't believe he'd once thought the west knew it all. God, had he grown up!

The air hostess arrived with the drinks trolley. Sino asked for a beer. He knew he'd regret it because he'd need to go to the toilet soon and would have to disturb the man next to him. But he wanted a drink. Maybe he could hold it in until they got to Dubai?

He couldn't help feeling guilty about Jane. He'd known he was going to feel guilty about her one day. There was no reason to. He'd never intended to have a relationship with her; he'd tried to avoid it. He'd told her from the very beginning that he was only in England temporarily and that he was going back to China, but it was inevitable that she would start to assume he was staying. You couldn't blame her. If an Englishman had talked about something for as long as he had without doing anything about it, you'd have known he was full of shit.

Sino had never worked out how seriously to take Jane. She complained all the time about the same things, but never did anything about them. A while ago, she'd started talking about the two of them in the future tense. She'd started buying things that 'they' needed for the flat, and asking him to contribute. She'd even suggested a few times that they start looking for a new place because their's was a bit like 'student digs'.

Sino was pretty sure she didn't really love him. They were just two people who'd wound up together and got used to each other. When she'd first taken an interest in him, he'd been flattered, but not for long. It was obvious she was looking for a man and was having trouble landing a western one, so she'd settled for him. Jane was a good person, but she wasn't good-looking.

Sino remembered an ugly woman in his village whom no-one had wanted to marry. She ended up with a much older man, who was as a mean as shit. "A woman will marry anyone – eventually," his grandfather had whispered to him at the wedding. It hadn't bothered him that Jane was no beauty. Most westerners were funny-looking in one way or another. It had been nice to have a woman around and the sex had been welcome.

Sino looked at the flight map on the screen in front of him. They had already flown over the English Channel. England was already behind them. It was such a small country. Europe was such a small place. Sino remembered a Chinese acquaintance at university telling him that the longest route across western Europe – from Dublin to Athens – was not much further than the trip from Beijing to Hong Kong. They would be flying over China for hours before they reached Shanghai.

It was hard to believe that England had once ruled over more than half the world. The countries it had colonised must have been appallingly run, or not run at all. Sino's grandfather had never been impressed by empires. Whenever he talked about the communists or the emperors, he would always shake his finger, and say, "Don't mistake the rain for the weather."

Sino looked at his vague reflection in the window. For years, he'd nodded knowingly whenever his grandfather said that, without having the foggiest idea what the old man was talking about.

His grandfather had said a lot of things Sino didn't understand. "Children don't understand most of what they see and hear," the old man would retort when his wife laughed at him for discussing such subjects with a child. "They just store it all in their heads until it comes in handy."

Sino still missed his grandfather. Sitting in this plane, over Europe, he could marvel at how much he'd learned since he left China. But the really important stuff – the knowledge that had made it possible for him to survive London, and to get back home – he'd got from his grandfather.

As much as he loved his parents, Sino wasn't sure how well he knew them. His most enduring childhood memory of his father and mother was saying goodbye to them as they packed up after the holidays to take the train to work in the city. Then he and his grandfather would walk back home together, the old man's arm around his shoulders, as Sino tried to hold back the tears.

But he never missed his parents for long. Life with his grandfather was too interesting. On weekdays, he would rush home from school to tell the old man what had happened that day, who had said what, how the other kids and the teacher had behaved. When the weather was nice, they would go and sit together on the battered wooden bench outside the house, and his grandfather would interpret it all for him.

Sino's favourite activity was sitting with his grandfather watching the villagers go by. As soon as each person was out of earshot, his grandfather would tell him all about that person. Not the boring, mundane facts, but the wicked secrets and the shameful pasts and what that person or that person's family had been doing when the communists were wreaking havoc across the country. Sino's grandfather was full of stories. The best one was how he had beaten the communists.

His grandfather had been the rock of his life, and the rock of the village. He was there when the communists arrived, and he was still there – still in charge of his village – after they'd turned back into imperialists.

"It's the Chinese way," his grandfather would tell him. "In China, we don't overthrow our oppressors, we 'Sinicise' them – we turn them into 'Sinics', like ourselves. Sometimes, it takes a long time, but in the end they always become like us. We did it to the Mongols, the Manchus, and the communists. We'll do it to the next lot, too."

Sino had spent many afternoons, spellbound, as the old man puffed his pipe and recited memories of his past. In old age, his grandfather was an ancient, wizened creature, who walked almost bent double and couldn't muster much more than a loud whisper, but he was still the most powerful man in the village.

"When the communists arrived, they humiliated me," his grandfather would say, haughtily. "They beat me and treated me like an animal."

Then he would turn to Sino and give him a wicked grin – "But they couldn't keep it up for long. The clever ones had to leave; they had a country to ruin. Here, in my village, they left behind a small man, with a small mind."

In the early days, the man that the Communist Party put in charge had tried to win over the villagers, but it wasn't long before he and his cronies started throwing their weight around. As the food became scarcer, and the demands for crops from the central government more outrageous, the party man abandoned any pretext at building support and simply used intimidation and violence to extract supplies out of the villagers.

"The year the crop failed and the stores ran out, I left the village," Sino's grandfather told him. "Everyone knew I had stores of grain underground, and everyone knew that I was the only one who knew where they were. I wasn't afraid of what they would do to me, but I feared what they would do to my family. So I left. There was no point in torturing my family if I wasn't there to see it."

When people in the village started dying of starvation, the party man panicked. He and his family were hungry, too, and the party was nowhere to be seen.

While telling his tales, Sino's grandfather would often pause to whack his pipe against the wooden bench on which they sat. "It's difficult to throw your weight around on an empty stomach," he would grin, scraping out the remnants of ash.

That was Sino's cue. "How did you save the village?" he would ask, even though he'd heard the story hundreds of times before.

He didn't mind; he enjoyed listening to his grandfather. He even encouraged the old man to repeat things, and would remind him when he left out important details. Sino had no idea why he liked hearing the same stories over and over again. There was something soothing about listening to his grandfather and knowing what was going to come out of the old man's mouth. It made him feel safe and secure.

His grandfather would raise a finger – a sign that something profound was coming. "There are few better ways of putting a man in your debt than to feed his family," he would say.

With his hidden stores of food, Sino's grandfather had won the villagers over and tamed the party people. "The communists always abandoned their people in the end," Sino's grandfather told him. "You just had to be there to catch them when the ground gave way."

When he was older, Sino heard and overheard different versions of the old man's tale. It was whispered in the village that his grandfather had intimidated and in some cases starved the villagers into submission. There were even rumours that he'd joined the communists and been appointed party man himself. His grandfather certainly wasn't loved, but he was respected. It was generally accepted that, because of him, most of the villagers survived. Because of him, many of the old people outlived Mao himself.

Over time, Sino learned about his grandfather's strategy – how he took control from the communists and made the village his own.

"I simply filled holes," was how his grandfather explained it. But Sino hadn't understood; not for years.

"Wherever you are, you will find holes," his grandfather would say. "Holes are things that should be done, but are not done. They are everywhere. They exist because no one regards them as theirs to do. You must fill these holes," the old man would say. "Every hole is an opportunity."

Sino would pretend to understand.

"Filling holes is an excellent way to increase your power and influence," his grandfather would say. "Not because it's clever, or novel, or easy but for the simple reason that no-one else ever does it. It's the one strategy that you, and you alone, will be using."

"How do you spot the holes?" Sino would ask. It was important to ask questions occasionally, otherwise his grandfather would think he wasn't interested.

"It's easy," the old man would say. "Whenever you encounter a question without an answer or a problem without a solution, you have a hole. People always react in the same way to holes; they ignore them. They pretend not to see them. They step over them, they walk around them. If the hole is too big – too obvious to ignore – they stop and complain that someone has left a hole. What they almost never do – what never occurs to them – is to fill the hole themselves."

Once, when Sino's grandfather had been explaining his theory of holes during a walk, they came across a family stranded on the road. The front wheel of their cart had gone into a hole, and was stuck fast. The horse was pulling and the family were pushing, but the cart wouldn't budge.

"Watch!" Sino's grandfather whispered to him, excitedly.

Neither Sino nor his grandfather could help; Sino was too small and his grandfather too old, so they simply stood there, watching.

Soon more people arrived and a discussion ensued about how the cart could be extracted. The owner of the cart was complaining about the state of the road, which was full of holes. It was because of the recent rains, said one man. Another blamed the government for not looking after the roads. Eventually, a volunteer was dispatched to borrow another horse to lend extra pulling power.

Then Sino's grandfather stepped forward. "Why not simply fill the hole with stones?" he said, pointing to several large stones lying around.

No-one moved.

"You might have to wait a long time for another horse," his grandfather warned.

Slowly, reluctantly, the family started gathering stones and dropping them into the hole. Soon the hole was full and the cart was free. It was a blindingly obvious solution but no-one had thought of it.

"People are funny about holes," Sino grandfather observed as they trundled away. "They always try to get out of them, but they never think to fill them up." The old man shook his head, slightly sorrowfully. "So the holes never go away."

Sino remembered his grandfather stopping, raising a finger and pointing it at him. "When you grow up, you must fill holes," he instructed. "You must do it of your own accord. You must do it without being asked."

Sino hadn't understood why.

"You must do it, because each hole is something to make your own."

To Sino, it sounded like a lot of work for no benefit, or worse, work that could be for someone else's benefit.

"It is," his grandfather said. "That's why people avoid holes. There is almost never a reward for filling them. Most of the time no-one notices and, if people do notice – because filling a hole has brought a benefit or attracted praise – you can count on someone else being there to claim the credit."

"So what's the point?" Sino asked.

His grandfather gave him one of his patient smiles. "What happens when you fill a hole?"

Sino tried to think of an answer, but couldn't do better than: "You don't have a hole anymore."

The old man nodded gently. "You create a surface, a fundament, a place on which something can be built, can grow. That's what happens when you fill a hole." He stuffed his pipe. "Few people are willing to take the time to create a fundament; it's much easier to squat on someone else's. That's what the communists did. They squatted on the fundaments of the peasants. They didn't grow crops, they stole them; they didn't produce steel, they melted the steel that was there."

His grandfather's face twitched slightly. "The communists destroyed the fundament of my village, utterly. They extracted every bit of value out of it and left nothing but holes – the worst holes in the world; the holes of hunger, fear, pain and grief."

"How did you beat them?" Sino asked.

The old man shook his head. "I didn't fight them; I just filled the holes they left behind. They came and swept away the ground beneath our feet. They left us suspended above a void. For the communists, it was too much trouble to replace the fundament. The big ones were too busy trying to reinvent the world; the little ones too busy feathering their nests."

The old man lit his pipe. "In this village, I created a new fundament. I had enough stores to fill the holes of hunger. When I was gone, the children died of malnutrition and starvation. When I came back, they stopped dying. The women never forgot that." He paused. "Incidentally, a woman is a much more reliable ally than a man." He smiled at Sino. "You never know what a man really cares about. With women, it's always the children."

The old man had evidently considered it important that Sino

understand the 'fundament strategy' because he had returned to it repeatedly. Resuming the discussion was easy – he only had to refer to 'the holes' or 'the fundament'.

Gradually, Sino began to understand. "How will people know?" he asked. "When I have filled a hole, when I have created a piece of fundament, how will they know it's mine?"

His grandfather grinned at him. "People always know what belongs to whom. They may pretend otherwise, but they know."

"Even thieves?" said Sino.

"Especially thieves!" his grandfather exclaimed. "That was the communists' big mistake. They thought people could be educated not to care about what was theirs." The old man shook his head and snorted: "People will share anything – provided it doesn't belong to them!" He lifted a finger. "When you create a fundament, people will come to you. They will come not because they like you, or because they trust you, or because they respect you. They will come only because they know you have the power to do something for them. With every hole you fill, every problem you solve, every question you answer, your fundament will grow and grow, and more and more people will come to you. And they will send other people to you because there is credit and kudos to be gained from knowing who knows."

During these conversations, Sino's grandfather would continually pause to empty his pipe and re-stuff it. "During communism, we smoked everything," he would grin wryly, banging the old tube on the bench. "We learned what could be smoked and what couldn't; what burned and what didn't, inside and out."

One day, during one of the old man's stories, a question occurred to Sino. "So you have the 'fundament' to help everyone else," he said. "You are at the centre, everyone knows you and comes to you. Where does that leave you?"

His grandfather laughed. "That is one question you must answer yourself!"

Sino knew his grandfather enjoyed giving him advice; he was the old man's only grandchild. Over the years, Sino came to realise his grandfather only ever told him *how* to do things, and only ever answered his questions about the 'hows' of the world. He never said anything about the 'whys', about *why* it was necessary to do something, *why* he had done what he did, *why* Sino should do what his grandfather was suggesting. Indeed, the old man consistently ignored all of Sino's 'why' questions. When Sino eventually worked this out, he asked the old man: "Why?".

To his surprise, he got an answer. "There is no need for you, or any man, to rediscover the 'hows' of the world," his grandfather said. "Everything I know how to do, I will share with you. But the 'whys' of the world, these are different for every man – these you must work out yourself."

Sino had immediately asked "Why?", but the old man only smiled at him. When Sino repeated the question, again and again, in a voice that got louder and louder until he was on the verge of tears, his grandfather leaned forward and gently stroked his face; but not another word came out of his mouth.

Sino remembered that day; he had walked away, his back to the old man, angry and frustrated. His grandfather called after him: "Don't waste your time thinking about what other people ought to be doing. Concentrate only on what you can do."

Sitting on this plane, heading home after all those years, Sino knew he still hadn't answered those whys. Sometimes – most of the time – he could pretend that he knew what was he doing and why he was doing it, but really, he had no idea. He wanted to go home. He wanted to run his own business. He wanted his parents to be proud of him. He wanted to be taken seriously, to be respected. He wanted to be rich. Wasn't it normal to want those things? Did there have to be a reason why?

His grandfather had thought so. "You must know yourself."

"Why?" Sino demanded.

"Otherwise, you will make slaves of your allies and enemies of your adversaries."

Sometimes, it all got a bit too much. "I don't want a fundament," Sino said one day, sulkily. "I don't want power."

His grandfather chuckled and patted him gently. "Power is like blood. You have to have a certain amount of it to live."

Sino hadn't properly understood what that meant for many more years, not until he started working in London. Not until he was cast into an environment where he had nothing – no friends, no allies – and no clue what he was supposed to be doing. In the beginning, his lack of power had nearly finished him. At times, he'd been so powerless, so at sea, he'd thought about jumping off a bridge. So he'd done the only other thing he could think of doing. He'd gone looking for holes. At first, he'd wondered whether there would be any holes. After all, London had been here for millennia. It was the capital of what had once been the biggest empire the world had ever known. How many holes could there be? Surely the fundament here would have been finished long ago?

He needn't have worried; he'd never seen so many holes in his life. As soon as he started looking, he saw them everywhere. No-one seemed to know the answer to anything. At first, it seemed so unbelievable that Sino assumed the chaos must be an illusion – something that would disappear once his eyes attuned to the greyness. It was only a matter of getting used to things, of figuring out how it all worked, how things got done, who was responsible for taking care of things.

After all those years, he still wondered, occasionally, whether he might be missing something, but he knew he wasn't. The chaos was real. Things didn't get done. What was supposed to happen didn't happen. No-one – but no-one – was taking care of anything. How could London be like this? Had it always been like this?

The whole city seemed continually balanced on a knife edge; the slightest disruption could bring everything to a halt. People just did, or didn't do, whatever they liked. No-one seemed to feel responsible for anything; no-one showed the slightest sense of obligation towards anyone. Everything had to be enforced with threats. In China, a threat was an absolute last resort, proof that any remnant of trust or goodwill was gone. Here, relationships were started on the strength of threats, presumably on the presumption that they would collapse. Normally, it seemed, they did. At work, people came and went all the time. Politicians were being sacked all the time, but in all those years, nothing had changed.

Sino's private theory was that it was all because of the strange relationships between people. Often, they seemed to trust strangers more than colleagues or even friends and family. That was the fundamental difference between home and here. Relationships here were fluid and temporary. It seemed you could instantly be friends with someone and equally quickly be enemies, and then friends again. You couldn't rely on anyone. Sino had met people who didn't talk to their parents!

Their society, they seemed to think, was the pinnacle of civilisation; the most advanced there had ever been. Jane had told him that this was where China was heading. "You'll see," she'd said, "one day the Chinese will want democracy." He hadn't argued. What was the point in arguing with someone who had always voted for a political party precisely because they were never going to get in, and then was upset when they did get in? The English had a strange aversion to responsibility. Sometimes, Sino had the impression that they didn't want anyone in charge, that they were happier living in a shambles.

What was really strange was that this attitude seemed to be shared by the people at the top; the ones with the power and the authority. They were supposed to be in charge, making the decisions, guiding the people, but they weren't. In all his years in London, Sino couldn't remember one boss who took his role seriously. The first one had been a case in point. On Sino's first day at work, the man had welcomed him enthusiastically and then spent the rest of their meeting interrupting himself to answer 'important' calls on his mobile phone. At the end, when Sino had stood there waiting for instructions, the man had waved him towards an empty desk, and said, "make yourself useful".

That was his department head; someone whom he saw occasionally in the corridor, who would wink at him and say: "Keeping busy?" or "Alright?" while talking into his mobile phone, or hurrying somewhere.

In the beginning, Sino survived only by filling any holes he could find to fill. In the beginning, he pretended to himself that he was following his grandfather's fundament strategy, but really he was just doing whatever he could find to do. Occasionally, someone would appear – usually his boss – and ask him to do something, or ask him why something hadn't been done. The man had an irritating habit of asking questions about himself. His favourite question was: "Why didn't I know about that?"

Sino had never worked out what the answer was. He supposed the boss was really upbraiding him for not having told him whatever it was he was supposed to know about, but sometimes Sino hadn't known about it himself. He quickly learned to apologise and to promise that he would make sure his boss would not, not know about whatever it was, again. In the beginning, he'd worried about how to make good those promises – how do you make sure someone knows about something you yourself might not know about? But it didn't matter. His boss never kept track of anything. It was tempting to lie to the man, like his English colleagues did.

In the beginning, his biggest problem was working out what his job was. It had never been explained to him and the only instructions he ever got were about things he was evidently supposed to have done but hadn't. On some days, he seemed to be responsible for everything; on others for nothing. Whenever anything went wrong, he seemed to be somehow responsible. He was never told he'd done anything right. For a long time, he'd been convinced he was just one more mistake away from being sacked, but gradually he came to realise they weren't going to throw him out.

They weren't, because he was the one who did the work. He made mistakes, he got things wrong, he misunderstood things, but that was because he was always doing something. Whenever something needed to be done, whenever something couldn't be found, whenever there was a job no-one wanted, Sino filled the hole. After a while, he didn't even have to go in search of holes. Holes were simply presented to him. He was the automatic hole-filler. He frequently overheard people saying it: "Oh, the Chinese guy will know." Or: "Ask Sino. He won't mind doing it."

Sino quickly discovered where the biggest holes were. They turned out not to be holes at all, but attenuated or non-existent lines of communication between and among the various departments and offices in the company. Worst were the holes between head office in London and the subsidiaries scattered around the world. At first, Sino had assumed his boss and the other managers were in close contact with the people on the ground, but over time he realised that no-one had a clue what was really going on outside head office. As long as the money came in, no-one gave a damn.

Sino had stumbled upon this bizarre state of affairs early and quite by accident. By simply answering questions from people in other offices he suddenly found himself submerged under a flood of emails and telephone calls. People in places he'd never heard of were suddenly deluging him with questions and requests about every subject under the sun. When he told them he didn't work in the relevant department, and asked them why they were contacting him, the answer was simple: "Because no-one else answers our questions!"

It was ridiculous – and exhausting. He could have worked 24 hours a day and still not finished solving people's problems. But he'd found a crucial hole; a way of establishing ties with people outside his department, and instilling in them a sense of obligation – to him. It took more than a year of thankless, hard slog until he was on first-name terms with people in every office, but it happened. Most of his contacts weren't important people, but they had access to people who were. Suddenly, for the first time, Sino's department was able to have some measure of influence in other parts of the company. Of course, they were hopelessly ineffective. What they were doing found hardly any traction, but they found some, and that was a first.

No-one admitted it, but the people around him were impressed. His superiors were impressed, his colleagues were impressed and people in other departments were impressed. What was particularly interesting was that they all behaved in exactly the way his grandfather had said they would. It didn't occur to them, for a moment, to try and emulate what he had done, to fill holes to establish their own fundament. Instead, they simply started using his. People he'd never heard of would suddenly appear at his door, or on the other end of his phone, asking for information, asking him to get things done. Without a thought, they jumped directly on to his fundament as if it was the most natural thing in the world.

His boss just assumed he'd struck gold; that he'd found a peculiar type of individual who was intelligent enough to follow orders (that he hadn't actually been given), but too dense to have any thoughts of his own. Of course, the man had a ready explanation. "He's Chinese," Sino had heard him say. At first, he'd assumed his boss had never set foot in China, but he'd later learned that the man had spent three years in Shanghai. "The Chinese are great to work with," he'd heard his boss say, "provided you don't ask them to think creatively. They're good at doing what they're told, and they don't ask questions. It's the education system. Rote-learning. They learn to follow orders, but not how to think." It was a strange comment from a man who never gave anyone a direct order and generally only spoke to Sino when he needed something explained to him.

Over time, Sino got braver, and started to be a bit more strategic about the holes he filled – to concentrate on those that were likely to improve his position further.

It was easy to find out what was important and what not. One thing the office did not lack was people who liked the sound of their own voices. The years of listening to his grandfather had taught Sino how to look like he was interested, and also how to steer a monologue on to subjects that did interest him. Occasionally, he would make a remark or ask a question that implied a sense of purpose that he was assumed to lack, or an interest that he was not supposed to have, but these slips could easily be neutralised with an innocent look. The fact that he was Chinese could excuse almost anything.

When Sino found a better job and resigned, without warning obviously, the reaction had been surprise and disbelief. They'd thought he was happy there. Why hadn't he said something? He didn't have to leave; they could work it out. He declined the offer politely. As if he would have stayed – as if he would have taken them into his confidence!

What was strange was that they really hadn't had the faintest clue who he was. He'd been there for three years and they hardly knew him better than the day he arrived. He hadn't fitted into their world, so they'd reinvented him to be something they could deal with. They'd even renamed him. His real name was Jinping. When he arrived in England, he'd called himself Harry to make life easier for everyone. But his boss hadn't liked the name. "You don't look like a Harry," he said, after a few weeks of calling Sino nothing.

"It's not my real name," Sino had said.

His boss suddenly rounded on him: "Sino!" he exclaimed, grinning at him.

Sino looked at him, confused.

"Why don't we call you 'Sino'? It's a perfect name – fits you like a glove." The boss's tone was friendly. It sounded like a real question.

Sino didn't reply.

After a few more weeks of calling Sino mainly nothing, but dropping in a "Sino" occasionally, always in public, his boss achieved his objective. Other people started calling him Sino. At first, he objected, but the name quickly stuck. It took Sino a while longer to accept that he'd been renamed by an Englishman he hardly knew, but in spite of himself he actually liked the name. So did other people. "Cool name," the pretty girl at the reception desk said, when she first heard it.

So he'd kept it. It was the only thing he'd taken away from that job.

Around him, westerners found it easy to let their guard down. At first, Sino assumed it was his foreignness that somehow made them feel safe, but later he realised it had more to do with his accommodating manner. Westerners could be very pushy and aggressive, especially the Germans. They seemed to respect aggression. Passivity and a cooperative attitude were seen as a sign of weakness. There was conflict all around. It was difficult to know when people were serious or not.

His ethnicity gave him some measure of protection from the politics, but the downside to the fundament strategy was that his desk was used as a rubbish bin. He'd worked for three companies in London in various roles and, in every single one of them, the pattern was always the same. He'd start by filling holes and quickly impress his employer and colleagues. They wouldn't admit it, but they were always delighted to have found such an intelligent imbecile. They would react in the same way: by heaping work on him. With the work would come the pressure, the problems, and the blame. It would all start flowing to him. Soon, the flow would become a torrent. Sometimes, people would comment on how helpful he was, how hard he worked, but no-one ever offered any help or support. Never once did a boss wonder whether he was doing too much – whether he might be in danger of the 'burnout' that everyone seemed to be suffering from. Based on what he'd overheard, people just assumed he had no life outside work. They usually ascribed it to something 'typically Chinese'.

"They're workaholics," was something Sino overheard fairly frequently. "It's a Confucian thing."

Not everyone was fooled; some of the older ones didn't buy it and they kept him firmly at arm's length. Sino supposed they knew the world too well to believe he was breaking his back for someone else's benefit, but it didn't matter. In London, the old ones were few and far between: either they were in the executive suites or, most often, they weren't there at all. That was another weird thing about the west. The greatest repositories of experience and information were regularly and routinely tossed away like rubbish to be replaced by over-confident graduates, as avaricious as they were ignorant. From Sino's point of view, it was better that way. The younger ones were a lot easier to deal with. They were like greedy birds, always loitering at a safe distance; far enough away to escape any work or blame, but close enough to snatch any credit that might be there for the taking.

It was difficult to reconcile the conflicting sides of his colleagues. At work, they could be the most arrogant, hateful, infuriating, useless individuals it was possible to imagine, but in the pub at the end of a day, they could be very good company indeed. Even the brusque, belligerent ones. Sometimes the rude ones were the best company – at least among the men. Some of the women were brusque and belligerent, too. They weren't good company; not under any circumstances.

In the beginning, Sino felt he understood his French colleagues better. He'd noticed early on that the French were quite like the Chinese in that they didn't seem to worry too much about how things got done as long as they got done. They always knew who was in charge, and there was always someone in charge, and they were polite and friendly and considerate. They always came to greet you when they were in your part of the building, even if they didn't want anything. None of his English colleagues ever greeted him first.

For a while, Sino had been seduced by the French exception. Their attitude was so much more constructive than that of the English, and it helped that they had such beautiful accents – even though he couldn't understand what they were saying.

But it turned out that there was one big problem with the French. Sino couldn't spot the holes in their fundament. The holes must have been there because, for one thing, no-one French was ever able to answer a question – no matter how simple or straightforward – without consulting someone else first. Yet somehow they always managed to give the impression that their fundament was fully intact. Partly it was because you could never pin them down to anything unless they had suggested it first, and partly it was because they somehow managed never to get involved in anything that didn't have a French person in charge.

The upshot was you had to rely on them completely to tell you what needed to be done. Then there was that irritating problem that whatever work you did on a French project was never seen or heard of again – at least in any recognisable form. And even though they gave you lots of the credit – usually more credit than you deserved – it was never clear what you had actually done, other than that you'd helped them to do whatever it was they were doing.

Sino was pretty sure that these difficulties would have gone away if he'd been able to speak French. Everything important was discussed in French – or at least nothing important was discussed in English – and sometimes Sino wondered whether his French colleagues remembered that he didn't understand a word of their language. They sometimes invited him along for a drink after work, only to spend the evening speaking nothing but French and ignoring him completely.

It was difficult to know how seriously to take his French colleagues. They went on about how important China was, but spent a lot of time talking about how it would have to change into something very like France before it would be truly successful. It was a bit like having a geriatric telling you to take him as a role model.

Still, at least the French were proud of their country; unlike the British. The only Brits who ever had anything good to say about Britain were journalists and television personalities. They seemed more or less continuously at pains to convince the entire population that Britain was the best place in the world. Sino didn't know why they bothered.

He had once got drunk in a pub and told some English colleagues what he really thought of their country. It had been inexcusable. He would have been livid if a foreigner had dared to say such things about China. He would have been lynched if he'd been talking to the French about France, but the English just laughed.

"If you think it's bad here, you should go north," one man said. Then one of the women patted his arm and, in a kind, sympathetic voice, said, "Don't worry, you'll get used to it."

She'd obviously assumed he was staying.

The English were right about one thing: the Germans. The two who were on career programme assignments in London were the most diabolical people Sino had ever met. The Brits and the French tried to take advantage of him, but they weren't very persistent, and at least they were polite about it. But the two Germans wouldn't leave him alone. They were constantly badgering him, constantly trying to persuade, cajole or coerce him into doing their work for them.

At first, Sino had actually warmed to them because they were less trivial and familiar than the English, but as he got to know them, he realised that they were as insensitive and arrogant as the English always said they were.

In the beginning, sensing a hole, he'd helped them with some of their work, but soon he realised there were no holes. They were obligingly *making* holes for him. Sino figured it out one day when he skipped lunch to prepare a presentation in English for one of them. The notes were so garbled that Sino couldn't read half of it, so he'd gone looking for Hannes. When he eventually found the bastard on the end of his mobile phone, it was obvious he was in a local restaurant, stuffing his fat face.

Instead of being mortified and apologising, Hannes acted as if nothing had happened. He and Wolfram even had the nerve to carry on barging shamelessly up to Sino's desk and pressuring him to do their work. They were the most insufferably arrogant people he had ever met. Hannes in particular would regularly and brazenly define Sino's job as being precisely what he wanted done. At times, Sino could have strangled the man. He had tried to get across that they weren't being reasonable but they just wouldn't get the message. Eventually, out of desperation, he turned to an English colleague for advice. It was in the pub again, after a few drinks. "What did you expect?" the man said, in a mock-German accent. "They are Germans!"

Then he loudly and comically told all the other people there about Sino's problem. They all started laughing, even someone whom Sino discovered to his horror was German.

The Englishman clapped the German guy on the back, and then, in the same heavy German accent, started carrying on about how the EU was a German plot to take over Europe.

When the German next went outside for a cigarette, Sino followed him out and apologised. The man waved a dismissive hand at him. "Don't worry about it," he said. "The guy sounds like a real arsehole." He took a long drag on his cigarette and pointed to a pile of rubbish bags lying on the pavement nearby. "The English are so relaxed about everything," he said. "That's why I like London. Here, nobody worries about anything."

He clinked his glass against Sino's, and then in a low, slightly slurred voice, whispered: "Let me give you some advice: this German guy – the one who's giving you a hard time…"

Sino nodded.

"The next time he comes with something," the German continued, "you must agree to do it, and then keep him waiting, right until the last minute, until he absolutely can't wait any longer."

Sino nodded.

"Then, when he comes asking for it, when he really needs it, tell him…" – the man stopped and held up his hand like a traffic cop, while he poured the rest of his drink down his throat – "… tell him to go and fuck himself."

The German started laughing, and clapped Sino on the shoulder. "I promise you," he said. "He won't ask you again."

The next time Hannes came, Sino just said no very politely and then sat there in silence until the man had stormed away. But before he'd gone, Hannes had stuck a finger in Sino's face and threatened him. Sino tried not to take it seriously – he knew Hannes was just letting off steam – but he also knew he would never forgive him. No-one had ever spoken to him like that before. If he saw Hannes lying in the street, bleeding to death, he would step over him.

Aside from the problems with the Germans and the French, the fundament strategy was working perfectly. Sino had started as a satellite, a barely noticed speck on the radar, but with each problem he solved, each call he returned, each piece of knowledge he acquired, each relationship he established, gradually, imperceptibly, he became more and more critical to the functioning of the whole. Eventually – and it didn't actually take that long – he gravitated towards the centre and became more and more part of the mass around which the activity revolved.

As his role became more pivotal, a colleague would occasionally made a sarcastic comment, or suggest that a re-ordering of responsibilities might be advisable. Less often, a boss might turn up to say something syrupy and insincere, but no-one seemed unduly concerned. He was no real threat; he was Chinese. They had the ideas, he did the work. They took the credit, he took the blame. They were moving up in the world, he was learning the ropes. That was how it worked; that was how it had always worked – at least with the British. With the Americans, it was different. The Brits and the Europeans could be avaricious, unreasonable and arrogant, but they were usually vaguely reasonable. They tried to take advantage of you, tried to pull the wool over your eyes, but in the end, you could come to an agreement with them. In the end, they came to the negotiating table expecting to negotiate.

The Americans were a different proposition altogether. If dealing with his employers in London was a nuisance, dealing with headquarters in New York was a nightmare. The Americans didn't discuss, explain or negotiate anything. They only thing you ever heard from them was "deliver, deliver, and deliver again". If there was ever a problem or a delay or a complication, the response was always the same: this is how it is done in America, so you'd better adapt and quickly. In London, everyone complained about the Americans and belittled them, but no-one had a clue how to deal with them.

Until the Italian showed up. Sino noticed almost immediately that he – alone – had no problems with Americans. While everyone else was avoiding them, or passing the buck or running around like headless chickens trying to give them what they wanted, the Italian somehow merrily managed the American exception.

"How do you do it?" Sino asked him one day. They were waiting at the bus stop.

The man shrugged.

Sino decided to force the issue. He looked the man in the face. "You know something we don't."

The Italian smiled at him. "I've been with this company for a long time."

Sino smiled back. "I would appreciate some help here."

The Italian shrugged again. "It's easy. Just give them what they ask for. They never ask for anything difficult."

"I try," Sino protested. "But it doesn't work!"

"No," said the man, shaking his head firmly. "You don't give them what they want. You try to understand what they want. You interpret their instructions. This is your mistake."

"I don't," Sino protested. "I try to give them exactly what they ask for. But most of the time I can't deliver it. No-one can!"

The man laughed. His name was Gelsomino, but no-one could remember how to pronounce that, so they just called him Gino.

"Let's go and have a drink," said Gino.

He led Sino to a nearby café with tables outside, and ordered a small bottle of red wine. The waiter, who was also an Italian, obviously knew Gino. Sino took a beer.

Sino was pretty sure the Italian was pleased to have some company. Since he had arrived in London, no-one had paid the slightest attention to him. There was no point; he was old – he looked around 60 – and he was only there temporarily. He was a specialist. The company sent him all over the world to train youngsters to do his job.

"I used to run the company's subsidiary in Italy," he told Sino. "In those days, the big boss – Sam – was the CEO. Now he's the chairman."

Sino nodded. He knew that.

Gino smiled at him, and lit a small cigar. "That's where I learned how to deal with head office. That's when I learned how to deal with the Americans."

The Italian leaned back in his chair and looked at the sky. It was grey, as usual, but it didn't look like it was going to rain.

Sino waited.

"Chinese people are very focused," the Italian said. "Very focused."

Sino nodded. He didn't know what to say.

"Just like the Americans," the Italian continued. "They're very focused."

"I don't think the Chinese are like the Americans," Sino said.

The Italian sipped his wine.

"What did you learn about the Americans?" Sino asked.

"You want me to tell you about my experiences?" Gino asked.

Sino nodded.

"I remember one time in particular. I was running the subsidiary in Italy – the local head office in Milano – and we had a new guy in the spare-parts department."

Gino puffed his cigar and inspected the end of it. He was obviously in no hurry.

He smiled at Sino. "He was a real ambitious guy. You know the type – impatient, only interested in himself, in a hurry to change the world." Gino puffed away. "Anyway, he decides we need to professionalise the place – to put everything on the computer. So, without telling anyone, he asks head office for a computer program; some sort of customer database."

He was shaking his head while he was speaking. "There was no need. We didn't have a super-efficient system. But we didn't need one; we knew the customers, we didn't need to computerise everything." Gino sipped his wine. "But this guy – he wanted to impress us, you know. He wanted to set up a whole fancy system and then unveil it to a big fanfare."

The Italian looked across the table at Sino. Sino would have preferred him to get straight to the point, but he could tell Gino was enjoying himself. He could also tell that the Italian was not going to be hurried. He was almost equally certain that Gino was eventually going to tell him something useful.

"Anyway," Gino continued, "when the people in New York looked at the specifications for this computer program, they realised that we were probably quoting different prices to different customers. I didn't know about this – the request for the computer program, I mean." Gino smiled again. "It was nothing crooked. In those days, it was normal that everyone had his own price. It was how customer relations worked."

He looked inquisitively at Sino.

Sino nodded, reassuringly.

"Anyway," the Italian went on, "suddenly a lawyer from London appears in my office and wants to know what's going on. Wants to know how the pricing works."

Gino sighed. "This is very Anglo-Saxon. They get very pushy when they want something." He shook his head. "Being pushy never works. When you push people, they either cover their asses or they push back. What they don't do – what they never do – is what you actually want."

He shrugged. "Anyway, this pricing system we had for each customer, it wasn't against the law. The lawyer knew that, obviously, but the legal people were very jumpy because they were having problems in other countries."

The Italian wagged his finger. "In other countries, they were having problems," he stressed, "not in Italy."

He gave Sino a slightly wounded look. "In Europe, they blame everything on the Italians. They think we are a bit… dodgy." He pronounced 'dodgy' with an English accent.

"But the real crooks are not in Italy." He shrugged. "The Italians are small-time crooks; we just test the rules. It's in the other countries – in northern Europe and America – where you find the real crooks; the ones whose 'activities' bring down entire economies, and that's where the company has the big problems."

Gino leaned forward and knocked the ash off his small cigar.

Sino sipped his beer and waited for him to continue.

"Anyway, this lawyer wants to start looking around," Gino went on. "I tell him not to waste his time, but he insists. So…" he raised his hands and gave another gentle shrug. "Later, he comes to me with a piece of paper that he's dug up from somewhere. It's a competitor's letterhead. He wants to know what it says. It's nothing – a photocopy of a price quote for a job. A customer had given it to one of my salesmen to prove he could get a lower price. Anyway, this lawyer goes back to London, and tells head office that all manner of dodgy things are probably happening in Italy."

Gino refilled his wine glass. "You want another beer?"

Sino nodded. Gino looked around for a second or two. The waiter appeared and took the order.

"Anyway," he continued, "a little while later, who should appear? The man himself – the CEO, Sam. Suddenly, he's in my office."

Sino adjusted his position slightly.

"He starts giving me a really hard time." Gino's tone was by now rather indignant. "Remember, nothing has happened in Italy. We're not doing anything wrong. The problems are in other countries. But Sam is suspicious. In fact, he's more than suspicious." Gino held up his finger. "He's convinced that we're up to no good. He tells me that he's got incriminating evidence."

The Italian started laughing and, shaking his head, repeated, "Incriminating evidence."

Sino's beer arrived.

"That's when I knew what kind of a man I was dealing with," Gino said. Sino could see the man's jaw muscles clenching between pauses.

"I try to reason with him, but he doesn't listen. He tells me there's bad stuff going on in my company. He says if anyone in my company is caught doing anything wrong – paying bribes, fixing prices, whatever – he's going to fire me, take away my pension and make sure I never get another job in the industry again." Gino shook his head. "That's what I had to deal with – from the CEO."

The Italian suddenly seemed a little upset, as if he had travelled back in time and was reliving that moment. Sino didn't know what to say.

The man rubbed the sides of his mouth with his thumb and forefinger, his eyes fixed on the table.

After a few seconds, he started talking again. "You must see that the CEO doesn't ask me if there's anything illegal going on in my company. He doesn't tell me to make sure that nothing illegal goes on in my company."

Gino emptied the remains of the small bottle of wine into his glass. "He's the CEO. I'm the country manager. He's entitled to ask me if there's anything illegal going on. He's entitled to tell me that I have to run a clean operation. He's entitled to tell me those things." The Italian grinned at Sino. "Incidentally, if he had told me those things, I would have felt obliged to do some work – some real investigating – just to make sure everything was clean."

Gino leaned forward, and raised his index finger. "But he doesn't. He tells me that if anyone in my company is caught doing something illegal, I'm in for the high jump." He paused and leaned back again. "Can you believe it? He comes all that way – goes to all that trouble – to tell me that I have to do absolutely nothing!" As he said 'nothing', Gino flung his hands outward.

He smiled at Sino. "You understand?"

Sino frowned. "But you did have to do something. What about the incriminating evidence?"

Gino blew a contemptuous blast into the air. "There was nothing."

"But he said he had something."

"He was lying."

Sino didn't understand.

Gino waved at the waiter. "In Italy, if you find incriminating evidence on someone, it can only mean one thing…"

Sino waited for him to continue, but the man said nothing.

"What does it mean?" Sino asked.

Gino grinned lazily at him. "It means he's innocent."

Sino frowned.

"It means someone put it there," Gino's tone was slightly impatient. "To frame the guy. You understand? No Italian would ever be stupid enough to get caught with incriminating evidence." He drained his glass. "In this company, everything is run by lawyers. There is no trust, even now. After 25 years, they don't trust me."

"Why do you stay?" Sino asked.

The Italian swayed his wine glass to and fro, watching the few remaining drops climb the sides and roll down again.

Sino waited.

"The world changes when you get old," he said, grinning at Sino. "You don't, but everyone else does."

The waiter arrived with the bill. Sino put his hand in his pocket, but the Italian already has his wallet out.

Once the waiter had gone, Gino stood up. "With the Americans, just do everything they say, to the letter. You will find – most of the time – you don't actually have to do anything at all."

Sino stood up.

Gino tapped his head. "America is a nation of lawyers; they think like lawyers. As long as everything is written down, as long as everything is signed, they feel happy and secure, and they don't worry too much about what really goes on."

He put out his hand. Sino took it.

"Don't wait too long," he said to Sino.

Sino frowned. "For what?"

"For whatever it is you want to do," the Italian continued.

Sino felt a little uncomfortable.

"You've still got time," the Italian smiled, looking him up and down. "But not that much."

Sino watched the man walk away. His walk was still relatively sprightly, but from the back, he looked like any other little old man.

Settling back into his seat somewhere over Europe, Sino sipped his beer. He wondered if he'd miss England. Probably not; he couldn't think of anything he'd miss, except maybe Jane.

There was too much conflict in the west. They were always looking for someone to blame, even though most things were nobody's fault. He'd said that to Jane, told her that, most of the time, things were caused by a confluence of unpredictable, unforeseen circumstances, too complicated to unravel. It had taken him a while to talk her round. But he couldn't convince her that blame could be out of place. She always insisted that someone had to be held accountable, that it was just as important for something to be seen to be done as is was for something to be done. He understood her point, but she'd got the wrong end of the stick. Sometimes, you needed to make examples of people, to force a change or as a means of stamping out a practice, but that wasn't what they did in the west. In the west, they were only interested in finding someone to blame, so they didn't have to change anything.

Sino wondered what it would be like to work in China. How different would it be? The products and processes and company rules and regulations would be the same, but the culture of the company was bound to be Chinese. People would know what their responsibilities were and would take them seriously. Things would change, improve, move forward. It wouldn't just be a perpetual blame game, where the only thing that changed was the faces. Finally – after all these years – he was going back to civilisation.

CHAPTER 7

Rosemary

Rosemary dialled Sam's office in New York. Even though he was her half-brother, the fact that he was so much older – almost the same age as her mother, Catherine – made him seem more like an uncle. She felt uncomfortable. Gideon was sitting on the couch behind her, watching her, listening to her.

"And how much will you be investing?" Sam asked sarcastically, when she told him why she was calling.

"We don't have any money to invest. We're proposing a 50-50 stake you put up the money, Gideon runs the business."

Sam started laughing. There was genuine amusement in his voice, but not much of it. "And how does your industrious, hard-working husband expect to turn a profit?"

Rosemary hesitated, and then simply repeated what Gideon had told her. "Gideon expects to break even within a year."

"Yes," said Sam. "That was in the business plan he sent me. He was very clear about when he expected to make a profit; he just left out how he was going to get there."

"That was a draft – he's still making the finishing touches."

"And it all adds up to a profit within a year?" said Sam. He was speaking in a slightly sing-song voice.

She nodded tentatively, forgetting for a moment that he couldn't see her.

Sam waited a few seconds. His tone became more serious. "Come on, Rosemary. Let's get real. Do you honestly think he's ever going to be able to get a business off the ground?"

She said nothing.

"Look," he continued. "You're my baby sister. If you need money, you only have to ask…"

"It's for the business," she said.

Sam was losing patience. "For Christ's sake, Rosemary, there is no business. What the hell is wrong with this guy? He couldn't stick with the job that we gave him in London. Then he refused the one that Catherine insisted I offer him in Johannesburg, and now he expects me to sink thousands of dollars into some ludicrous start-up that we both know he couldn't get off the ground, if his life depended on it. Who the hell does he think he's dealing with?"

Rosemary took a deep breath. She could feel Gideon's eyes on her from the couch, trying to work out how the conversation was going.

"I'm sorry, Rosemary," Sam said. "I don't know why you let Gideon put you up to this, and I dislike his attempt to use me as an alibi."

"What do you mean?"

"Well, I suppose that's what this is about," Sam went on. "If I don't invest, then he can say that it's all Sam's fault that he couldn't start his business."

"What? Don't be ridiculous," said Rosemary, a little stunned. "We're just asking if you're interested in a business venture."

Sam laughed down the phone. "Gimme a break, Rosemary. It's Sam, remember. Let's be honest with each other. I understand that he's your husband and maybe you love him, but you know as well as I do that he's trying to pull a fast one. He's not interested in working. He's hoping for a handout that will allow him to sit on his lazy ass for a few more years."

Rosemary was close to hanging up the phone.

"Are you there?" Sam asked.

Rosemary made a sound, but couldn't quite get a word out. Gideon was leaning forward, a deep frown on his forehead. He could tell she was upset.

"I helped him before – against my better judgement – because of you, Rosemary," Sam went on. "Christ, he couldn't even hold down a job that was handed to him on a silver platter in London, now he wants to run his own business."

"The labour market here is tough," she said softly. "Anyway, based on his past experience, he thinks he'd be better suited to running his own business."

Sam exhaled into the phone. "Listen honey, you know as well as I do that people who want to work, find work. He's not interested in working, that's why he's getting nowhere. Anyone can see he's a loser – he's never done a proper day's work in his life. I don't know why you married him – it was obvious he was going to live off you."

She said nothing.

Sam took a deep breath and started speaking in a more reasonable tone. "I'm sorry, Rosemary, I'm interfering. I just wish you'd married a man who was at least capable of doing an honest day's work and bringing home a paycheck." He paused for breath. "Don't you see that if he can't even hold down a job, he's never going to have the discipline to run a business? Being your own boss is the hardest thing in the world."

"We asked you if you wanted to be a partner, Sam. That was all."

Behind her, Gideon threw up his hands and exhaled loudly.

"Okay, Rosemary," Sam continued. "If you want to play this straight, let's play it straight."

He paused, and then started speaking in a businesslike tone: "I only in invest in companies if I believe in the quality of the management," he said. "It won't surprise you that I don't have any faith in your husband whatsoever. So based on what's on the table, the answer's a resounding no."

Rosemary forced her shoulders to relax. She was slightly out of breath. "Thank you, Sam. That's all we wanted to know."

Sam ran his tongue around his mouth. "So what are you going to do?"

"I don't know."

"Why don't you come to the States? I'll give you a job."

Rosemary said nothing.

"What kind of future are your kids going to have there?"

She still said nothing.

Sam looked at the clock on his wall. "Okay, Rosemary, this is the deal. The job offer at our Johannesburg office is still open. If your husband deigns to accept it and he manages to stick with it for a reasonable period of time, then I might – might! – consider helping him set up a business, but he better prove that he's capable of doing something."

Sam waited.

"Okay, Rosemary?"

"Okay."

"I love you, Rosemary."

"I know." She put down the phone. Gideon was on his feet, coming towards her. He stared at her with an incredulous face. "He said no?"

She nodded.

"I can't believe it," Gideon hissed. "The bastard! The mean, miserable bastard!"

Then she had to get away from Gideon. She pushed past him and ran and shut herself in the bedroom.

With hindsight, Rosemary couldn't believe she'd been naïve enough to think Sam would have given Gideon the money. She'd let Gideon persuade her, against her better judgement, to ask Sam. She shouldn't have done it. Now Sam was wondering about her.

Why had she listened to Gideon? He didn't know Sam like she did. Gideon always jumped to conclusions. If someone did something nice or generous, Gideon assumed they would always be nice or generous. Sam had helped before. It didn't occur to Gideon that he might not always be willing to do so. Also, Gideon had far too much faith in his own powers of persuasion. He had no idea that the more he said, the less Sam thought of him.

She went into the bathroom. Her make-up needed retouching. When she came out again, Gideon was sitting on the couch, smoking. She hated it when he smoked inside.

She went and stood at the open trellis door that lead out on to the veranda. "Sam offered me money," she said.

Gideon looked up, and exhaled loudly. "Well, that's mighty generous of him. He won't invest in a business venture, but he will give us a handout. To hell with him! We're not taking his money – not after this!"

"He'll tell my mother."

"Tell her what?"

Rosemary turned to look at Gideon. "He'll tell her what I asked for, and he'll tell her that he offered me money."

"So what?" Gideon said.

Rosemary looked out of the doors. "She's going to think we're being ridiculous."

"What are you talking about?"

"I can't tell her we're not taking Sam's money and then, in the next breath, ask her for a handout."

Gideon got up and went outside.

Sam was the pits; everything he touched turned to disaster. Anyone else would have just said no, but not Sam. He was the only person who could screw up everything from his penthouse office on the other side of the world.

Gideon sat down on the edge of the veranda. He wondered how long it would be before Sam's offer could be 'forgotten' to the extent that they could ask Catherine for money.

They didn't have time; they needed money now. Christmas was just around the corner.

"What about asking him for a loan?" he said loudly over his shoulder.

Rosemary walked out on to the veranda. "He wouldn't lend me money, nor would my mother. They'd insist I take it." She sucked her lips into her mouth and bit them gently. "Why don't I just take his money? What's the difference?"

Gideon frowned at her. "Take money from him? After this?"

She nodded.

Gideon shook his head. "It's simple, Rosemary. If we accept something from him, then we accept he's right."

"Right about what?"

Gideon turned his head and looked at her. "The man treats us like kids. He's constantly trying to tell us how to live our lives. He can't imagine that we might not want to live his way or to be like him." He paused, and took a drag on his cigarette. "Anyway, he's not your father, he's your brother. And he's not even a full brother. He's a half-brother. And in more ways than one! Who the hell does he think he is!" Gideon got up and went and stood in front of her. "I'm not going to live like that, Rosemary. I tried it. I did my best to live like that, to be that. I hated it. I'd rather be dead." He moved to her side and put his arm around her. "It's our decision how we live our lives, not his."

Rosemary stared out into the garden, still biting her lip. "We need money," she said.

"We've managed so far."

She looked up at him. "We can't keep asking my mother for money, Gideon. She pays for everything already."

He dropped his arm and took a step away from her. "Rosemary, the money is yours. Don't you understand? It belongs to you as much as it does to them. They're using the purse strings to control you, but it's your money, too."

She shook her head. "It's not."

"It belongs to your family. It belongs to all of you. It belongs to the kids – our kids."

"I didn't make it. It's got nothing to do with me."

Gideon laughed cynically and looked up at the sky. "So who made it? Did your mother make it? Did Sam make it?"

"He made some of it," she raised her voice.

Gideon laughed again. "How did they make it? How did your ancestors make it?" He looked her hard in the face. "They made some of it here, in Africa. My ancestors might even have helped them, but my family doesn't have anything to show for it."

"Please, Gideon, don't let's go through that again." It was a plea, but she was more irritated than upset.

Gideon threw his head back and began to stalk around the veranda. "I don't want your family's money. I was born with nothing – I'm used to it. I don't need anything. I can live in a shack and eat mealie-meal." He went and stood in front of her. "But you can't and our kids can't. Your mother and your brother are trying to control us, using money that you have as much right to as they do!" Gideon turned away and carried on walking around. "Just because your demented old father signed everything over to your mother. He should have left you your share, then we wouldn't be in this mess."

He sat down again on the edge of the veranda and started smoking again. Gradually, his muttering died down. Rosemary stared at the back of his head. On it was a small scar, where the hair didn't grow – a wound from a policeman's rubber bullet, he'd said, when she'd first asked him about it. She hadn't believed him, and she still didn't. It could just as easily have been from a fall, like the scar on her head. She'd got hers as a child, falling against the radiator. It had long since been hidden by her hair.

Gideon exaggerated, and he wasn't above telling downright lies. He'd had a harder life than she had, but it hadn't been as bad as he made out. Rosemary knew that from what his mother said. His mother had had a tough life, like most African women. The women here were the ones who really had it hard.

Gideon still thought she was one of them, that she didn't quite trust him, that she worried he was trying to get his hands on her family's money. It had been like that for a while – how could she trust someone who lied like he did? – but she was starting to see through him. It was hard. For all Gideon's moaning about being misunderstood, he didn't make it easy for outsiders to understand him and his world. Even Africans from other clans were kept firmly at arm's length.

Rosemary went and stood behind him and rubbed his head affectionately. He pulled away, but not very convincingly. She knew he wasn't interested in her family's money, or at least not much of it. His event horizon extended as far as the next thing he was looking forward to. Money in his hands was like sand. He couldn't understand why her family were so mean, why every handout came with strings attached, and he had no idea how much they were really worth. It was obscene, actually.

Gideon had tried – in Sam's books, not hard enough, but for Gideon, it was probably the most effort he'd ever expended on anything in his life. In retrospect, it had always been hopeless; like trying to get a hippo to adapt to life in the desert. She remembered that dinner in London, when she'd first brought Gideon to meet her mother. It had started off okay, but with every mouthful, every sip of wine, every word, Catherine had become progressively more horrified. Her mother's face when Gideon picked up his knife and fork...

An involuntary giggle escaped Rosemary's mouth. Gideon turned his head and looked up at her suspiciously. She pretended it was a cough. It worked. He turned away, still ignoring her, but letting her rub his head.

She was glad he was home; she had horribly vivid memories of their time in London. It had nearly destroyed their marriage. She admired Gideon for surviving there as long as he had. But he had changed, become dark and brooding; horrible to live with. It was as if the damp and the greyness had sucked the sunshine out of him. He wasn't made for London. Within days of being back in Africa, he'd turned back into himself. Rosemary still didn't understand what made him tick. She knew him well enough to be able to predict how he might react, but still she had no idea what really went on inside his head.

Her mother was convinced that African society – at least here in South Africa – had been destroyed by apartheid. She'd tried hard to persuade Rosemary not to move to Johannesburg. It was the crime that worried Catherine most. It was difficult to live behind bars. The children couldn't ride their bicycles, couldn't go out on the street. But there was a society here. It was not just chaos. Rosemary was too much of an outsider to understand how it worked, but the rituals, codes and rules were unmistakably there. For her, the impact was fairly negligible – they lived away from the rest of Gideon's family in a well-to-do, predominantly white suburb, but she'd been surprised at how rigid, judgemental and uncompromising African society was. For some reason, she'd assumed it would be open and tolerant – apartheid had been over for so long.

The reality had surprised her; people were frighteningly unforgiving. It could be terrifying here, particularly because you never knew what was going on. In the beginning, it had seemed like England with African accessories and nice weather, but the veneer had soon worn off. She'd assumed they would be away from the crime and violence because they lived in a rich suburb, but if anything, the crime here was worse because every criminal south of the Sahara seemed to be making a beeline for their neighbourhood. Those carrying out robberies, car-jackings, murders and rapes never seemed to get caught.

Over time, Rosemary realised that – among the Africans – what went around, eventually came around. The rich had the impression that crimes went unpunished, but that was only because they lived in an artificial world, suspended above the ground. In the indigenous communities, when a crime was committed, people generally knew who was responsible. Most criminals were gang members or drifters. If they stuck around too long, retribution would come. When it came, everyone would know, and no-one would say a word.

Rosemary found this out by accident one evening, when a local thief called Douglas appeared at the door of her mother-in-law's house in Soweto. Blood was pouring from a huge gash in his head. The guests did nothing – they simply stood there staring at him for a while, before going back inside. Rosemary had been horrified. "Call an ambulance!" she'd shouted at Gideon, but he and all the other Africans just looked at her as if she was mad, as if she'd committed some sort of dreadful *faux pas*. All the time, Douglas was standing there bleeding, slouched against the wall, pathetic and helpless, saying nothing.

Eventually, Gideon had gotten the car keys. He opened the back door of the car, and then stood there like a chauffeur, waiting for Douglas to get in, even though it was obvious he wasn't going to. "Help him!" Rosemary shouted, pulling at Douglas's arm, while trying to avoid getting blood on her. Gideon shuffled across the driveway like someone wading through molasses. It was if everyone – including Douglas – was being subjected to some sort of huge inconvenience. Throughout the whole process, the Africans were incommunicado – just the odd murmurs and mutters among themselves in languages she didn't understand. It had been the most frustrating experience she could remember – a man bleeding from a terrible head wound, and all around people behaving as if he wasn't quite there. Eventually, they got Douglas into the back of the car and drove him to hospital.

The next day, at home, when she'd interrogated Gideon, he told her that Douglas had had it coming, and professed to know nothing more about it. He complained for days afterwards about the blood stains on the back seat of his car.

At difficult moments, the Africans were like stones. They saw nothing, heard nothing and said nothing. Sometimes, she would scream into Gideon's face like a hysterical banshee, but it made no difference. He would simply sit there in silence, unmoved and immovable. At times like these, it worried her that he was the father of her children.

She had stopped stroking his head. Gideon stood up and walked back into the house. She could tell he wasn't speaking to her. That meant he wouldn't speak first. He would reply, if spoken to, and if confronted he would deny anything was wrong. This would continue until she made things right.

She hadn't meant to suggest he was living off her family. Of course, he was – they both were – but that was beside the point. The way he saw it, none of it had anything to do with him. It was all because of her. If she hadn't been there – if she'd never been there, if she'd never come into his life – he wouldn't need her or her family's money. He had never been explicit about this, but the fact that the point remained unmade didn't make it any less of a point. For him, this position was very convenient. It freed him from ever having to say thank you. It freed him from having to be responsible for her and the kids. In fact, it freed him from having to do anything.

That was life with Gideon; everything was always down to her. Everything was because of her. They'd met because she had come here on holiday. Because of her, they lived in an expensive house, in an expensive suburb. Because of her, they had kids. Because of her, they needed more money than he could scrape together. Because of her, his life was completely different to what it otherwise would have been. It wasn't that she was wrong, or bad, or to blame – quite the opposite. She had changed his life; she had opened his eyes to things he'd never seen and could never have experienced. Because of her, he'd been given opportunities that had once been inconceivable. Because of her, his life was better than he had ever imagined it could be. Everything was because of her. Nothing was because of him.

To make things right again, she would have to affirm this. Otherwise, they would never get back to normality. That was always the way with Gideon. He wouldn't – couldn't – imagine that he might somehow bear some measure of responsibility for something, however microscopic.

In the early days, she'd promised herself that one day she wouldn't make it right; that one day, he would have to make the first move, but the problem was that it was always so easy to make it right. She hardly had to do a thing. She had to do so little that it really wasn't worth not doing it, so she did it – for the children's sake, for her sake, for his sake. She feared that if she didn't, then the strange state, in which he would not speak unless spoken to and would not acknowledge that something might be wrong, might persist for the rest of their lives.

She wasn't ready to do it yet; she was still too upset with him. There was no hurry. There was never a hurry. It could be done quickly, in an instant. It was only a question of pushing the reset button, of removing the suggestion – however inadvertent – that his existence had somehow made him responsible for something. Once that had been done, he would immediately revert to normal. He could be forgiving, magnanimous, even grateful, at least momentarily. But never responsible. Responsibility was woman's work.

Rosemary couldn't figure out why he behaved in this way. In the beginning, she assumed he was just manipulating her. That was the obvious assumption. It was always she who backed down, she who swallowed her pride, she who compromised.

Was he manipulating her? Occasionally, he tried, but more often his reactions and his behaviour were so harmful to himself – so self-destructive – that what was going on seemed not to be about her at all. At times, she felt utterly incidental, as if her involvement in his life, her presence, was simply getting in the way of the more serious business of harming himself. But why? For what?

She was sure he needed her. Not for the money, but because, after his mother, she was all he had. His relationship with his mother was another mystery. He was quite happy to talk about the mortality of anyone else, but if the subject of death came up anywhere around her, he would literally shut down, like a machine that had been turned off. It was bizarre. Often, he didn't even seem fond of her. Sometimes, when he talked about her, his face would take on a look of disgust.

Gideon's relationship with his mother was not Rosemary's

problem. What she wanted to know was why – like now – he insisted on pushing her away but not letting her go? Why did he adamantly refuse all offers of help and assistance, and at the same time accept everything that was put in front of him? Why did he make himself powerless by giving her the power to destroy their relationship? At times, she supposed he hated himself; that he thought himself worthless, but this was difficult to reconcile with the fact that he was fiercely proud, not inconsiderably conceited, and seemed very happy in his own skin.

Rosemary had tried hard to confront him with these questions. She had told him repeatedly that he was handing her – forcing on her – the power to determine the outcome of his life. If, one day, she chose not to give way but to walk away, she could deprive him of everything in an instant, including his children. They both knew he would do nothing to prevent it.

But he didn't, or wouldn't, understand.

"Don't you get it? I can shut you down?" she would scream at him. "Anyone can shut you down. They just need to push a button and you stop functioning."

But he'd just stare past her, at the wall. He never responded when she said such things. But at other times, on occasions when messages could be delivered independently of context, he would say cryptic and disturbing things like: "We are born alone, we live alone and we die alone."

When these things came out of his mouth, she didn't know whether he was trying to communicate with her – perhaps to scare her – or simply repeating the words because he liked the drama or the sounds. Sometimes, she wondered whether he was pretending to be someone else. He must have been trying to tell her something, but it made no sense. He couldn't stand being alone. It wasn't that he needed to be close – to some extent, he was incapable of being close – but he needed people nearby. When she went away, he did nothing. When she wasn't there, he simply waited for her. She knew that because when she got back, nothing had ever changed; it was as if time had stood still.

She ran her fingers through her hair and unclenched her jaw. Her teeth were hurting from the pressure. Why did she stay? She stayed because of the other side of him; the side she had fallen in love with, the side she had married. Sometimes, she wasn't sure whether she was in love with him, or in love with the person she could be around him. It sounded dreadfully corny, but there was no other way of saying it. It wasn't that he helped her be that person. It was more because, as usual, he did nothing at all. At first, she'd imagined that he'd allowed her to discover her real self, that he had somehow made it safe for her to unearth the person who, presumably, had been barricaded away as a child and had retreated so far into herself that she'd forgotten she was there. But that wasn't it. The real reason was because, for the first time in her life, she had to be herself. With Gideon, she was the one they relied on. It wasn't because he trusted her, or had faith in her; it was simply because if she didn't take control, no-one would.

Before Gideon, she had spent her life surrounded by people who were in charge, who made all the decisions. Even now, as a grown woman with children of her own, her mother was still lurking in the background like some protective beast. Sam was the same. He had no children. She was his future, too. Once she met Gideon, she realised that they weren't helping her. They weren't equipping her for the future, instead they were trying to prepare her to inherit their legacies. It wasn't their fault; they couldn't imagine doing anything else.

All the other men in her life had been the same, always expecting her to fit into their worlds. Before Gideon, she'd felt like a garment – something that men tried on, perhaps wore for a while, and then lost or discarded.

Gideon had been a breath of fresh air; an opinionated, intolerant, judgemental breath of fresh air. He hadn't tried her on. If anything, she'd tried him on. He had no expectations; he hadn't wanted her to be anything. He hadn't even expected her to be responsible. That was her decision. She could be anything, do anything and say anything. The things that made normal men freak out or scurry for cover, simply amused him or piqued his interest. Most of the time, he simply watched her, simply observed her being herself. On occasions when she was over-reacting, or being purposely petulant, perhaps to get his attention, he might mock her gently. But the mocking was never malicious, never chastening, never an attempt to change her. Mostly, it was simply an acknowledgement of her; a nod to her existence, her right to be Rosemary. He was the only man she had even known who was happy to discover her – to find out who she was. With other men, she'd been all sorts of things – a doll, a trophy, an heir, a means of impressing the boss, the baggage that came with a vagina – but never her, never just Rosemary.

She sat down on the edge of the veranda and stared up at the sky. She'd been grateful for Gideon for a long time, but it was starting to wear off. The fact that he was the best man she could find just proved how bad men really were. Most women she knew went on about men being bastards, but that wasn't it. They were just disappointments, like holidays and sex. Her mother had warned her about men when she was young, but Rosemary hadn't understood. As a girl, she hadn't realised that at some deep level of her being she obviously had a lot of expectations about men. She supposed they'd come from her father, or maybe from books and films. At times, she wondered if such expectations were programmed into her DNA – into women's DNA.

The disappointments had started with her first sexual experience. She'd anticipated it for years. It was going to be the most wonderful moment in her life; a memory she would cherish forever. She'd spent a lot of time thinking about who it was going to be with. In the end, she'd settled on Paul. He was a nice guy and his hair and clothes were always clean. She'd kidded herself she was in love with him, but even as she was getting ready to let it happen, she'd known it had more to do with the fact that she was the last virgin she knew, and he was the least bad of all the rich boys she had to choose from. Eventually, she'd let him screw her on a friend's bed at a party, after they'd both drunk too much. It had been like an injection – painful and over before she had even had time to start thinking about what it was like. When he'd finished, she'd looked down and noticed that he hadn't even taken off his trousers.

With men it was better. At least, with the ones who could control themselves, but sex had always been more of a pain than a pleasure. You read about all the sex that people were supposed to be having all the time, but, apart from a brief period in her early 20s, when she'd had a few boyfriends in quick succession, she had never been particularly sexually active. She supposed it was the combination of being terrified of venereal disease and the way that men usually behaved when sex was involved that put her off. For some reason, men just didn't *get* women and sex. It was as if they didn't understand that the two things were connected. That was presumably why they could screw prostitutes. That was why Gideon had screwed that girl; at least, that was his excuse.

Rosemary had tried to believe it; tried to believe that a man could love you, and want to be with you, and have no intention of leaving you, and still screw someone else. Her mother had told her it was normal – it was how they were – the night she walked out on Gideon.

"It's no reason to break up your marriage, my darling," Catherine said, as if they were discussing photosynthesis. "All men have affairs. You'll just wind up in the same situation with another one."

Rosemary remembered turning on Catherine, determined to unsettle her. "What about Daddy? Did he screw around?"

Her mother's face surprised her. It was almost mournful. "Your father had two affairs…" Catherine paused, "…At least, while he was married to me."

Rosemary remembered being totally stunned. "And you forgave him?"

Her mother looked away. "I was very upset when I found out about the first one, but he was very calm about it and simply told me that he loved me and I shouldn't worry about it." Catherine looked at Rosemary again. "Of course, I lost my temper, but later he asked me whether I wanted to have sex with him."

Rosemary sat up straight.

Her mother tilted her head slightly to one side. "Of course, I didn't. I was never very keen on sex and I lost interest in it completely after I had you." She poured the tea. "Your father understood that; he accepted it. He never tried to have sex with me after you were born." Catherine picked up her cup and saucer and held it in front of her. "It would have been unreasonable for me to expect him to be celibate for the rest of his life," she continued.

Rosemary remembered being utterly at a loss for words.

Catherine smiled and started drinking her tea. "Men never lose interest in sex. I think, for them, it's rather like golf; they don't really mind who they do it with, as long as they can do it. It's not something you should worry about."

Gideon knew nothing of this; he assumed their marriage had survived because of his powers of persuasion. Sometimes, when he said nasty things about Catherine, Rosemary was tempted to tell him that it was his 'bitch of a mother-in-law' who had saved his marriage.

The best sex Rosemary had ever had was with a married man. She'd never told Gideon or her mother about her affair, which was just as well because he would have thrown it back in her face. But her affair was different; she wasn't the one who was married, and it was in no way comparable with what he had done. She'd been young and naïve, and lonely. She couldn't stand the boys she had to choose from. Adam had been the first man – the first adult – who'd ever paid any attention to her. She'd really believed he was going to leave his wife – not because he said he would, but because he already had. That was how they met. They'd been introduced at a party, after he'd left his wife. That was when they started seeing each other.

He wanted them to keep a low profile – "just while the lawyers are preparing the divorce," he'd told her. She should have known from the presents of sexy underwear and the toys and the weekends away that he wasn't looking at her as a wife-to-be. He talked about his old wife all the time; how glad he was to be free of her and how he just needed to get through the divorce and make sure the kids were okay, and then they would plan their future together. It took her a while to twig that he hadn't left his wife at all. He'd been a stockbroker or something like that, who lived in London during the week, and spent weekends with his family in the country. The bastard had never come clean with her. The day she dumped him, he was still saying he was going to leave his wife "as soon as the kids are sorted out". Rosemary knew it wasn't all a total lie. At some level of his being, he meant it, but it was never going to happen. His wife wouldn't have allowed it.

It was all such a cliché, because it always happened like that.

Maybe she should have told Catherine – her mother would have opened her eyes – but she'd been afraid to tell her. Catherine was so protective, and when she turned against someone, it was very difficult to control her. Rosemary had been afraid of what Catherine might do. It was ridiculous – protecting her married lover from her mother. She was still afraid to tell her mother. She didn't know why – it had all been so long ago. But still, Catherine was a funny woman. Most of the time, she was harmless, but she had a streak of ruthlessness which could appear unexpectedly. She also had a long memory. Sometimes, Catherine would remember things as being worse than they really were.

It surprised Rosemary how indulgent Catherine was about Gideon; probably it was because nothing bad he did was intentional. He could be a sly, wicked, unpleasant, deceitful bastard, but there was no malice in him. Whenever he hurt her – or anyone else – he was always more surprised than anything else. He was a child, really.

CHAPTER 8

Missing fathers

Gideon waited for Rosemary to come inside and then went back out again, ignoring her as they passed each other. He sat down on the edge of the veranda and lit a cigarette. Everything was going wrong, as per effing usual. How could they have been stupid enough to think Sam would have lifted a finger to help them? Most rich people had short arms and long pockets – that's why they were rich – but Sam was in another category altogether. Usually, favours came with strings attached, but with Sam, they came with ropes. Chains, even.

Well, it didn't matter. He didn't need Sam, or any of them. They could all go to hell. They were all pissed off with him for walking out of their crappy job in London, including Rosemary, but he couldn't have stayed – not for another winter.

He didn't blame Rosemary for taking him to London. He'd allowed it to happen; he hadn't had anything better to do. It was exciting; he'd never been overseas. Everyone had told him to go. It was a once-in-a-lifetime chance, an opportunity to be jumped at, but in the back of his head, he'd known it wouldn't last. He didn't want to move away – he'd never had any desire to leave Africa – all he'd wanted was a holiday. It had been nice to have money for a change, too, not to have to worry about where the next meal was coming from. But money or no money, he couldn't live like that. Once the fun of being a tourist had worn off, he'd turned into a zombie, a creature in a daze, an automaton. Rosemary had no idea what a nightmare the whole experience had been for him. He remembered one night in particular, sitting on the tube, staring out of the window into the blackness, not even noticing the stations passing by. He'd been so disconnected, so blinded by alienation and depression, that he'd wound up at the end of the line, nine stations beyond his destination. That disconnectedness had lasted a long time. Life had become nothing but a succession of functions: wake up, wash, dress, commute, work, eat, work more, commute again, eat again, pretend to play with the kids, and then collapse for the night to try and recoup enough energy to do it all over again the next day. He couldn't believe people spent their lives doing that; he would rather have killed himself.

The day he escaped had since become one the fondest memories of his life. London, as usual, had been wet and freezing. He'd been glad to be leaving, but too tense and exhausted to enjoy the feeling he was going home. After a bad night's sleep on the plane, he'd woken up, cold and thirsty, wondering how much further they still had to go. He remembered leaning over Joshua and pushing up the plastic cover on the aeroplane window. Instantly, the African sun had pierced the cabin like a laser beam. It was so bright and powerful that he and Joshua both recoiled like terrified vampires. "For God's sake, close it," Rosemary whispered loudly from across the aisle, as the sleepers around them started to stir.

Gideon laughed aloud at the thought of it. He remembered stepping off the plane into a typical Jo'burg morning. The air was already warm and above them, in all directions, stretched an endless blue sky, marked only by the occasional smear of a harmless cirrus cloud.

Walking into the arrival hall, full of colours and crowds, he'd almost started to cry. In Europe, airports were like mortuaries: no friendly or familiar faces, just rows of stiff bodies waiting to be claimed, but here, it'd felt like the world had come to welcome them. There was a sea of smiling faces and waves of arms and hands and, as he approached the barriers, one of his nephews had come forward to drag him to where his family was waiting. His mother had been dancing and whistling as if she'd won the lottery. Then, the rest of his nieces and nephews, urged on by his sisters, cautiously came forward, more interested in the presents they expected to find in his luggage than in the uncle they hardly remembered.

Gideon put his head back and blew a smoke ring into the air. Thank God he was home; job or no job, money or no money. He knew Rosemary and her family were going to start pressuring him to work – she'd already told him he should be doing something with his life, which was classic white-speak for 'get a job!' – but at least he was home.

Gideon glanced behind him into the living room. Rosemary was playing with the kids. She was probably thinking about leaving him. Sometimes, he wished she would; she'd turned into a real misery guts. Before the kids, they used to have fun; now they hardly did anything together and when they talked it was only about the future. For a while, he'd tried to pull her back into the present, but she always had a reason to forget about the here and now and to worry about what might happen. Once, he asked her if she'd like to know the future. "God, no," she said. "I'd probably commit suicide." Then she promptly carried on worrying about it.

Her biggest worry was money, and especially how they were going to be able to pay for things they hadn't even decided to buy. Whites were funny about money; they couldn't share it, even among family. They had some sort of inherent insecurity about it. They could still feel poor even when they were rolling in it.

He probably should have married an African woman, like his mother. Well, not like her, but a resilient woman, who didn't worry so much and who wasn't so infuriatingly weak. Rosemary was so fragile that Gideon was sometimes surprised she'd survived to adulthood. Her arms were like sticks, her wrists like twigs. When he hugged her, it felt like she would snap. When she was naked or in a swimming costume, you could see the bones sticking out of her chest and shoulders. She'd once twisted her foot and had been unable to walk for days.

Her physical condition he could handle, but it was the moaning he couldn't stand. She was always complaining about something. She couldn't cope with pain, illness, lack of sleep or anything like that, and there were so many things that bothered her. It was always too hot, too cold, too wet, too dry, too dark, too light. Jesus, it irritated the hell out of him. She spent her life trying to achieve a state of complete comfort and equilibrium based on some unmeasurable standard that she had stored away in the back of her fragile little head.

The truth was that she simply refused to put up with anything remotely uncomfortable or difficult and that was final. No discussion. If it didn't match up to Rosemary's expectations, it was not tolerated. Sometimes, he wondered why she'd settled for him.

He'd never met anyone as pathetically powerful as Rosemary. That was sort of what had attracted him to her in the beginning, although it was really she who'd chosen him. He didn't know why. But she'd been interested, and what did he have to lose? She was rich and good-looking – a perfect person to have as a girlfriend – and he'd often wondered what it would be like to be with a white woman. Marriage hadn't entered his head. She'd wanted it; she was just the girlfriend he wound up marrying. It was the same with the kids. She'd asked him what he thought about having children, and then been upset when he told her it was up to her. What was he supposed to say? She was the one with the uterus, the birth-control pills; and the money.

Rosemary had been born lucky; had had everything handed to her on a silver platter. That was why she complained so much, Gideon supposed, because she could afford to. People like him didn't complain. When you had nothing, you were more concerned about finding something to be happy about, to be proud of.

He'd been proud of his parents once; even though they were poor and uneducated and had nothing. That wasn't their fault; that was the whites' fault, or maybe it was God's fault. Or the fault of evolution, or of climate or something. Whoever's fault it was, Africa – and Africans – had been dealt a shit hand. At least his parents had been good for a while. The hardest had been finding out who his mother was.

She'd been his life when he was a boy; much of his childhood had been spent waiting for her to come home. Normally, she came home once a month, sometimes not even that often. The rest of the time she lived in a white family's backyard in Jo'burg where she worked as a maid. He lived for his mother's visits; there was nothing else.

The best times were the evenings, when she would put him to bed and tell him stories about his father: a man from the Shangaan tribe, called Joseph Mathonsi, who had worked on the gold mines.

She'd tell how she'd fallen in love with him the moment they met, because he was the kindest, gentlest, most considerable man she'd ever known, and clever and handsome and brave. She told him how lucky she was that he had chosen her.

"You are just like your father," she would say, stroking Gideon's head. "You are all the things he was."

Then she would tell Gideon that good people like his father often died young because God couldn't bear to be apart from them for too long.

"But I have spoken to God," she would say. "We agreed that you will live to be an old, old man." She would stroke his head. "God doesn't mind waiting for you because he has your father with him."

He could understand why she had lied to him. He had nothing; they had nothing. Although he'd never met Joseph Mathonsi, it had never occurred to Gideon that his mother might not have been telling him the truth about his father, until he reached his 17th birthday. He was celebrating with friends in a shebeen when, amid much wicked laughter, he was introduced to his 'uncle'.

At first, Gideon assumed the man was from his mother's village; virtually every man from the village was an 'uncle' to some extent or another. But this one, who didn't have much to say for himself, was a Zulu. There was no way he could have been Gideon's uncle.

Gideon wondered, if he'd walked out of the shebeen there and then and put the matter out of his head, maybe it would have been possible to forget about this 'uncle'; to carry on as before, believing his father was Joseph Mathonsi, believing his mother. But he'd been the only person in the shebeen who didn't seem to know that he had this 'uncle', and the man wasn't denying it. Eventually, after many quarts of beer, the 'uncle' started talking about Gideon's mother, Grace Mathonsi, and his brother, Reginald Gumede, who was apparently alive and well and living in Jo'burg. The 'uncle' professed not to have seen Reg for years, but he remembered how much his brother had liked Gideon's mother.

At first, Gideon tried not to take it seriously. The man had been drunk and vague, and could easily have made up the whole thing. But why would he? Also, everyone in the shebeen seemed to know all about it. And how did he know who his father was? He only had his mother's word for it.

For a time, Gideon had been tempted to confront her, but how could you broach such a subject with your mother? She was bound to deny it – she would have to deny it – and it never did any good to dig up old skeletons. It was so long ago now. She'd probably convinced herself in the meantime that Joseph Mathonsi was his real father. When he was a child, she'd often talked about how they had intended to move in together as a family as soon as they could scrape together enough money, but then his father had been killed in a mining accident.

Maybe it wasn't so important. As long as he didn't think about it, he could still feel he was Joseph Mathonsi's son. He'd spent his entire youth believing it. The problem was that he'd been brought up by his grandparents and indoctrinated with all their superstitions about the dead. This meant he had a close relationship with the late Joseph Mathonsi, as well as with many other deceased relatives. The fact that he hadn't met most of them was almost incidental. As a child, he had developed such close and profound relationships with them – and especially with Joseph Mathonsi – that it was like trying to imagine that a person who you'd grown up with and loved and cherished had never existed.

He could reason away Joseph Mathonsi if he really tried. But as soon as he stopped reasoning – as soon as he forgot to forget – Joseph Mathonsi would appear, often in his dreams, as his real father. His re-appearance was always the most wonderful thing in the world; like suddenly finding out that someone whom you thought was dead wasn't.

It was his mother's fault. If she hadn't insisted that Joseph Mathonsi was his father, hadn't spent his childhood continually telling him about his father and likening him to the man – if she'd just shut up about it – he could have just grown up without a father, like so many other people he knew.

Now he had to get rid of Joseph Mathonsi – a person he'd spoken to almost every day of his life, whom he still spoke to when he needed advice or help or just someone to talk to. It was ridiculous. The only man he'd ever been close to, the only man he'd ever been able to confide in, the only man he'd ever loved or given a damn about, had turned out to be a figment of his mother's fucking imagination!

It had been almost as difficult to get used to the fact that his mother was a whore. He still loved her; he couldn't help it, but he wished she wasn't his mother. He wished he could have kept Joseph Mathonsi and got rid of her. The only reason he still went to see her was because she would know something was wrong if he didn't. He'd learned over the years to block out of his mind what she was, so that when they saw each other he could be normal. He'd never told Rosemary the truth about his parents. How could he? How could you tell your ridiculously respectable wife that you were the illegitimate son of a whore?

Gideon got up and went inside. Rosemary wasn't talking to him. This was the usual routine. He knew what was coming next; soon she would make peace with him and then start leaning on him to go and work for Sam, as if a crappy job was the most important thing in the world. He got a beer out of the fridge and went back on to the veranda.

For the first 17 years of his life, he'd had the best parents in the world. Then, in one night, they'd turned into the scum that the whites had always said they were. Instead of being the son of man he'd idealised and a woman he doted on, he'd turned out to be the by-product of a union between a whore and a man that nobody wanted to know. Gideon knew next to nothing about Reg Gumede. In the beginning, he'd tried to find a out a bit about Reg, but he'd noticed that, whenever the name Reg Gumede was mentioned, people immediately changed the subject, so he'd dropped it. The truth was, he wasn't interested in Reg Gumede. If Joseph Mathonsi wasn't his father, he didn't want one.

CHAPTER 9

The Fu partners

Sino looked at his watch. He'd been waiting more than half an hour, but he didn't dare leave. He knew Miss Li would appear sooner or later. She always did. If he left now, he'd just have to come back and then she would be in a filthy mood and make his life miserable for weeks.

He hated Miss Li. It wouldn't have been so bad if she hadn't been so ugly – if she'd been pretty, or even plain, that would have been something! – but she was by far the most revolting-looking person he'd ever laid eyes on. He hadn't seen that straightaway. At first, she hadn't seemed so bad. He'd even admired her, briefly, because she had crippled feet, but wouldn't accept anyone's help to move around. But that was then, before he'd seen what she was really like. Now he couldn't detect one redeeming feature about her.

Normally, when he was around people for long periods of time, they got better-looking or at least less ugly. That was what had happened with Jane. She was certainly no oil painting, but after working with her for a while, she became easier to look at. Then, after more time, he'd started to like the look of her. At some angles, and in some lights, she'd started to look quite alluring. One night, after a few drinks after work, he'd wound up at her place, and seen that picture of her on the bookcase. It was just an ordinary photo, of her on holiday somewhere, but that night he'd seen something in her face that he'd never noticed before. Maybe it was the wistful smile, or the tender look in her eyes. He didn't know what it was, actually, but it had been enough to make him almost fall in love with her. He missed Jane. She still emailed him, but she'd accepted he was never coming back to London.

Miss Li just got uglier. Sino was in no doubt that it was because she was such an unpleasant woman. Jane had been beautiful inside and that had gradually changed his view of her outside. With Miss

Li, it was the opposite. It had now reached the point where Sino could hardly bear to look at her; her face had actually started to haunt him. Sometimes, he couldn't get it out of his head. Sometimes, it appeared in his dreams, as a floating head. Sometimes, he'd see it on a billboard, or flashing by on the side of a car. The worst was when it appeared suddenly and without warning. In one nightmare, he'd seen it in the basin, alive, staring up at him while he was brushing his teeth.

He could see it now; the bulging eyes surrounded by loose bags of skin; the nose, flat and wide, with those disgusting nostrils. On the sides, they sort of turned inside out so that the hairy skin was exposed. She trimmed the hairs but there were always stray ones sticking out. Worst was her mouth. There was no other way to describe it – it looked exactly like a chicken's anus. The lips were always pursed in a silent, spiteful growl, and when she was angry – which was most of the time – they would contract like a sphincter, sometimes so hard that the tendons in her stringy neck stuck out like washing lines. Sino didn't remember her mouth as having been that bad at first. It was probably the horrible things that came out of it all the time that made it seem so revolting.

He had just managed to force Miss Li's ugly face out of his head when she appeared in person, hobbling towards him, followed by Mr Zheng. Thank God, Mr Zheng was always there to dilute her. He was just a businessman who'd got lucky – or maybe unlucky. Poor Mr Zheng had Miss Li around all the time.

She didn't stop but simply pressed on, yelling at Sino to follow her. As he rose to his feet, Mr Zheng reached him. They shook hands in mid-stride and both fell into step behind her.

Sino came regularly to see Miss Li and Mr Zheng. He had a standing appointment with them once a month, but they were always calling him to come over at short notice when they wanted to know something. They never came to Sino's office, and they refused to talk to anyone else from his company except the chairman.

Miss Li, as far as Sino knew, was simply Mr Zheng's business partner, the other shareholder in the company. She and Mr Zheng were scrupulous about presenting it in this way, but it hadn't taken Sino long to work out that she was calling the shots. Mr Zheng's authority extended only to the operational business. That was obvious because most of the time, Miss Li didn't even bother to listen when they were discussing operational matters. Even more obvious was the fact that she didn't have a clue how the company was run and seemed to care even less.

On matters of strategy, and especially when it came to investments, Mr Zheng deferred to her absolutely. He would even rouse her if the subject of an investment came up during a discussion about operations. Sino had no idea how she made her decisions and he suspected Mr Zheng didn't either. It was obvious she wasn't working alone, but no-one knew who she talked to and to what extent she might be taking orders. Of course, no-one dared ask. Sino had never seen anyone initiate a discussion with Miss Li. He certainly wouldn't have. Whenever the chicken's anus opened, everyone just said or did whatever they could think of to get it to close again.

When he first came back to China to manage the 'Fu partnership', as the chairman called it (*Fu* was Chinese for luck), Sino had thought about one day approaching Mr Zheng for a job, but as long as Miss Li was around, he couldn't imagine it. Anyway, it was obvious that both she and Mr Zheng wanted him right where he was.

To them, he was a mine of information and they were constantly pumping him about everything the company was doing. It was industrial espionage, plain and simple. Mr Zheng's ambitions were fairly modest – he just wanted to steal the company's customers and learn a few things – but Miss Li was obsessed with the company's strategy, its plans for the future, and especially its research and development. Sino was pretty sure she didn't have a clue what to do with most of the information she got, but she demanded it anyway.

The first time they'd asked him intrusive questions, he'd politely evaded them, hoping they would get the message. They got the message alright; when he got to work the next day, he'd been summoned by the CEO, no less.

"The Fu partners called the chairman last night," the CEO told him. "They told him you were uncooperative and insolent."

Sino tried to explain, but the CEO wasn't interested. "If you want my advice, just do what you're told," he said. "This partnership is important to the chairman. If they complain about you again, you're out."

Downstairs, the Chinese MD patted Sino on the back; messing with the Fu partners was about as good for your career as screwing the chairman's wife.

By the time they got to the meeting room, Miss Li was embroiled in an argument with someone on her mobile phone. Sino and Mr Zheng sat in silence while she screeched into the device. The Fu partners didn't stand on ceremony with Sino. Since he'd been given that dressing down for not cooperating, they'd been treating him as if he was one of their own employees – albeit a slightly untrustworthy one. Occasionally, Sino gently tried to remind them that he represented – and was paid by – their business partner, but it made no difference. As soon as the Fu partners got wind of something, they would haul him over and, after upbraiding him for not having told them first, would set about extracting as much information out of him as possible. The first time, he'd been completely honest. He'd known nothing and told them as much, but that hadn't got him very far. Miss Li had such a pathologically suspicious nature that she'd been convinced he was hiding something and interrogated him relentlessly for hours. Eventually, he'd started making things up just to try and get out of there.

By now, he was fairly expert at being interrogated. The trick was to be a little reticent at the beginning. If you were too accommodating too soon, they got suspicious, and if you held back too much, they would call in provisions for the long haul.

Once the interrogation was underway, Sino would take what he called the 'Italian approach' – the one he'd learned from Gino in London. He would answer every question as openly and completely as possible, without making the slightest effort to understand what the Fus were really trying to find out. The result was that they would quickly be overwhelmed with information, but usually not much closer to the answers they wanted. This kept individual interrogation sessions short – since the Fus needed to go away and digest the information – and, over time, they increasingly took

Sino into their confidence to try to extract more precise answers out of him. He didn't yet know what they were up to in detail, but it was obvious that they were planning to diversify and to expand their activities abroad.

It was also obvious that the Fus assumed Sino was a more important employee than he actually was. Presumably, this was because they considered themselves to be more important than they actually were. They were encouraged in this view by the chairman, who personally kept in contact with them through his Chinese advisor.

What the Fus didn't know was that the chairman did this with all the company's Chinese partners. It was his way of keeping them sweet and keeping his ear to the ground because the chairman didn't trust anyone in China, especially not his own people. The Fus were working on the assumption that a joint venture with the company was simply a matter of time. Sino wondered how long it would take them to figure out that the company had no intention of sharing control of anything with the Fus – or anyone else in China, for that matter.

In the meeting room, Miss Li ended her phone call and complained that the tea was cold. Mr Zheng called for more. Sino waited.

Miss Li dumped a pile of papers on the table and started thumbing through them. "Do you know anyone in Africa?" she barked at him, without looking up.

Sino was taken aback. It was a typical Miss Li question – as absurd as it was unanswerable. It was the first time Africa had ever been mentioned by either of the Fu partners.

Sino shook his head, looking blank.

"The company has subsidiaries there," Mr Zheng pointed out, helpfully.

The Fu partners always referred to Sino's employer simply as 'the company'. They never used its name or gave any indication of its ownership. An eavesdropper could easily have assumed it was their company.

Sino nodded.

"Where are the company's subsidiaries?" Mr Zheng asked. His

tone was friendly. He was a nice, polite man. Sino was pretty sure he knew the answer already.

Sino explained that Africa for the company meant primarily Egypt, Morocco, Nigeria and South Africa. He didn't bother to mention the small branch offices in shitholes like Luanda.

"What are the company's activities?" Miss Li demanded.

Sino hadn't expected these questions. He started reeling off the types of businesses that he knew the company was involved in.

"Where do the raw materials come from?" Miss Li interrupted. Her mouth was looking more like a chicken's arse than ever, and she clearly wasn't listening.

Sino gently shook his head. He was thinking fast now; he needed to come up with some sort of answer fairly soon, otherwise he'd be here all day.

The door opened and Mr Zheng's secretary came in with the tea. She smiled at Sino, replaced the cups and poured steaming tea into them. Sino and the Fu partners sat in silence.

As soon as the woman left the room, Mr Zheng quickly asked if Sino knew anyone in Nigeria or South Africa. Presumably, he wanted to get the question in before the chicken's arse opened again.

Sino lifted his head slightly and looked thoughtful. He didn't know a soul in Africa. He'd never known *anyone* in Africa. In London, he'd purposely avoided the subject of Africa like the plague, because he'd been terrified of being sent there.

He could feel Miss Li's eyes boring into him. He desperately tried to think of something he could tell them; something he could plausibly back up, when the next question came.

Then he remembered the African guy he'd met on the career programme. He hadn't thought about him in ages. He'd been from Johannesburg. What the hell was his name? Something with a G; something like Ged… something biblical…

"Gideon," Sino exclaimed, almost with relief.

The Fu partners looked at him suspiciously.

"I know a man in the London office who's from Johannesburg," Sino said. "I haven't seen him for a while"

"He's African?" Mr Zheng asked.

Sino nodded.

Sino could tell from their faces it had worked. They'd release him now; send him off with instructions while they plotted their next move. Whenever possible, it was best to be truthful. Nothing was as convincing as the truth.

"We want to know about the company's activities in Africa," Miss Li barked. "We want to know what the company buys, who the suppliers are, and where they are, and who to talk to."

Sino nodded.

"We're looking for ways to expand our partnership," added Mr Zheng, smiling.

Sino kept nodding.

"The company has a very well-established presence in Africa," Mr Zheng continued.

"Is there anything in particular you are interested in?" Sino asked, aware that he sounded a bit like a shop assistant.

"Contacts!" barked Miss Li.

Mr Zheng nodded back at Sino. "We're looking for someone we can communicate with." He gave Sino a funny look.

The Fus stood up. Sino was dismissed. He probably had a week to come up with a victim that had the potential to be cultivated.

Sino stopped for lunch on the way back to the office. Whenever possible, he tried to avoid the office canteen.

Sino had twelve subordinates sitting in low-walled cubicles outside his glass-walled office. Officially, they were sales and marketing people whose job was to find new customers and to build up relationships with existing ones. In reality, they supported a network of freelance agents who sold the company's products, and made sure the company didn't get close enough to the customers to put them out of business. Most of Sino's team were little more than glorified secretaries to the agents. As their boss, Sino took care of the important agents. The most successful one was an ugly little swine with yellow teeth and a bad wig. He would regularly swan into the office and treat them all like shit. He even shouted at the branch manager in front of everyone. No-one ever said a word; no-one dared. The bastard's last contract alone made him more valuable to the company than everyone in Sino's department put together.

The company had been trying for years to deal with the market directly, but it couldn't get a foothold on the ground, especially among the big customers, who were beholden to government officials. It was like being stuck on stilts.

Sino got back to the office and set about trying to track down Gideon. He had no idea what Gideon's last name was, so he had to go through all the names in the UK directory of the company's electronic phonebook. There were no Gideons. He rang the main reception. The receptionist was new, and had never heard of an African called Gideon. "Maybe he's left, or been transferred somewhere else," she suggested. "Maybe he's gone back to South Africa."

Sino looked through the phone book for South Africa. There were four Gideons. Only one of them had bothered to enter his personal details into the company phonebook, even though it was supposed to be mandatory. Sino checked the time difference. Johannesburg was an hour ahead of London, so it was still morning. He picked up the phone. He'd start with the Gideon whose direct line he had. The man's last name was 'Swanepoel'. Sino dialled his number.

Sino knew it wasn't the right Gideon the moment Mr Swanepoel answered the phone, even though he couldn't remember what Gideon sounded like. He replaced the receiver without saying anything and dialled the reception desk.

Working in reverse alphabetical order, Sino asked for the next Gideon, one called 'van der Merwe'. The receptionist corrected his pronunciation and put him through. Mr van der Merwe wasn't the right Gideon either; his accent was thicker than Mr Swanepoel's and he'd never been to China. Sino asked him to put him back to the reception desk, but the man cut him off. Sino dialled reception again. This time he was looking for 'Gideon Mathonsi'. This Gideon was not answering his phone, the receptionist told him.

"In that case, may I speak to 'Gideon Gcwabaza'," Sino asked. He had no idea how to pronounce the name, so he spelt it.

"He's not here," she said.

"Do you know when he'll back?"

"He won't. He's left the company."

Sino paused. If Gideon was in Johannesburg, he had to be 'Mathonsi' or 'Gcwabaza'.

"Are you looking for someone called Gideon?" the receptionist asked.

Sino admitted he was.

"What does he look like?" she said.

Sino tried to think of a description but could only come up with "he looks African".

The woman said nothing.

"He used to work in London. I met him in China about a year ago," Sino said.

"You're looking for Gideon Mathonsi," the receptionist confirmed.

"Am I?" said Sino, relieved.

"Yes, but he's not available," she said.

"Do you know when he'll be back?"

"No."

"Can you give him a message," asked Sino.

"Okay," answered the woman.

"It's confidential," said Sino, "but it's very important that I speak to him urgently. Please tell him to call me as soon as possible. I'll give you my mobile number."

The following day, Sino called again. Gideon was still unavailable. The day after, it was still the same story.

"Are you sure there's no other way I can get hold of him?" Sino asked the receptionist.

"Yes."

"Are you sure he got my message?"

"Yes."

"Did he say anything?"

"No."

"Do you still have my mobile number?" he asked.

"Yes."

Sino scratched his head. The whole way through the conversation – if you could call it that – he could hear the receptionist talking to someone else.

"You're absolutely sure he got my message?" Sino said.

The receptionist made a noise that could have meant anything.

"It's essential that I speak to him very soon," Sino continued, in the most serious voice he could muster. "I have an important business issue to discuss with him."

The woman made another noise.

"Please," Sino said, aware that his tone was by now becoming slightly desperate. "It's really important that I speak to him."

"Why?" the receptionist asked suddenly. Her tone was slightly aggressive.

Sino hesitated. By now, he was pretty certain the woman knew Gideon personally. He decided to take a chance. "I have a business proposition for him," Sino said. "It would really be in his interest to call me."

There was a moment of silence. "Okay," the woman said. "I'll give him the message."

"Thank you!" said Sino.

He hoped it would work this time; he had to have something for the Fu partners.

It was late; time go home. The cubicles were empty – the workers tended to leave at 5.30pm on the dot, unless they were told to stay. They were all better off working for a western company than a local one but Sino wanted out. He'd had a few offers since coming home to China, but only from western companies which weren't likely to be any different from this one.

What he really wanted was to run his own business, but he didn't know anyone.

The call from Gideon came in the middle of the night. He obviously wasn't concerned about the time difference.

"I heard you had a business proposition for me," Gideon said.

"Possibly," said Sino, half asleep.

"I'm listening."

"How are you?" said Sino, trying to get his eyes accustomed to the light.

"Fine."

"It's been a while."

"Yes."

Sino glanced at the screen of his mobile. He couldn't see

Gideon's number. He thought of asking whether he could call Gideon back in the daytime, but decided against it. Better to get things moving as soon as possible. The Fu partners would be wanting answers soon.

"How's the new job?"

"Fine."

"What are you doing now?"

"The same," Gideon said.

"Remind me what you do?" Sino said.

Gideon said nothing for a second or two. "What are you calling about?"

"It's not actually about work, *per se*," Sino said.

"What is it?"

"I'm looking for some contacts and I was hoping you could point me in the right direction."

"Contacts for what?"

"Well, anything really. People who do business in Africa."

"What makes you think I can help you?" said Gideon.

"I don't know anyone else in Africa."

Sino waited. After a few moments of silence, he said: "Hello!"

"Yes, I'm here," Gideon replied. He went silent again.

Sino clenched his teeth. He remembered that Gideon had been difficult to communicate with. "Actually, this has got nothing to do with the company," he said. "I'm calling on behalf of a Chinese company. They're looking for partners."

"Yes?" said Gideon, sounding a bit more interested.

"They're looking for people they can do business with."

"I have some contacts," Gideon said, immediately.

"Oh, what line of business are they in?"

"Oh, import, export, that kind of thing."

"Anything to do with raw materials?" Sino asked.

"Mainly raw materials, but also agricultural products and, you know, parts – for cars and things," Gideon said.

"Sounds promising," said Sino. "Can you give me some more information about these people?"

Gideon went silent again.

"Even a website, or something?" Sino asked.

"I can give you a long list of websites," Gideon replied. "But you don't need me for that. Google would probably be better."

Sino smiled into the phone. It would probably never happen, but he would really enjoy introducing Gideon to Miss Li.

"Can I tell these people in China that you might be able to help them?" he said.

"Sure," said Gideon. Suddenly it sounded like he didn't give a damn one way or the other.

"How can I reach you again?"

Gideon hesitated.

"I might need to contact you at very short notice," Sino said firmly. "In China, things move very quickly. It won't work if I can't get hold of you."

Gideon didn't respond.

"Are you interested or not?" said Sino, impatiently. "You could make a lot of money out of this."

"I'll give you a mobile number," said Gideon. "You can reach me on that anytime."

"One more thing," said Sino.

"Yes?"

"What do you do?"

"I work in sales and marketing."

"What's your job exactly?"

"I try to sell the company's products."

Sino went straight back to sleep. It was a weight off his shoulders.

Two days later, he was summoned by the Fus for the next interrogation. It didn't take them long to extract all the information Sino had about Gideon.

They lapsed into silence and stared at the table. They were obviously thinking hard. Sino was slightly surprised; he'd been expecting his next set of instructions.

"Are you having some trouble getting hold of raw materials?" he asked, in the most sympathetic tone he could manage. The question was addressed to Mr Zheng.

Miss Li suddenly sprung to life. "No!" her mouth farted, ominously. "We have no problems – with anything! If you tell anyone we have problems, you will be the one with the problem!"

Sino immediately dropped his head and nodded apologetically.

"We are thinking about the future," said Mr Zheng, watching Miss Li out of the corner of his eye. "We are expanding and Africa is an up-and-coming place, with huge natural resources. We want to find partners there. It's important for us." He paused and leaned forward. "It's important for China."

Sino nodded.

Miss Li was still glaring at him.

"Do you need to use the bathroom?" Mr Zheng asked Sino.

Sino stood up immediately. "Yes, thank you."

When Sino returned, both the Fus were sitting in exactly the same position, watching Mr Zheng's pretty secretary pouring fresh tea into their cups.

Sino sat down opposite them. He had no idea whether he'd given them more or less than they'd been expecting.

Mr Zheng smiled at him. "This man, Mr Ma… Ma…"

"Mathonsi," Sino supplied.

Mr Zheng kept smiling. "I suppose he's a very career-minded person, having been on the career programme?"

Sino looked at the table. "I'm not sure about that."

"Oh," said Mr Zheng, sounding surprised. "Would you say he's more interested in position and authority or in money?"

"Oh, money, definitely," said Sino without hesitation.

"But he's an honest, loyal employee, who always puts the company's interests first?" said Mr Zheng, in an unusually firm tone. He sounded almost angry.

Sino was surprised. He looked at Mr Zheng, but said nothing.

"I'm sure the company carries out very careful assessments of each candidate before allowing them to join the career programme," said Mr Zheng, speaking normally again.

"Well?" demanded Miss Li, when Sino didn't respond.

Sino stiffened slightly. "To be honest, it's not that difficult to get on to the programme; you just need to be the right age and to have the right qualifications, more or less."

Mr Zheng was about to say something else when Miss Li leaned forward and pointed her finger directly at Sino's face. "You call this man again!" she instructed.

Sino nodded.

"You tell him that a company in China is interested in doing business in Africa." Miss Li paused. Both she and Mr Zheng were staring intently at Sino.

He didn't react.

"Are you following?" Mr Zheng asked in a friendly tone.

Sino immediately nodded.

"You tell him that anyone who can put this company in touch with people they can do business with stands to make a lot of money in facilitation fees." Miss Li was still stabbing her finger in Sino's direction.

Sino nodded again.

"These are the activities that the company is interested in," said Mr Zheng, sliding a sheet of paper across the table towards Sino.

Sino knew better than to pick up the paper. He waited.

"You also find out what raw materials the company buys and where it gets them," instructed Miss Li.

Sino resumed nodding.

Miss Li stopped and leaned back in her chair. The sphincter in her face relaxed slightly. That meant she was finished.

Slowly, Sino put out his hand and drew the piece of paper towards him. It was a plain sheet, torn from a notebook, containing a hand-written list of products and services that the Fus were professing to be able to offer.

He stared at the list, waiting.

"Do you think Mr Ma – your contact in South Africa – will be interested in facilitating business opportunities for us?" asked Mr Zheng.

Sino nodded enthusiastically. "Yes."

Miss Li stood up and hobbled out of the room.

Mr Zheng showed Sino out. "If we can secure some business agreements, everyone wins," he smiled. "It would be good for us" – he pointed at himself and at Sino – "and good for China."

As soon as he was alone, Sino realised he was shaking slightly. As usual, he'd been tense during the discussion and the implications were still unfolding in his mind, but it was clear he was in a very tricky situation.

Until now, the Fus had used him only as a source of information. This was the first time they'd instructed him to represent them, even though he obviously wasn't to admit it. What was making him uneasy was that they were both clearly nervous about the whole thing. Even Miss Li seemed uncertain, which was a first.

Sino knew himself well enough not to do anything straightaway. That was a mistake he'd made time and time again in London; always trying to deal with everything immediately, always responding to emails the moment they landed in his inbox. In those days, he'd hardly reflected on anything – he'd just acted, acted, acted. Over time, he'd realised that many problems were like patients on life-support. In many cases, it was much more sensible to leave them alone and see whether they survived the night. Sino would leave the Fu problem in the back of his mind and see what he thought about it tomorrow.

Whatever he did, though, his job was going to be at risk. If he didn't help the Fus, they would make sure he was replaced. If he did help them, and the company found out, he would be out on his ear.

The problem was that there were no good guys. The Fus were milking their partnership with the company for all they could, and the company was milking them for all it could. They were both trying to squat on each other's fundament.

Sino would have liked to ask his grandfather for advice. The old man would probably have told him to walk away from both the Fus and the company. But that was hardly sensible. What was the alternative? To go and work for someone else and, in a year's time, be stuck again between a rock and a hard place?

As Sino drove back to work, he recited over and over again some of the things his grandfather had told him during their interminable conversations.

"Understand the nature of power," the old man had been fond of saying, "and you will always know how to be powerful."

What the hell did that mean? How could he be powerful now? Both the Fus and the company had him by the balls. Maybe his grandfather hadn't had everything covered, after all.

Sino glanced at his face in the rear-view mirror. He was being childish because he was nervous and didn't know what do. He knew better than to second-guess his grandfather, even from this distance. The old man was too sharp to have missed anything.

The damned Fus; why couldn't they just treat him like a regular business partner, instead of sucking him into their shenanigans?

The real problem was the company. He couldn't forgive the fact that they had sided with the Fus against him. He'd believed the company, taken it at its word. He remembered the words of the Chief Integrity Officer: "No-one in this company has anything to fear from coming forward with the truth."

How stupid he'd been to believe it! He should have listened to the Fus. He remembered Miss Li's horrible face when he first evaded her questions, and afterwards Mr Zheng sidling up to him and whispering that the Chinese had to stick together. He should have listened. Culture was thicker than commerce. As long as he sided with the Fus, they would never betray him to the company. That was the difference. Provided he was loyal, he could trust the Fus. With the company, loyalty counted for nothing. Of course, they said it did – they even paid loyalty bonuses to the suckers who survived the repeated restructurings – but it was all a lie. Everything the company had said had turned out to be a lie.

On one level, you had to admire the CEO and his type. Machiavelli would have been impressed. With their earnest eyes, smart suits and presentations full of Chinese proverbs, they really looked like they meant what they said, but it was all bullshit. They weren't interested in China or building partnerships or any of the noble things they professed to care about. Why they insisted on dressing it all up, why it had to sound like they gave a damn, Sino had never understood. They didn't have to say it. If they couldn't be honest about it, they didn't have to say anything. Maybe it was all intended as a distraction – a cover – because they weren't willing to share the power and the profits.

Why shouldn't he help the Fus? What were they doing wrong? They were just trying to expand their business activities into Africa. And why not? Chinese companies were doing very well in Africa and the Africans were doing very well out of it, too. Thanks to China, Africa had an alternative to the west.

Sino arrived back at work. Without realising it, he had solved his dilemma. It was merely a question of priorities. Where was his future? It was here, in China, and China was the future. One day, China would be the superpower. The west was an old donkey on its last legs. Once, it had carried the world into the future, but its best days were behind it. Now the rest of the world – led by China – could stand on its own two feet.

Sino walked to his office. On one side were the low-walled cubicles full of Chinese workers; on the other was an almost unbroken glass wall, behind which were managers' offices. On his floor, most of the managers were Chinese, but the higher you went, the fewer Chinese faces you saw. It was an absurd situation. He, a Chinese, sitting in Shanghai, with a team of Chinese workers was helping Chinese agents sell products made in China to the Chinese. And they were doing it for a company run by people who didn't know enough Chinese to order a beer in a bar.

Sino sat down at his desk and started checking his emails. Already, it was hard to believe that he had even considered siding with the company against the Fus. It was because of the lies the company told. Their lies were so convincing; it was as if they believed them themselves. Perhaps they did. Sino had noticed that people could convince themselves of almost anything, if it was in their interest to do so.

CHAPTER 10

Chinese waves reach Africa

Gideon put down the phone and felt in his pockets for his cigarettes. He was getting excited. He stuck his finger into the cigarette packet. There was always one left; one slightly battered fag hidden away in the deepest corner of the packet. He dug around but couldn't feel it. He ripped the top off the packet. It was empty. Shit!

He walked downstairs, searching his pockets for his lighter. It wasn't there. Someone must have 'borrowed' it. He would go past the smoking area on the way out – someone was bound to be there. The Chinese guy's words were buzzing around in his head.

A bunch of technical people were smoking. Gideon extracted a cigarette out of one of them and headed towards his car, puffing away. Down here, he always had the feeling he was being watched from the offices above. Sometimes, he had the same feeling in the toilets, that there was a camera behind the mirror. He knew there wasn't – probably. He started walking faster, keeping his head down. His feet felt like they had a mind of their own.

He got behind the wheel and reversed out of the parking place. He really wanted to rev the engine and shout out of the window, but he was also getting a kick out of keeping his excitement bottled up. He drove through the car park with an absurdly straight face, nodding solemnly at everyone he saw. Usually, he found it a struggle to act as if he was as boring and pathetic as the rest of the sad people who populated this dump of a company, but not today. Today, he was enjoying himself.

He waved at the security guard, who gradually opened the barrier to let him out. As the car hit the road, Gideon took a last drag of the almost-finished cigarette and flicked the stub out of the window. Then he let out a yell that hurt both his throat and his ears.

Finally, his luck was changing. Finally, something good was coming his way. Finally, he was going to make some money! With the 'facilitation' fees the Chinese guy had been talking about, he was only going to need one big contract to be able to walk away from this shit company for good. Soon he'd be out of here, away from all these idiots. No more taking shit from his bastard boss and arsehole Annabel! Soon he'd be free! Free! After all those years of being ordered around by everyone under the Sun, he was going to be able to tell them all to go to hell.

He yelled again. It was amazing how the world worked. When he woke up this morning, it had been just another shit day; another struggle to get out of bed to go to a shit job in a shit company owned by his shit in-laws.

Who would have believed that, by mid-morning, a Chinese guy he'd met a year ago in Hong Kong was suddenly going to call out of the blue with an offer that was going to change his life? You had to admire the Chinese; they didn't screw around. He hadn't thought much about Sino's first phone call, but a week later, the Chinese were ready to move. It was amazing – so different to dealing with whites and Africans.

By the time he reached the petrol station, Gideon had his whole strategy mapped out. He would have to involve Sango. He didn't want to, but Sango was the only person Gideon knew who could put him in touch with the kind of people the Chinese wanted to meet.

Sango's contacts were the reason he had his job. Through them, he helped the company win lucrative government contracts. In exchange, he got a fancy office, a fat salary, and a seat on the management board. Gideon and Sango knew each other because they smoked together and they both lived in the northern suburbs. In the mornings, he often saw Sango in his silver BMW, picking his nose while he waited at the robots.

Gideon had been intending to go and talk to Sango as soon as he got back to work, but – surprise, surprise – ugly Annabel was waiting for him. She was like a puff adder: fat, lazy, speckled and poisonous, and always lying in wait to bite some unsuspecting victim. He and Annabel had hated each other on sight.

She was supposed to be the department's 'coordinator', but the bitch couldn't coordinate a sneeze out of her fat, freckled nose, let alone manage an order book. She couldn't keep track of the mindless, menial, moronic tasks she was always dumping on to Gideon. She never knew where anything was, or when anything was supposed to be ready. In the months that Gideon had worked there, he couldn't remember her knowing the answer to one single question. When he'd eventually had enough and suggested that the place might be made to function slightly better if they occasionally stuck to a process – as opposed to running around like headless chickens until everyone was stressed and exhausted – arsehole Annabel had gone crying to the boss.

Gideon didn't find out until the following day, when the boss – who turned out to be an even bigger arsehole than Annabel – appeared at his desk to give him some 'helpful advice' about being 'empathetic', and not "undermining unity, because what you said had really upset Annabel".

Gideon remembered shaking his head in disbelief. Of course what he'd said had upset Annabel! It was supposed to upset her! That was why he'd said it! Annabel was the most useless piece of blubber ever to have washed up on the company's doorstep. They should have fired the bitch years ago!

But that had done it for him. He'd spoken out; he'd stuck his head above the parapet. After that, he was the bad guy; the ogre in the corner, the one you didn't want to get too close to. Meanwhile, the rest of his pathetic, little colleagues sat twittering away behind their little screens, keeping a low profile and putting up with stupid Annabel and her moods and mistakes.

Ironically, his comments had made things easier with Annabel – at least for the moment. Now she was walking around him on eggshells, and he was largely ignoring her. You couldn't ignore Annabel completely – for one thing, she took up too much space – but it wasn't that difficult to forget she was there. She was like something stuck to the bottom of your shoe – it bothered you while it was there, but once you scraped it off, you quickly forgot about it. Gideon wondered whether Annabel and the boss were having an affair. Maybe that was how she kept her job.

Gideon stood there while she waffled on. She was panicking, as usual, for no reason. He couldn't be bothered to listen. He should have used the fire escape – that way he might have avoided her. Now she was asking questions. He watched her mouth move up and down. She looked like a fat fish gulping air from the surface of a pond.

He played dumb. That was his usual tactic; pretend he didn't know what she was talking about, pretend he didn't understand. She was no threat, nor was the arsehole boss. It had taken Gideon a while to work that out. They didn't dare antagonise him too much, let alone fire him – he was married to the chairman's little sister.

It was less of a privilege than people thought. The family had forced him into taking this job, presumably in the hope that, with the passage of time and enough brainwashing, he might still turn into something resembling the little white boy they wished Rosemary had married. They probably knew it was hopeless – he'd told Rosemary as much – but Sam was determined to try. It was ridiculous. How could they possibly imagine he could ever become one of those pin striped, presentation-wielding MBAs that were squatting on the career programme? He couldn't do it. He *wouldn't* do it. He'd rather sleep on his mother's floor.

Annabel raised the decibels. She was trying to extract a promise out of him to do the work that probably could have been avoided if she hadn't been such a clueless bitch in the first place. He could have got out of doing it, but he really wanted to go and see Sango.

"No problem," he told her. "You'll have it by Monday."

She went off, looking relieved. They thought he was stupid. Annabel really believed it was going to take him two days to do the work she wanted. He'd crank it out in a couple of hours. It was donkey work – work they knew he hated. He supposed they gave it to him on purpose. To remind him that – no matter whom he was married to – they were calling the shots, and he was just the office boy. That was why he hated this company; they were constantly trying to squeeze him into a box. They'd been doing it since the day he arrived. The more he refused to fit into the box, the harder they pushed. It was ridiculous. He couldn't have fitted in, even if he'd wanted to; it was like trying to put shoes on an elephant. Gideon wasn't sure why they were doing it. Maybe it was just because they needed someone to do the dirty work, maybe it was just about showing him who was boss, but they were really trying hard. Extremely hard. So hard that he couldn't help thinking there was more to it than met the eye.

Sango was playing games on his computer when Gideon put his head around the door.

"Just a minute," he said, pretending he was working. Gideon didn't know why he bothered.

"Feel like a cigarette?" Gideon asked.

They went downstairs together. It was best to avoid the lifts; you never knew when there might be a power cut.

Gideon moved away from the other smokers. Sango followed him, looking curious. He decided not to beat around the bush. "If a foreign company wanted to bid for government contracts here in South Africa, how would they go about it?"

Sango looked surprised.

Gideon waited. He wasn't worried about being blunt. The worst thing Sango would do was nothing.

"Who wants to know?" Sango asked cautiously.

"A company in China," said Gideon, blowing smoke into the air.

"You know people in China?" Sango's tone was sarcastic.

Gideon nodded patiently. "I met someone when I was there last year."

"Who does this person work for?" said Sango.

"It's a Chinese company."

"What's it called?"

"I can't say it – it's a Chinese name."

"Try."

Gideon invented a few sounds that he thought sounded Chinese. They both laughed.

"I thought you might know if there were any big projects planned that a Chinese company might be able to bid for," Gideon continued, "who they should talk to."

"What kind of projects?" asked Sango.

"Anything," said Gideon. "The bigger, the better."

Sango stared at him for a few seconds and then lit another cigarette. "What makes you think I might be able to help you?"

"You're the business development manager."

"Yes," said Sango, in a very serious voice. "For *this* company." He pointed a finger at the ground.

"Yes," said Gideon, in an equally serious voice, "but presumably you know about contracts that we aren't interested in, or that we're not eligible to bid for."

Gideon waited.

Sango just stood there, saying nothing. Gideon could almost see his brain working. He was wondering whether Gideon was trying to trap him.

Sango ran his tongue around his teeth. "Why would we pass on such information?"

Gideon started laughing.

Sango didn't react.

"Look," Gideon said, "I'm in a hurry. If you can't help or you're not interested, just say so. I'll make another plan."

He stared directly at Sango.

"Let me talk to some people," Sango said.

"When?"

"Soon."

"I need to tell them something by Monday," Gideon said. Then he put out his cigarette and strode away, trying not to make his exit look too theatrical. He was almost certain Sango would come up with something. He'd seen the dollar signs in the man's eyes.

Back at his desk, Gideon stared at the world map on the wall. It had been put there by his predecessor – or maybe his predecessor's predecessor, or the one before that. Everything around him was inherited from previous incumbents. The only thing that was his was a mug that Rosemary had bought for him after he complained that all the ones in the office were either stained or chipped, or both. His successor would soon inherit it all. He might even leave him the mug.

There was an email from Annabel to the whole department. Gideon deleted it without opening it. Sometimes, he was tempted to put mails from Annabel on to automatic delete, but that would probably have been going too far. Anyway, he didn't know how and he couldn't be bothered to find out.

Now he had a more pressing problem: how was he going to keep Sango and the Chinese apart for long enough to get his facilitation fee. He knew Sango would exclude him as soon as he had someone to talk to in China. Gideon had to find a way to keep himself in the game – or to keep Sango on the straight and narrow.

Underneath the waning excitement, Gideon was feeling nervous about the whole thing. He didn't have the first clue about arranging a business deal, especially with someone on the other side of the world, but how difficult could it be? He wasn't interested in the details – or even the deal, for that matter. He just wanted to make the introductions and then do a duck with his commission.

He would have liked to talk to Rosemary. She was smart about these things, and always had a friend or relative she could call on, but he couldn't very well ask her to help him snatch a deal away from her family's business.

Maybe he could find a way of separating the deal from the company. Gideon sat up straight. That was it! As long as he was working here, he couldn't legitimately help another company bid for contracts that might interest his employer, but if he didn't work here, there was no problem! Biting his bottom lip, Gideon stood up and went and looked out of the window. On the ground below, he could see people moving around. It was his turn to watch them.

He could feel the excitement rising again. What had he been thinking? He didn't need to wait until the deal was done. Now that he had the contacts, his job at this shit company was more of a hindrance than a help. He only needed to stay for as long as it took to set things in motion.

Suddenly, Gideon could imagine himself leaving soon – much sooner than he'd ever thought possible. Technically, he had to give three months' notice, but he could skip out sooner than that. If he left, he would have Sango by the balls because Sango would be the one with the job to lose. It wouldn't come to that, but one word to his in-laws and Sango would be out on the street.

Maybe he shouldn't have involved Sango. He'd moved too quickly; he should have thought about it for longer. He should have asked around outside the company first – he might have found someone else, who knew someone who knew someone.

Gideon felt like another cigarette. He went back downstairs, hoping Sango wouldn't be there. If he was, he would go and smoke in the car.

He was almost alone in the smoking area. It was situated some distance from the door to comply with the no-smoking law but was otherwise completely exposed – presumably so the smokers could be watched. As if smokers gave a damn who was watching. Gideon lit up.

Suddenly, it struck him. What the hell was he thinking? He was handling this all wrong. Jesus, he'd nearly messed up the whole thing. He was so fixated on getting his fee as fast as possible that he'd almost handed the whole deal to Sango on a plate.

Gideon shook his head. This was what happened when you were squashed into a box and treated like an idiot. You stopped thinking; you lost the power of thought. Why the hell was he worried about Sango hijacking this deal? He didn't need to put Sango in touch with the Chinese at all. Sango was working for *him*. Sango was going to put him in touch with someone whom he was going to introduce to the Chinese. He would pay Sango a facilitation fee for his trouble – and then tell him to piss off. Sango wouldn't like it, but what could he do?

Gideon slapped himself gently on the head; he had to stop thinking like an employee. He was the boss now. He was going to keep both sides as far away from each other as he needed to until he was assured of getting paid. Without him, no-one was talking to anyone.

He was tempted to resign right then and there, or just to leave and not come back. But Rosemary would freak. He'd better talk to her about it first. What could he tell her? There was no way she would be persuaded that he should leave. That was okay – he didn't need her permission. Actually, he could be honest with her; tell her he was opening his own business as he'd intended to do in the first place. She didn't have to know the details; she'd do her best to dissuade him anyway, because at the end of day she had no faith in him. That was the problem with whites. They measured your success by how well you fitted into their boxes. Well, he was going to prove her wrong.

*

In the event, Gideon left the company the following day. He hadn't meant to, because he hadn't yet mentioned his plans to Rosemary, but the arsehole called a department meeting out of the blue, and having to sit there listening to the fool for three hours on a Friday had pushed Gideon over the edge. Anyway, he really didn't need to stay any longer. Sango said he already had a contact who was interested, and Sino had responded with an SMS confirming that the Chinese were ready to talk.

You had to admire them; they didn't fart around. When they wanted something, they just went for it. No wonder they were taking over the world. When the Africans were in charge, nothing ever happened, and when the whites ran things, everything immediately degenerated into a never-ending nightmare of tension, stress and boredom.

The unexpected Friday meeting called by the arsehole was a case in point. Because it wasn't scheduled, Gideon expected it to be marginally less dull than usual, especially since everyone freaked out instantly when they read the arsehole's email, which referred to 'minor changes in the department'.

But what followed turned out to be the most mind-numbingly boring meeting in the history of the Universe. After two hours, the level of boredom was so extreme and so overwhelming that Gideon was almost in tears. At times, he wanted to blow his brains out just to relieve the tedium. Why were these people so boring? Why did it all have to take so long? Why did they have to go over everything again and again and again? It was always the same. Just when you thought it was over – because every facet and nuance had been scrutinised, analysed and discussed until you were ready to rip out your hair – some flabby-faced bastard would resurrect some obscure point and the whole process would start all over again. If it had been complicated, if it had really been necessary to pick everything apart over and over again, it would have been one thing. But it was all so obvious – so unbelievably and incredibly obvious. The budget had been cut again. The arsehole needed to fire someone. That was all.

When he finally admitted it, Gideon had nearly got up and smashed the man's face in. Not for what he had to do – he was just following orders – but for taking so long to get to the bloody point!

For a moment, he'd considered jumping up and down and laughing hysterically, just to freak them out. By then he was so infuriated by the stream of shit pouring out of the arsehole's mouth that nothing except mad, maniacal, monstrous violence would have been enough to express just how furious he was.

Instead, Gideon had done what he always did: clenched his teeth and his fists and stared at the floor. Only someone sitting very close to him, who was very sensitive to vibes, would have noticed that he was boiling.

It wouldn't have been so bad, had it not been for the bastard's voice. In conversation, it was bad enough, but whenever the little sack of shit got agitated, his squeaky, shrill monotone would reach a new pitch of irritating-ness. If it had just been the words – if it had just been the usual pathetic, meaningless, anodyne, corporate shit-speak – it would have been one thing. But because he was going to have to throw someone out, his words and tone melded together into a slimy, sympathetic-sounding ooze that seeped into your ears like quicksand, and filled up your skull until you literally wished your head would explode!

By this stage, Gideon was almost shaking. He'd had enough. He wasn't going to put up with this anymore. It was over. If life was about spending your days in confined spaces with arseholes like this, he wasn't interested. He stood up.

"Excuse me," he said as normally and as pleasantly as he could, and then – without looking at anyone – he picked his way through the seated bodies and left the room.

Outside, he took a few deep breaths. It felt like he hadn't taken a proper breath for ages. He went into the toilet, loosened his tie and rinsed his face with cold water.

Gideon looked at his face in the mirror. If he went back, it wouldn't matter. His short absence would be put down to a toilet break, or an emotional pause – something that should have been avoided, but nothing more. If he stayed away, the arsehole would demand an explanation. He'd have to come up with a reason. He'd have to engage in polite conversation with the man. He'd have to stay silent while the inevitable shards of sarcasm spewed out of the arsehole's mouth.

The alternative was simply to ignore the man, like he was doing with Annabel. He could just show up for work and not engage, simply do nothing, and wait. Eventually, they would sack him, but he could squeeze many months of income out of them in the process and then blame them for it.

Gideon looked at himself again in the mirror. He couldn't do it. He wasn't made that way. It was the arsehole's company. You either accepted that or you left. He couldn't stay.

Gideon went back to his desk and looked around. There was the mug from Rosemary. He would take it with him, to remind him of how bad life could get. What else was his? He looked in the drawers, then in the cupboards. They were full of files that he'd never opened. His successor would probably never open them, either. Why they were left there was a mystery. He'd thought about clearing them out, but he'd been concerned that it might seem rude or somehow imply that he knew better, so he'd left them. His predecessor's pot plant was still there, too. Actually, it was more of a tree now. Gideon had never really noticed it. He didn't even know who watered it. Someone must have been watering it. It wasn't a bad plant, actually, for an office plant. It had probably been there for years, just living next to a desk that kept changing hands. Plants were amazing; they could survive anything.

Gideon wondered whether to wait for the meeting to finish to tell the arsehole that he was leaving. There wasn't much point; he'd just go. He'd call him on Monday. He was doing the man a favour – now he wouldn't have to sack anyone.

On his way home, Gideon wondered what he was going to tell Rosemary. He had no idea how she'd react. He'd just walked out of her family's company, without a moment's notice, and until he got his fee, she was going to have to support them – the kids, herself and him, unless she decided to kick him out.

It wasn't a problem in any practical sense. Her family were rolling in it.

Gideon pulled up at a red robot. A man was standing on the traffic island, holding up a cardboard wall of sunglasses. Gideon looked at the collection. The man lifted up the board and moved it closer to the window.

"Let me try those," Gideon said, pointing at a pair that would probably suit him.

The man glanced at the opposing robot to check it was still green, and then handed Gideon the glasses.

They felt cheap – they were cheap – but in the rear-view mirror, they looked good on him. Gideon paid the man with the last notes in his wallet. If Rosemary's family wouldn't cough, he knew a man he could borrow money from until the Chinese came up with his commission. Normally, he wouldn't deal with a loan shark – they tended to break your legs if you missed an instalment – but he knew he'd be able to pay him back shortly.

*

Rosemary didn't take it well, which was hardly surprising. She was ridiculously calm, and sat there in silence not looking at him. Gideon would have preferred her to freak out; it was always easier when females got things off their chests immediately. Now he'd have to wait for her to get it out, and that could take days or weeks. Why did women always have to make you suffer?

"Are you sure you're doing the right thing?" she said. It was like being asked whether becoming a heroin addict was the right thing.

He played it cool, acting as though she'd asked a real question. He told her straight that he hated the job, and needed to go his own way.

"And where is that exactly?" she asked.

Gideon watched her warily. "I'm going to set up my own business."

She sucked her lips into her mouth. He smiled at her.

"Doing what?" she asked.

"Business development," he said, confidently.

She frowned. "What does that mean?"

"I'm going to advise companies overseas on doing business in South Africa."

Rosemary blinked, turned away and raised a hand to her mouth. She had a funny expression on her face.

He stared at her for a moment and then realised she was grinning into her hand.

He should have known this was going to happen. She had no faith in him – none of them did. Well, he wasn't going to react. He wasn't going to let her freak him out. He would bide his time, then show her and her stupid family what he was capable of.

She looked at him again, with a more serious face. "What advice are you selling, exactly?"

He went and looked out of the trellis door that led on to the veranda.

"Like I said, doing business here. What they need to do, who they need to talk to."

She raised her voice. "I'm sorry, Gideon, but what do you know about it? You're not a lawyer. You can't even fill out a passport form correctly."

He could feel the anger rising. That was a typical female, always dredging up the past and throwing it in your face. What the hell did it matter whether the passport form was in blue or black ink? It was ridiculous.

"For your information, I already have a client," he said.

She stood up. "Who?"

He immediately regretted saying it.

"Who?" she said again, coming towards him. She seemed genuinely curious.

"Don't worry about it," he replied, unlocking the trellis door. He went outside and lit a cigarette.

She didn't follow him.

He sat there on the edge of the veranda smoking and kicking his feet on the grass. He'd show her. It wouldn't be long until he'd fixed things up with the Chinese and got his fee. Then she'd see what he was capable of. He'd enjoy that day; he'd come home with a bottle of expensive champagne and tell her they had something to celebrate.

He could imagine her face. She'd wonder what the fuss was about but assume it was something trivial, something unimportant, like all the things he celebrated. White people only celebrated monumental things.

He'd pour the champagne and tell her that his first deal – in his new business – had been successfully concluded. Then he'd let her slowly extract the information out of him: how he'd been instrumental in brokering a deal between a Chinese company and the government, how he'd organised the negotiations, how he'd made possible a major cross-border business deal, and how he'd earned some serious money.

And then he would turn to her, and smile and say: "You were right, baby, I'm no lawyer. So I hired one."

That would shut her up – her and her fucking family.

Sango called the following day. He'd arranged a meeting with a company called Julius Investments.

"The chairman is very well-connected," Sango told him. "He knows everyone and everything."

"What's his name?" Gideon asked.

"Julius."

CHAPTER 11

The man at the trellis door

Rosemary pointed the remote control at the gate and pushed the button as hard as she could. The damn gate hardly ever opened first time. After another push, it started to slide open. They lived in a townhouse complex, north of Johannesburg. The place was typical of the northern suburbs. The 'townhouses' were actually flats in rows of buildings two floors high. Those on the ground floor had small gardens, enclosed by low walls. The complex was pleasant. It had a swimming pool, nice grounds with enough trees and was surrounded by a three-metre-high wall topped with electrified barbed wire. Inside the complex, it was relatively safe, although everyone kept their security gates locked at all times. Occasionally, someone got burgled. Everyone said the burglaries were inside jobs; no-one was ever caught and nothing was recovered.

Rosemary looked around for the security guard but he was nowhere to be seen. Usually, he was in the guardhouse next to the gate, or sitting on a white, plastic garden chair just behind it. She drove down the driveway, keeping an eye on the closing gate in the rear-view mirror to see if anyone followed her in.

Coming to live in Johannesburg had been a big adjustment, but Rosemary had learned how to handle herself. The serene surroundings could be deceiving – you could be murdered on your way from the car to the front door.

Poor Sally had been grabbed as she was walking into her house. They'd taken her inside and – apparently – raped her and burned her with cigarettes before shooting her in the head. Rosemary had heard all about it at a dinner party. She wasn't sure whether to believe all the gory bits. How did the people at the party know? These kinds of horror stories were the staple of South African dinner parties. When she'd first come to live here, Rosemary had found it difficult to believe them. Most of the time, the details were vague and the victims were always friends of friends or friends of colleagues – people she hadn't known directly. Until Sally.

Rosemary had known Sally quite well. She was someone they had seen fairly often, and she was definitely dead – definitely murdered. What had happened to Sally had made Rosemary think – again – about whether she could stay here.

Sally's death had brought the danger and the fear that much closer. She had lived just down the road; she'd been almost a neighbour and almost a friend. A harmless creature; someone who got weepy when she drank too much and never remembered what she'd said the next day. She'd been a pain in the neck, and a bit of a bore, and vain, and much too self-obsessed to really get close to. But she'd been someone you could let your hair down around; someone you could have fun with, someone you could spend an afternoon or an evening with and not regret the time wasted. Someone who talked all the time, but who never said anything. Someone you often wished would go home, but whom you missed now that she wasn't there.

What had happened to Sally didn't bear thinking about but Rosemary couldn't help it. What did Sally do when they attacked her? Did she scream and struggle? Did she beg them to spare her – or did she simply 'switch off' and let it happen, knowing her time was up? Rosemary hoped she'd been drunk, but probably not – it had happened at eleven o'clock in the morning. Rosemary had no idea how Sally reacted. She had no idea how *she* would react if she were attacked in her house, raped, tortured and murdered; better to concentrate on making sure it didn't happen, *couldn't* happen. But it could. It had. Sally hadn't deserved to be murdered, especially not like that. The randomness of it was what scared Rosemary most; here, things just happened. There was no sense to it. Sally had been unlucky, that was all. It was easy to be unlucky around here.

Rosemary was about to turn into the parking area in front of their flat when she saw that someone had taken her parking place. Shit! She hated it when people did that. She turned the wheel the other way and drove into one of the visitors' parking spaces opposite.

There was a shiny new black BMW a few spaces away from hers. South Africans liked fancy cars. Rosemary preferred a cheaper, nondescript vehicle because you were less likely to be hijacked or to have it stolen – unless you were unlucky.

The boot was full of shopping bags. Rosemary contemplated trying to lug them all in at once but then decided against it; Gideon could come out and get the heavy ones. She picked up the bags with stuff for the fridge and walked to the front door. As she passed the car that was in her space, she was tempted to let down the tyres. Once, she wouldn't have dreamt of doing such a thing, but since moving here – to South Africa – she'd noticed her patience threshold was a lot smaller. She'd better not. You never knew how the driver might react. He could come to the front door with a gun – or let down her tyres. Gideon was no help. It didn't bother him when people parked in his space; he just parked in the visitors' parking, or in someone else's space.

The front door was closed. That was strange; Gideon always left it wide open, except during the short winter. She opened the security gate. Every flat had security gates on all external doors. The front door was not only closed but locked. She unlocked it and went inside.

"Hello?" she called, locking the gate behind her.

There was no answer.

The townhouse was not large – just a lounge-cum-dining room, a kitchen and the three bedrooms. There were two bathrooms and one en suite to the master bedroom.

The trellis door on to the veranda was locked, but the sliding French doors were open. Gideon must have taken the kids out through the garden. Maybe they were at the pool.

Rosemary put the bags down in the kitchen and walked towards the bedrooms. The doors to the kids' bedrooms were open, but the master bedroom door was shut. She pushed down the handle. It was locked. She was slightly startled. She shook the handle. "Gideon! Gideon?"

She heard whispering inside and then the key turning in the lock. Joshua opened the door. Lydia was sitting on the bed. There was no sign of Gideon. "Where's your father?" she demanded.

She looked down at Joshua. "Where is he?" she said in a louder voice.

"I don't know," he said, shaking his head. He told her that Gideon had told them to lock themselves in the bedroom and not to come out under any circumstances.

Rosemary went back into the living room to call Gideon. She was angry and tense and walking quickly – so quickly, in fact, that she was already almost in the middle of the room before she noticed the man standing outside the trellis door. He was leaning against it; he must have climbed over the low wall to get into the garden. The garden gate was supposed to be locked. Rosemary stopped dead.

"Where's Gideon?" he asked her casually. He was tall and thin with very dark skin, and his head was shaven. He didn't look South African.

Her mouth was suddenly as dry as a bone. She just managed to swallow, but she couldn't get a word out.

"Is he here?" the man asked.

By now, the panic was rising within her. "No," she managed to say. Her voice was a growling whisper.

The man had been picking at his fingernails and was looking more at his hands than at her. He stopped and took hold of the bars of the trellis door with both hands, like a man in a prison cell. He studied her for a few seconds.

"Where is he?" he said. His voice was completely expressionless.

Behind him another man appeared. This one was much bigger. They were both decently dressed. Rosemary was absolutely terrified.

"I don't know." She managed to speak a little louder, but it sounded like she had gravel in her throat.

Out of the corner of her eye she saw Joshua slowly emerging from the bedroom. She surreptitiously shook her hand at him, clenching her teeth. He stopped. She turned her head slightly and gave him a furious look. He retreated back into the bedroom.

By now her limbs were shaking, and her stomach fluttering uncontrollably. She tried to breathe through her nose but her lips were trembling so much that she couldn't quite keep her mouth closed. Her breaths were short, sharp and quaking and sounded incredibly loud. She hoped the man couldn't hear them. For a few seconds, she contemplated running back into the bedroom, but she couldn't. The children were in there. The back of her eyes started to fill up with tears. Every muscle in her face was trembling.

The other man was walking around the garden, peering into the windows.

She stood there, shaking. She'd always assumed the flat was secure – that even if they got into the complex, the security gates would stop them. Standing there now, even in her terrified state, it was obvious that this man was not wondering how he was going to get in.

The other man returned to the one leaning against the trellis door and said something to him. He nodded.

"Let me in," he said to Rosemary. "I want to check that Gideon is not here."

She stood there, looking at him. "I promise you, he's not here." Her voice was weak; just loud enough for the man to have heard her.

"Who's in the bedroom?" the man said.

Rosemary took a deep breath. "My children."

The man put his forehead against the bars of the trellis door and stared at her.

She stared straight back at him. "I promise you, Gideon is not here."

After a few seconds, the man turned around and said something to his accomplice in an African language. They had a very short conversation, then the man who had been speaking to her turned and tapped the bars of the trellis door with the nail of his index finger. The taps were loud enough to give her a jolt.

"You give Gideon a message," he said.

Her legs were really beginning to wobble now.

"You tell Gideon that Simon is looking for him."

She nodded like a terrified schoolgirl.

"You tell him I want to see him by tomorrow." He paused and stared at her. "You understand me?"

She nodded again, furiously.

"Don't forget!" he said, tapping the bars again. The two men turned and walked away.

Rosemary stood there, frozen, until they were out of sight. Then she moved forward carefully, like a nervous animal. The garden seemed empty. She edged closer to the trellis door until she could see the entire garden. There was no-one in it. At the far end was the locked gate leading to the visitors' parking. She pushed the side of her head against the trellis door, trying to hear something. Then she heard the car. She rushed across the room to the front door.

The black BMW was heading up the drive. She watched until it was out of sight, then she collapsed on to the floor, shaking and sobbing.

She sat on the parquet floor, her legs underneath her, her right shoulder propping her up against the wall. She was panting like a dog and letting out occasional involuntary sobs. Suddenly, she sensed someone behind her. She jumped. It was Joshua. She burst into tears as soon as she saw him.

He stood there still in front of her, a worried look on his face. She couldn't stop crying.

She managed to get to her feet and lead him to the couch. They sat down together, holding hands. He was six years old. Lydia appeared at the door. She was four. Rosemary beckoned to Lydia, who immediately rushed over and climbed on to her lap.

Both children sat there looking at her, saying nothing. Rosemary tried to clear her throat. She desperately needed a glass of water. Calmly, with a rasp, she asked Joshua to bring her one. He ran off to the kitchen.

She and Lydia sat there, waiting. They heard him open the cupboard, take out the glass, open the fridge, pour the water.

By the time he was back, Rosemary had more or less composed herself. Gulping down the water, she thought for a second about calling the police, but there was no point.

Her mind was starting to work now, thoughts spiralling around in her head. She swallowed and took some deep breaths. Where the hell was Gideon? What had happened to him? Where was the security guard? There was always supposed to be someone at the gate. She was tempted to put the kids into the car and just drive away, but where would they go? She looked at the clock. It was nearly 11.30. There was probably a direct flight to Zurich leaving that night. They could spend the afternoon in a hotel while they waited.

She tried to calm herself. What would they do in a hotel all day? The kids were already getting restless just sitting there. She put Lydia down on the couch next to her and turned on the TV. Both of the children immediately started watching it.

She got up and took Joshua's hand. "Come with me," she said softly.

He hardly heard her. She gently pulled him out of the room and led him to his own bedroom.

"I want you to tell me exactly what happened," she said, sitting him on the bed.

She felt calmer now. She could feel some strong emotions building deep inside her; there was anger there, and the beginnings of something worse, but these feelings were still forming, she could still ignore them. She didn't want to get angry with Gideon, or anyone else, until she knew exactly what had happened and what she was going to do next. The man at the trellis door wanted to see Gideon tomorrow. That meant they had the rest of the day.

"I want to watch TV," Joshua said, trying to get off the bed.

She held him firm. "Just tell me what Daddy said."

"I told you," he said, obstinately.

"Did Daddy say where he was going?" she asked him.

Joshua shook his head. "Who was that man?" he asked.

She shook her head. "I don't know."

"Did someone phone or ring at the gate before Daddy went out?"

Joshua frowned, irritated at having to think. Then the memory kicked in. He nodded. "Someone rang at the gate."

"Tell me again what Daddy said."

Rosemary listened patiently while her six-year-old son haltingly and confusingly repeated his father's instructions. He told the children to lock themselves in the big bedroom and stay quiet until he came back. He'd been in a hurry. He'd made them turn off the TV and go straight to the bedroom. He'd been angry. He had shouted at Joshua to lock the door.

Rosemary went back into the living room with Joshua and gave the children some biscuits. She looked at the phone. She couldn't call Gideon from here. She went into the bedroom, and rang him on her mobile. His phone wasn't on. She tried two more times, then decided to go and find the security guard.

He was sitting in his plastic chair outside the guardhouse. She knew his name was Thomas. They'd never had a proper conversation, but they always exchanged pleasantries. She gave him the children's old clothes and toys for his family, and they gave him a small amount of money at Christmas. They had never been burgled.

As soon as he saw her, he jumped to his feet.

"Did you see a black BMW leaving just now?" she asked him, looking into his face.

He moved his head very slightly, not quite shaking it, more waving it very gently from side to side. His face was expressionless. He wasn't looking her in the face, but he seldom did.

"Where were you?" she asked.

"I was here," he replied. His eyes were on the ground. He wasn't allowed to leave his post while he was on duty.

"You weren't here when I came home," she said.

"I was there," he said. He waved his arm vaguely towards his left.

"But you didn't see the black BMW that drove out about 15 minutes ago?"

Again he moved his head slightly.

"You didn't see it?"

He waved his head.

"If you were here, you must have seen it," she persisted. Suddenly, she knew she was going to get nothing out of him.

He didn't disappoint her. He simply stood there, totally silent, staring at the ground, waving his head gently.

She raised her voice. "They were bad men! They came into my garden!"

She was shaking now with anger and frustration. "My children are in that house!" she almost shouted, pointing down the drive.

She stopped, breathing heavily.

The guard simply stood there, looking at the ground.

"Did you see Gideon leave?"

The man lifted his head suddenly. He seemed surprised at the question, then he shook his head.

"All these things happened this morning, but you saw nothing," she hissed. She wasn't asking a question – there was no point.

The guard looked at her. "I think Gideon is there," he said. He walked into the driveway and looked down it.

"He's not," she snapped.

The guard looked puzzled.

"But his car is there," the guard said, pointing down the driveway.

The guard was right. She'd forgotten that Gideon's car was there. Where the hell was he?

"But he's not," she said, confused.

The man frowned. "I didn't see him go. I think he is still there." It wasn't clear whether he was speaking in the present or past tense.

"And you were here all the time," she said again.

He nodded.

Rosemary turned and walked back down the drive. Africans could be infuriating. She couldn't blame him. He'd probably been paid, or threatened, to turn a blind eye. Why should he do otherwise? He had his own life to worry about. Why should he risk his life for a stranger?

Walking down the drive of her Johannesburg townhouse complex, Rosemary suddenly saw how vulnerable they were. The realisation hit her like a punch. She started shaking again. She'd been bullshitting herself that they were safe, lying to herself that the walls and the electric fences and the security guards and the gates were enough to keep the criminals out. It was a fantasy. She'd wanted to believe it. Maybe the petty thieves could be kept out – the bag snatchers and the pickpockets – but against the really dangerous ones, all this security was useless. The killers didn't need to figure out how to get over the fences, or break through the gates; they just drove in whenever they wanted to. Suddenly, she was angry; angry at the security guard at the gate, angry at the man who'd sold them the flat, angry at the bastards who'd installed these useless security systems. Angry at everyone.

She stormed down the driveway, breathing heavily. Despite wanting to strangle all of them, she knew this anger was harmless. It was the anger you felt towards strangers and the world; the anger that frustrated and infuriated and chipped away at one's diminishing faith in human nature. But that was all it was. The real anger – the one that grew and festered and spawned and had the potential to evolve into real, lasting, furious hate – was still building. She could feel it forming deep inside her, down in her gut. It was like there was something rotten inside her that her body was getting ready to expel. It wasn't a pleasant feeling, but she was looking forward to it. A part of her would have liked to force it out, the psychological equivalent of sticking your finger down your throat, but she couldn't get this anger out by herself. Only he could do that. It would stay inside her until he appeared.

She couldn't quite bring herself to think about what he had done. That would have to wait. That would be something he would have to explain. Then she would move on to thinking about what it meant and what was going to happen next. But that was getting ahead of things. First, they had to confront what he had done, and he wasn't going to get away with it. Not this time. His dissembling, his silence, his arguments, his temper, his refusal to take responsibility, were not going to save him. This time, he was going to have to face it.

She went back into the flat and called her mother. Catherine wasn't home. Where the hell was she? Then Rosemary remembered – she'd gone to New York for another board meeting. She tried her mother's mobile.

Catherine answered the phone almost immediately. As soon as she had adjusted to the slight delay on the line, she fell silent. Rosemary could picture her mother's face; that silent, pursed look that always came over Catherine when she knew something was wrong but not what. As Rosemary started to talk, she started crying again. The words just tumbled out. She had no idea whether Catherine was able to follow what she was saying; her sentences were all over the place. She wasn't even using names – just words like 'he', and 'the man at the trellis door' and 'the guard'.

As she sobbed her way through her story, she wondered whether she should be telling Catherine what had happened, but she had no-one else to talk to. Sally was dead. There was only her mother. She could picture the change in Catherine's face. To anyone else, it would be almost imperceptible. They might notice the skin turning a shade paler; the eyes a touch narrower; maybe they would see the cheeks drawing in minutely, the jowls sinking a millimetre or two. But they wouldn't notice the change to the face itself. You had to know Catherine to be able to notice it; to tell the difference between the normal face, and the face of stone.

Her mother no longer criticised Gideon to her face – Rosemary suspected she had even developed a certain fondness for him – but she knew Catherine thought the marriage had been a mistake. To her mother, the purpose of a husband was to look after his wife and their children. If he was not able to do that, he was useless. "Would you keep a guard dog if it didn't scare away burglars?" her mother had asked her once.

Rosemary paused in her monologue. She always felt better when talking to her mother. No matter how worried or scared she was, as soon as she said something to Catherine, it all suddenly seemed to be less serious, but telling her mother things was dangerous. All she had to do was nothing. Her mother would take control.

Now that she'd finished her story, Rosemary knew what was coming. Catherine would ascertain whether she was able to deal with the situation.

The question came on cue. "What do you plan to do now?" Catherine asked. Her tone was completely expressionless, as neutral as an executioner's.

Rosemary said nothing.

"You can't stay there," Catherine continued. "You must leave that house. You said it yourself."

"I'm waiting for Gideon."

"Where will you go?"

"A hotel, I suppose," Rosemary shrugged. "I'm not worried about that. We can be out of here in minutes."

"And if he doesn't come back?" Catherine said.

Rosemary could feel herself getting tense again. "Why wouldn't he?" The thought hadn't occurred to her.

Catherine said nothing.

"He'll be back," said Rosemary. "He just ran away."

The words came out calmly, as if she was talking about the weather, but the act of saying them, of putting a voice to what she'd refused to think about, suddenly brought the fury to the surface like vomit. She snarled into the phone. "He ran away and left my babies alone!"

Now she was no longer talking to her mother. She squeezed her hands into fists. "The bastard," she muttered through clenched teeth. The muscles in her face were shaking. "The bloody, fucking bastard!"

The fury was tumbling out now. If Gideon had walked into the room at that moment, she would have killed him. "I'll call you back," she said into the phone.

"Okay," her mother said. It was like they were in the room together. They both rang off simultaneously.

Rosemary couldn't keep it in any longer. She closed the bedroom door, then walked into the bathroom and closed that door, too. Then she opened the cabinet above the basin. She picked up Gideon's aftershave and hurled it at the shower. The bottle smashed into smithereens against the tiles. Then she really let rip. Within seconds, every bottle in the bathroom had been smashed in the shower. The plastic ones had ricocheted off the tiles, and one had hit her on the head, making her even more furious. Some of the tiles were cracked. Surveying the damage, she felt a little better; a little more in control. But the fury wasn't going away. He was going to pay for this. If he thought that he'd suffered after that little affair of his, he was in for a real wake-up call. This time, he was going to pay. Her teeth were hurting from the clenching.

She checked her appearance in the mirror and went back into the living room. The kids were arguing over which TV channel to watch. Joshua was standing on the couch, holding the remote control out of Lydia's reach and trying to ignore her. She was attempting to climb up his body to get it, and getting progressively more frustrated and angry with each futile attempt. She would flip out soon, Rosemary knew. Rosemary stepped into the fray and was about to start mediating a truce when she saw Gideon at the small gate leading into the garden.

He hoisted himself over the gate and walked up to the trellis door. "Knock, knock," he said, tapping on the hollow bars with his index finger. He was acting normally – overly normally.

Rosemary swallowed. "Where have you been?" she asked, surprised at how normal her voice sounded.

"I had to go out suddenly," he said, retrieving his keys from his pocket and unlocking the trellis door.

Lydia was now starting to cry and shout at the same time.

Gideon walked into the room and approached Rosemary warily. He was looking closely at her face but avoiding direct eye contact.

"Where were you?" she asked again. Her tone was ominously pleasant.

Gideon took a breath and kissed her on the cheek. She did not respond. He retreated slightly.

Lydia started screaming.

Rosemary turned to Joshua. "For Christ's sake, give her the fucking remote," she hissed loudly. He looked up, aghast at her sudden anger. Then he threw the device on to the other couch and ran into his bedroom, shouting, "I hate you." He slammed the door.

Lydia picked up the remote control, changed the channel and sat down as if nothing had happened.

Rosemary turned her gaze back to Gideon. "Where were you?" she asked again. This time the anger in her voice was unmistakable.

Gideon ran his tongue around his teeth for a few moments. Then he said, "Look, I'm sorry I left the kids alone. I just had to go out suddenly. It was very important."

Rosemary turned on her heel and walked into the master bedroom.

He followed her. "Do we have to make a big deal out of it?" he said to her back. "I wasn't gone long – they can be left alone for half an hour."

It had been at least an hour since Rosemary had returned home. She turned around and faced him. "Close the door."

He did. She saw his face change; that look was appearing.

"Why did you go out?" she asked.

His eyes became evasive. He didn't react.

"You went out and left my babies alone!" she screamed. Now she was shaking.

He looked her in the face. "Joshua is nearly seven years old!" he said in a loud voice.

Rosemary moved away from him, to the far side of the bed – his side of the bed. He was still near the door. They were at opposite ends of the room.

"Why did you go out?" she demanded.

He shrugged and looked away.

"Who is Simon?" she asked suddenly. Her tone was flat now, the volume almost normal.

Gideon stiffened slightly but he didn't react.

"You went out because you knew they were coming," she said. Her voice was low. Her back was very straight, her entire abdomen trembling. It was obvious she was on the verge of exploding.

He seemed unsure how to respond. For a few moments, he just stood there. Then he shrugged again slightly. "They were looking for me. I didn't want to see them. That's all."

She inhaled sharply. "You left my babies alone in this house when you knew those bastards were coming!" She was screaming.

That look was now plastered across his face.

She waited.

"They were never in any danger," he said, staring at the floor.

Rosemary stared at him in total shock. "You left my babies here – alone, unprotected, in this house, when you knew those men were coming." Halfway through the sentence, she burst into tears.

Gideon threw up his hands. "It's no big deal. I owe them some money, that's all."

"What?" she hissed.

He looked at the floor. "We needed money and your family weren't willing to help. So I borrowed some."

Her mouth was hanging open. She stared at him, blankly, through the tears.

"Don't you understand? If I'd stayed here, they would have come in to get me," he said. He was speaking as if what he was saying was the most obvious thing in the world. "That's why I went out."

She carried on staring at him, stunned.

"They're just loan sharks. I didn't want a scene in front of the kids, so I went out. That's all."

She didn't reply; just stood there, unable to believe what she was hearing.

"Well, did they come in?" he said. He was speaking to her as if she was an idiot. "Did they? I don't see any signs of a break-in!"

He waited. She could feel the thing building up inside her; it was like waiting to vomit.

"What happened?" he asked. His voice was loud and unpleasant. "Did anything actually happen? Everything looks fine to me."

Suddenly, the tsunami of anger broke. "You fucking bastard," she shouted. "You fucking coward."

She snatched the bedside lamp and hurled it at him. He ducked, but it didn't fly far; it was restrained by the cord in the plughole and fell harmlessly on to the bed.

The fury flowing through her surged to a new level. She grabbed the clock radio and yanked it towards her with all the strength she could muster, making sure she ripped its cord out of the wall. Gideon was already halfway out of the room when it smashed into the door, close to his head. He quickly stepped out and slammed the door behind him. She threw the rest of the stuff that was on his bedside table at the door and sat down on the bed.

Now she was weeping with exhausted, desperate fury, mouthing the words: "coward, coward, coward".

Her shoulders sagged, as if her spine was unable to hold her upright.

When she re-emerged from the bedroom, he was sitting in his usual place on the edge of the veranda, smoking. She walked to the trellis door. He just sat there, sort of looking in her direction, but not looking at her.

She went to Joshua, who was still sulking in his bedroom. He ignored her, but let her sit next to him and stroke his head.

Rosemary wondered what to do next. In the past, she'd forgiven Gideon everything – all the lies, the deceptions, the cheating and even the affair – but this was different. She couldn't believe what he'd done. If he'd admitted that he'd run away and abandoned the kids in a moment of terror, she could have at least understood it, but what he'd said had been incomprehensible. She couldn't understand how anyone could leave a six-year-old and a four-year-old locked in a flat. What if there'd been a fire?

But to do that when he knew – *because* he knew – that two crooks, murderers, she didn't know what, were trying to get in, just beggared belief. What if they'd heard the children in the bedroom? They were bound to have heard them. The bedroom windows opened on to the garden and the fanlight was always open. Those men would have broken into the house, and then broken down the bedroom door… Rosemary shivered and started weeping again, imagining the children, hiding in the bedroom, terrified out of their little minds as those men smashed their way into the house. She could picture Joshua hugging his sister – trying to calm her – as they heard people breaking in. Then, when they started on the bedroom door, she could imagine Joshua desperately looking for a place to hide himself and Lydia. He probably would have pushed Lydia into the cupboard and then hidden himself under the bed. She could see them trembling in their little hiding places as the door gave way. She could see the man with the fingernails trampling over the broken door into the room. She could see him looking around, shouting for Gideon. She could see him ripping open the cupboard doors, grabbing Lydia. She could imagine little Joshua struggling out from under the bed to protect his sister. Her babies, having to face such things, because their fucking, cowardly, shit father…

Rosemary stood up, staggered out of the room and on to the veranda. Gideon saw her coming and quickly jumped to his feet. Then she started trying to hit him, but she had almost no strength left, and simply pounded uselessly against him. After a few moments, he pushed her away and walked inside. She dropped into a chair on the veranda and stared at the ground as if in a daze.

After a few minutes, she went into the bathroom and stared at her bloodshot eyes in the mirror. She washed her face, brushed her hair, and went to the toilet. She was finished – cried out. She'd had enough. She went into the bedroom, got two suitcases out of the cupboard and started packing. Gideon was back on the veranda, smoking, when she came out of the bedroom. She took the children into their bedroom and told them they were going to Switzerland to see Grandma. It took a few minutes to silence Joshua, then she called her friend Belinda and packed their clothes.

A little while later, Belinda rang the buzzer at the gate. They would spend the rest of the afternoon at Belinda's house and she would drive them to the airport that evening. Rosemary phoned her mother in New York again and told her they would be landing in Zurich the following morning. Catherine told Rosemary that the neighbour had a spare key to the house.

"We're going now," she said to Gideon in a completely bland voice, once they were ready.

Still sitting, he shrugged, half of his back to her. "Say goodbye to Daddy," she told the children.

She and the kids were all crying by the time Belinda drove them out of the complex. Gideon had hugged and kissed the children and whispered into their ears, but had said nothing to her.

It was a relief to get to Belinda's. She had a big garden and a nice swimming pool – plenty for the kids to do for the rest of the day while they waited to go to the airport.

Rosemary took the children into the guest bedroom and started helping Lydia get undressed.

"Where's my blanket?" Lydia demanded, as Rosemary was digging around in the suitcase for her swimming costume.

As Lydia said it, Rosemary knew she'd forgotten her daughter's security blanket. "I left it at home," she replied without looking up, hoping vaguely and in vain that Lydia might tell her not to worry about it.

There was a second of silence. Rosemary glanced at Lydia. The child's face was starting to crumble.

"We'll go and get it," Rosemary said, as Lydia burst into tears. "I promise you, we'll go and get it."

Lydia took a breath. Rosemary decided to take a chance. "We'll pick it up on the way to the airport."

It didn't work. The crying resumed. "I want it now," Lydia insisted. She was starting to get hysterical.

Belinda appeared at the door with a knowing look on her face. "You can leave the kids with me," she said. "Take my car."

The last thing Rosemary wanted to do was go back there, but it was better to do it now. Better to go straight away and grab the bloody blanket. There was no point in waiting. She couldn't put Lydia on that plane without her blanket, and the last thing she needed now was a hysterical child.

"I'm going," she said to Lydia. "I'm going right now."

The child immediately started to calm down. Rosemary kissed her, picked up her handbag and said goodbye.

Gideon was the last person she wanted to see again. She knew what was going to happen; he wouldn't say anything. He would just look at her in that 'way' – the way Africans always look at you when you aren't welcome somewhere.

She wasn't going to let him get to her. She wouldn't even look at him; wouldn't even stop to acknowledge him. She would just walk in and, on her way to Lydia's bedroom, she would just say, cool as a cucumber: "I've come to get Lydia's blanket." Then she would pick it up and walk out again.

She pulled up at a traffic light. A man selling flowers approached the passenger side of the car. She always kept the windows wound up, except for a small space to let in the air. Belinda had a nice car – an expensive sports car. Rosemary wasn't even sure what make it was, but the man with the flowers was definitely going to think she was rich.

He grinned at her through the window. "How are you today, Mama?"

She smiled back at him and shook her head.

"Come on, Mama," he said, grinning with lots of teeth. "They're nice fresh flowers. Make my day."

Suddenly, his face changed. He slapped the window hard. "Go," he shouted, and dashed off.

Rosemary turned. A man was coming towards her. She could see a gun in his hand. Her blood went cold. She slammed her foot down on the accelerator and took her foot off the clutch. The car shot forward and stalled in the middle of the intersection.

The man ran to her window and banged on it. Rosemary didn't look at him. She just turned the key back, pushed down the clutch, and started the engine. She was pulling off when she heard a loud noise and felt something on the side of her head.

CHAPTER 12

Uncle Joe

Catherine checked the screen of her mobile phone to make sure the call had been disconnected. She felt the hate rising in her. At that moment, she had never hated anyone as much as Gideon. She could quite easily have killed him. She looked down at her hands and opened and closed her fingers. She could have strangled him. She could imagine sticking her fingernails into his neck; cutting into his throat, watching the blood starting to flow, squeezing the life out of him. She could imagine him choking, gasping for breath. She would keep on squeezing, watching his eyes, watching him die. At that moment, Catherine wasn't afraid of anything – not Gideon, not prison, not death, nothing. She always got like this when someone hurt her daughter. She wanted to kill him. She *could* have killed him. Normally, she was incapable of violence and feared it, but when it came to Rosemary, she changed. It was the fear; that hideous fear of losing her child.

She'd first felt it when Rosemary was three years old. She was running in the living room and tripped on the rug. She'd gone flying. Her head had smashed into the radiator, right against the sharp metal edge. There had been blood everywhere. Rosemary hadn't screamed or cried. She'd just lain there, silent, next to the radiator, staring at the ceiling. Catherine's blood had literally gone cold. She remembered Joseph. He'd been a typical man – calm and rational – telling her not to panic; telling her that a head wound always looked worse than it was. He'd been moving so slowly; picking up the phone, dialling the ambulance, telling them what had happened, telling them the address, repeating it, explaining everything so slowly and carefully. She'd wanted to kill him. She had just stayed right beside Rosemary.

Then they tried to stop her getting into the ambulance. "We'll follow in the car," Joseph said, restraining her, pulling her back.

That was when she lost it. She hit him over the head with her handbag and forced her way into the ambulance. They tried to get her out; told her she couldn't stay in the back, but she refused to move. She'd known she was making things worse; delaying things, wasting precious time, but she couldn't let Rosemary out of her sight. Something inside her was compelling her to stay close to her child. She remembered that feeling; the abject terror that if she was separated from Rosemary, even for a moment, the child would die. Eventually, they capitulated.

At the hospital, it had been the same. They tried to stop her going into the casualty room, but she forced her way in and refused to leave. Every time they came near her, she panicked, and started grabbing things to defend herself. She had these visions of sitting in the hospital corridor, waiting desperately for news, and then eventually a serious-looking doctor coming out, taking her aside and telling her that her child had died. Every time the thought started to crystallise, she panicked. That wasn't going to happen. Eventually, they stitched up Rosemary's head with her and Joseph in the room. Rosemary had been awake throughout the whole thing. It turned out to be a flesh wound; the only lasting damage was a scar that was quickly covered by her hair.

Then there was that teenage boy – the one at school who'd punched Rosemary in one of her small, growing breasts. The pain had been so bad that the child had spent the night crying. The following day, after the seeing the doctor, Catherine had dropped Rosemary off at a friend's and gone to the school. The boy had been summoned. The headmaster had been the classic mediator, trying to find out what had happened – as if it needed explaining. Catherine would never forget the boy's face. He had eyes like a pig and a mouth with a permanent smirk. She had positioned herself carefully and then slapped him across that revolting face – as hard as she could. She could still hear the crack as her palm connected with his horrible little cheek. It must have hurt his face because it had hurt her hand. The headmaster had nearly had a heart attack. She'd wanted the boy to hit her back more than anything else in the world, because then she could have killed him. But he didn't – so she slapped him again. Then he pushed past her and tried to get out of the room. She hit him across the head with her handbag. She'd chosen the bag carefully – it was the old leather one with the heavy, metal buckle. She'd purposely put a hard-cover book inside it. By the time she was finished, the headmaster's office looked like a bomb had hit it. The boy had managed to get out of the office, but before he'd escaped, she'd beaten him black and blue.

She had been charged with assault, found guilty, fined and given a suspended sentence, but no-one at that fucking school had ever bullied her daughter again.

Catherine had always had doubts about Gideon. She liked him. He had nice eyes, and he wasn't a bad person, but this was too much. He would have to change. Otherwise, Rosemary would have to leave him. Most men were cowards – you had to expect that. Catherine suspected it had something to do with the fact that they had testicles. Her father and Joseph were the only men she'd ever known who weren't cowards – that was why she'd left her first two husbands. That was why she'd married Joseph. She'd been grateful that Gideon at least wasn't a bully. But a man who put his family in danger, who didn't protect them – you couldn't stay with a man like that.

Gideon had been lucky – lucky his family had escaped harm, and lucky his children were probably still too young to realise just how badly he had let them down. Maybe he would learn from the experience, but probably not. People who let you down seldom learned. Catherine's mother had never learned. Usually, it was because they didn't realise they'd let you down in the first place.

She'd never forgiven her mother. She'd tried to, but she couldn't. It didn't matter that her mother was dead. Well, maybe it did matter, because being dead meant she could never redeem herself. So their relationship could never recover. What was that saying she'd heard once? Something about children starting life by loving their parents, and then judging them, but rarely forgiving them.

Catherine couldn't remember when she'd started judging her parents, but it had obviously been from an early age because, by the time she was 12 years old, she'd condemned her mother for life. It was a lesson in how careful you had to be as a parent. Things were sent to test you when you least expected it. You had to be very attentive because you could easily fail without even knowing you were being tested. That was what had happened to her mother. Her poor, stupid bitch of a mother, so wrapped up in her pathetic, snobbish little reality.

For years, Catherine had tried to blame everything on Uncle Joe – a revolting, terrifying, despicable specimen who'd done *that* thing to her. But even at the time, she'd known that he had simply been the trigger, the catalyst that exposed the fault lines in her relationship with her mother.

She could picture him still, even though she hadn't laid eyes on him for more than half a century. The first time she'd seen him, she'd thought him handsome and dashing. He had been, with that thick crop of hair and that big moustache. He looked so much more of a man than her father did. The first time she'd seen them together – the first time she'd met Uncle Joe – her father had looked like a scarecrow standing next to Zorba the Greek. Everyone fawned when he was around.

But her fascination with Uncle Joe had worn off fast. He wasn't her uncle at all – he wasn't even a family friend. He was just her father's business partner. She would have preferred to call him 'Mr', but he insisted she call him 'Uncle Joe'. Actually, she would have preferred to call him nothing at all. Even better would have been if she'd never met him in the first place; better still would have been never to have known of his existence. Better than *that* would have been if he'd never existed at all. He was so dreadful that he didn't even belong in fairy tales or horror stories.

But he'd been real and terrifying. Grown-ups hadn't understood what was so bad about him, but they'd never seen or felt the real Uncle Joe; never been held in his iron grip and pulled towards that horrible face. Never been forced to be kissed on the mouth by those disgusting, wet, rubbery lips. Catherine could still smell that smoke-laden breath, still picture the tiny flecks of snot that flew out and dotted the hairs on his upper lip when he was breathing heavily.

Worst were Uncle Joe's hands. Whenever she came to greet him – as she was expected to do – she wouldn't at first notice the hands because she was always desperately trying to avoid having to be kissed by those lips. But as soon as she was imprisoned on his lap, as soon as he had one hand free, it became like a spider crawling all over her body; under her arms, across her chest; along her bottom and, when no one was looking, between her legs. To an observer, to other adults, it obviously looked like harmless affection, like a family friend cuddling a favourite child.

She'd taken to hiding under her bed when Uncle Joe rang at the front door. She hadn't planned it, but one day when she knew he was coming and the doorbell rang, she'd instinctively scrambled under her bed, and lain there, determined not to come out, determined not to be discovered.

It had worked. It had been excruciatingly uncomfortable and boring, but it had worked! She'd escaped those lips, not had to feel those hands crawling all over her. So she'd done it again, and again. The third time, he'd come looking for her. She remembered the door opening and, from her hiding place, seeing his shoes shuffle into the room. As soon as she saw them, she'd known it was him. It had been a nightmare from hell, lying there frozen in terror while he stalked the room. She'd held her breath and waited, hoping, praying, desperately, that he wouldn't bend down and lift up the bed skirt.

He'd fiddled with things on her dressing table, opened a drawer. She'd felt his legs brush against the bed, but he didn't look under it. She remembered that feeling of absolute, sheer, utter, marvellous, indescribable relief when those shoes padded out of the room. She'd stayed hidden for ages, until she was certain he must have gone.

"Where were you?" her mother asked. "Uncle Joe was looking for you."

That was the first time she'd hated her parents; really hated them. She hated her stupid, snobbish bitch of a mother for not having the nous or the imagination even to wonder why a hideous, middle-aged thug of a man was looking for her daughter. Her father she hated for bringing the monster into their house in the first place, for allowing that revolting specimen into the one, single space in the world where she was supposed to be safe.

But it was the bathroom incident that had changed everything: redeemed her father and destroyed utterly any remnants of a bond that she had with her mother. She'd been in the bath. She hadn't even heard Uncle Joe arrive. Lying there in the water, languishing, day-dreaming, she hadn't even heard the bathroom door open or close. Then, sensing something – feeling a change in the atmosphere – she'd opened her eyes. There he was, right there, standing above her, staring down at her, grinning like a hobo who'd just seen a coin on the ground. She sat up in shock. He crouched next to the bath, right beside her and his hand slid between her legs. She desperately started scrambling backwards, trying to escape those fingers, but her back was against the wall of the bath.

He leaned towards her and pushed his face against hers. She could feel his fingers trying to poke into her. He was whispering things, but she didn't register a word. His fingers were hurting her. She tried to stand up. That was a mistake; his hand went underneath her, his fingers stabbing her from below. All the time, it hadn't even occurred to her to scream. The pain between her legs was unbearable. She grabbed hold of his arm and, using it as a support, desperately tried to hoist herself higher, to get away from those dreadful fingers, which were digging deeper and deeper into her.

Then she heard her mother coming down the passage. Instantly, the fingers vanished. She slid back into the bath. The door opened. She turned and saw him backing out of the door.

"Oops," he said, "I'm sorry. I didn't know there was anyone in here."

His voice was like one you know you've heard but you can't recognise.

She heard her mother saying something.

"I'm sorry, I accidentally walked in while the young lady was taking a bath," he said, chuckling.

She heard her mother giggle.

They were both standing at the door of the bathroom. He was just inside, her mother in the doorway.

"You don't mind Uncle Joe seeing you in the bath, do you?" her mother said, smiling at him.

Catherine said nothing; just lay there, waiting for them to go away.

Her mother stepped into the bathroom and looked at her. "Time to get out of the bath," she said. The stupid bitch hadn't even noticed that his hand was wet. Catherine could see the soggy thing dangling at his side, the hairs on his fingers arranged in damp rows.

"Bye," he said cheerfully, and walked out.

"Time to get out," her mother said again.

Catherine stayed put.

"Now," her mother said.

Slowly, carefully, Catherine stood up. Her mother left the room.

There seemed to be blood in the water. Catherine felt between her legs. She could see blood on her fingers. She squatted in the water and rubbed the facecloth between her legs. Then she dried herself quickly, put on her dressing gown, and went to her bedroom.

She got into bed and lay there. She felt strange, as if she was with another self who she didn't know very well. She lay there for a long time without moving. The area between her legs was tender, but it didn't really hurt, as long as she didn't move.

After a while, her mother appeared.

"Supper time," she said, putting her head around the door.

She was startled to see Catherine in bed. "What are you doing in bed?"

"I want to be alone," Catherine said. Her voice came out completely flat, as if she was reciting sounds in a language she didn't understand.

"Nonsense," her mother said. "Get up. It's time for supper."

Catherine simply curled up more tightly into a ball and lay there with her back to the door.

Her mother came into the room. "What's the matter with you?"

After a few seconds of silence, the woman let out a long breath. "Is this about Uncle Joe seeing you in the bath?" she exclaimed.

Catherine said nothing.

"Oh, don't be ridiculous!" she went on. "There's nothing to see. You don't even have breasts yet."

To Catherine, the voice was like a radio playing in the background – a noise that she wasn't the slightest bit interested in listening to.

Her mother raised the volume and demanded she get up.

Catherine ignored her.

"Very well," she said. "I'll get your father."

Then she went away.

Catherine was shaking and on the verge of tears. She knew she wouldn't be able to ignore her father like this, but she couldn't get up. She couldn't stand up. She just wanted to stay tucked up in her bed forever.

Presently, her parents came into earshot. She could hear them coming down the passage. "I don't know what's got into her," she could hear her mother saying. "She won't get out of bed and she won't talk to me."

Then they were there, in the bedroom. Her mother was still talking.

"She's being ridiculous. I think it's all because Uncle Joe saw her in the bath."

Then her father spoke. "What is it, Catherine?" he said. His voice was calm and expressionless.

She didn't react.

Then she felt his hand on her shoulder. "What's the matter?" he said. His voice was changing, getting softer.

Slowly, she turned her head to look at him over her shoulder. He was standing looking down at her, leaning over the bed.

Their eyes connected momentarily before she looked away.

He sat down on the bed and put his hand back on her shoulder. Her mother turned on again, like a radio, "She's being ridiculous."

"What is it, Catherine?" he repeated softly. She could feel he was staring directly at the side of her face.

She didn't react; she couldn't.

Her father tightened his grip on her shoulder. "Look at me, Catherine," he instructed. Her father leaned closer towards her. He was staring intently, like a cat waiting for something to appear.

It was an enormous effort. She forced herself to look at her father. As soon as her eyes met his, she fell apart, sobbing uncontrollably.

Her father leaned forward and with one swift movement swept her into his arms. It was like being pulled out of a frozen pit into warm sunshine. She curled up tighter into a ball and just sank into him.

Her mother started crackling again.

"Leave us alone for a moment," she heard her father say to her mother.

Her mother protested.

"Please, Joan," her father said. His tone was soft and gentle, the one that came out when his patience was running thin.

Her mother retreated, whining like an accomplice accused of the crime.

For a while, her father said nothing, just sat there holding her.

Eventually, Catherine looked at him.

"What happened?" he said.

She looked away. For some reason, she was afraid to tell him. She didn't know why. She didn't know *how* to tell him. How would she explain it? She couldn't bear the thought of being questioned about it.

"Did Uncle Joe do something to you?"

She shuddered, like an old woman.

Her father's eyes changed. "What?" he said. "What did he do?" He sounded nervous. His voice was almost hoarse.

She started sobbing. She couldn't tell him; she couldn't get the words out.

He stared at her for a little while and then pulled her closer to him. They sat there like that for a long time, until she looked into his face.

To her surprise, his eyes were wet.

She stared at him in shock.

"Did he hurt you?" her father asked. His face was unstable. His features were moving in strange ways.

She shook her head. "Mummy came before he did anything really bad."

Then she told him what had happened. That he had come into the bathroom; that he had tried to stick his fingers into her.

"I'm sorry," her father said. "I'm so sorry." She'd seen the tears coming out of his eyes.

Catherine remembered hiding her face in her father's chest. He must have assumed she was shaken because of Uncle Joe, but really, she'd been hiding from him, from his tears. She'd never seen her father cry before. She would almost have preferred that he didn't believe her.

He held her a while longer, then he took her by the shoulders and looked into her eyes. He was back in control of himself.

"I'm sorry," he repeated. "I didn't think he was capable of that." He paused. "It will never happen again. I promise. You will never see him again. He will never come here again. I promise you."

She never did see Uncle Joe again. His name was mentioned only once more, by her mother, at the dinner table. As soon as it came out, Catherine dropped her head and stared into her soup. Her father waited a few seconds and then started talking about something else. Catherine still didn't know whether her mother had ever found out what had happened. She died five years later.

Catherine remembered her mother as a pale, distant, helpless creature, from another time. Her father had always done everything. For years afterwards, she tried to picture her mother as she had appeared in her wedding photo – young, healthy and smiling – but she'd never known that woman. Her most vivid memories were of a stiff, familiar stranger – always calling for something, always needing assistance, always ruining the games and mischief that she and her father would get up to. Her father became her life, until he died and she'd gone to live with Aunt Caroline before running off with her first husband. Looking back, it was obvious that her husbands had been replacements for her father. Only Joseph, the third one, had come close to making the grade.

Catherine didn't like to admit it but, like her mother, she'd left a lot of things to men over the course of her life. Looking at her parents, she had noticed – couldn't fail to notice – that men can be left, or induced, to take care of most things. As a woman, you could get away with doing very little, even as a mother – especially as a mother. That was a woman's little secret: leave it to a man to do everything and then blame him for it. Her mother had been the undisputed master. Catherine wondered whether the feminists had been in on it.

She had unconsciously done the same thing to her husbands. Well, at first, it had been unconscious. Men were so easy to handle. Catherine supposed it was because they found it easier to act than to think – and they certainly preferred to act than to argue. Women were made completely differently.

But manipulation had its drawbacks, she'd discovered. At the time, it had seemed like a good idea to pass on all the burden to the men in her life. But what she hadn't considered – hadn't even imagined – was that she was handing over more than the burden. The men she manipulated had done what she wanted, but they'd had their own reasons for doing it. Over time, they'd earned and accumulated position and power and had found a role for themselves in the world. She'd been left with nothing, except her husband's money, which she couldn't forget wasn't rightfully hers. At one point, it had gone so far that she'd lost the ability to deal with the outside world. She'd isolated herself, wholly and totally, and become dependent on men to interact with the world on her behalf.

It was Rosemary who had saved her in the end; her little girl, who she was determined she would never fail, never let down, never disappoint. Rosemary had turned her into an adult. Not right away – it had taken years – but Rosemary was the first thing she'd ever had that was too important, too valuable, to leave to a man to take care of.

Catherine looked at her watch. She'd better hurry, otherwise she was going to be late for the board meeting. She'd had enough of men. Enough of Sam and, after what had happened, enough of Gideon. Now she was going to take control.

CHAPTER 13

Mama Africa

The doorbell went. For a second, Gideon thought Rosemary might have come back, but she wouldn't have rung. Maybe it was someone who lived in the complex, or his mother. She was the only other person who had a buzzer for the gate. Gideon looked through the peephole.

His mother was standing there; the last person he wanted to see. He opened the door and then the security gate.

He leaned forward and kissed her stiffly. He'd had trouble touching her since he'd found out what she was. She walked past him into the living room, and stood there, handbag in hand, like someone waiting for a train.

"Do you want a drink?" he asked her.

"Tea."

She always wanted tea. It was a hassle. "You wouldn't prefer something cool?" he asked hopefully, almost adding, 'like a normal person'. It was around 30 degrees.

She didn't answer.

"Sit down, Mama," he said, walking into the kitchen.

Gideon started putting the tea things together. His mother hadn't changed much since he was a child. She'd always reminded him of an elephant. Although she wasn't the least bit tall, she was very wide with large, heavy arms and legs like tree trunks. She was also covered in a good layer of fat, which hid the fact that she was incredibly strong.

She'd got even wider with age, and now he looked down at her, rather than up, but her face was still round and smooth, and her eyes still shone. She had always had the most wonderful eyes. Everyone remarked on them. It wasn't that they were especially large, or bright or unusual in colour, it was just that they shone like little suns embedded in her face. Sometimes, when she was morose or brooding, her eyes didn't seem to belong to her. He remembered those eyes from childhood. They were one of the strongest memories he had. He imagined he could remember them looking down at him when he was a baby…

The kettle started boiling. Gideon prepared her tea in a mug. She took it exactly as he did: almost three sugars, filled to the brim with enough milk to cool it to the point where she could start drinking it straightaway. He placed the mug on the coffee table in front of her.

His mother picked it up and immediately started drinking it.

"Where's Rosemary?" she asked. "And the children?"

He looked down at her, wondering whether to be honest. He may as well be; she was going to find out soon enough anyway. "She's gone," he said.

He walked to the trellis door and looked out into the garden. He knew his mother hadn't understood.

"Gone where?" she said.

"She's left me," he replied, turning around to face his mother. "She's left me and taken the children to Europe."

His mother sat up very straight.

"Yes," he said, as if they were discussing the price of butter, "just a few minutes ago. We had an argument. She decided I was a bad husband and a bad parent" – he stressed the word 'parent' – "so she left me."

His mother simply sat there staring at him, her eyes wide open.

He stared back, getting some satisfaction from the fact that she was so disconcerted.

After a while, she shifted her gaze to the coffee table and just sat there, taking sip after sip of tea.

Gideon was used to silence when he was with his mother. They didn't talk. They'd hadn't talked for years; they had nothing to talk about.

He missed his old mother – the one he'd had as a boy. Now he was stuck with this old whore, who had nothing to say; whose life had been a waste and wasted. Sometimes, when he looked at her, and forgot what she was, he could still see the old Grace Mathonsi; the one he used to wait for.

He looked at her hands grasping the mug. They were not large and the fingers were slim and elegant, and looked out of place at the end of her heavy arms, but her grip was fearsome. He remembered it from his childhood, when she used to squeeze his hands. That had been his favourite game – taunting his mother until she caught him, and squeezed his hands until he said sorry.

They used to play it whenever she came home. He would wait until she was sitting on the grassy bank in front of the huts, then he would sneak up behind her and pinch her, tug at the scarf on her head, pull her ear, or do something else not allowed. Sometimes, she would shoo him away, but if she was in the mood for a game, she would immediately freeze, purse her lips and give him an exaggerated, dangerous stare. That meant the game was on.

Keeping out of range, he would start to taunt her and provoke her. At first, it would be easy; he was far quicker than she was. He would literally be running circles around her; touching her, prodding her, flicking her, pinching her. She would be casting around like some sort of gigantic, beached whale, immensely powerful but also helpless because she couldn't do more than flail about. Eventually, he'd have to get closer. He didn't have a choice – it was either move into the danger zone or run away. But running away, which he did occasionally, would end the game, and he was the one who wanted to play.

He'd move within her grasp, still taunting her, still evading her clumsy lunges, but not for much longer. Eventually, he would stray too close, or slip, or miscalculate, and inadvertently put himself within her reach long enough for her to grab a piece of him. Sometimes, she managed to seize an extremity – an arm or a leg – but more often it was a loose piece of clothing; the back of his shirt, perhaps, or a sleeve of his holey jersey, which in winter was usually tied around his waist. Occasionally, very occasionally, if she hadn't managed to get a proper grip, he could still get away, but that was only to delay the inevitable. At some point, she would have him, then would come the slow, protracted reeling in. Once she had something of him in her grasp, there was no escape. Suddenly, the tables were turned and the helpless whale was back in the water.

The reeling in was the best part. He'd be struggling – pulling frantically, trying to free himself – but it was always futile. Her grip was simply too tight. Now it would be her turn to taunt him. She was never in a hurry; she would begin drawing him towards her, slowly, deliberately, purposefully. "I warned you," she would hiss, in a threatening voice, as her hands – slowly, inexorably, marvellously – drew him closer. Until this point, he would have been fixated on her, the whole of her, but now it would be the hands, the hands alone, that he would be trying to escape. They were like claws or talons. As they pulled him towards her, he would wait with anticipation until one of them touched his flesh. Even though they hadn't played the game for years – decades – he could still remember perfectly well the feeling when talon hit flesh. Goosebumps would break out all over him as a mixture of gentle pain and ticklishness spread out from the point of contact. Then, with one arm, she would pull him close to her, against her, and hold him so he couldn't escape. With the other, she would go for his hands. He would try as much as possible to keep them out of her reach by moving them, flapping them, so she couldn't get hold of one of them but eventually the talon would fasten itself on to one of his arms, somewhere near his shoulder. Then it would start inching down his arm. This was the really tantalising part; every time the talon moved, the grip would momentarily loosen, and it would feel like he might just be able to wrench his arm away.

But of course he couldn't and finally the talon would reach his hand. It couldn't envelop his hand – it wasn't much bigger than his – but the bones in her fingers were like small steel bars attached to an immensely powerful piston. As her hand closed on his, he could feel her fingers against his; bone touching bone through the thin layer of flesh between them.

Then she would begin to squeeze: slowly at first, in punctuated, rhythmic contractions. "Say you're sorry," she would command softly, in a voice that no-one could take seriously.

He'd refuse, or giggle. The talon would tighten.

"Say you're sorry," the voice would repeat, on the verge of breaking into laughter.

He would laugh again, or squeeze back, or pull a face, and the talon would tighten further. So it would go on – the continual contractions – until his hand was aching.

Then he'd start to protest, start to complain, start to accuse and threaten, and all the time the grip on his hand would be getting tighter and tighter. He would keep doing it – keep provoking her – knowing that at some point her grip must eventually reach the limit of its squeezing power. Eventually, half-sobbing, half-giggling, he would scream "I give up" and desperately try to wrench his hand away. That was the best part. That was when she would pull him close to her, until their faces were almost touching, and then slowly and with ridiculously exaggerated seriousness, she would say, "Do you promise, promise, promise, to never, ever, ever do that again?".

He would hesitate, knowing that her grip couldn't possibly get any tighter, knowing that if he held out just a moment longer – just long enough to prove that the grip had done its worst – he would have won... But then, impossibly, unimaginably, absurdly, the grip would tighten further. By now his hand would have disappeared into hers, his fingers protruding from her fist like a bunch of twisted sausages.

Then she would say it again; this time for the last time, because as she said it, her grip would be contracting – tightening and loosening – again and again, reminding him that the tightness threshold was a long way from being exhausted. Finally, he'd give up. Sometimes, with a full stomach and nothing on his mind, he would accede gracefully. Other times, he would give in and then immediately lose his temper. Occasionally, they would have a fight. Occasionally, if she wasn't willing to console him and make things better, the game would ruin the day, and she would threaten never to play it again, but more often, she would hold him, envelop him, and keep him pressed against her until the warmth of her body and the closeness sapped away his anger and frustration. That was when he would feel his mother was the most wonderful, powerful person in the world, who could protect him from anyone and anything.

That was the mother he wanted. Not this fat whore, who was taking up his living room.

"So, she's gone," said the mother, who was sitting on the couch. She was still staring at the coffee table.

Her remark brought him back. "Yes, she's gone."

His mother didn't react.

Gideon turned around again and stood looking out into the garden. The atmosphere had suddenly got very tense.

After a while, he felt obliged to say something. "I'm not unhappy about it, you know. It's better this way."

He was aware that his mother had stood up. He turned around. She moved closer to him until she was less than an outstretched arm away.

He looked down at her. "I'd had enough of her. She was getting on my nerves; always hassling me."

His mother just stood there.

"She wouldn't leave me alone," he went on. "It was ridiculous, like living with a policeman. Everything I did, everything I didn't do…"

Suddenly, his mother slapped him on the arm, hard. "Stupid!" she said loudly.

He stopped, astounded. Then she seemed to lose control slightly. "Stupid, stupid, stupid," she repeated in a loud voice, slapping him on the arm.

He stepped away, surprised. He had never seen her like this. "What's the matter with you?"

His mother moved back to the couch and sat down. She was very agitated. She picked up her mug of tea in both hands, but they were shaking so much that she had to put it down again.

"Do you think she'll come back?" she asked, after a few seconds.

He shrugged. "How the hell do I know?"

"You must get her back. She's your wife." Now she was looking at him.

He exhaled loudly. "I don't want her back."

"You must get her back," his mother persisted. It was an order, an instruction. She hadn't given him one in years.

Gideon was surprised at her. He nearly told her to mind her own business. "What do you care?" he said, instead.

"She's the best thing that ever happened to you."

Gideon stared at her, astonished. His mother was full of surprises today. "Do you think I need her?"

He moved back to the trellis door and stared out at the garden. "Do you think I need anyone? Especially a woman?" He turned to look at his mother. "Any woman?"

She was sitting very straight, staring ahead of her. He could tell from her mouth that she was very upset.

"I don't need her!" he said loudly. "I don't need anyone."

His mother sucked her cheeks, and began moving her jaw, but her eyes remained on the table. Gideon grabbed hold of the bars of the trellis door and started rocking himself gently from side to side.

"If there's one thing I've learned," he said, "it's that you can't rely on anyone. We are born alone, we live alone and we die alone."

Still holding the bars, he turned his head slightly and glanced at her out of the corner of his eye.

"You never really know anyone," he continued. His tone was very unpleasant. "You think you do, but then one day something happens, and you realise that they're not the person you thought they were."

He turned back to the garden and carried on rocking. After a while, his mother came up behind him and tapped him on the shoulder. He turned his head slightly and glanced in her direction.

"What is it?" she said.

He looked away again, as if she wasn't there.

She repeated the question in a louder voice.

He turned his head. "What is what?" he said. Still holding the bars, he leaned towards her, letting his mouth hang open.

Her eyes narrowed, and her lips moved into an angry pout. He could tell she was getting angry, very angry. Her moods were like smells – you couldn't mistake them.

"I want more tea," she said, walking back to the sofa.

He went and made it and brought it to her.

As he placed the mug on the coffee table, she grasped his wrist. He tried to shake it free, but she had it in one of those grips. She pulled him towards her. He tried to pull himself back but she just tightened her grip. He tried to stand up, but to do so he had to lift her, too, and she was much too heavy. His arm was beginning to ache. She grabbed his other arm and held him fast, right in front of her. The only escape would be to wrench himself free, but that would mean pulling her on to the floor, and she probably still wouldn't let go.

He could feel her eyes fixed on the side of his face.

"What is it?" she said. Her teeth were clenched.

"Nothing. What are you talking about?"

She pulled him closer. As always, her strength surprised him; it was like being held down by a lion.

"You tell me," she said. He could tell that she was absolutely furious.

"Tell you what?"

She squeezed his arms harder. Now it felt like the tips of her fingers were between his arm bones; as if they had bored holes into his arms. "Tell me what the problem is," she said. She was pulling him downwards. He was having to resist, having to hold himself on his feet to stop himself from tipping over and landing on the floor.

He was getting angry. "Let me go," he said, through his teeth.

She ignored him, simply holding him there. He was losing patience fast. If she really wanted to know what was bugging him… He hesitated a moment longer. But the grip didn't weaken.

"I know what you did," he said. His voice was horrible. It sounded like he was spitting out something rotten.

The lines in her forehead deepened and her head shook slightly. Her face showed no sign of having a clue what he was getting at.

He looked her in the face. "I know about Reg Gumede."

Her grip relaxed immediately. Her hands fell off him. He saw her shoulders slump. Gideon moved back, finally free. He surveyed her from a safe distance.

It seemed as if she had suddenly shrunk, as if the elephant had crumpled under a bullet.

For a second, he enjoyed her discomfort, but the sight of his mother looking so deflated, so weary, so frail even, quickly made him uncomfortable. Seeing her like this was suddenly disconcerting. He moved towards her.

He could see her trying to compose herself, trying to get a grip. After a little while, she looked up at him. "What do you know?" she said.

But he wasn't going to let her get away with that. They'd come this far; now she was going to admit what she'd done.

"How could you have done that?" he demanded. His voice was a whispered shout.

She frowned. "Done what?"

Gideon clicked his tongue against the roof of his mouth, and walked away.

He stood with his back to her for a few moments, and then turned round. His patience had run out. "Why didn't you tell me Reg Gumede was my father?" he hissed. "Why?"

His mother's mouth literally fell open. Her expression was so incredulous that he had no idea what to say next.

"Who told you that?" she said.

"I heard it in a shebeen," he snarled at her. "It seems the whole of Jo'burg knew about it, except me!"

She was still looking stunned, like an amnesiac who hasn't yet worked out what's happened.

He just stood there, staring at her.

"When did you hear this?" she said, shaking her head.

"A long time ago," he said, leaning forward and sticking out his lower jaw. "When I was a teenager." His tone was turning sulky. He didn't like her reaction.

She kept shaking her head. "And you never told me?"

He shrugged. "What was I supposed to say?" He wanted to call her a whore, but he couldn't; she was still his mother.

She straightened up, and lifted her head. "Reg Gumede is not your father." Her tone was decisive and haughty.

"How do you know?" he demanded. He'd wanted to sound bitingly sarcastic, but even to his ears, he sounded more like a suspicious child.

She turned back to him. "What?" It was obvious that she found the question incomprehensible.

"How do you know Reg Gumede is not my father?" he pressed. "How can you be sure? Did you have a DNA test?" He knew his mother didn't know what DNA was, but that was beside the point.

She stood up and went and stood in front of him. "What is this rubbish you are talking? Your father is Joseph Mathonsi. You know that."

"That's not what I heard," he snapped back.

She gave him a dark look. "I don't know what you heard," she continued, "but you can be sure I know who your father was." The corners of her mouth turned down. She was insulted.

She looked directly into his face. She was still very agitated, and there was something about her expression that made him uneasy.

"How can you be sure?" he pressed. He didn't want to, but he believed her. She was speaking as if she was stating the most obvious thing in the world.

"How can you ask me such a question!" she said, trying to sound composed.

"How do you know?" Gideon insisted. "How can you be sure?"

Her eyes were wet and shining more than ever. It was difficult to keep this up.

"Joseph Mathonsi is your father! I promise you." It sounded like a plea – a plea for him to stop asking questions.

"How do you know?" he demanded.

Her eyes dropped again. Her features started to tremble. Then, fighting back the tears, she forced herself to look him in the face. "I know..." – her voice failed momentarily – "I know because... Because Reg Gumede's child is dead."

Then the tears started to pour down her cheeks in torrents.

Gideon shook his head as if trying to clear water from his face. Then he took her by the shoulders and shook her gently. "Mama, what is it?"

For some more seconds, she simply stood there, sobbing in silence, staring at the floor, tears pouring like waterfalls. He shook her again. "Mama, please. Please stop. Please tell me what's the matter."

He hated it when she cried like this. She hardly ever cried like this – only when she heard about deaths of old people from the village.

He dropped to his haunches in front of her and looked up into her face.

Her legs instantly crumbled and she collapsed on to the floor. He tried to pick her up, but she simply sat there, sobbing and heaving, too heavy to move.

He lowered himself further. "Stop it," he told her. "Pull yourself together. What is it, for God's sake?"

But she simply sat there, rocking slightly from side to side, crying like an abandoned child. He wished she'd stop. His mother could be a real drama queen, could burst into tears at the drop of a hat, but these tears were different. These were terrifying tears. When his mother cried like this, it was like the world was about to end.

He fell forward on to his knees and started hugging her. "Please stop," he whispered. "Please, please stop." He was weeping too now. He should never have allowed this to come out. He should have let sleeping dogs lie. It was her fault. She had provoked him; she should have minded her own business. If she'd kept her nose out of his life – out of his marriage – none of this would have had to come out.

"Please, Mama!"

After a while, she gradually stopped rocking and fell silent. Gideon released her. She struggled to her feet. "Can you make me some more tea?" she said.

He jumped to his feet. "Yes, Mama, yes!" He grabbed her mug and hurried into the kitchen.

As he was preparing the tea, he became aware that she was standing at the kitchen door. Her shape filled the width of the doorway.

"The people in the shebeen don't know what happened," she told him.

Gideon found it very difficult to look at her.

"When I knew I was pregnant with Reg's baby," she went on, "I went to see the Sangoma – the medicine man. He was an old friend of my father's and he gave me medicine to get rid of the baby. I was sick for two weeks. I thought I was going to die, but the baby came out. I don't know exactly when it happened – I was so sick – but the Sangoma's medicine got rid of Reg Gumede's baby."

"Why did you do it?" Gideon muttered. "How could you do it?"

His mother stepped into the kitchen. The kettle had just boiled and was slowly falling silent.

She came and stood next to him. He was looking down at the kitchen counter. She put her hand on his arm.

He turned to her. "How could you?"

She held his arm. "I did nothing wrong, Gideon."

He inhaled accusingly.

She looked at the floor. "He raped me, Gideon. He raped me and left me with his baby." Then the tears started again.

Gideon's head jerked back slightly. He felt like an electric shock was passing through his body.

She nodded. "I loved your father, Gideon. He was the only good man I ever knew."

Gideon tried to speak, but his throat closed as he tried to utter the first syllable.

His mother pushed a glass towards him, and released his arm. Gideon filled it up at the tap and gulped half of it down. "Did you tell him? He must have known."

His mother looked down at the floor.

Gideon grabbed her arm. "Tell me!" he shouted.

She took a step back and shifted some of her weight so she was leaning against the kitchen counter. "When your father found out, he went to teach Reg a lesson." She looked at Gideon. "They had a fight." Then her face crumpled up again.

"What?" Gideon demanded. "What happened?"

She shook her head, unable to speak.

He shook her. "Tell me."

"They had a fight on the mine," she whispered. "Near the hostels."

She was shaking helplessly again now, but the tears were not the same as before.

"What happened?" Gideon insisted.

"Reg killed him. With a knife."

Gideon stared at her in total disbelief. "But you always told me he died in a mining accident."

She nodded.

"It wasn't true?" he said.

She nodded again. "He died in hospital after that fight with Reg Gumede."

Gideon looked around the kitchen. He didn't know what do with himself.

"I'll kill him," he muttered. "I'm going to kill him." He smashed his fist on to the counter. He was crying now. "I'm going to kill him. I'm going to rip his heart out."

"No!" His mother's voice filled the kitchen.

He turned to look at her. She was shaking her head. Her eyes were wide open and terrified.

"You think I can't handle Reg Gumede?" he said, incredulously. "You think I can't handle him? I'll kill him with one hand tied behind my back."

She shook her head. "No."

He stared at her as if she was some sort of apparition. "He raped my mother and killed my father. I'm going to rip his heart out of his chest and stuff it down his throat."

She moved back until her bulk filled the doorway.

He walked up to her. "Get out of my way," he instructed.

"Where are you going?"

"I told you," he said. "I'm going to kill Reg Gumede."

She shook her head again. "No. It's over."

"What the fuck do you expect me to do?" He never swore in front of his mother. Gideon tried to push past her, but she refused to give way. He pushed harder and forced her back into the living room. Then he disappeared into the bedroom to get his things.

When he returned, she was blocking the front door.

"Get out of my way," he ordered her.

She just stood there. He grasped her by the arms and tried to pull her towards him. After a short struggle, he managed to unbalance her and yank her into the room. He stepped past her and grabbed his keys, which were hanging next to the door.

"No," she shouted and lunged at his back. He shook her off and went for the door.

That was as far as he got. Behind him, she simply sat down on the floor and wrapped her great arms around his legs. By now she was wailing.

"Let me go," he hissed. It was a ridiculous picture; she, sitting behind him, clutching his legs; he, standing there, unable to move, looking at his closed front door.

"Please, Gideon," she wailed. "Please, I beg you."

He knew there was no point in struggling. There was no way she would let go and he would certainly hurt her if he tried to free himself.

"Alright," he said, hanging up his keys. "I'm not going."

He looked down at her over his shoulder.

She slowly relaxed her grasp, as if testing him. He remained totally motionless until she had let him go. Then he turned, helped her to her feet and led her to the couch.

He would humour her; wait until she was gone, and then go and find Reg.

He brought her a fresh mug of tea and then sat down opposite her.

Leaning forward and staring into the coffee table, she cupped the mug in her hands and sipped the tea, rocking gently backwards and forwards.

"If you kill Reg, they will put you in jail," she said.

Gideon laughed cynically at her. "I can handle myself. Not many killers go to jail in this country."

She nodded, and then looked up at him. "But you will go to jail."

He frowned.

"They will know it is you," she said.

"How?"

She shrugged. "You said it yourself: the whole of Jo'burg knows, and they know Reg killed your father."

Gideon shrugged back. "They still have to prove it." He got up from the couch and walked to the trellis door. "Anyway, it would be worth it. At least he'd be dead."

"He will be dead soon enough," she said.

Gideon spun round. "What?" He paused. "Where is he?"

His mother turned down the corners of her mouth.

"You know where he is," Gideon said. "Tell me!"

"Killing him will change nothing." She started imploring again. "It will just ruin more lives – yours and mine."

He shrugged: "Yours is already ruined, and mine, well –"

He got no further. She jumped off the couch like someone who has sat on a bee. "How dare you say that!"

He recoiled.

She stuffed her face into his. "How dare you!" She was hissing through clenched teeth.

"Take it easy," he said, patting the air around her head. "What's the matter with you?"

"My life is not ruined!" she exclaimed indignantly. "It could have been. It could easily have been, but it's not. I've spent my whole life making sure it's not ruined."

Gideon had never seen her like this.

"I did everything I could so that our lives were not ruined," she went on. "Now that I'm old and helpless, *you're* going to ruin it all."

"Oh, God," he said, lifting his eyes.

"I did it for you, you stupid –" She was spluttering now.

He raised his finger. "Don't hold me responsible for your life and problems."

She shook her head. "Stupid, stupid, stupid. You don't understand. You never *listen*."

Before he could say anything, she raised a finger and stuck it into his face. "Don't you understand? Reg Gumede is not worth killing. He's not worth getting into trouble for. The best thing you can do is just forget about him and get on with your life!"

"Why are you protecting him?" he said. "You're not telling me things."

She shook her head and waved her arms frantically, as if trying to ward off a stinging insect. "Don't you understand? Reg could have ruined my life – our lives – but I didn't let him. I couldn't stop him raping me, but I could refuse to have his baby. I couldn't stop him killing my husband – who also wouldn't listen! – but I could take care of myself and my child, and make sure that we both survived and that we had a future."

He frowned at her, still wary that she was trying to pull the wool over his eyes.

She moved back to the couch and sat down. "I only want you to do one thing. There is only one thing I ask of you."

Gideon's lips tightened.

"Just get your wife and children back. They are the only thing in the world that matters."

"She left me," he pronounced, imperiously. "If she chooses to come back, I will consider it."

His mother stood up and picked up her handbag. "You don't understand anything. It's my fault. I should have brought you up differently."

He watched her walk to the door.

She turned as she got there. "You're just like all the other African men in this country – and you're going to make the same mistakes."

"Oh, yes," he said.

She turned her back on him and unlocked the door and then the security gate.

"You think I'm stupid and I don't know anything," she said, locking the gate from the outside and tossing the keys into the room. They landed near Gideon's feet.

She raised her eyebrows. "If you kill Reg Gumede, you will go to jail, and your children will grow up without a father – just like you did. Just like so many other children in this country did when we still had apartheid."

She was gone before Gideon could say a word.

He hadn't understood her point, but it didn't matter. He knew what he had to do now. He only hoped he would have enough time to tell Reg why he was going to die before he blew the motherfucker's brains out.

CHAPTER 14

The board meeting

Sam looked at the faces around the boardroom table. He was surprised Catherine wasn't there yet; she'd said she would be coming. Maybe she'd changed her mind and gone shopping with his father's money.

Just as he was starting to think she really wasn't coming, his secretary appeared at the door of the boardroom and showed her in. There she was; his stepmother, a jumped-up secretary, hardly older than he was, who'd screwed his father's fortune and power-of-attorney out of him.

Sam stood up. She came up to him and proffered her cheeks. As if he wanted to kiss them – he'd rather siphon gasoline. The skin on her face was loose and furry, like mangy velvet. Kissing her always left him with a face full of powder.

She was more confident than in the last meeting; he could tell that by the way she was moving. God knows what she had in mind to say today. Sam watched her glide into a chair next to the former head of the audit committee. The old goat shakily poured her a glass of water and turned on what was left of his charm. The rest of the board members were admiring her, too. Even George was inspecting her, in that non-committal way of his.

Sam had to admit, she was looking good, even with the jowls and the lines. She'd aged well – better than Mary – and it didn't look like she'd had plastic surgery. His father had had a good eye for pulchritude.

The meeting started. As in the last one, Catherine sat there in silence, just observing. It was impossible to know how much she understood of what was going on. Occasionally, one of the men on either side of her whispered something to her; Sam supposed they were explaining whatever it was that was being discussed at the time. Most of the time, she just nodded. By now the former head of the audit committee was almost salivating.

As usual, the meeting was about legal issues. These days it was always about compliance. Sometimes, it felt like they were in business simply to pay the lawyers.

Then it was time for any other business. If Catherine had something to say, this was when she would say it. A few points were made by the other directors. Sam was watching her like a hawk, but the meeting ended without her saying anything. The directors were standing up.

It was too good to be true. Sam couldn't believe she'd come all the way to New York to say nothing. She was a woman, after all.

Then she asked her question. The directors were starting to file out of the door – some of them were almost out of earshot when she said it. It was a typical Catherine question. It sounded like nothing, but it was calculated to scare the shit out of everyone.

"What's going on in Shanghai?" she asked, in a tone that you would use to ask about the weather. The question was directed at Sam, and was said in a personal way; as if it wasn't meant for anyone else but him, as if the other directors could carry on leaving.

Sam felt the tension shoot through his body. It was supposed to have been a normal board meeting. It was a Friday; most of the board members were on their way home for the weekend. Sam was looking forward to spending the night with Rosa.

The directors stopped, unsure whether to stay or go. George, who'd been on his way to the door, moved back into the room and started staring out of the wall.

"You know as much as I do," Sam muttered, turning his back on her and looking for someone to talk to.

He could feel the bitch's eyes boring into him.

"All I know is that our joint-venture partners have been raided by the police," she said.

Sam finished shaking hands with a retired ambassador and turned around to face her. It was difficult to keep his voice steady. "We don't know anything. There's nothing to discuss."

She was doing this on purpose – to make his life difficult.

George walked to the boardroom table and put his hands on the back of his chair.

All the directors who weren't hard of hearing were back in the room. Sam could feel them watching him.

"It's China," he shrugged, "we won't know what's going on until something happens." He looked at Catherine. She seemed to think the world should follow her rules, as if she had it all figured out. He was sick of her.

He could feel everyone's eyes on him. Everyone was waiting for an explanation. Sam felt like exploding but you couldn't do that in board meetings. That's why the bitch was bringing it up here. She hadn't listened to a word he'd said after the last meeting. She wasn't going to be invited to the next one, whatever the fucking rules were.

"We're ready to cooperate fully with the authorities, if necessary," Sam continued, "but so far they haven't been in touch and our inquiries have got nowhere, so we're waiting."

Catherine looked at him. "One of our South African managers was murdered in Angola on Tuesday."

Some of the board members shifted their positions. George cleared his throat gently.

At that moment, there were few people in the world that Sam hated more than Catherine. This was a complete non-story; it didn't concern the board for a moment.

"He was hijacked in his car," said Sam. "Happens all the time. It's got nothing to do with anything!"

"Who was he?" George asked. From his tone, the question didn't sound important at all.

"The business development manager," replied Sam.

"It wasn't thought worthy of mention?" said George, smiling.

"The man was unlucky," said Sam. "It's not a business issue."

"What happened?" George asked. Sam could tell he was getting impatient.

Sam shrugged. "He was ambushed at a traffic light. They shot him and his driver dead on the spot. It was a classic hijacking – happens all the time."

"They were robbed?" said George, in a concerned voice.

"No!" Catherine interjected. "Nothing was taken."

"The hijackers were probably interrupted," Sam said slowly,

glaring at Catherine. He paused and looked around. Most of the directors were staring at the table. There was little on it, except untouched notepads, glasses and bottles of water. George was looking at him.

"And China?" George said, looking out of the wall.

Sam shrugged. "At the moment, we don't know anything. No-one on our side has been contacted by the police, let alone questioned."

"What do the locals say?" asked George.

"No-one knows anything." Sam looked at George. "But it's got nothing to do with us. If it turns out that our partners are crooked, we say goodbye to our investment. That's all."

The room went silent for a while.

"It's got nothing to do with us," Sam repeated. "These partners were just glorified suppliers. We bought a stake in their company to improve our political position. It's not our problem, it's the partners who are feeling the heat. Like I said, we haven't even been contacted by the authorities."

"How did you find out about all this, Catherine?" George asked suddenly, smiling at her.

"She's got moles," said Sam, staring at her. "Old employees who knew my father."

"And what's their opinion?" George asked, still looking at Catherine.

"They don't know what they're talking about," Sam said loudly.

George carried on looking at Catherine.

She glanced at Sam. "They don't know anything more about the situation in China. In South Africa, they think their colleague was murdered because he was trying to do some sort of deal in Angola and the local mafia decided to put him out of business."

"Do you have any idea who he was representing?" George asked.

"Gimme a break," said Sam. "The guy was probably there on holiday."

"Would you go to Angola on holiday?" Catherine snapped.

Sam shrugged. "Maybe, if I was African." He stopped and looked around at the directors. "Look, this guy wasn't smart enough to negotiate a discount on a used car. The only reason he was hired was because we needed some more black people on the management board. He had a desk, a car, a fat salary and an expense account – everything, except a real job. That's why his death – tragic as it is – is not a business issue. It's an inconvenience. The local police aren't even following it up, except as a classic hijacking."

"And the journalists?" said George, shifting his gaze to Sam.

"It didn't get beyond the carnage pages of the local newspapers. Our press people are keeping an eye on it."

Sam looked around at the directors. "This is a simple hijacking. No connection to the company."

George stared at Sam silently. The other directors looked at the table.

Sam rubbed the skin under his eyes with his thumb and index finger and looked around the table. "Anything else?"

After the meeting, he pulled Catherine back into the board-room and sat her down. "What the hell was that about?"

She gave him a bitchy look. "Come on, Sam. What did you expect me to do? I've been trying to get answers out of you since I first heard about all these things."

"It's nothing, for Christ's sake!"

"A man is dead," she said, "and in China, it looks like bribes are being paid…"

He looked at her, saying nothing.

"And not only in China and Africa," she went on, her voice raised. "Everything is opaque as hell. God knows what's going on in the Gulf. You're using money from our pension fund to invest in projects and bidding for the contracts to build them."

Sam shook his head. "I don't understand. What's got into you?"

"The world has changed, Sam. We can't operate like this."

He laughed at her. "You don't get it, do you? It's incredible. You Europeans are incredible. You colonised the fucking world and then, when that didn't work, you abandoned it. Now you're trying again – except this time, you're trying to impose the rules from a distance: 'Do it our way or we won't do business with you.'" He laughed again. "I can appreciate that it was a brilliant strategy. It worked for a long time. The only problem with it is that the rest of the world is now saying: 'Up yours!'" He shrugged. "If you want to marginalise yourself, that's your business, but this is my business, and I have no intention of being marginalised – by anyone."

She shook her head. "There are so many things wrong with what you're saying, Sam, I don't even know where to start."

He opened his mouth.

"So we just forget who we are?" she snapped.

"Don't you get it, Catherine? We're living in a different world. They've got everything – the workers, the raw materials, the factories, the consumers. What have we got? We've got nothing. We're just a bunch of old people, getting weaker and poorer all the time."

She looked around the room. "This used to be a real company. We used to make things, we used to add value. That was the business you inherited."

She stared back at him. "Now we do nothing. We make nothing. We just insert ourselves between people who make things and people who buy things." She shook her head and looked at her hands. "I let you do this. I trusted you, and now you're turning the business into a racket."

"Listen –" he said.

"We're like the mafia, for God's sake!" she burst out. "Now even dead bodies are turning up!"

He threw up his arms. "You don't know what you're talking about. Don't you understand? The guy was killed in a hijacking. It's a coincidence. It's got nothing to do with the business. For Christ's sake, Catherine, don't you read the papers? The difference between Luanda and Caracas is that the Africans don't bother taking hostages." Sam leaned forward. They were sitting at one end of the boardroom table, almost facing each other. He took a deep breath. "Catherine, you can leave this to me. There's nothing to worry about. We are doing fine. Nothing has changed. In China, it looks like we did a deal with the wrong people, that's all. Whatever they're involved in has nothing to do with us." He put his hand on top of hers. "I'm sorry I didn't take the time to fill you in when you asked. You know what it's like – things fall by the wayside; especially if they're not critical. Next time, I'll make sure you're informed, I promise."

She gently withdrew her hand and straightened up. She glanced at his face and then looked down at the table again. She swallowed. He could see her jaw muscles contracting.

"The deal in the Gulf is legit. The investment was made on its own merits by the pension fund. They didn't even know we were tendering for a contract." He paused, looking at her closely. "The Chinese walls are fully intact, I promise."

She carried on staring into the table.

"Okay?" he asked, craning his neck slightly to look her in the face.

She swallowed again. "Okay." She didn't look at him.

He ran his tongue around his teeth. She sat there, motionless.

"I have to go," he said. "I'm due in DC." He put his hand on her shoulder. "When are you leaving?"

"Tomorrow."

He leaned across and kissed her cheek. "Have a safe trip home."

She nodded.

He stepped back, then turned and left the room.

Catherine stood up and walked to the wall. She stared out across Manhattan. In the mist, the skyscrapers looked like shards of glass. Below, the cars and cabs inched along like lines of beetles. A sudden shiver ran through her body. She folded her arms across her chest and rubbed her shoulders with her hands.

She heard a knock. She turned around. Sam's secretary was at the door. "There's a phone call for you," the woman said. "From South Africa."

Catherine was surprised. It must be something urgent, otherwise Rosemary would have waited for her to turn her mobile back on. "Where can I take it?"

The woman closed the door, and pointed at the phone on the boardroom table. Catherine looked at her a second or two, wondering why she wasn't leaving the room, then leaned forward and reached for the receiver.

As she picked it up, Sam's secretary came up to her and gently pushed a chair against the back of her legs. "Have a seat," the woman said, in a considerate voice.

"Hello," Catherine said into the phone.

"Catherine," she heard a voice say. "Catherine, it's Gideon."

"Hello, Gideon," she said, wondering why on earth he was calling her here.

Out of the corner of her eye, she could see Sam's secretary had opened the drinks cabinet and was pouring a shot of something that looked like whisky into a glass.

"Catherine, are you sitting down?" she heard Gideon say.

Sam's secretary walked towards her with the glass.

CHAPTER 15

Ganging up on Gideon

By the time they got home from the funeral, Joshua was really getting on Gideon's nerves.

The kids had been quiet and well-behaved the whole way through the service. They'd just sat on their grandmothers' laps and cried occasionally, but as soon as they were in the car, Joshua had started.

Gideon's patience had lasted all the way home, until they were inside the house. By then, he'd had enough.

"You promised," Joshua shouted.

"I did not promise," Gideon muttered through his teeth. "I said we might do it if we had time. That was all I said."

Joshua ran crying to his African grandmother, who was sitting on the couch. She enveloped him with her great arms and started kissing him all over the face.

"I did not promise," Gideon insisted. "Either he's lying or he's forgotten what I said."

His mother gave him a poisonous look. "Shut up!"

"Why are you telling me to shut up?" Gideon complained. "He's the one making all the noise."

"He's a child," his mother said loudly. She kissed Joshua again. "He's just lost his mother," she mouthed silently at Gideon.

"And I've just lost my wife," Gideon mouthed back.

Gideon looked across at Catherine, who was sitting in an armchair with Lydia on her lap. She hadn't said a word for ages, she'd hardly cried at the funeral, and she was just sitting there.

He knew neither of them trusted him to look after his children. They had no faith in him as a father. They thought he'd didn't give a damn; he could see it on their faces. They both had that same look – the one that females give you when they don't trust you. At the end of the day, women were all the same. It didn't matter that one was an African maid and the other a European millionaire.

His mother turned to his mother-in-law. Now they were looking at each other. They weren't saying anything, but he could see them communicating, just by looking at each other.

"You mustn't worry about them," his mother said to his mother-in-law.

"What does that mean?" Gideon said.

His mother gave him a dirty look. He looked at Catherine, who stared back at him. They were just sitting there, holding his children.

"Come here!" he said to Lydia.

She didn't move.

He took a step closer to her. "Come here!"

She immediately started crying and snuggled deeper into Catherine. He took another step forward. Catherine wrapped her arms more tightly around Lydia. Then his mother was on her feet, Joshua firmly enclosed in one giant arm, between him and his daughter. "You leave her alone," his mother shouted, waving a threatening finger at him with her free hand.

They were ganging up on him now – these old women. It was like being trapped between an elephant and a crocodile.

"They are my children!" he said in a threatening voice.

But he couldn't scare his mother. She flung her free hand into the air as if shooing away an animal. "You don't deserve them! You don't care. You only think about yourself!"

Both children were crying now.

"Come to Daddy!" he said to Joshua in a gentle voice, putting out his arms. "Come to Daddy!"

But his son just clung more tightly to his grandmother. He seemed scared; tears were rolling down his cheeks.

Gideon turned on his heel, furious. Why were his children behaving like this? He'd never hurt them – never laid a finger on them. Why were they punishing him? Maybe they blamed him for Rosemary's death. But why? How could they? He clucked his tongue, went out on to the veranda and lit a cigarette.

He walked to the edge of the terrace and sat down. As usual, everything had turned into a disaster. As usual, they were blaming him for everything. Maybe he should kill himself. Maybe that would make them happy; maybe then they'd feel he'd been suitably punished. As far as he was concerned, Rosemary was lucky. She'd got off this fucking planet. He was stuck here with the kids and those two old witches.

His backside was hurting. He shifted his position, but for some reason he couldn't get comfortable. He tried standing up and sitting down again, but it didn't help. Even his veranda was against him. To hell with it, he'd stand.

He got up and carried on puffing. He could hear noise coming from inside. He glanced around surreptitiously. The women were holding the kids on their laps and talking to them. The children were already calm again. Joshua even seemed slightly animated as his African grandmother held him on her lap and rocked him like a big baby. Lydia was sitting on Catherine's lap, facing her and touching her lined old face.

Gideon put out his cigarette and went back inside. As soon as he walked through the trellis door, the children fell silent. Neither of them looked at him. He looked around for a moment and then walked through the room and went to the bathroom. He didn't need to go but he went.

What the hell was he doing? Why was he feeling uncomfortable? It was his house. He went back into the living room. Again, the children turned silent and looked anywhere but in his direction.

"Anyone want a drink?" he asked as normally as he could.

The two women muttered something that indicated no.

He got a beer and went and sat on the couch opposite his mother. Now they were carrying on as if he wasn't there. He couldn't stand this; his mother was the only one acting normally. Catherine looked like a zombie and his children were behaving in the way that children do when they want you to know that they've got something against you.

He had to get out of there. He drank some more of the beer and got up. "I'm going out," he said.

"I should be going too," Catherine said. "Back to my hotel."

Gideon looked down at his mother-in-law. She looked terrible, like the life had been sucked out of her.

His mother smiled at Catherine. "First, let me make you a cup of tea? I think you need some tea, with sugar."

Catherine nodded. "Thank you."

"You should go and lie down," his mother said.

They were acting as if he wasn't there. Well, let them. He had things to do. Now that the funeral was over, he could go and do what he'd been planning to do all along. He could go and find Reg Gumede.

CHAPTER 16

Morning-after pills

Finally, Catherine was home. She had spent so much time travelling lately that the place was starting to smell musty. There was a note from the neighbour saying that flowers had been delivered and Catherine could come and collect them. She put on the kettle and lugged her suitcase upstairs to her bedroom. Outside, the lake and the suburbs of Zurich were lying peacefully in the weak spring sunshine.

Catherine stared at the view for a while. It was one of the most expensive views in the world; she'd thought it was worth it when she bought the house. At the time, she'd thought the view looked like a mural. She hardly ever looked at it anymore. She only noticed it when she came home from a trip – that was the only reason she was looking at it now. Sometimes, she felt she should look at it more because she'd paid so much for it.

She went into the kitchen and hunted around in one of the cupboards for a particular bottle of pills. She hadn't seen it for a long time, but she knew it was there – right at the back, behind the painkillers.

She put the bottle in her pocket and put on the kettle. She'd planned to have a cup of tea before going to lie down, but standing there waiting for the kettle, she didn't feel like going to all the trouble of making the tea and then sitting down to drink it. It would take so long. Not that she was in a hurry; she'd been putting things off for so long that a cup of tea wouldn't make much difference now.

Instead, she took a glass out of the cupboard and filled it with tap water, then she went upstairs to the bedroom. She put the pills and the glass of water on the bedside table and lay down on the bed.

She stared at the ceiling and took a deep breath. She could think about it now. She'd been keeping the thoughts out of her head for well over a week – she'd thought about everything else under the sun so as to keep those thoughts away. The tranquillisers had helped. That woman, Belinda, had been very helpful, with her stash of tranquillisers. They'd both been popping them like crazy since before the funeral. Belinda had given Catherine enough of them to last her all the way home to Zurich. Well-to-do South African women seemed very well-stocked with pills. But now she didn't need them anymore. Now she was home and alone and everything was done and she could think about what had happened.

She swallowed. She could feel currents of pain and anguish swirling somewhere deep within her. That bitter taste was surging into her throat and the tears were climbing towards her eyes, but they were still falling back. She couldn't bring them out; not just yet.

She glanced at the bottle of pills. They were Joseph's. The doctor had given them to her to put him to sleep when it looked like he was getting out of control. They were serious pills. One had been enough to knock him out for a whole night and to keep him in a daze for most of the next day. A handful would knock out an elephant.

She could take them now – right away. She didn't need to wait. Why wait? What was the point? Why go through the pain? It would be so easy just to swallow them all. She'd been swallowing so many pills since the hysterectomy that they went down like water. She could down the whole bottle in just a few gulps.

Catherine leaned across and picked up the bottle. She shook it. The pills rattled. She wasn't supposed to have them. When Joseph went into care, the doctor had asked for them back. She'd lied and said there weren't any left. He'd known she was lying, but they were too valuable to give back. She didn't mind lying to doctors. They lied to you – for your own good, they thought. Well, she'd lied to him, for her own good.

But she couldn't take the pills yet. First, she had to say goodbye – to the most important person in the world. To the only person in the world that mattered. Her lips were trembling, her eyes stinging. It was time to say goodbye… to… to… Rosemary.

As her mind voiced her daughter's name, a spasm shot through her. Her stomach muscles contracted, pulling her abdomen upwards in a sudden retch. Her eyes were on fire; the muscles in her face wobbling uncontrollably. Her throat was burning from the bile.

Rosemary's face started to take shape in her mind. It was the first time that Catherine had allowed Rosemary into her consciousness since she'd got the phone call. Every day for more than a week, she'd concentrated on not thinking about Rosemary. She'd thought about anything and everything else; constantly analysing and re-analysing, she had taken pills, hurt herself, shouted, screamed – anything, not to think about Rosemary.

Now, in her mind, she saw her daughter as she'd last seen her. As usual, she'd been complaining about Gideon, and then one of the children had come in. Catherine remembered watching her daughter, worrying that she was too thin, worrying about that small, troubled frown on Rosemary's forehead. Worrying that she never sat still; worrying that she was always getting up to do something. Worrying that she was so busy and never took time for herself. She remembered just watching and worrying about this young, hagged, beautiful person, so full of emotions, the only thing in the world she cared about.

She started writhing around the bed. The grief was coming in waves now. Each seemed to be stronger, like birth contractions. She started struggling for air, struggling to breathe. Then her throat closed completely. She tried to breathe but couldn't. Her mouth opened in a gape and she started sucking at the air, but with each gulp her throat slammed shut, blocking the passages. She was suffocating; she lay there gulping like a drowning fish. For a second, it occurred to her that the grief itself might kill her – that it would suffocate her to death.

Then something else appeared. Anger, hideous anger; fury; hate. Catherine rolled away from the pills – she didn't want to break the bottle – to the other side of the bed. Suddenly, she hated the world, everything and everyone. Her mind filled with obscenities; words she hadn't thought of for years. Her whole body shook. She slithered around. How could this have happened? Jesus Christ, she hated this world. She wished she still believed in God because then she could have hated Him, too, and vented her hate on Him. She could have tempted Him with her hate; tempted him to hurt her, to kill her, to send her to hell. God was a bastard. How could he have done this? He could he have allowed this? What kind of shit, crap, useless disaster of a world had He made where it was possible for things like this to happen? He wasn't a creator; he wasn't even a fucking handyman. He should be ashamed of Himself. What kind of disgusting, hideous, abominable, abysmal Universe had He made where such things could happen?

Things like this were not supposed to happen. Children were not supposed to die before their parents! That was not how it worked. It was children's responsibility to bury their parents. That was what they had to do; that was how the world was supposed to work.

Now, some fucking miserable, son-a-of-bitch, bastard, swine had screwed it all up and taken away her child. Now she was alone; without her daughter, with nothing – and it was all her fault.

She was being ridiculous. Rosemary's death had been a terrible accident. It had nothing to do with her, or with God, whom she didn't believe in anyway, or with Gideon. Or even with the man who did it. It was a shocking coincidence; a hideous outcome that no-one could have foreseen or prevented.

But if she'd stopped Rosemary from going to Africa, brought her up differently, been a different kind of mother... If she'd been more insistent... If she'd intervened when... These thoughts were useless, but she couldn't stop them. Without Rosemary, she had nothing. She *was* nothing. It wasn't so much that there was no point in being alive after your child had died. It was more that there was no point in ever having been alive at all. She was a waste of space; a waste of flesh, a waste of oxygen. Her very existence was a travesty, a cheat. She was worse than nothing.

She began smashing her fists against her head. She had failed, utterly. A mother's minimum responsibility was to make sure her children survived her. She hadn't even managed that. She was worthless. She didn't even deserve to die. She was worse than shit.

The anger was subsiding; the pain was coming back. She stopped hitting herself. Now she had no strength left in her arms. She couldn't even lift herself; all she could do was lie there, sobbing.

Sometime later she woke up, and wondered where she was. She looked around the room. She was home. Then she remembered, and collapsed again into fits of tears. She struggled to take back control of her mind. Eventually, she forced an image of Joseph into her head. It was the image she had made; the one she had chosen of him in his dinner jacket, in the entrance hall, waiting for her. She'd found the picture among his things after he'd gone into care. She didn't know who'd taken it; she didn't even remember the occasion. Actually, she didn't even know who he was waiting for. It might not have been for her at all, but that was all irrelevant. The important thing was that the man in the picture was Joseph. The real Joseph; the man she'd married, looking exactly as she'd always wanted to remember him. Like a ship's captain; someone who you entrusted your life to without a thought. Someone in command; someone in control; someone so obviously in charge that he could quite happily wait for someone else without feeling the slightest need to assert himself. That was Joseph. *Her* Joseph. It had taken her a while to get rid of that other man; the one that dribbled and soiled himself. The one she still went to see. The one that, if she was honest with herself, she had stopped caring about.

Gradually, the shaking lessened. Now she was just crying. She curled up tighter into a foetal ball and lay there weeping. She didn't have the strength to move; she just wanted to lie there until she died. Suddenly, she was freezing cold. She started shivering violently, as if gripped by a terrible fever. She curled up even more and lay there waiting for the shivering to stop, but it didn't. Eventually, she stretched out a quivering arm and pulled the duvet over her. She burrowed into it, like an animal in straw, until it covered her completely, even her head.

Gradually, the shivering died down and she felt lonely – really lonely – which was not surprising, because she was alone. Alone in the world. A lonely old woman with no-one and nothing. A pathetic, invisible creature; someone who talked to people at bus stops. The tears started coming in torrents again. The whole thing was so sad. Life was so sad, so terribly, terribly sad. Looking back from her age, she could see that life was really just a long succession of goodbyes. Now, there was no-one left to say goodbye to. Maybe that was why we grew old and died. Maybe it was because the human heart could only cope with so many goodbyes before it broke. Catherine had said goodbye to so many people that her heart was broken. Suddenly, she wanted her father, wanted him there to hold her and take away the cold and the pain. Suddenly, she missed being a child; she wanted to be a little girl again. Someone who didn't know what this world was like, how horrible and painful and sad it all was. Someone who forgot pain and goodbyes as soon as they were over and had no inkling of the terrible agony and anguish that life had in store.

She heard a noise and stayed still for a second and listened. It was the phone; the phone was ringing. She wouldn't answer it – she couldn't face talking to anyone. Who would it be anyway? There was no-one left.

She lay there, listening to it ring. After a while it stopped.

Catherine lifted the duvet and sat up unsteadily. She was utterly cried out. There was nothing left in her, not a shred. She could feel the emptiness spreading inside her. That was what she couldn't bear. There would be more tears and more pain – lots more – but those she could cope with. It was the emptiness – that dull vacuum, that dreadful nothingness – that she couldn't live with. She'd first felt it when her father died and it had never gone away. It couldn't go away; it was what replaced the pain and the grief. But this emptiness that was forming now – the emptiness of no Rosemary – was going to be worse; much worse. She couldn't survive it. You can live without a lot of things, but there comes a point – a moment – when you have lost so much that there is simply not enough left to sustain you. That was the point she was at now.

Catherine reached across and picked up the pills. She unscrewed the lid of the bottle and shook one into her hand. It was big and ugly. She remembered them well; remembered smashing them into little pieces so she could hide them in Joseph's food.

She put it in her mouth. It sat there on her tongue like a clueless grub waiting to be swallowed. She could taste it now. It tasted like a pill – chalky and medicinal. She picked up the glass of water.

The phone started ringing again.

She sat there, holding the glass with the pill in her mouth.

Suddenly she felt slightly self-conscious. Through the window, she could see the trees and the blue sky. The birds were chirping. The world was carrying on as if nothing had happened; as if there was still something left to carry on for. God, it was a fucking heartless place; and now the bloody phone wouldn't stop ringing. Irritated, she put down the glass and took the pill out of her mouth.

She walked on to the landing and picked up the phone.

"Hello," she said angrily into the receiver.

There was a slight delay. It was a long-distance call.

"Hello," she said again, even more crossly.

"Hello, Catherine," came a familiar voice. "It's Gideon."

For some reason, she was surprised to hear from him. "Hello," she said again, for want of anything better to say.

"We wanted to check that you were alright – that you got home safely."

She was surprised. "Really?" she said, without meaning to.

"Yes," Gideon said. "The kids are here, too, and my mother. She spent the night with us."

Catherine didn't know what to say. "Thank you. I'm fine."

There was a moment of silence.

"Catherine?" Gideon said.

"Yes, I'm still here."

"Lydia wants to speak to you."

He was probably lying – almost certainly lying. Children never wanted to speak to anyone on the phone, particularly old people. Still, it was nice of him, nice of them, to have bothered.

"Hello, Grandma," came a little voice down the line.

"Hello, my darling," Catherine said.

"How was the flight?" the little voice said, in exactly the same tone that an adult would have used.

"Fine," Catherine said, and told her a bit about it. Then she started asking questions. You had to with children on the phone, otherwise they just lapsed into silence.

"What have you been doing this morning?" Catherine asked.

"I woke up very sad this morning," Lydia said. "I miss Mummy." And then she started crying into the phone.

Catherine tried to say something to console her, but her voice had gone. For a little while, they both cried down the phone at each other.

Then Gideon came back on to the line. "She's very upset," he said. He told Catherine how things had gone during the night and then said goodbye. Just before she put the down the phone, he said: "Wait, Lydia wants to say something else to you."

"Grandma," she heard the little voice say.

Catherine tried to say something but her voice was still not working.

"Grandma," the voice repeated. "Mummy told me that if I ever had a problem and she wasn't there, I should call you."

Catherine promptly collapsed on to the floor. She covered the mouthpiece with her hand and sat there, her legs under her, slumped against the wall, quaking like a deprived addict.

"Is that okay, Grandma?" Lydia said. "Even though you're far away."

"Yes, of course," Catherine muttered into the phone. She sounded like an old man with a rasp. She cleared her throat. "You must call me, if you have a problem. You can call me any time – day or night."

"That's good," the child said. "That makes me feel better."

Catherine stood up carefully and went back into the bedroom. She picked up the pill she'd nearly swallowed, and the bottle, and took them downstairs to the kitchen. She dropped the pill down the plug-hole in the sink and put the bottle back into the cupboard behind the painkillers.

She was happy about what Lydia had said, but at the same time felt bad at having forgotten about her grandchildren. But that was understandable – under the circumstances.

She went and turned on the kettle again to make that cup of tea. It would take time to sink in. The reality that things had changed – that there was no escape.

CHAPTER 17

Killing Reg

It didn't take Gideon long to find out that Reg Gumede was running a protection racket in the south of Jo'burg. Most evenings, he could be found playing cards in a particular shebeen in Soweto.

Gideon took a minibus taxi to Soweto, and arrived at the shebeen around six. He got a quart of beer and lingered near a group of men playing cards.

He had a 9 mm pistol in a holster strapped to his left ankle. Sitting down, he could have the gun out and cocked in about a second. From a standing position, getting hold of the gun was awkward, but his plan was to get the pistol out in advance and have it ready in the back of his pants. He wasn't hopeful that he could kill Reg tonight. This trip was more of a reconnoitre, but you never knew. If he saw Reg and could follow him out of there unnoticed, and get him alone…

Gideon soon got into the card game, only to discover Reg wasn't one of the players. He played for long enough to make his presence unremarkable and then retreated to the sidelines, close enough to hear and observe the proceedings. Reg arrived about half an hour later. Gideon didn't notice him to begin with because he didn't resemble anything that Gideon had imagined Reg might look like – he was smaller than expected and had let his hair turn grey.

Once Gideon realised the man was Reg, he began to scrutinise him carefully. The first thing he noticed about him was the way he held his hands. They hung off his wrists as if the joints were somehow damaged, but from the way Reg skilfully manipulated the cards, it was obvious there was nothing wrong with them. His arms were slim and looked slightly robotic, as if the long, thin muscles under the skin were being controlled by wires.

The other thing Gideon noticed was Reg's eyes. The whites

were dark yellow, almost brown. As a child, Gideon had heard that that came from smoking too much ganja, but he didn't believe that anymore. Reg certainly didn't look like he'd been a dope-smoker. His pupils were surrounded by light grey circles and protruded slightly. They reminded Gideon of marbles. In fact, Reg's eyes looked so like glass balls that you could have mistaken him for blind.

At one point during the game, Reg became aware that Gideon was looking at him. He shifted his head very slightly and fixed his eyes on Gideon. It was like being stared at by a snake. It wasn't difficult to imagine that this man could kill someone; there was something about him that gave you the creeps. Gideon looked back at the game. He was quivering slightly and his stomach felt full of butterflies. Out of the corner of his eye, he could still see Reg's shape. The man's head didn't seem to have moved, although Reg must have taken his eyes off him by now – he was playing cards, for God's sake. But Gideon couldn't quite bring himself to look again at Reg. Anyway, he had to be careful. He couldn't let Reg know he was interested in him.

After a few more minutes of not looking at Reg, Gideon went inside for another beer. He hadn't intended to drink any more, but for some reason he really felt like a drink. When he got back outside, he positioned himself so that Reg wouldn't easily be able to look at him. Reg wasn't talking much. He seemed distracted, as if he was not really interested in the card game. Gideon wondered why he was bothering to play.

After a while, Gideon got the distinct impression that Reg was waiting for something. He looked like a man who expected to be called away at any moment. Every time a new hand of cards was played, Reg would seem to hesitate before joining in. Gradually, Gideon became aware that Reg himself was watching someone. It was the way he held his head; all the other card players were facing the table, and were usually looking in the direction of the person who happened to be playing his hand at that moment. They were also continually laughing and joking, and trying to unsettle each other. Reg was leaning on one arm of his chair – a piece of plastic garden furniture – and had his head tilted slightly to one side. It looked like he was keeping an eye on someone to his right.

There were several people in Reg's line of vision. After observing him for a while longer, Gideon decided that Reg was watching a group of three men sitting on a bench against the wall of the building. One of the men rose and went inside. Reg seemed not to notice. That left two. With the next round of drinks, another of the three got up. Again, Reg didn't react. By now, Gideon was convinced that the third man was Reg's target. Gideon finally finished his beer. He'd been drinking it as slowly as he possibly could because he didn't want to get drunk.

The third man got up. Reg didn't react. Gideon was surprised; he was certain Reg was watching this man. At the end of the next hand, Reg stood up. The others didn't try to persuade him to stay. The third man was already back with his group's drinks. Reg went back to the bar, got himself a quart and then went and sat down on a plastic chair some distance away, near the entrance to the shebeen garden. The three men were still in his line of vision, but he seemed not to be paying attention to them any more. Gideon had by now given up trying to figure out what Reg was up to. He contemplated getting another drink but decided against it. Reg was clearly as sober as a judge.

The shebeen was filling up and Gideon was finding it more and more difficult to keep Reg comfortably in his sights. Another hour passed. Then, one of the three men left the shebeen. Reg, partly obscured by people, appeared to be staring into space. Gideon decided to get another drink but as he stood up, he saw that Reg's chair was empty. He must have slipped out after that man. Gideon immediately rushed to the shebeen gate and looked out into the street. Reg was nowhere to be seen. Shit! He'd spent the whole evening watching him and now he'd lost the bastard. Momentarily unsure of what to do, Gideon stood there, frantically looking around. There was no way he was going to find Reg; it was too dark to go looking for him.

Down the street was a taxi stop. Gideon lit a cigarette and walked towards it. As he reached it, a man emerged from behind a tree. He looked like the man who had left the shebeen before Reg.

He nodded at Gideon and asked for a cigarette.

Gideon had just lit it for him when a minibus taxi pulled up. They both got in. The man was going to the southern suburbs. Gideon had been wondering whether to go home, or to spend the night in Soweto with relatives. He decided he might as well go home. It meant crossing town but it wasn't yet eleven.

Gideon glanced at the man from the shebeen out of the corner of his eye. He had no idea whether Reg had been watching him. Gideon asked the man where he was from. He was a Zulu – like Reg – and originally from Natal-Kwazulu. That was all Gideon got – the man obviously wasn't interested in talking. Gideon tried to think of a way to bring Reg's name into the conversation. For a moment, he thought about taking out his mobile phone and pretending to call Reg, but he knew he would feel too self-conscious to make it plausible.

They were approaching the outskirts of Jo'burg. The man got out at a red robot. From his seat in the minibus, Gideon watched him cross the road and disappear down a side street. As soon as he was out of view, a car pulled up next to Gideon's window. The robot changed. As the car pulled off, in the same direction the man had gone, Gideon caught a glimpse of the driver. It was Reg.

Gideon jumped up and hauled open the minibus's sliding door as it was pulling away. The driver hit the brakes and yelled at him. Gideon ran out in front of the vehicle and paused momentarily to pull a note out of his pocket. He threw it into the driver's window and ran off after Reg.

Down the side street, it was very dark. The only thing on the road was Reg's car. Gideon could see the other man in the headlights, walking along the pavement. Reg pulled up alongside him and said something, then he stopped the car and got out. Gideon approached slowly, careful not to be seen. The two men were arguing now. Gideon moved closer. They were too far away for him to hear what they were saying but the other man was doing most of the talking. He was bigger than Reg and was pointing at Reg; he seemed to be threatening him.

After a few seconds, Reg got back into his car and reversed as if he was looking for a place to turn around. The man started walking away. Reg stopped, then started to move forward again. Suddenly, he accelerated and the car mounted the pavement. The man turned at the noise. He jumped back but didn't manage to get out of the way in time. Gideon saw him bounce off the car's side fender. The impact flung the man backwards against a wall that ran along the pavement. He did a clumsy pirouette and collapsed. The car stopped some metres away, back on the road. The lights went off.

Gideon stepped into a driveway and sunk down on his haunches out of sight. He was expecting Reg to get out of the car or drive off, but he didn't; he just sat in the car with the engine running. For a while, nothing happened. Then the man, lying on his back on the pavement, moved.

Reg reversed the car until he was parked directly next to the man. Gideon saw his shape move across to the passenger seat and look out of the window. The man on the ground rolled on to his side. Reg opened the driver's door, and got out. The light in the car did not go on. Reg walked around the car and crouched down next to the man, evidently trying to inspect him. The car engine was still running. Gideon saw Reg kneel down and say something in the man's ear. Then he stood up and started kicking him. Gideon could hear the man's grunts as Reg's foot collided repeatedly with his face and abdomen.

Suddenly, Gideon remembered what he was doing there. He had been so distracted by what was happening that he'd forgotten he was supposed to be killing Reg. He reached down to his ankle and touched the butt of the 9 mm. He unclipped the flap of the holster that was holding the gun in place and slowly withdrew it. As he brought the gun up, he realised his hand was shaking like a leaf. Leaning against the wall, he placed his left hand across the barrel to try and steady the gun. He tightened his grip, ready to cock it, but the weapon was wobbling almost uncontrollably. By now, Reg had stopped kicking the man and was crouching down next to him again. Gideon tried to pull back the slide of the pistol but his hands were sweating and shaking so badly he wasn't sure he was going to be able to fire the thing. He hesitated. Even if he could fire it, he might miss. If Reg was armed…

Gideon took a deep breath. He wasn't even sure he'd be able to pull the trigger. He'd never killed anything before except insects, and once, as a youngster, a cat. He'd felt bad about that cat for years – he still felt bad about it; he never should have done it. Reg stood up and got back into the car. The man had stopped moving now. Gideon wondered if he was dead. Reg's car pulled away and disappeared around a corner.

Gideon put the gun away, got to his feet and ran over to the man. "Can you hear me?" he whispered. There was no response and he couldn't see very well, but he could hear the man's breathing. It was rasping and irregular. Gideon pulled out his phone and wondered what to do. Rosemary would have been shouting at him to dial the flying squad. After a second or two, he did. A voice came on the line. Gideon had no idea what street he was on and started running back to the intersection to see what the street name was. He panted an explanation into the phone. He said the injured man had been hit by a car – that he was a victim of a hit-and-run.

"How badly hurt is the victim?"

"How am I supposed know?" said Gideon.

"Is he conscious?"

"No, but he's breathing."

"Who are you?" the voice said.

"I'm just a passer-by."

"What is your name?"

Gideon reached the intersection and read the street name into the phone.

"Did you get the licence plate?" the voice asked.

"No," Gideon panted. "I just saw the man get hit and the car drive away. I didn't even see what kind of car it was."

The voice asked him his name again but Gideon didn't answer.

"You must wait there until the ambulance arrives," the voice said.

"I can't. I'm leaving now," he said. "Come quickly."

"You can't leave a man lying in the street," the voice said. "He could die at any moment."

Gideon was getting frustrated. He was being a good citizen – he was helping someone – why the hell did they have to give him such a hard time?

"It's got nothing to do with me," he said into the phone. "I could have just walked away."

"You must wait there," said the voice.

Gideon looked back down the street. He could see the shape of the man lying there. It didn't seem to have moved. For all he knew, the man was dead already.

The voice was still asking questions.

"Did you get the street name?" Gideon muttered into the phone. "Is an ambulance on its way?"

"The victim is much more likely to survive if you stay with him," the voice said.

"Are they on their way?" Gideon shouted.

The voice confirmed that they were but said it could take some time before they got there.

"You must stay with the victim," the voice said. Then it asked for his name again.

Gideon hit the 'end call' button. He was shaking worse than before. He started to walk quickly in the other direction, away from the man. There was not a soul in sight. He stopped. Should he quickly go back and check? The man was probably already dead, and even if he wasn't, what could Gideon do? He had no first-aid experience. The man probably had internal bleeding. There was nothing Gideon would be able to do about that.

He turned his head slightly. He could see the shape lying on the pavement. It still hadn't moved. Gideon felt his eyes welling up. The whole thing had turned into a real fucking mess. Reg Gumede was still fucking everything up, even after all these years. He hated Reg fucking Gumede. He should have killed him; he should have shot the bastard in the back while he had the chance, before he started kicking that man.

Gideon started walking back. The shape was horribly still. He started walking faster, then running. He dropped down next to the man's head. He couldn't hear any breathing. He grabbed a wrist and tried to find the pulse, but his hands were shaking so much that he had no hope of keeping the wrist still. Gideon dropped the arm and pushed the man on to his back. He cleared the jacket lapels away and stuck his head against the chest. Suddenly, it occurred to him that he shouldn't have moved him. Shit! All he could hear were his own arteries thumping. Gideon shifted on to his knees and started pushing the man's chest. Nothing moved; it was like trying to pound concrete. He started frantically thumping the man's torso.

After a few seconds, he stopped and leaned back on his haunches. "Calm down," he said aloud to himself. He took control of his breathing and slowed it with long, deep breaths. What the hell was he getting so freaked out about? If this man died, what did it matter? People were being murdered all the time. Gideon stood up. He needed to get out of there before the ambulance arrived. The man seemed to make a small noise. Gideon dropped down next to him. He could see moisture on the man's lips. It was probably blood. Shit! The man was probably drowning in his own blood. He shouldn't have moved him. Gideon hoisted the man back on to his side and moved his head so that anything in his mouth would drip out on to the pavement. Then he heard the sirens.

He looked around, trying to work out where they were coming from, but the sound just filled his head. He got up and started moving cautiously down the street, hoping he was going in the opposite direction. Both sides of the street were lined with walls – there was nowhere to hide. Suddenly, he remembered the 9 mm strapped to his ankle. He'd bought it a few days ago, no questions asked. It was definitely a stolen gun. If the police found it. Fuck!

He pulled out the gun and wiped it furiously with his shirt to get rid of the fingerprints. Then he threw it over a wall. The holster followed. He started walking fast, but not running. A police van came round the corner. He was fully enveloped by the headlights. An ambulance was behind it.

The police made him come to the station to give a statement. He tried to get out of it – said he would come tomorrow – but the cop had been adamant. They didn't trust him. He wasn't carrying any ID. He decided not to argue.

For some reason, they were taking the whole thing very seriously.

Gideon didn't know why. As far as they knew, it was a hit-and-run, and he was just a passer-by. He was pissed off. He should never have called the fucking flying squad. He should have shot Reg and left the man to take his chances. The poor bastard was still alive, but the medic had been worried about the bleeding from the mouth.

They took him to Jo'burg Central police station. Gideon had never been there before but he knew it had been John Vorster Square, where they used to torture people during apartheid. They put him in a room with a table and chairs and gave him a plastic cup of water. He supposed it was an interrogation cell. It was a horrible experience, sitting there in the cop shop. He should have remembered his mother's advice: never get involved, always just run like hell. She'd being saying that to him ever since he was a little boy. Running away was not something you could be proud of, but as a survival strategy, it couldn't be beaten. He should have done it tonight. He wouldn't be sitting in this bloody place.

They took ages to come and take his statement. Eventually, a young policeman arrived with a form. He wrote slowly and kept asking Gideon to repeat everything. Once he'd taken down all Gideon's particulars, the door opened and another policeman walked in, a big, white man. He nodded at Gideon and sat down.

"Please tell me what happened," the young policeman said.

Gideon shrugged. "I just saw him get hit by a car, so I went to see if he was okay. When I saw he was unconscious, I called the flying squad."

The young policeman started asking questions. Gideon hadn't expected to have to provide this degree of detail. He told the policeman that he'd been crossing the intersection, when he'd seen the car hit the man, down the side road.

"Was the car coming towards you or going in the other direction?"

"It was driving away. I could only see the back of it."

"Did it stop after it hit the man?" the policeman asked.

"Briefly."

"Did the driver get out?"

Gideon shook his head.

"Did the car mount the pavement, or was the man walking on the road?"

Gideon hesitated.

"Couldn't you see?" the policeman asked.

"I can't say for sure," said Gideon. "I think the man was on the road."

"What happened then?"

Gideon explained that he'd run to the man to see if he was okay. "Then I called the flying squad."

Once the statement was complete, the white policeman leaned across and picked up the form and inspected it. "What were you doing there?" he asked Gideon. He was obviously an Afrikaner.

Gideon was surprised by the question. "I was on my way home."

"Where from?"

"Soweto."

"How did you wind up on that street?"

Gideon was getting impatient. Ever since he'd called the police, all they'd done was ask him questions. Why were they so suspicious? All he was doing was trying to help.

"What do you mean?" said Gideon.

"I mean how did you get there?"

"A minibus taxi."

The policeman looked at the form again. "You live in the northern suburbs?"

Gideon nodded.

"So you were taking a taxi from Soweto to the northern suburbs?"

Gideon pursed his lips. He was sick of being asked stupid questions, especially by this bloody Dutchman. Who did he think he was?

"Why are you asking me all these questions?"

The policeman smiled at him. "Just a formality." He glanced again at the form. "Why did you take a taxi to the south if you were going to the northern suburbs?"

Gideon shrugged. "I took the first taxi that came. Some of the passengers were going south." He paused. "It's quite common that taxis don't take the most direct route, you know."

The policeman smiled at him again and put the form back on the table.

Gideon leaned back in his chair. "Is that everything?"

"What happened to the taxi?" the policeman said.

Gideon hadn't expected the question. He felt his shoulders tense slightly. "What do you mean?" he asked, slowly.

"You must have got out of the taxi."

"Yes," said Gideon.

"Why?"

Gideon hesitated. "The driver wanted to pick up some fares that would have taken me further out of my way." He stopped. "So I decided to find another taxi."

The policeman looked around the room for a moment as if trying to spot a buzzing insect before his eyes settled again on Gideon. "So you got out of the taxi, in the middle of the night, in a deserted area of the south, because you were in a hurry to get home to the northern suburbs?"

Gideon rubbed his chin with his hand. "Look, why are you asking me all these questions? If I had done something wrong, do you think I would have called the flying squad? I saw a man get hit by a car and I wanted to help. That's all."

The policeman leaned forward and put his elbows on the table. "I just want to know what you were doing there. That's all."

"I don't have to answer your questions."

The policeman rubbed his chin. "No, you don't."

Gideon put his hands on the table.

The other policeman smiled at him. "If we straighten this out tonight, we won't have to bother you again."

"It's late. I'd like to go now, please," Gideon said, looking at the table.

The white policeman stood up. He didn't look happy; he walked out without a word. The other one asked Gideon a few more questions and then asked him to read and sign the statement.

As Gideon was leaving the building, the white policeman appeared again. "Wait," he said.

Gideon stopped.

The policeman smiled at him. "I can give you a lift home," he said.

Gideon was slightly taken aback.

"I'm going home now myself," he said. "I live quite near you. I can drop you off on my way."

"It's okay," Gideon muttered.

"What? You worried I'm going to rob you or something?" the policeman asked, still smiling.

Gideon smiled back, politely. The last thing he wanted to do was ride home with this man.

The policeman beckoned him, holding the door open. Slowly, Gideon walked through it.

"I called the hospital," the policeman said, once they were in the car. "The man's condition is stable. It looks like he's going to be okay."

Gideon stared out of the windscreen.

The policeman glanced at him. "You saved his life. If you hadn't called, he probably wouldn't have been found till the morning."

Gideon said nothing.

"Did you know the victim?" the policeman asked.

Gideon looked at him. "No," he said. His tone would have dissuaded most people from asking any more questions.

"You'd never seen him before?"

Gideon was ready for that one. "I don't think so, but I don't really know what he looks like. I couldn't see his face properly in the dark."

"And you didn't notice what kind of car it was, or the licence plate?"

Gideon shook his head. "It was dark and it all happened so fast."

"But you saw the car hit him?"

Gideon nodded.

"You saw the car hit him, while he was walking along the road, and you saw it stop briefly and then drive away?"

Gideon silently repeated the policeman's sentence to himself, before answering. "That's right," he said. "It was a hit-and-run."

"Funny," said the policeman.

Gideon took a breath.

"The hospital said they found injuries that were not caused by the car hitting him. It appears that he was hit or kicked repeatedly in the face and the stomach around the time he was run over."

Gideon kept his eyes fixed on the road in front of them.

"The victim must have sustained the other injuries after he was hit by the car," the policeman went on. "If he'd got them beforehand, he wouldn't have been walking down the street."

Gideon said nothing.

"Was he out of your sight between the time he was hit and when the police arrived?" the policeman asked. The question was very matter-of-fact.

Gideon swallowed. "Briefly."

"Yes?" the policeman said.

"I didn't know what the street was called," Gideon continued. "So I went back to the corner to find the street name."

"How long were you away?"

"Not long," said Gideon. "A few minutes."

"Do you think it's possible he could have been attacked during that time?"

Gideon looked at the policeman. "Why would someone do that?"

The cop shrugged. "Who knows? Maybe the driver who hit him came back to finish him off."

Gideon tried to think of something to say.

"Did you think he was hit by accident?" the policeman asked. "Or was it done on purpose?"

Gideon shrugged, and exhaled loudly. "I don't know. Like I said, I was just walking past the street and suddenly I saw a car hit this man."

The policeman nodded, and sucked his lips into his mouth.

They drove the rest of the way in silence.

"I didn't do anything wrong," Gideon said to the policeman, as he got out of the car.

"I believe you," the policeman smiled.

Gideon didn't believe him.

"Thanks for the lift."

The policeman nodded and drove away.

Gideon walked down the driveway. Thank God that night was over.

CHAPTER 18

The Bereaved Bitch

Sam stared out of his wall at Manhattan. Life was a bitch. There were millions of scumbags out there that the world would have been better off without, and some piece of shit had to go and kill his little sister.

He felt bad about not having gone to the funeral, but things here were getting out of hand. Anyway, what was the point in travelling halfway across the world to see a box? He felt bad about having never got to know Rosemary, but they'd spent their lives on different continents. They were a different generation – she was young enough to have been his daughter. He hoped she'd known that he loved her.

He'd had high hopes for Rosemary. He'd figured that, being raised by his father and her gold-digging bitch of a mother, she'd be perfectly suited to running the company, but she hadn't been interested. She'd been a sensitive soul. Even as a kid, there'd been something gentle and fragile about her. Sam clenched his fists under the table. If only they knew who had done it; he'd wring the bastard's fucking neck.

But he couldn't think about Rosemary now. He had other things to worry about – like the BB. That's why they were here; to discuss the BB case. He wasn't hopeful the board would have any useful ideas but they had to do something. The whole thing was getting out of hand.

Sam drummed his fingers on the boardroom table while his secretary set up the film. He looked around at the other board members. Fewer than half of them were present, because he'd called the meeting at short notice. They were waiting for George, who was on his way up.

Sam looked across at Peter, the company's great legal expert. He was wearing one of his fancy suits – you could tell it was tailor-made and must have cost a fortune.

Sensing Sam's eyes on him, Peter looked up. He gave Sam a polite smile and carried on looking through the folder that had been prepared for the meeting.

Peter was a very convincing person. He was the kind of lawyer who you would have expected would have gone into politics. He always seemed totally at ease and he had that ability to make you feel as if he had everything under control. Sometimes, even Sam felt slightly awkward when pressing him on something. It was no surprise that Peter had got as far as he had. Because he was relatively young – not yet 50 – he could also still rely on his looks, to some extent.

Sam inhaled through his nostrils. Peter had disappointed him. For five and a half years, the man had swanned around in his fancy suits, acting like the great legal intellectual. Now the shit was hitting the fan in ever-increasing quantities and it was becoming clear that Peter was out of his depth. Instead of getting on top of the situation – instead of taking control – he and his team were just fighting each case as it came.

If there was one thing Sam couldn't stand, it was arrogance combined with incompetence. He could put up with people who thought the sun shone out of their asses, provided they were still able to shine when clouds started coming in, but it had turned out that shiny Peter couldn't handle bad weather. He was the only board member whom Sam had taken a chance on. The rest of them knew how the world worked but Peter had only ever been a lawyer and an academic. Sam didn't know which was worse.

Sam was angry with the board about Peter. Against his better judgement, he'd been too patient with Peter. That was the board's fault. They were so scared about how complex the legal and legislative environment was becoming that they had started assuming the company couldn't do without him. Sometimes, when a really complex issue came up, Peter could literally seem like an oracle with his reassuring manner and his grasp of arcane legal bullshit.

Then there were his 'connections'. Peter knew everyone and

everyone knew Peter. If anyone was able to get in a word into the right ears in DC, it was Peter. At least, that was what they'd all assumed; that was the impression Peter gave. It was hard not to be convinced because of whom his father was. In five and a half years, Peter and his army of lobbyists had spent a fortune in time and money wining and dining the whores in DC but they hadn't made a whole lot of progress. The laws were weighing more heavily on the company than ever before. To be fair to Peter – even though he didn't deserve fairness – it was a sign of the times, but that didn't make him any less of a useless bastard.

Sam looked out of the wall in the direction of where he thought DC might be. Those fucking righteous bastards were determined to regulate the United States out of business. They were becoming like the Europeans. Between the ever-rising tax burden and the waves of ridiculous rules and regulations, it was becoming impossible to do business in large parts of the world. The whole thing was calculated to kill entrepreneurship. What entrepreneur in his right mind was going to want to open a business in this kind of environment?

George arrived.

The moment he walked into the boardroom, Sam could tell he was seriously upset. When George was pissed, you knew. There were never any outward signs – apart from a minute tightening of the skin under the mouth. Sam could see them now; the faint lines leading from George's chin to his mouth. It was as though the skin was being ever so slightly tugged upwards by invisible strings.

Then there were the eyes. Those snake eyes. They appeared whenever George was in a mood. It was because the skin on his upper eyelids was slightly droopy. Normally, this gave him the appearance of being sleepy, but when he was angry and frowning, his eyes took on a hooded appearance. With those eyes and his long neck, he looked exactly like a hovering cobra. It gave Sam the creeps. It was difficult to look George in the eyes for more than a few moments at the best of times but when he was in a mood like this, it was difficult to look at him at all. He could make you uncomfortable by just being in the room. Sam had noticed long ago that George could communicate without saying a word.

At that moment, in his seat at the boardroom table, George was communicating serious displeasure. What the hell was it? What had George found out?

Sam was getting angry at himself now. What the hell did he have to fear from George? The bastard was his director, on *his* payroll. Who the fuck did he think was, marching in here, into Sam's boardroom, on Sam's time, giving off vibes like that? George was the one who should be worried. Lately, he was being a real pain in the ass. Either he wasn't paying attention or he was dominating the proceedings with intrusive questions, and generally acting as if he was entitled to be consulted about everything. The world was full of intellectuals. Sam hated fucking intellectuals.

It was probably Japan. That was it! George must have heard about the letter that Sam had sent to Japan. Or was it that? George seemed very pissed; hugely pissed. Would he be that pissed just because he hadn't been consulted about the letter? Sure, the Japanese had reacted like they'd had a rocket stuck up their asses, but that was typical of the Japanese. The vaguest suggestion of untoward behaviour, couched in the most anodyne form, was enough to trigger an outpouring of hysteria across the Tokyo bureaucracy. Surely George was more mature than that?

Well, Sam didn't give a damn. George could sit there steaming like a fresh turd. Sam had been complaining about Japanese protectionism for years, and the whores in DC had never done a thing about it. It was time he took matters into his own hands. Any reasonable person could see the whole thing was totally absurd: huge swathes of the Japanese market were effectively off limits to American companies and no-one in DC said a word. What the hell were they afraid of? Japan was yesterday's country – the land of the setting sun. The whores were always complaining about the Chinese, but you could sell anything in China. In Japan, you didn't have a hope of flogging a rubber duck without an armada of lawyers and product designers to break through the labyrinth of legal requirements. What the hell was the World Trade Organization there for?

Sam glanced again at George out of the corner of his eye. The bastard was just sitting there, watching him, waiting to get him alone.

He tried to concentrate on the presentation that was going on at the front of the room. To fill the time while they waited for George, Sam had pulled in the head of compliance – one of shiny Peter's subordinates – to update the board on the bribery investigation. The company had lawyers going through every subsidiary with fine-tooth combs to see what the bastards were up to. Sam was pretty sure nothing would be found, but the point wasn't to find anything – the point was to convince the politicians and the prosecutors that they were doing everything possible to prevent bribes from being paid.

Trying to run a business in this world was becoming impossible. Every time you turned around, some politician or policeman was breathing down your neck. They didn't give a damn about business; they didn't appreciate for a second that without Sam and entrepreneurs like him, they would be running a bankrupt banana republic.

"Ironically, our real worries are closer to home," the lawyer went on. "We are most vulnerable here and in Europe because the likelihood of being prosecuted is so much higher."

"They're not getting any tougher in Asia?" asked one of the directors.

The lawyer shook his head slowly. "They say they are, but there's not much evidence for it."

"Tell them about Japan!" Sam interjected.

The lawyer nodded. "We recently found out that one of our companies in Japan had been colluding with the competition to divide up the market, possibly even to fix prices." He paused. "It happened before we took it over. We immediately informed the Japanese competition authorities and sent them all the information we had."

"So we would get leniency," Sam interrupted.

The lawyer waited.

"What happened?" asked one of the directors, looking at Sam.

Sam nodded at the lawyer.

"Nothing," said the lawyer, "we never heard back from them."

"Here and in Europe, we would have been raided within 24 hours!" Sam said loudly. He stood up and leaned forward over the table, resting on his knuckles. "We're being crippled by legislation while the rest of the world is doing exactly what they damn well please."

Sam looked around the table. George was just sitting there, watching him. He decided to ignore him, even though it was George he was actually talking to. He still didn't know if it was the letter to Japan that George was pissed about.

"We're ready," Sam's secretary told him.

He nodded at her and she started the video.

It was a recording from last night's TV news. The newsreader finished talking about something and flashed a big smile at the camera. Then her face took on a more serious expression: "And now we turn to a case that's been making headlines in Florida…"

They listened as she reminded the viewers about what had happened. Two teenagers had been electrocuted on the site of a new eco-friendly power plant that Sam's company was building in Florida. The kids had broken into the site and got fried. It was as simple as that. One of them was a Cuban-American. He was only 15, but in his passport picture – shown on local TV – he looked more like an 18-year-old thug. It was obvious that they were looking for something to steal.

At first, it had seemed an open-and-shut case. Sam's company had said very little on the assumption that they would settle quietly out of court, but then it turned out that other dead boy had an aunt who was a lawyer – one of the best in the state.

The newsreader continued with the story so far. Sam could almost recite it word for word.

It was the boy's aunt – and not the police or anyone in Peter's team – who had found out that the perimeter fence around the plant was not alarmed. Since there was no way the two sweet, innocent, little bastards could have cut a hole in a heavy-duty security fence, it was the bereaved lawyer's contention – by now being presented as fact – that there must have been a hole there already.

Sam rubbed his cheeks with his hand. What the fucking newsreader *hadn't* mentioned was that site security was supposed to be the job of a local security company, which was now nowhere to be found. She'd also neglected to point out that two 15-year-old thugs with a pair of bolt cutters could quite easily have cut a hole in the fence themselves.

The bereaved bitch of a lawyer – since shortened to BB – had started with a simple lawsuit, but when she discovered that the company might be vulnerable to a charge of criminal negligence, she'd upped the stakes. Sam's company was the least well-connected of all the bastards on the ground, so she'd scared the shit out of the locals until they closed ranks behind her. They were now putting up a united front that Peter hadn't been able to crack.

Sam hated the lawyer's guts. At first, he'd liked the look of her – she was well-built and photogenic, even if her mug was a bit pockmarked and chiselled – but after months of hearing that Florida drawl and listening to the bitch telling lies about his company, he'd started to hate her like poison.

Peter had badly underestimated her. She might have been as rough as a bear's ass, but he should have known that you didn't need to know how to hold a knife and fork to make mincemeat out of a multinational.

With her backyard secure, the BB had moved on to DC. She had a story that hit all the right notes: she, the grieving relative, was determined that no other family would have to go through what her family had suffered because of the negligence and carelessness of profit-obsessed corporations like Sam's. Fucking bitch!

The newsreader on the screen started interviewing a muckraker on the ground in DC. Sam couldn't remember the scumbag's name but he was always on camera. Sam hated journalists at the best of times, but the smug, self-righteous bastards on this channel were worse than most.

The little shit had been trying to find out how the company handled safety and security, and how much it spent on these things. Sam shook his head. Obviously, he'd got nowhere – as if the company would give out such information!

"But the company refused to give us any information," the hack went on. "So we did the next best thing – we went to the federal authorities to find out what they knew about the company's safety record."

"And what did you find?" asked the newsreader, pretending to give a damn.

The scumbag journalist made a big deal about looking surprised. "It's hard to believe, but there is no data. There is absolutely no way of knowing how many incidents involving death or injury have occurred on this company's construction sites."

The whole thing was a fucking farce!

The newsreader looked concerned. The journalist quoted a letter from the relevant government department, admitting that such statistics were not available. The letter appeared on camera; the passages in question were marked in red.

Then the journalist gave the newsreader a knowing look; one of those typical self-satisfied looks that you see smeared on reporters' faces before they dress up bullshit as fact.

"But what is well-documented is fatal accidents involving employees in this industry," the hack said, leering into the camera like a peeping tom. "We did a background check on this industry's employee safety record because we reasoned that this would be a good indicator of its attitude to safety overall."

The newsreader nodded eagerly. "And what did you find?"

Sam leaned forward. This wasn't journalism; it wasn't even fucking entertainment.

"The mortality rate of employees in this industry is more than one in 20,000 per year," the bastard said, gravely. "That is much higher than the homicide rate in your average American city!"

Sam clenched his fists. Jesus Christ!

"Do you know how much this company invests in the safety of its employees?" the newsreader asked.

Some of the board members moved in their seats. The employee safety budget had been cut the previous year.

Sam clenched harder. These fucking journos were doing their goddamned best to make the company look as bad as humanly possible.

The journalist looked grave. "We worked out that companies in this industry are spending less than 500 dollars per employee *per year* on safety training and protective equipment," the journalist paused for effect, "in what is one of the most dangerous industries in America."

Then the BB came on. In spite of himself, Sam was impressed; she knew exactly how to talk to the camera and exactly how to sound intelligent and sincere while still making sense to the average pleb. In a few short months, she'd evolved from boondocks lawyer into a media-savvy DC attorney.

"If you take the fatality rates for employees in this industry as a whole," she said, "and I'm talking only about fatalities, not injuries in general, which are much more common, you see there has been virtually no improvement in the last 10 years."

The journalist added: "In other words, these companies are satisfied with death rates of more than one employee in 20,000 per year?"

The BB said nothing, but every line on her smug, make-up-caked face was quivering in agreement.

Sam looked around. The fucking journalists were working for her. "She knows this is meaningless bullshit," he said in a loud voice.

Some of the other directors made noises.

The BB went on about how disgusting it was that companies like Sam's were raking in record profits and paying their executives multi-million dollar salaries, while spending proportionately the same amount on safety as 10 years ago.

The journalist appeared back on the camera. His concluding line was typical of the kind of trash that passed for journalism these days: "It seems some companies in this industry have worked out how much a human life is worth – to them."

Sam's secretary turned off the machine.

Sam slapped his hands on the table. "How the hell do they get from a freak accident in Florida to concluding that we value human life at less than 500 dollars apiece?"

No-one said anything.

"So what do we do?" Sam asked. He looked around the table. "Every time we say something we look worse than we did before." He looked at shiny Peter. "What's your advice?"

He knew what was coming. The serious stare, the pathetic-looking creases that always appeared on the man's forehead when he wanted to look earnest, and then the usual non-committal answer. Who the fuck did he think he was dealing with?

"I don't think we should underestimate this one," Peter said, shaking his head solemnly.

Sam stared at him blankly for a while, just to make him feel stupid and uncomfortable, then he opened the paper folder in front of him. The other directors had already looked through their copies while they were waiting for George.

"This angle has been picked up by several other media," Sam said, looking at George.

The retired senator started looking through his folder. He seemed calmer.

Sam looked around the table. "There's a debate scheduled on at least one channel this week about the price that businesses put on human life."

"Let's hope they ask the airlines and the aircraft manufacturers," said an economist on the board, who had once worked in aviation. He was British and tended not to look at anyone when he spoke.

Sam looked at him. "What?"

The economist smiled. He was over 60 and had seen his reputation trashed in the last banking crisis. Sam knew better; he knew the old goat had sounded the alarm bells when the bankers really started losing the plot. Naturally, no-one had listened. They were worse than lawyers.

"Well, it was worked out rather precisely at one time," the economist continued. "The conclusion was that a human life – an American one, anyway – was worth about 10 million dollars. Or perhaps it was 20 million. I can't remember."

Sam didn't know what to say.

"Yes," the economist went on, getting into his stride, "that report..." – he waved his hand in the direction of the TV set – "was obviously not very scientific, but you have to stop spending money on security at some point. It's a fact of life."

"But that's not the same as putting a financial value on human life!" Peter, the lawyer, protested.

The economist looked through one of the walls.

Sam frowned.

"It was worse in the automobile industry," piped up the former head of the audit committee. "I remember reading that at least one company actually calculated that – based on accident mortality rates – it was cheaper to pay grief settlements to bereaved relatives than it was to improve safety with airbags and things."

"Yes, yes, we all know that one," said the economist. "But that was in the '50s. The aviation industry is still…"

George cleared his throat. Everyone stopped and looked at him, but he was still reading his papers.

Sam turned to Peter. "What's your opinion?"

"I think we most definitely need to act," said Peter, "and quickly."

Sam carried on looking at him.

Peter looked at the papers in front of him. "What we need is a diversion. Maybe we should sue the security company."

The old economist let out a small sigh. None of the other directors said a word.

"What's the situation in Florida?" asked the former head of the audit committee.

Peter started to speak but was interrupted by Sam.

"The whole thing is like an Italian farce," said Sam. "The owner of the security company, which was supposed to be guarding the site, is related to the mayor, who is closely connected to people in the state administration. They're all blaming us."

"It's a funny place, Florida," the old economist observed. "Once, everything used to start in Florida; now everything seems to end there."

After the meeting, George, who'd said nothing, lingered in the boardroom, looking out of the glass walls. When the others had gone, Sam came and stood next to him.

"What have you got against that lawyer of yours?" George asked.

Sam turned his head slightly and looked at him out of the corner of his eye. "Peter? He's not up to the job."

George tipped his head slightly to one side. "What's the problem?"

Sam stared out of the wall. "I thought I'd hired an arsonist, but he's turned out to be a fire fighter."

George frowned. "But he's got things under control?"

Sam shook his head. “He’s totally screwed up this Florida case and it looks like we’re going to get busted for paying bribes.”

George stiffened and inhaled sharply. “I thought these things were under control.”

Sam glanced at him out of the corner of his eye. “They should have been. Peter’s got an army of lawyers working for him, but they haven’t managed to stop the bastards on the ground from handing out brown envelopes to corrupt officials.”

George turned down the corners of his mouth. “How many people have you got working in compliance?”

Sam looked at him. “Peter’s got eight lawyers.” He grinned. “We call them integrity officers.”

“I mean globally,” said George.

“Eight,” said Sam.

The old senator turned his head and stared at Sam. His eyes were more like a cobra’s than ever.

Sam swallowed. “We’ve done and we’re doing everything humanly possible to stamp out bribery, but it’s impossible. These people are crooks, plain and simple. They’re not susceptible to persuasion. They’re morally bankrupt – irredeemable.” He paused. “And the politicians are out to get us – in DC and in Brussels.” Sam turned to look at George. “And now we’ve got this bitch from Florida to worry about.”

George’s mouth tightened. “I wouldn’t worry too much about that case. The only legs on that story are hers.”

Sam growled: “She’s making us look like shit.”

George inspected the view. “Things happen, Sam. People understand that.”

“Even in DC?”

George turned back to him. “It’s a Florida story, Sam.” He was speaking slowly. “And old people don’t like thugs or smartass lawyers.”

“The bitch is spending a lot of time in DC.”

George gazed at the side of Sam’s face. “She sees this as her big chance, Sam. My advice? Just sit it out.”

Sam said nothing.

George turned his head to look out of the wall. “Your real problem is this bribery investigation.”

Sam looked away.

George put his hand on Sam's shoulder.

"Forget about going on the offensive with this one, Sam," he said softly. "This is about settling as quickly and as quietly as possible."

Sam nodded unconvincingly. George could see his jaw muscles contracting.

"Damage limitation," George repeated softly.

For a while, the two men stood there, looking down at the skyscrapers of Manhattan arrayed in front of them. They hadn't done that for a while. At one time, it had almost been a ritual.

CHAPTER 19

George

The car was waiting for George in front of the building. He got in and greeted the chauffeur. The man, who had instructions to stay behind the wheel, pulled out into the traffic. For the first time that week, George was alone.

He looked at his briefcase. Usually, he read through what the week had produced on his way home, but not today. He was tired and jet-lagged and fed up. It was bad enough that Sam had insisted he attend that 'emergency' board meeting about that Florida case but now the old fool was about to be had up for bribery. This was the last straw.

George stared out of the window at Manhattan passing by. He should have resigned from Sam's board when he'd first made up his mind to do so. Now it was going to look like he was jumping ship because of the bribery case, and it was going to be even harder to find someone to take his seat.

The way things were going, his successor was going to have to be very well connected – and an expert in damage limitation – and indulgent and patient enough to deal with an ageing adolescent like Sam. But who, with a resumé like that, was going to want the job? It would have to be someone old. For a moment, George was tempted to leave the search for a successor to Sam – he certainly wouldn't be thanked for finding his replacement – but it would be like abandoning a child on the subway, and he still felt a slight sense of obligation to the old bastard.

He should have seen this bribery problem coming. It was inevitable that Sam was going to be had up for something sooner or later. Most big companies were little more than a breath away from prosecution or at least a PR disaster. It was what happened when you cut corners; when you tried to police a global business empire with eight lawyers. The only thing that had saved Sam so far was the fact that his businesses were too boring to investigate, but the climate was changing.

George still couldn't make up his mind whether Sam was good or bad for the company. For a long time, he'd dismissed him as a lucky dinosaur, but now that he had some experience on company boards, he had noticed that, for all Sam's faults, at least the old bastard gave a damn. That made a change from most of the other pompous asses you found squatting in executive washrooms. Maybe Sam's longevity wasn't such a coincidence after all.

Sam's problem was that he was old and stubborn. And while he talked about handing over to a younger successor, it was the one subject on which he was remarkably unconvincing. George had tried to imagine Sam stepping aside, had tried to picture him passing on the reigns to a smart 40-something technocrat, but the image just wouldn't crystallise in his mind. He could picture Sam being wheeled out feet first. It was not beyond the bounds of possibility to imagine Sam being ousted by a coalition of angry shareholders, but Sam stepping aside of his own free will while he was still *compos mentis*? It was about as likely as a general election in China.

Once, it had been possible to get through to Sam. It had never been easy, but in the old days he'd at least been able to accept that someone else might have an answer or an idea that he himself hadn't already discounted. But that was the old Sam – or rather the younger one. Nowadays, the only discussions around Sam were about tactics – all the fundamental questions had been answered. God forbid you inadvertently gave the impression that one of Sam's ideas might be lacking in some way; he would immediately retaliate with an aggressive: "What's the alternative?" He never waited for an answer.

George was used to dealing with closed minds. Over a lifetime in DC, he'd watched plenty in the process of closing. It didn't happen to everyone, but it was definitely an affliction of age. George didn't know why; presumably it was because the brain stopped producing enough neurons to create new thoughts – or maybe the pathways left by old thoughts gradually became so entrenched that they couldn't be over-ridden? If George was honest with himself, he hadn't had a genuinely new thought in years, but at least he hadn't succumbed to the absurd notion that there weren't any to have. That was why he travelled and always tried to meet new people, especially young ones; they had thoughts and ideas that could be appropriated.

Of course, Sam had no idea that his mind had closed. He'd been listening to himself and having his own opinions fed back to him for so long that he'd forgotten that reality was not something you defined in a boardroom. In Sam's little mind, he was still the ultimate entrepreneur – the exhibit A of unfettered, free-market capitalism – but somewhere along the line, he'd ceased to be a real entrepreneur and instead become just another one of those corporate welfare cases, whose lobbyists clogged the corridors of DC.

George glanced at his chauffeur. Actually, it was his wife's chauffeur. Sometimes, he had the feeling the man was watching him in the rear-view mirror.

In the old days, Sam had been on the road all the time. Now he hardly ever left New York, except to kiss ass in DC or woo a dithering customer. Once, he'd been a pioneer and a risk-taker, who boasted that he treated his mistakes like mistresses and took success with a pinch of salt. Now, Sam's idea of a risk was committing himself to a profit target. Mistakes were ignored, his mistress was a prostitute, and successes were things dreamt up by the marketing department. Even his meetings, once vaguely entertaining, had turned into dreary séances with the dearly departeds there in person.

George liked to be hard on Sam. He deserved it; he believed his own lies. George had believed his own lies, too, once, but at least he'd seen through them in the end. And he had the excuse of his upbringing. Sam had no excuse; he was simply a narcissist – and an ugly one at that.

It was going to be a relief to finally get away from Sam. Businessmen were all the same; they took credit for sunshine and blamed everyone else when it rained. They were pathetic. George had had enough of them.

He wasn't looking forward to telling Sam, even though there

would be some satisfaction at watching the old fool throw an apoplectic fit. He had never forgiven Sam for that year when he worked for him – when he'd been in the shoes of that unfortunate lawyer who was the target of Sam's latest hate campaign. From the moment George started work – literally the day he arrived – Sam had ignored him. He'd pretended he was listening, but it hadn't taken long to work out that he wasn't. At no point had George been in a better position to advise him, yet Sam ignored him completely. The situation had been intolerable.

After George resigned, they hadn't talked for years – until he retired from the Senate. Almost immediately, the phone had rung. It was Sam, greeting him like a long-lost friend. He hadn't wanted to talk about the past. He seldom did, especially if it interfered with his plans for the present. In that sense, Sam could have been a lawyer; the past was simply a library of evidence to be dredged up at his discretion.

Sam jumped straight to the point. He wanted George on the board. "When can you start?" he bellowed into the phone.

Even after all those years, George could still picture him grinning into the mouthpiece, convinced his offer would be accepted. Flattery was how Sam hired everyone. He overwhelmed you with flattery and plenty of other gifts into the bargain. You had to know yourself very well to resist him. The flattery lasted until the day you started work – then you became just another one of his intelligent imbeciles.

George refused, point blank. He had to. He gave no explanation – just 'no thanks'.

"Come on," Sam roared, "you know I never take no for an answer."

George stayed firm. He wasn't keen, but if he was going to work for Sam again, it would be on his own terms. There would be no repeat of the past.

He knew Sam had his back to the wall. In those days, the bankers were still riding high; they had a seat for any bum that had once sat in the Senate. No ex-senator in his right mind would have bothered with Sam's boring old board.

Sam had pestered him for more than a year; it had been a long, tedious process. Every time they seemed to be on the brink of a meaningful discussion, Sam would back off at the last minute. His favourite line was: "Do you want me to grovel?"

Eventually, George had gone to Sam's office. "This will be the last time I discuss this with you," he warned.

"What do you want from me?" Sam asked, almost plaintively. It was pathetic.

"Do you know why I resigned before?"

Sam shrugged and avoided George's eyes.

"I resigned because you hired me to advise you and then you ignored me."

Sam retreated behind his big desk and started fiddling with things.

George had been amazed at how difficult it was for Sam to talk about it. "I want to know why!" he demanded.

"It was so long ago. Can't we forget about the past?"

George shook his head. "I want an answer!"

He remembered the fool's look of total bewilderment. Sam couldn't understand why George wasn't letting this go. It was unbelievable that a man who was running a multi-billion dollar global enterprise didn't understand why this was so important. It was like dealing with a schoolboy who thought he'd got away with stealing.

The man had carried on vacillating between aggression and conciliation until George finally announced he could not accept the seat and would no longer be taking Sam's calls. As he was walking out of the door, Sam gave in. "Okay," he said. It took a while longer, but eventually George got him to admit what he'd done. It hadn't been an enlightening experience, but at least he'd acknowledged that George wasn't making it all up. George had hoped for more; hoped they might at least touch on why Sam behaved like that, but the old delinquent wasn't capable of that level of introspection. Still, he'd gone far enough. George joined the board.

In truth, he'd only done it because, on the bank board that he was on, they paid even less attention to their directors than Sam did. They were just more tactful about it. He'd known from the start that he wasn't going to last there – amid the pinstripes, gold watches and dental implants, he'd felt like an old whore trying to land a last trick.

George smiled at his reflection in the car window. Leaving that bank had turned out to be the best-timed decision of his life. He'd been owed some luck. As a boy, everyone had always told him how lucky he was, but he'd never felt lucky – until the banks failed. Suddenly, everyone was scrambling for cover and he, George, had woken up with a reputation for wanting nothing to do with banks. It had helped that he was on Sam's board – boring old companies that actually made things were back in vogue.

It wasn't fair. He'd been in politics all his life and not once had his face, much less his achievements, made the front pages. Then one day, out of the blue, completely by chance – after he'd retired! – he was suddenly handed the greatest gift a politician could hope for: the presumption of intellect and integrity combined! He hadn't had to do a thing or say a word. The only question he'd been asked was: why hadn't he warned them?

George remembered looking at the interviewer and then into the TV camera. He'd put on that slightly weary look; the one that said: 'I did every thing I could.'

"This is not the time for recriminations," he pronounced, magnanimously. "First, we have to heal the financial system."

Before, he'd been too aloof, too stuck up – too New England. Now he was a man of principle, respectable, old school, who understood the difference between veneer and value. It was almost perfect. It would have been the perfect moment to exit the grubby world of boards and business and stage a political comeback, but this world was too enamoured of irony to let him off the hook like that. What no-one but his wife knew was that the banking crisis that had made his reputation had also wiped him out. Only Mary knew that he knew as much about finance as he did about futurology. Why would he know anything? You didn't need to know anything about business and finance to be a politician. It was better not to know anything, especially if you were going to sit on company boards.

George looked down at his patent leather shoes. It had been a bitter pill. After a lifetime in politics, he'd been reduced to working for money. Mary had said he didn't have to, if he wanted to go back into the Senate, but the truth about his financial affairs was bound to come out if he did. Anyway, he was too old and too tired to go back. He'd been looking forward to the day when he could concentrate on his reading and his memoirs; maybe think about accepting a post as an envoy or even as an ambassador, if one of his protégés was ever lucky enough to make it into the White House. Thank God he had a rich wife. At least he could keep up appearances.

It was hard to believe how fast everything had evaporated. It was like he'd gone to bed one night and woken up in a completely different world. It was partly perception, he knew: the Cold War had been never-ending, until it ended, but still… His retirement – like the future – was over before it even began.

George missed the old days, before the bankers buggered everything up. Back then, it had still been possible to pretend that America knew better than the rest; that the western model was one worth emulating. Now it seemed the only people who took America seriously were the fundamentalists.

The Chinese certainly didn't. The trip George had just returned from had been calculated humiliation from day one. In the old days, an American senator – even a retired one fronting a delegation of boring businessmen – would have been given something resembling the red-carpet treatment, but times had changed. When they landed in Beijing, there wasn't even a doormat laid out. The reception committee consisted of a fresh-faced technocrat called a regional vice-president – whatever that was – and a bunch of local shysters looking to fleece the foreigners.

Of course, George had protested immediately. He hadn't expected the prime minister, but they could at least have wheeled out an official with a mind of his own. In the end, they'd had to wait until the following evening before a heavyweight of sorts appeared to host a dinner. It was like trying to do a deal with the emperor after the gunboats had weighed anchor.

Worse was to come. The new man, whose name was Yang, was evidently one of the Communist Party's rising stars. He was smart, westernised, and clearly put out at having to play host to such a motley crew at short notice. He got stuck in before the duck arrived.

"It's been a while since I was in America," he said, in a voice loud enough to silence the table. "Do people there still talk about the free market?"

The man chuckled to himself and took a sip of his Chinese Cabernet Sauvignon. Then, turning to his aides, who showed no sign of being able to understand English, he said in a loud voice: "In America, they used to allow the private sector to run the economy, but that didn't work, so now the government does it – just like here."

George glanced across the table at Harold. Thank God Harold had been in Beijing. He was the son of an old friend from George's Oxford days who'd recently joined the Foreign Office. He was in China to improve his Mandarin and to learn how to stand firm with nothing but Britain behind him. Mr Yang might just be the man to put Harold through his diplomatic paces.

Their Chinese host smiled at George. "Politics and economics have become so much more simple since…" he paused. "Well, haven't they?"

"How so?" said Harold, picking up his chopsticks.

Mr Yang glanced at him and then went back to looking at George. "We used to be communists, you used to be capitalists, but now we're all pragmatists."

George smiled back, and glanced in Harold's direction. The entire table had gone quiet. George wasn't surprised; businessmen were incapable of an intelligent riposte and they never had anything to say when serious subjects were discussed.

"I do hope I'm not speaking out of turn," said Mr Yang, apologetically. "But we're all men of the world here – surely we can be honest with each other?"

Harold moved his head in Mr Yang's direction and murmured something about the exceptional nature of the last economic crisis. Then, expertly wielding his chopsticks, he plucked a boiled duck's heart from the Lazy Susan in the middle of the table and chewed it up enthusiastically.

"You really must try these ducks' hearts," he said to the businessmen present. "Boiled in malt, they are quite out of this world." Then, in a voice as loud as Mr Yang's, he started gushing about the food, and sending his compliments to everyone who had had anything to do with it. It was a very convincing performance, especially for someone who'd eaten nothing up to that point.

George relaxed slightly. Like most Englishmen, Harold couldn't talk for toffee, but he was very good at changing the subject and even better at ignoring people in the most withering way. When he got into his stride, Harold could literally ignore the life and soul out of the party.

The young diplomat enthusiastically gobbled up a second duck's heart and then set about ignoring Mr Yang. George leaned back with his glass of Chinese Cabernet. He was familiar with Harold's act, but it was still worth watching.

Harold started by striking up an intimate conversation with the two people between himself and Mr Yang. Soon, other people at the table defected into their own conversations. George joined one himself, but kept a close eye on Harold. Suddenly, Harold fired a question at the person on the other side of Mr Yang and expertly pulled him into their conversation. That did it. Mr Yang was isolated, surrounded by a conversation that he had no part in. Soon, he was turning his head from side to side like a spectator at a tennis match.

George watched the man trying for an opening. But Harold kept the pace perfectly timed to prevent anyone from interrupting. Jumping in to a conversation under these circumstances was extremely risky; the slightest error in timing could undo any reputation for civility. A normal person wouldn't have tried, but Mr Yang had to. He was hosting a dinner for a retired senator, a British diplomat and a bunch of boring businessmen; he couldn't very well spend the evening talking at his aides. He waited a few more seconds, and then took the plunge.

As soon as Mr Yang opened his mouth, Harold immediately drew a sharp breath and started acting as if the man had committed some sort of mortifying *faux pas*. Then, as Mr Yang retreated into silence, Harold hurriedly resumed the conversation with the people around him, as one does when trying to pretend that what has just happened hasn't. It was truly a performance to behold.

It took Mr Yang a little while to grasp just how ignored he was being. As it dawned, he started to change colour. Then, he spent some time considering his position and decided to ignore Harold back. But doing that only reinforced his isolation because Harold took the opportunity to divert the people around Mr Yang into separate conversations with people even further away. By the time Harold was finished, Mr Yang could do nothing but look around at other people talking to each other.

George watched Mr Yang as he sat there, spinning the Lazy Susan in the middle of the table, morosely snatching morsels with his chopsticks.

It wouldn't last; the man would say something soon enough, but he'd been punished, and he knew it.

Mr Yang held his tongue until their wine glasses were filled for the last time. Then he stood up and raised his. "To our guests," he said, graciously.

They raised their glasses.

"To the health of our respective economies…" he continued.

The atmosphere was getting tense again.

"And most important of all," Mr Yang said loudly, raising his glass even higher. "To pragmatism…"

Harold put down his glass immediately, with just enough of a bang to ruin the toast. Then he raised it again. "To China," he said. "To the future. To the free market!"

They could behave like this here. It was a dinner for businessmen.

George decided to take Mr Yang outside. That way, they could find out what the man really thought, and nudge him on to the straight and narrow – if necessary. He was too cocksure, and considering his English and his table manners, he would soon be representing China abroad.

George got into position and signalled to Harold to do the same. At the end of a meal, the Chinese tended to leave the table *en masse* without warning. If you bent down to retrieve your napkin, you could wind up alone in the room. The moment Mr Yang moved,

George and Harold were on their feet, following him out. Harold elbowed one of Mr Yang's aides out of the way and left his interpreter to block the door. It worked; they got Mr Yang alone in the car park.

George decided to let Harold do the talking – at least to start with. As a rule, he always let the British do the talking (except in the Middle East) because their accent had an authority and a pitch that tended to drown out other voices. Anyway, it was better for him to stay out of it. He didn't want Mr Yang to dream for a moment that he considered him an equal.

"Thank you for a marvellous meal," Harold smiled. "We enjoyed your comments almost as much as the food."

Mr Yang stared at him, bemused.

"We don't blame you for gloating," Harold continued. "I think it's fair to say that we all learned a few things from the last financial crisis, but it's all history now."

Mr Yang smiled politely. "What have you learned?"

Harold was slightly taken aback. "I beg your pardon?"

"You said we'd all learned a few things," said Mr Yang. "What have you learned?"

The corners of Harold's mouth dropped slightly. "Mistakes were made," he nodded. "Regulation was found lacking, rules were not always properly enforced." He paused to re-hydrate his mouth. "But the important thing is that we acted quickly and decisively in our common interest."

The Chinese man stared blankly at him for a few seconds, then guffawed like a determined drunk being told not to drive.

Before George could stop him, Harold lashed out in the most patronising tone he could muster: "We learned our lessons two centuries ago."

It was understandable; Mr Yang was a provocative man and Harold had drunk too much, but it was a pity. He'd put Mr Yang in control. Now they would have to start again.

George interrupted. "Mr Yang knows all that, Harold," he said, smiling at Mr Yang. "I'm sure Mr Yang knows far more about these matters than we do."

The Chinese man tilted his head slightly to one side.

"Are you an economist, Mr Yang?" George asked.

The man nodded. Then he straightened up and smiled politely at Harold. "With respect, I'm not sure you've learned anything at all – in this century."

"Well, you certainly have..." Harold muttered.

"Yes," said Mr Yang. "We've learned a lot – in particular about what happens when control of the economy is handed over to banks and businessmen."

"Ah," said Harold. "So, in other words, you've learned nothing at all."

"China didn't cause the problems," Mr Yang replied. "We just helped to clean up the mess – the mess of the west."

George stepped forward, closer to Mr Yang. "Gentlemen," he said, cheerfully. "We have much too much in common to argue. We have to stand together." He looked at Mr Yang. "Our two countries are on the bridge of the world economy. We can't afford to rock the boat, much less jump ship."

Mr Yang turned to George. "I can assure you that China has no intention of rocking the boat or jumping ship. Quite the contrary! We are on the bridge precisely because we believe the ship must be steered."

George took a step back.

"What we will not do," Mr Yang continued, "what we will *never* do, is allow the technicians in the engine room to take control of the ship."

George smiled at him with gentle eyes.

Mr Yang softened his tone. "Ships need a captain, someone to plot the course. The people in the engine room can't see where the ship is going. All they can do is keep the engines running."

George smiled at him. "I understand you perfectly, Mr Yang." He smiled more broadly. "As a matter of interest, where is your ship heading?"

Mr Yang smiled back. "To where we should have been all along."

George tilted his head inquisitively.

"To where you are," finished Mr Yang.

"As long as you're happy to follow us," Harold interjected.

Mr Yang gave him a sideways glance. "We overtook you a long time ago."

"And when you get there – to where we are," said George. "What then?"

Mr Yang bowed his head slightly. "I can assure you, China doesn't want to take over the world. We only want to be able to make our own decisions, about our own future."

"Yes, I've heard that," said George. "And your future?"

Mr Yang smiled. "It's very simple. We want stability and progress. That's all China has ever wanted."

"Is that why you don't like freedom and democracy?" said Harold.

George stepped forward so he was almost between Harold and Mr Yang. "What interests me more, Mr Yang, is just how far you believe your policy of pragmatism is going to take you?"

The Chinese man grinned. "We'll stick to it for as long as it works."

"Yes, of course," said George. "But you do see that governing according to outcomes can only take you so far."

Mr Yang said nothing.

George gave him a very friendly smile. "The world is very complicated, Mr Yang. At the moment, you might be able to agree on where to go, but there comes a point when the course is no longer clear. Then, you need a moral compass – a set of guiding rules and principles – to show you the way when you've sight of your destination."

Mr Yang nodded. "I see what you mean, but in China, a moral compass is the last thing we need now. It would sink us straightaway."

"Why?"

"Because we need legitimacy!" Mr Yang exclaimed. "We need the support of the people."

George and Harold glanced at each other.

Mr Yang laughed at them. "Yes, gentlemen, we need legitimacy, just like you do, and we all know what brings legitimacy!"

"Democracy?" said Harold.

Mr Yang laughed at him. "Please, don't insult my intelligence."

George and Harold carried on looking at him inquisitively.

"Success!" exclaimed Mr Yang. "Success brings legitimacy. It took us a long time to work this out. But we understand it now. It's all about success! There is no other source."

He paused and looked at them shrewdly. "You can attribute your legitimacy to things like capitalism and moral compasses and democracy, if it makes you feel better, but let's not pretend that you really have any confidence in those things. We've all seen that you're ready to drop them like hot cakes when the situation demands it."

Harold took a deep breath. "You're quite sure democracy wouldn't make China even more successful?"

Mr Yang turned to him. "It would be a dangerous distraction. It would compromise our ability to grow and progress, just like it has yours."

"Well, that would be up to the people," said Harold.

Mr Yang shook his head. "In China, we learned the hard way what happens when power fragments, when there is no strong central authority. We're not going through that again."

"How can you be so sure that's what would happen?" asked Harold.

"This is not Britain or Hong Kong," replied Mr Yang. "This is still a nation of peasants. They would interpret an election as an admission of weakness; as an abdication of power and responsibility. The country would become ungovernable." He paused and looked around. "China has always bordered on the ungovernable!"

"And when you're no longer successful?" asked Harold.

"Well, then, you're finished," said Mr Yang. He stepped back so he could look at both of them. "It really is that simple. Success sustains the system. Democracy is, at best, window-dressing, at worst, a destructive distraction." Mr Yang shrugged and dropped the corners of his mouth.

George stuck out his lower lip. "You speak very convincingly, Mr Yang, but are you sure that the single-minded pursuit of success is the best way of achieving it?"

Mr Yang laughed heartily to himself. "That, of course, is the ultimate question. You could say that success is God: the answer to everything except itself." He grinned at George. "In China, we believe that success, like man, holds the answer to its own existence.

Bringing things like God and moral compasses into it is simply answering questions with questions."

Mr Yang looked around for his aides. They were waiting in a line, in silence, at a respectful distance from him. George's businessmen had found the bar. You could hear their voices floating out into the parking lot.

"You seem to have an answer for everything, Mr Yang," said George.

"I have a good memory," smiled Mr Yang.

"Thank you for a very interesting evening," said George.

"May I now ask you one question?" asked Mr Yang.

"Of course."

"Do you think the United States can imagine a world in which it is not the pre-eminent power?"

George smiled at him. "I'm afraid we don't think that far ahead."

Mr Yang gave a small bow, and shook hands with George and then Harold.

They stood there watching as he led his little party away.

"Why didn't you answer his question?" asked Harold.

George carried on looking after Mr Yang. "I don't know the answer."

Harold looked at him. "I had a horrible feeling you were going to say that."

★

They were out of New York City and on the road to Connecticut. George glanced at the chauffeur in the rear-view mirror. The man's eyes seemed to be firmly on the road. He was no wiser after his trip to China; but he felt better. Listening to the Chinese was always reassuring. They only wanted stability and prosperity; they weren't interested in taking over the world or even expanding their borders. They were always respectful, modest and reasonable – so long as they got their own way.

Suddenly, George missed the State Department; missed being a diplomat, missed the Cold War. In those days, you were either a capitalist or a communist, and everyone knew the difference. Now, it was all a mess. The communists were capitalists, the capitalists were interventionists, and the free market was run by the government. What made it worse was that it was all so dull. Once, going to work had really been about saving the world but now all they could do was worry about the deficit, wonder about the Chinese, and try to tune out the economists.

It was quite a comedown, especially for a superpower. It was even more of a comedown for him, someone who was once going to be president.

It was his parents' fault. They had seemed to take the idea seriously.

"If you're going to be president, you should go and work for the State Department," his father had told him, while he was at Harvard. "Most of the great presidents were secretaries of state: Jefferson, Madison, Adams…"

George had wondered for years if his father had sabotaged his plans on purpose. The old man must have known that the State Department had become a graveyard of presidential ambitions.

He finally asked his mother at his father's funeral.

"You were too clever to be president," she said, wiping away a tear.

"What does that mean?" he muttered, as the box was lowered into the ground.

His mother stepped forward and tossed a spadeful of dirt on to her dead husband's coffin. "You think too much," she whispered, stepping back into line. "A president must be someone who can make decisions quickly, who can act, without knowing what's going on."

His mother put a hand on his arm. Anyone watching would have assumed she was seeking support in her grief. "That's not you, George," she whispered. "You're a thinker. That's why your father sent you to the State Department; you were needed there. We needed clever people to fight the Russians."

"You didn't believe in me," he whispered into her ear.

"Of course we did," she mouthed back, indignantly. "You just weren't made to be president, nor was your father. It would have been irresponsible to try and get into office. It would have been a disaster if you'd succeeded."

He surveyed the assembled guests. They all seemed remarkably similar, standing there in their black clothes, looking serious and sad.

"Would you really have wanted to be one of those idiots who insists on humiliating themselves and wasting the country's time whenever an election comes round?" she whispered. "It's like watching chimpanzees trying to master cutlery."

"You always told me I could be anything I wanted to be," he whispered, holding his hand over hers.

She looked up into his face and stroked his cheek. "It's important people believe that, George, especially when they are young."

George looked at his reflection in the car window. His mother had been right, of course. He'd never been any good at making decisions. How could you be when decisions hardly had anything to do with the eventual outcomes that they were supposed to have led to? Decisions were for naïve people, for people who believed they could consciously influence events, for people who took themselves seriously.

George had never been able to take himself seriously. How could he? It was embarrassing enough watching other people take themselves seriously. People always looked like primates when they took themselves seriously; being in a room with serious people was like a trip to the zoo, or to a board meeting. George smiled to himself and glanced into the rear-view mirror. The chauffeur smiled back.

CHAPTER 20

The legacy

Gideon stared at the ceiling. He knew Catherine would call back – she must be flying or somewhere without a signal – but he couldn't relax. He needed money fast. Shit! He should have called her last week; that way he would have had the money by tomorrow. Now, it could take till Thursday.

He was dreading the conversation to come. He knew she was going to lecture him – whites always lectured him. Gideon suspected they couldn't help it; that they were genetically programmed to bore you to tears with their stupid ideas about how everyone else should be living their lives. Normally, he would just switch off and let her drone on, but this time he needed cash – and fast. Because he'd asked her for money not that long ago, she'd be in full lecture mode – and he couldn't lose his temper with her because then he'd have to wait for her to call back and apologise.

Still, at least he could count on Catherine. Sam had treated him like shit since the day Rosemary… well, since he could remember. "Get a job," was all he ever heard from Sam. His voice was like a recorded message playing down the line from New York.

Gideon knew the family couldn't stand him. The only reason Catherine kept in touch was because of the kids, and the only reason she gave them any help was because she was terrified they would show up on her doorstep in Switzerland. Family meant nothing to her or Sam. They were loaded – rolling in the stuff – but God forbid he asked for a pittance to put towards raising their relatives! You'd have sworn he was asking them to part with a bloody kidney or something.

He'd tried to please them but it was impossible. Having a conversation with either of them was like trying to communicate with another planet – you were constantly being pulled backwards and forwards in time. Catherine was always going on about things he couldn't remember and Sam never spoke about anything but the future. The last conversation with him was the worst Gideon had ever had, just a bombardment of questions and orders: "Where are you going?", "What are your plans?", "You need some to find some direction", "When are you going to get a job?", "What's going to happen when you're too old to work?".

People were being murdered every day and he was being interrogated about his retirement plans by a mean, miserable bastard sitting in a penthouse office ten thousand miles away. It was so absurd, Gideon couldn't even get angry. He didn't have any answers. Retirement was not exactly a priority. He owed money, he had bills to pay; it was almost the end of the month.

Gideon got out of bed and walked into the living room. It was a nice day. He unlocked the trellis door and went outside. The bright sunlight hurt his eyes. It was going to be really hot. He went back inside, got his cigarettes, and came back out again. The stone ashtray was full of emaciated cigarette stubs; the ash had long since been blown away by the wind. He sat down on the edge of the veranda and lit a cigarette.

Gideon had never been able to imagine the future; the present was where he lived. The past was a succession of events – mostly unpleasant, better forgotten. The future was a closed door that opened sporadically and spat things out. Most of the time, what came through that door didn't make much sense in the grand scheme of things, but occasionally something big showed up. Usually, it was something bad; something that knocked you flat – that killed you, if you were unlucky – but once in a while, something good appeared. It had been a long time since anything worthwhile had come through that door. At some point, his luck had to change.

He'd had high hopes of doing a deal with the Chinese – then, he would have been able to pay back the loan shark and get back on his feet – but he should have known Sango was going to screw everything up. His mother always said you should never speak ill of the dead, but in Sango's case, Gideon felt justified in making an exception. When he first heard that Sango had been killed in Angola, he'd felt sorry for him, but that was before he found out the bastard had been out there looking for partners for the Chinese.

Sango's dodgy buddy, Julius – of 'Julius Investments' – was still pushing him to call Sino back. But what was he supposed to say? "Don't worry, we'll make sure the next guy stays alive for long enough to cut you a deal!"

Anyway, he and Julius had since discovered that the Chinese were even worse than the whites, with their arrogant attitude and ridiculous demands. They'd even insisted on being allowed to bring in their own workers, for God's sake. What the hell was that about?

"We need special skills," they'd said, during that first fiasco of a phone call – as if you needed special skills to dig holes and lay bricks. It was obvious they didn't trust Africans to do the job properly.

One day, the Chinese were going to be running the world. That was something to look forward to. With the whites in charge, everyone else got the dirty work; with the Chinese in charge, it looked like nobody else was going to get any work!

"It's okay," Julius had told them, once the phone call was over. "I'll talk to some people. We'll find a way around this. Money talks." Gideon remembered him rubbing his fingers together.

Julius's next coup had been a cringe-making meeting with that official from the department of trade. They were sitting in leather armchairs in an over-priced bar when the man arrived. "Let me do the talking," Julius whispered.

The man, who was coloured, started rolling his eyes almost as soon as Julius opened his mouth. "So let me get this straight," he said. "You're asking us to invite a Chinese company to tender?"

They were talking about a lucrative government contract.

Julius nodded.

"Even though," the man continued, "this company is not even present in South Africa and wants to bring its own workers in from China?"

Julius hesitated.

The man leaned forward and grasped a handful of peanuts from a bowl on the table. He had a slightly constipated look on his face. He tilted his head back and, holding his hand above his mouth, let the nuts trickle into it.

Julius started saying something vague about facilitation fees.

The man swallowed his nuts and took a long swig of beer. Then he leaned forward and looked Julius directly in the face. "You're in the wrong country, my 'China'," he mouthed, as if Julius was slightly deaf.

Gideon remembered taking out his mobile phone and looking at the screen. Sango was staring at something on the ceiling. The man from the department of trade leaned over the side of his arm chair and dug a document out of his briefcase. He dumped it on the table in front of them. It looked like a brochure. "I suggest you give that to your friends in China," he said, in a more normal tone. "It explains the basics of investing in South Africa."

He drank some more beer and then looked at Julius. "I'll give you some advice – for free. The way it works with the Chinese in Africa is that they hand over a lot of cash to government officials in exchange for being able to dig up raw materials. Then they build the roads and railways and harbours – with Chinese labour – to get the stuff back to China." He drained his beer and stood up. "We don't operate like that in South Africa. We're interested in serious investors – people who are here for the long term."

They sat there in silence, watching him walk away. Gideon remembered Julius trying to put a brave face on it: the brilliant deal-maker who'd managed to find the only civil servant south of the Sahara that wasn't a crook.

But Sango had obviously been paying attention. He'd gone straight to Angola to find the kind of partner that the man from the department of trade had been talking about – and got his brains blown out in the process.

The phone was ringing. It had to be Catherine; she was the only person who still called on the landline. Gideon got up. It was lecture time.

"Gideon? Can you hear me?"

Catherine always took a few seconds to cope with the long-distance delay.

"Hello Catherine, I can hear you perfectly. How are you?"

Gideon lay down on the couch and lit another cigarette. This was going to take a while.

"Gideon," she paused, and said nothing for while.

"Yes?" he said cautiously.

She cleared her throat. "I want to talk to you about the children."

"Yes?"

"About their education," she went on. "It's very important that they get a good education."

He waited.

"It's very important that they attend good schools, where they get the support and encouragement that they need."

"I couldn't agree more," he said, pleasantly.

"There is some money…" she muttered. Her voice started to go funny.

Gideon sat up. He'd never heard a white person raise the subject of money before, except when he owed them some.

"What money?" he said. Rosemary had left no will and had no assets that he knew of.

"We – Rosemary's father and I – set up an investment fund for her when she was a child…" Catherine's voice petered out. He could hear her covering the mouthpiece as she broke down in tears.

He waited a few seconds. "Yes?" he said, gently.

Catherine cleared her throat. It was obviously a huge effort for her to speak. "Well, that money is for the children now," she said, hoarsely. "To make sure they have everything they need. To give them a proper education – a future."

It was like listening to someone who had throat cancer. "I see," he said. "That's very generous of you."

"It's not a lump sum," she muttered. "It's a monthly income – for the children."

"That's great," he said, wondering how many more times she was going to try and get her point across. "It's a real load off my mind."

"There should be enough to buy them everything they need, and to pay for school fees and the occasional holiday – for all three of you."

"Thank you, Catherine." He meant it.

"An accountant in Johannesburg will be in touch in the next day or two to make the arrangements," she said.

Gideon waited.

"Hello?" she said.

"Yes, I'm here."

"He will take care of all the arrangements with your bank and handle all the payments to the schools."

"I'm perfectly capable of arranging everything, Catherine."

"Of course you are," she said, in a friendly tone, "but this accountant is being paid, so he should earn his fee."

"I can handle it, Catherine. You don't need to pay an accountant."

"Don't worry," she said, "it's all arranged. In any case, you have enough on your plate with two children to look after."

They talked for a bit longer. Gideon tried to think of things to tell her about the kids. He really wanted to talk about Rosemary. Catherine was one of the few people he could have talked to about her – she was the only person he knew who really knew Rosemary – but he couldn't mention her name, not to Catherine. It would be like sticking a red-hot poker into her.

The children were coping well – surprisingly well – thanks in part to his mother, who was continually fussing over them. Lydia was already starting to forget things. Gideon knew that because she'd asked for a photograph of Rosemary to keep next to her bed. He'd assumed she wanted it for comfort, but that wasn't it.

"It's so I don't forget what Mummy looks like," she explained, placing the picture carefully among all the things she kept on her little bedside table. "I need to be able to recognise her when I meet her again in heaven one day."

Joshua was recovering, too. In the beginning, he'd fallen apart every time his mother was mentioned, but now he just sat there with a face of stone, tears rolling down his cheeks. It would take longer for him, but he would get over it, too.

Now Gideon's eyes were watering. He found it painful to talk about Rosemary, but he preferred the pain. It was better to have the pain, because if no-one talked about Rosemary, if no-one acknowledged her existence – and since the funeral, only the children had – then… It was better to talk about her, even with the pain. Sometimes, it was like she'd just gone out – like she'd be back later, or tomorrow – because the house still looked exactly the same as the day she left, except for the mess, and the dirty ashtrays. At least he didn't have to listen to her moaning about the mess.

Gideon cupped his hand over the mouthpiece and sniffed furiously. Catherine had stopped talking but he could hear her breathing. She was in a state. He had a strong feeling she was never going to be able to talk about Rosemary again; not properly. He said goodbye and put down the phone.

He stood up and went into the kitchen to put the kettle on. The money was a relief, a big relief. It was something he would normally celebrate. Cash on the way – a regular supply of it at that – and no lectures. He hadn't even had to bullshit Catherine with a sob story. Maybe he should celebrate. It wouldn't be bad to cheer himself up; everything had been so depressing for so long. He wondered what to do. Maybe he'd go out for lunch – to a nice restaurant, with someone fun. He was free till the evening – till he had to pick up the kids from his mother's.

He pulled his mobile out of his pocket and started scrolling through the contacts list. There were lots of people he hadn't seen or heard from in ages – some names he didn't even recognise. His thumb scrolled faster. The names whizzed by. He stopped. Who the hell was Sabrina? He hit the button and opened Sabrina's entry but there was only a mobile number. He always meant to put in more information but never got around to it.

He opened the dishwasher and took out a clean mug. He took a tea bag out of the box and tossed it into the air. It landed squarely in the mug. That only worked when you weren't concentrating. Three spoons of sugar followed the tea bag. The kettle was starting to make a noise. Sabrina? Sabrina, Sabrina, Sabrina. He murmured the name aloud, letting it vibrate in his head. His brain was getting closer to unearthing her; it hadn't been that long ago. He waited for the kettle to boil and then poured the boiling water into the mug. He agitated the tea bag for a while and then filled up the mug with milk. Then he vigorously stirred the whole mixture before tossing the tea bag into the sink on his way out of the kitchen.

He suddenly remembered. Shit! Sabrina had been the arsehole's secretary. Yes! Nice arse, nice legs. He couldn't quite picture her face but he'd recognise her if she walked into the room. He hadn't seen her since he left the company. God, she might still work there.

Gideon put the mug on the coffee table and looked at his mobile. His thumb hovered over the call button. He was hesitating because he wasn't sure he wanted to go back there. Maybe she didn't work there anymore. She hadn't been one of them; she'd been on his side. Wasn't she the one who'd coined the nickname 'arsehole' for the arsehole? She was probably still at the company; she'd had it too good to leave, unless she'd found a rich husband. She'd been screwing the CFO when Gideon arrived. That poor fool hadn't survived for long. He was a nice guy, but hopeless. After he got the boot, Sabrina went to work for the arsehole.

Gideon sat down and slurped his tea. It was a tiny bit too sweet – he'd been a bit slapdash with the sugar. Shit! Now it would never be perfect. It was a pity Rosemary wasn't there – she knew just how he liked it. He went back to the kitchen to try and fix the tea. Perfect was two and three-quarter spoons of sugar – this was more like three. He added a tiny bit of hot water from the kettle and a drop of milk. Now it was just that little bit too watery. A mug of tea was one thing that couldn't be repaired – it had to be perfect first time. He looked at the phone again. What the hell! He pressed the call button.

He recognised Sabrina's voice. She knew who he was instantly. He could tell from her slightly mocking tone that she remembered every single detail of what had happened when he left. "Free for lunch?" he asked her.

"You must be kidding. What do think I am? A nun?"

"If you were a nun, you'd be busy – it's Sunday."

They bantered for a while, getting reacquainted. A few minutes later, the arrangements were made. He felt a bit uneasy – and guilty – but what the hell. He hadn't done anything fun for a long time.

Lunch was fun; Sabrina was fun, but he made the mistake of letting her follow him home from the restaurant and getting into bed with her. From the moment she took off her clothes, he wanted her gone. It took the rest of the afternoon to get rid of her.

Calling her had been a mistake. He wasn't the least bit interested in her; he'd known it the minute he'd laid eyes on her again. The sight of her had jerked him back into the past, back to the world of the arsehole and his spotty sidekick. For a little while, he'd enjoyed hearing about the arsehole and his problems. He was hanging on by his fingernails, Sabrina said. Sam's lawyers had flown in and torn the place apart after Sango got blown away. Then it had got too much. The images of ugly Annabel lying in wait for him in the corridor; the arsehole and his vomit-inducing pep talks. Gideon didn't want anything to do with anyone remotely connected to that world.

Really, he wanted to get away from everyone and everything, including Catherine – especially Catherine. For a second, when she first mentioned the money, he'd been tempted to turn it down. To tell her he didn't need her – that he would do it all on his own. But he did need it. It wouldn't be forever. One day, in the not-too-distant future, he'd be free, independent, not need anyone. Maybe he should call Sino back; maybe they could work something out together – something legal. It was tempting. Sino was a nice guy, someone you could get through to – not like those other Chinese who'd wanted to bring in their own workers.

Gideon looked at the clock. It was almost time to go and pick up the kids. He looked at the phone. Should he call Sino? He put out his hand and picked up the receiver. He stared at it for a while, then put it down again. He had a feeling he'd better think things through – work out exactly what he wanted – before getting hold of the Chinese again.

What did he want? He wanted money. For most of his life, that was all he'd wanted; he'd wanted it so badly that he hadn't thought about anything else. That was poverty for you – all-absorbing. So absorbing that he'd assumed he'd do anything for money – and he had. He'd begged, borrowed and stolen; he'd done all the worst things you could do for money, but with hindsight, what he'd done hadn't been that bad. Begging wasn't so bad, if you didn't have a choice. Borrowing was fine – everyone borrowed – and where was the shame in stealing when the state was the biggest criminal of all?

Then he'd gone to work for Sam and it had turned out there were things he wasn't prepared to do for money. It wasn't because the job was that bad – he'd been through far worse – and it wasn't that there was anything to be ashamed about; most people were impressed when they found out who he worked for, but he couldn't do it. He wasn't sure why. It had something to do with the fact that he had to exert himself, to motivate himself, to do something he didn't give a damn about. Before, in the old days, you could survive anything because you didn't give a damn and you weren't expected to. Back then, it was exactly the opposite; you were a slave. You were only doing it because you had to – because you were forced to. Everyone understood that – the oppressor and the oppressed – and that had made it easier.

Now it was different. Now you were expected to give a damn – to care about things that nobody normal could possibly give a damn about, like selling stuff that nobody really needed. That was it. Before, you could be honest. You could hate people, and be sullen and obstructive, and no-one was surprised. Actually, it was easier to be those things, because then you lived up to everyone's expectations – everyone's worst expectations – which made them secure and by extension made *you* secure.

Now, different things were expected, and when you behaved in the old way, you made people insecure, and that made you insecure. That was why everyone was walking around pretending to care, pretending to give a damn. Maybe some of them did, but most of them didn't. They couldn't have, because he didn't, and he was pretty much like everyone else.

What could he do instead? He had no idea, but with the legacy from Catherine at least he had some breathing space. He needed it. There was so much still to absorb and to do. It had been a shock finding out the truth about who he was; a nice shock, but still a shock. Then that policeman had freaked him out – and he still had that loan shark, Simon, breathing down his neck. With Catherine's money, he could pay him now. That was a load off his mind. It meant he was free again to focus on unfinished business...

CHAPTER 21

Changes in China

Sino could sense something was not right the moment he walked into the Fu partners' offices. The people who manned the reception desk were behaving normally, but they kept him in the reception area rather than letting him go upstairs as usual. Mr Zheng's secretary appeared a few minutes later to fetch him.

They knew each other quite well and normally they chatted while he waited for the Fus, but today she simply greeted him and took him directly to Mr Zheng's office without saying another word. She'd been the same on the phone; curt and to the point. It was the first time Sino had ever been to the top floor of the Fus' building, let alone into Mr Zheng's office.

Mr Zheng came round the desk. He was pale and his eyes were all over the place. There was no sign of the usual grin and welcoming words. Miss Li was nowhere to be seen. He motioned Sino to a chair and asked him if he wanted tea, then simply stood there, quivering slightly. Sino waited. A few minutes passed. Mr Zheng was obviously extremely upset.

"What is it?" Sino asked, suddenly impatient. "Where's Miss Li?"

Mr Zheng opened his mouth but seemed unable to utter a sound. Sino got up and went and stood in front of him. Suddenly, the man stumbled and clutched at Sino. He caught Mr Zheng under the arms and put him back on his feet. Mr Zheng stood there swaying for a few more seconds and then burst into tears.

Sino helped him to a chair and squatted down in front of him. The man was so agitated he couldn't speak. "What is it?" Sino said, trying to sound calm and polite.

"Miss Li's been taken away," Mr Zheng moaned.

Sino's back straightened. "What?"

"The police came and took her."

Sino was stunned. "What did they say?"

"Nothing. They just took her."

"What did she say?"

"Nothing. She just went."

"But she's got friends! She knows people!"

Mr Zheng nodded. He looked like someone who'd just heard he has only weeks to live.

"It must be a misunderstanding," said Sino. "What could it be?"

Mr Zheng didn't seem to hear him. He was staring fixedly at the wall in front of him.

Sino got him a cup of tea and helped him drink some. It was like handling an incapacitated patient.

Sino's impatience returned. Mr Zheng was over-reacting. Miss Li might be in some sort of trouble, but there was no reason to behave like this. Sino imagined her in the interrogation room. She would probably be scaring the police.

He put his hand on Mr Zheng's shoulder. "It'll be alright," he said. "It's probably a misunderstanding. She'll be back soon."

Mr Zheng shook his head, managing to look miserable and terrified at the same time.

"What's she done?" Sino demanded.

Mr Zheng said nothing.

"She must have done something really bad if you're this worried."

Mr Zheng looked up at Sino. Normally, the dyed hair and the suits took years off him, but now he looked old and weak.

"What's going to happen to her?" Sino asked. It was infuriating, standing next to this man, who seemed to know what was going on but who was saying nothing.

Mr Zheng looked away and started shaking his head.

Sino squatted down in front of him and held his shoulders, trying to make him look him in the eyes, but Mr Zheng just looked away.

"They're not going to kill her, for heaven's sake!" Sino exclaimed.

Mr Zheng shivered like a hypothermia patient.

There was no point in staying. Every word seemed to turn Mr Zheng into more of a nervous wreck, and it was clear he wasn't going to say any more. The whole thing was very strange. Sino had the impression that Mr Zheng had been about to tell him what was going on, but for some reason, he'd pulled back at the last minute.

By the time Sino got back to his office, he'd decided he better tell the CEO. He'd almost gone straight to the Chinese MD but he would probably have forbidden Sino from telling anyone else as soon as he heard the news, and if the chairman found out that he had known about Miss Li and said nothing…

Sino waited till lunchtime and then took the stairs to the top floor to avoid bumping into one of the MD's people. He knew the Chinese would have decamped to the canteen by now. The CEO preferred to have lunch in his office, so he would probably be there. Sino walked to the door of the executive suite and knocked. There was no answer. He opened the door. The outer office was empty – the secretary had gone for lunch. Sino moved towards the open door of the CEO's office. He could hear voices. Suddenly, a Chinese man appeared – it was the chairman's right-hand man.

"What is it?" he asked in English.

"I wanted to see – " Sino said.

The CEO appeared at the door. He smiled at Sino and invited him into the office. He frequently said his door was always open – that people should feel free to come and see him if they had anything to discuss, but no-one ever did.

"Have a seat," said the CEO.

Sino sat down. The CEO followed suit. The Chinese man loitered nearby, somehow managing to give the impression that he wasn't listening.

"I came to tell you that Miss Li has been arrested," Sino said.

The CEO raised his eyebrows but said nothing.

"Who told you?" the Chinese man asked.

"Mr Zheng."

"You went to see him?"

"Yes."

"Why?"

"His secretary called and asked me to come over," Sino continued.

"Why did he want to see you?"

Sino shook his head. "I don't know. He didn't tell me anything, except that Miss Li had been taken away by the police."

"He invited you over to tell you that Miss Li had been arrested?" The Chinese man was asking all the questions.

"That's all he told me when I got there." Sino paused. "Mr Zheng was very upset."

"Do you have any idea why she was arrested?" the CEO asked Sino.

Sino shook his head. He looked inquisitively at the Chinese man.

The man stared back at him but didn't react. It was impossible to know whether he knew anything.

Sino looked back at the CEO and smiled politely.

The man told him to keep the news strictly confidential and to inform him as soon as he heard anything else, then sent Sino on his way.

After lunch, Sino went to see the MD. Mr Wen got very excited and wanted all the details. He was a little disappointed that Sino didn't know anything; he reprimanded Sino for having told the CEO first and made him promise to report any new information to him the moment he heard anything. He also told Sino to keep quiet about the whole thing.

That afternoon, Sino called Mr Zheng, who still wouldn't discuss anything. It was obvious the man was terribly upset and worried. It was the same story the following day, which was a Friday. On Monday morning, the police came and took Mr Zheng away, along with his computer and most of his files. It was an exact repeat of what had happened to Miss Li.

Sino found out because Mr Zheng's secretary called him as soon as the police had gone. She was in a terrible state. Sino went directly over to the Fus' offices and comforted the secretary. She had no idea why her boss had been taken away; the only thing they'd told her was that he would be taken to the Shanghai detention centre. Sino went to talk to Mr Zheng's operations manager, who was responsible for the factory. He also knew absolutely nothing. Sino told him to keep everything running as normal and decided to go and see Mr Zheng's wife. When he got to the Zhengs' house, a relative told him she'd already gone to the detention centre.

Sino drove there and enquired about Mr Zheng. It was probably a risky thing to do but what could they do to him? Lock him up for asking questions? They asked him who he was and then told him to wait. He found Mrs Zheng among the despondent-looking people in the waiting area. She wasn't saying much but it was obvious she was in a worse state than Mr Zheng had been. She hadn't seen or heard anything of her husband. The police hadn't told her to wait; they hadn't told her anything. She was just sitting there because she didn't know what else to do.

A little over two hours later, Sino was summoned and shown into a room with a table and chairs and ordered to sit down. After waiting alone for almost another hour, two men appeared. One of them sat down and asked Sino who he was and what he wanted.

Sino told them. That was the only question he managed to ask. For the rest of the interview, which lasted about half an hour, he was subjected to a barrage of questions by both men in turn. By the end, Sino was just glad to get out of there. He shepherded Mrs Zheng into his car. She'd been quiet in the waiting area but went to pieces as soon as they got into the car.

As he drove her home, Sino realised he had no idea whether the men who'd questioned him even knew who Mr Zheng was, let alone whether he'd been arrested or what he was supposed to have done. They'd only asked him about himself and his relationship with Mr Zheng. Miss Li hadn't even been mentioned. The only thing Sino had learned was that there was no point in asking the police.

On his way back to work, Sino called Mr Zheng's secretary. The police had been back, the secretary said. They'd gone through the offices with a fine-tooth comb, even though there was nothing left to take. Everyone had been told to continue working as normal. There was nothing else to do. Sino told the secretary to keep an eye on things and to call him if anything went wrong.

Every morning after that, Sino stopped at Mr Zheng's offices on his way to work to check whether they'd heard anything and to make sure the business was running properly. There was no news until Friday morning when someone called Mr Zheng's office and told his secretary he would be back at work on Monday. She called Sino immediately. No other information was given. Sino called Mrs Zheng to find out when Mr Zheng would be home, but she hadn't been contacted – she'd heard nothing about her husband.

Mr Zheng was delivered to his office – without warning – the following Tuesday. He'd been held incommunicado for more than a week. He went straight home without saying a word to anyone. As soon as Sino heard he was back, he called the Zhengs' house, but Mrs Zheng told him there was no point in coming over – her husband was refusing to see anyone.

On Wednesday morning, Sino drove straight to Mr Zheng's offices. The employees at the front desk were almost as pleased to see him as they would have been Mr Zheng. There was no sign of the man. Sino decided to wait. The secretary stuck him in the usual room so he could work. Sino waited until late morning but Mr Zheng still didn't appear. He went and told Mr Zheng's secretary to call him as soon as Mr Zheng arrived, and drove to his office.

The CEO called him in as soon as he got back and demanded to know what was going on. Sino told him what he knew. The chairman's man was still there. He'd been in China for more than a week, which was rather unusual. During the conversation, it became obvious that the company was considering whether to dump the Fus as a supplier. At one point, the CEO said as much, but the chairman's man immediately corrected him, saying no decision had been made. He told Sino not to say a word about their discussion to anyone. If asked, Sino was to say that, as far as he knew, the company had no plans to change any of its suppliers. He was also to deny any knowledge of what had happened to Miss Li or Mr Zheng. As if anyone would believe that!

Mr Zheng's secretary called Sino after lunch. Mr Zheng was back in his office, acting as if nothing had happened. He had ordered a new computer and told her he was not to be disturbed.

Sino went over and was admitted immediately by the people at the reception desk, even though he wasn't expected. He supposed there was no point in treating him like a visitor anymore. They knew him and, anyway, he'd been keeping an eye on the place for more than a week.

Riding up in the lift, it suddenly occurred to Sino that he knew more about what was going on in the Fus' company than he did in the one he worked for. He didn't know much about either, but here at least he knew who was – or was not – making the decisions.

Looking at the loose lift buttons and the dirt in the corners, Sino felt more at home in this building than he did in his own offices. Mr Zheng's premises were anything but slick and fancy: the furniture was cheap, the floors stained and the plants artificial and dusty. In fact, the whole place was a bit of a dump. It looked clean-ish but wasn't, and in some places the paint was peeling off the walls.

In other words, it was a typical Chinese workplace. The doors and the walls were normal – that is, not see-through – and the small offices were stuffed to bursting point with people and papers. When you walked in to offices where the people knew you, they immediately jumped up to clear a space in the mountains of clutter, so that you had somewhere to sit.

It was a nice change from the uniform zoo of cubicles outside Sino's glass cage, where everyone was required to keep their workspace clean and tidy, like children in a kindergarten.

Stepping out of the lift, Sino realised he had never really noticed Mr Zheng's offices before. He supposed it was because Miss Li's poisonous atmosphere had crowded everything else out. It was incredible, but after just two weeks her odour of dissonance had disappeared completely. The place seemed utterly transformed; it was as if she'd never been here. For Sino, it was the first time he'd ever felt relaxed and comfortable in a working environment.

The people on Mr Zheng's floor greeted him as if he belonged there. That was a nice change. For some reason, westerners hardly ever greeted you. In all those years of working in London, hardly anyone had ever said good morning or goodbye. They didn't greet you at his company's Shanghai offices either – the company had brought its western manners with it. Only here – in Mr Zheng's shabby offices – did people seem pleased to see him.

He knocked on Mr Zheng's door and walked in. Unusually, Mr Zheng stayed seated behind his desk. He acknowledged Sino and waved him to a chair. He appeared to be re-arranging his desk, but it was obvious he wasn't actually doing anything.

Once Sino was seated, Mr Zheng stood up and came towards him with his usual smile on his face. To a stranger, he would have seemed completely normal, but he was moving slowly and carefully, like a man not too sure on his feet. Sino rose slowly and put out his hand. Mr Zheng's hand slid into his. The grip was weaker than before. Mr Zheng didn't look him in the eye and he was swallowing a lot.

Sino sat down and leaned forward. Mr Zheng lowered himself into a chair. As he sat down, he nodded at Sino, looking at the lower half of his face. "Thank you," he said, referring to what Sino had done while he'd been away.

Sino nodded back.

They sat, staring at the table, while Mr Zheng's secretary brought in tea and poured it out.

Mr Zheng leaned back holding his tea and sipped it in silence.

"Have they finished with you?" Sino asked softly.

Mr Zheng pursed his lips together and nodded. Moving his head seemed to require a lot of effort. His eyes were fixed on the table.

After a few seconds of silence, Sino mentioned that the company might be considering dumping Mr Zheng as a supplier.

Mr Zheng didn't react. It was as if he hadn't heard. For a while, they both sat there drinking their tea.

"Miss Li is not coming back?" Sino asked.

Mr Zheng started nodding and then suddenly shook his head.

Sino leaned forward. "Will you carry on?"

Mr Zheng nodded gently. At that moment, he didn't look capable of doing anything.

Sino leaned across and put his hand on Mr Zheng's arm.

Mr Zheng looked at it, and then at Sino. His eyes were wet but he was in control of himself. "There was nothing I could do," he said. "She was involved with people and things I didn't know anything about."

Sino just sat there listening.

"She wasn't as bad as they will say, you know," Mr Zheng went on.

"She didn't do anything wrong; she just did things the way they've always been done." He inhaled sharply and shivered. "Now, they've changed the way things are done. New people have taken over."

He stared at the wall.

"What does that mean?" Sino asked.

"We will have to learn to work with new people," Mr Zheng said.

Sino was dying to find out what had happened but it was obvious that Mr Zheng wasn't ready to talk about it.

They sat there for a few more minutes in silence until Mr Zheng stood up. "Come and see me next week."

As soon as Sino got back to his office, the CEO's secretary appeared and told him to go upstairs immediately. She beat the hapless MD by a millisecond. Sino shrugged apologetically as he walked passed the man.

"So what's happening with the Fus?" the CEO said in his overly friendly manner as soon as Sino had sat down. The chairman's man was nowhere to be seen.

Sino told him what he knew.

"So Zheng's in the clear?" the CEO said. "Free to carry on with the business?"

Sino nodded. "It looks like it."

The CEO turned back to Sino. "I suppose the whole of Shanghai knows about this by now?"

Sino nodded again.

"So the Fus –" the CEO stopped, and grinned at Sino. "I suppose we should stop calling them the 'Fus', since there's only one 'Fu' now."

Sino smiled politely back at him.

"And he's not had much 'Fu' lately," the CEO went on, still grinning.

Sino could see the man's tongue moving around his mouth. He had a habit of licking his lips when he talked. Sino wondered why he didn't drink more tea or water.

The CEO turned back to Sino. "How do people normally react when someone gets arrested like this? I mean, people who know the person?"

"I'm not sure what you mean," said Sino.

"Well, do they typically put some distance between them and the 'arrestee'? Or do they rally round?"

"I don't know… It depends."

"Well, if you were arrested in London," said the CEO, "you can be sure that everyone you know – friends, colleagues, customers, suppliers, the whole lot – would drop you like a hot potato. You know what I mean?"

Sino nodded. "Yes."

"Well, is it the same here? Or do people here stick together? Stand up for each other when the police come and kick their doors in?"

"It really depends on the relationship," replied Sino.

The CEO, who had stayed on his feet, looked down at Sino. "I thought maybe the Chinese were, you know, a bit more loyal. You know, because of 'old values'" – the CEO held up his hands and waved his fingers to indicate quotation marks – "and because these kinds of arrests are probably politically motivated."

Sino stared at the man, wondering whether to say nothing or to start waffling on about everything and nothing like he used to do with the Fus.

The CEO looked at him. "Did you know that we own nearly half of Zheng's company?"

Sino sat up a bit straighter. He hadn't known.

"Obviously not," the CEO grinned. "The question is, what do we do now?"

Sino decided to take a chance. It was the first time a westerner had ever consciously given him information that he didn't have already. "Is the company considering selling its stake?" he asked cautiously.

The CEO guffawed. "Are you interested in buying it?"

Sino didn't say anything.

"Seriously," said the CEO, "do you think this is it for Zheng's company, or do you think he can keep the thing going?"

"I really don't know."

"Come on," said the CEO. "You've been dealing with these people for a long time. You must know something."

Sino tried to think of an answer.

"Or don't you give a shit?" The CEO was watching him like a hawk.

"What?"

"Do you care about Zheng and his company – whether it survives or not?" The CEO paused. "It's a simple question."

Sino hadn't thought about the implications of Mr Zheng going out of business. His secretary might have to go back to her village, which was a long way away, in Sichuan province. He might never see her again. Mr Zheng would be finished; he was too old to do anything else.

"Yes, I do care," said Sino. "Mr Zheng is a good man. There are hundreds of people working for him – they would all be out on the street."

"Okay," said the CEO. "This is what we do. You go over there and find out what's going on. We need to be sure that Zheng is in the clear and to find out what his plans are."

"Why?" said Sino.

"Because if he is in the clear and he's looking for help, we might be willing to increase our stake, or even buy him out, if he's thinking about selling." The man paused and raised a finger. "But you had better not say anything to anyone, including him. We need to keep this under wraps until we have a clear picture of the situation. You understand?"

Sino nodded. He didn't, but he had a feeling the CEO wasn't in the mood to explain himself.

The following week, Sino went back to see Mr Zheng. He felt at home in Shanghai now. The city had stopped changing, at least as quickly as before. During his years away, every trip back had been to a different Shanghai. It wasn't so much that there were new buildings going up all the time – that had been happening for as long he could remember – it was more that so much was disappearing; houses, shops and old buildings were vanishing all the time. On some of his trips, he came home to find that entire streets, whole areas of the city, had disappeared completely.

Sometimes, it seemed the only thing that hadn't changed was Mr Zheng's place. The factory looked the same as it always had.

Sino remembered it vaguely. It was the only building in the area that was older than he was. Sino knew that inside it had been completely transformed into a modern manufacturing plant, but outside, it still looked the same. Only the signs had changed. It probably should have been knocked down. It looked out of place. It had that old drab, dilapidated appearance; what China used to look like.

Sino drove through the open gate towards the office building, which was situated at the far end of the factory. He parked in his usual space. It was some distance from the office entrance but he knew the car would be safe here. If you parked near the front door, where the cars were too close together, your doors could get scratched or dented by careless drivers.

Some of the factory workers were loitering nearby, smoking. Their overalls were cleaner than they'd once been and now they smoked outside but otherwise their habits had hardly changed. China was a bit like a new zoo full of old animals; the cages didn't stay clean and shiny for long.

Thinking about it, things hadn't actually changed that much. Sino could still navigate here without thinking too much. In fact, it was better *not* to think too much, especially when you thought about had happened to Miss Li and Mr Zheng. They still hadn't heard a word about Miss Li; it was as if she had disappeared off the face of the Earth.

Mr Zheng was reading a letter when Sino walked into his office.

He tossed it away with a resigned cluck.

"What is it?" Sino asked.

"Another customer giving us notice," Mr Zheng said.

"How important were they?" Sino asked.

"Fairly important," said Mr Zheng. He admitted that the company's customers were deserting them in droves. Sino's company was one of the few who hadn't yet said anything.

They went off to get some lunch together. Mr Zheng had recovered remarkably well since his arrest. He still wasn't talking about it or about Miss Li, but he was back to his old self – except he seemed slightly older. There was something about the way he moved and talked and generally conducted himself that made Sino think of an older person. Maybe he'd been like that before and Sino just hadn't noticed. Sino decided to tell him what the CEO had said.

Mr Zheng dug in his rice bowl for a while and then turned to Sino. "And what about you?"

"Me?"

"Yes," Mr Zheng said. "What are your plans?"

"I don't have any."

"I thought they might want to buy me out," Mr Zheng went on, "or failing that, they will cut their losses and walk away. They will never leave me in charge, especially after this."

"How do you know?"

Mr Zheng spat a fish bone on to his plate. "I won't sell," he said.

"Why?"

He grinned at Sino. "I can't afford to. My whole family works here – my extended family."

"But you're losing customers hand over fist. How will you survive?"

Mr Zheng took a slurp of tea and shouted for more. "We'll survive." He waited until the tea had been replenished and then, munching away, muttered: "Why don't you come and work here?"

The question was thrown out so casually that Sino almost didn't realise it had been asked.

"It would make my secretary very happy," Mr Zheng chuckled.

For some reason, the offer made Sino feel exhilarated. He didn't know why, it was meaningless; the company was on its last legs.

Mr Zheng patted him on the shoulder. "Think about it," he said. "I need a new partner."

"Have you heard anything of Miss Li?" Sino asked. He didn't know why he was asking.

Mr Zheng looked down at his plate, and then shook his head. After a few seconds, he looked at Sino. "She's not coming back."

Sino knew that already. He didn't know how he knew, but things had changed so much in the past few weeks that it was obvious they couldn't go back to the way they were. It was incredible how fast everything had changed. Sometimes, years went by and nothing changed – like when he was in London – but at other times, like now, everything could change within a matter of weeks. Miss Li hardly seemed real anymore.

Sino spent the rest of the week thinking about what Mr Zheng had said. It was obvious the man had a plan, otherwise he would have leaned on Sino to persuade the company to buy him out, but he'd been categorical that he wouldn't sell.

Ordinarily, Sino wouldn't have dreamt of giving up his job at a western company to go and work for a local Chinese firm, especially one in a position like Mr Zheng's, but Mr Zheng hadn't offered him a job. The word he'd used was 'partner'. That put things in a completely different light.

Thinking about it, the prospects for Mr Zheng's company might not be so bad. It made essential components for several types of machines and, thanks to the processes and quality-control mechanisms that had been foisted on Mr Zheng by Sino's employer, his products were among the best available. All he needed were some new customers.

On Monday, Sino went to see the CEO, who wasn't there. His secretary told Sino that his usual Sunday evening flight from Hong Kong had been cancelled so he was coming in on the morning plane. As Sino turned to leave the office, the chairman's man appeared in the doorway. Sino hadn't even known he was in the country.

He nodded at Sino. "How's Mr Zheng?"

He'd obviously overheard some of Sino's conversation with the CEO's secretary.

"He's okay."

"When did you last see him?"

"Last week."

"Why?"

Sino didn't know why. He saw Mr Zheng every week. "The CEO sent me to find out what his plans were."

"And did you?"

"Not really," said Sino, cautiously, "but he seems to be in the clear."

The chairman's man stared at Sino for a few seconds. "Don't go back there."

"What? Why?"

"We are no longer working with Mr Zheng."

"But he's done nothing wrong," said Sino. "They've let him go. It's Miss Li they were after."

The chairman's man took a step towards Sino. "As of now, no-one in this company is permitted to communicate with Mr Zheng or anyone connected to him." He leaned closer to Sino. "And that means privately, too."

He waited. Sino didn't react. The man turned on his heel and walked away.

Sino resigned the following day – or at least tried to. He'd woken up at two in the morning and tossed and turned for nearly two hours before deciding he was going to stay with the company. Then he fell asleep and woke up an hour and a half later, having decided he was going to resign. By the time he got to work, he was back where he'd been the day before – nowhere.

But when he walked into the room with all the cubicles and saw the wall of glass offices behind which he and the rest of the ground-floor managers spent their days, he made up his mind. He couldn't stay; he was already too far gone to come back. All he had was Mr Zheng's vague mention of a partnership, but the events of the past weeks had taken him too far away. It was like he'd jumped out of a plane. The only question was whether the parachute was going to open.

Sino felt uneasy about the prospect of working with Mr Zheng. The man was dodgy, there was no doubt about that, but Sino was certain that the only thing Mr Zheng ever broke was the law – and he didn't break it badly. The two of them had clicked from the start. Even in the poisonous atmosphere of the early days, they had developed a relationship that transcended Miss Li.

The Chinese MD took Sino's news very badly. Sino tried to make him understand that it had nothing to do with him. But Mr Wen wasn't having any of it. He refused point-blank to even discuss it, let alone accept Sino's resignation. Sino tried again the following day, but the man still wouldn't talk to him. Sino desperately wanted to avoid going above Mr Wen's head to the CEO, but the end of the month was approaching and Mr Zheng was impatient for him to start as soon as possible.

On the penultimate day of the month, Sino went to the MD again for the last time. If the man wouldn't accept his resignation today, he would have to tell the CEO. He opened the MD's door, and walked straight into the CEO, who happened to be in the MD's office. As soon as the man found out Sino was leaving to go and work for Mr Zheng, he ordered him out of the building. Sino waited in the driveway while a colleague retrieved his personal belongings from his office and handed them to him in a plastic bag. That was it. After more than four years at the company, they hadn't even allowed him to say goodbye to anyone, let alone to serve out his notice. He had seen people treated with more dignity in a public hospital. It was another marvellous display of the trust the company had in its employees and it was plain stupid. If he'd really wanted to steal something or sabotage the computer systems, he could have done it on the way to the MD's office to hand in his notice.

Still, at least it was over. He was *free*. It was a strange feeling, walking to his car. He'd spent his entire adult life doing the bidding of westerners and suddenly, in a matter of minutes, it was all over – all those connections, all his relationships, everything he'd ever done since leaving China all those years ago, were behind him. He'd imagined this moment for years, but there wasn't much to enjoy. He was now seriously worried about what was going to happen to Mr Zheng's company.

Mr Zheng was delighted to see him and even more delighted that he could start work immediately. He told his secretary to book a dining room at a nearby restaurant for a celebratory dinner that same evening.

"It's up to us now," Mr Zheng told Sino, as he showed him to his new office, which was in no way fit to work in. "We have to find new customers – and quickly – otherwise we won't be able to pay ourselves or the rest of these people." As he finished the sentence, Mr Zheng waved an arm at the factory building, which was visible through the window.

Sino stared at him.

"Are you with me?" Mr Zheng smiled.

Sino nodded eagerly. "Yes, of course." He didn't have a clue where to start.

That evening, they drove to the restaurant in Mr Zheng's car. Before they went in, Mr Zheng opened the boot and pulled out a few bottles of Chinese Cabernet from a box he obviously kept in there.

"For emergencies," he chuckled, handing Sino two bottles to carry.

In their private dining room, Mr Zheng proposed a toast to the company's future and then proceeded to order everything that Sino and his new colleagues couldn't normally afford to eat.

After they'd demolished most of the food and the wine, Mr Zheng started talking about – of all things – Sino's old employer.

"The agents that do the selling for your company – sorry, for your previous employer." Mr Zheng grinned. "I suppose they have exclusive rights to represent the company in the areas where they work?"

Sino shook his head. None of the agents had any special rights to represent the company, not even the ugly bastard with the yellow teeth and the bad wig. Sino was sure Mr Zheng must have known this already.

"So how did you stop them from selling other companies' products?" Mr Zheng asked.

Sino hesitated.

"Did they sell other companies' products?" Mr Zheng persisted.

Sino grinned at him. "Well, never to us."

Mr Zheng found that very funny. He nearly choked on the last piece of lobster that he had told Sino to eat and then reluctantly agreed to chomp himself.

"So your agents are free to represent other companies," Mr Zheng remarked.

"Certainly not," said Sino, still grinning.

"But the company hasn't given them any exclusive rights," said Mr Zheng, motioning to the waiter to fill up their wine glasses.

Sino shook his head.

"So it's not treating them fairly."

Sino shook his head again.

"This is typical of westerners," Mr Zheng said, shaking his head indignantly. "They're as bad as the Japanese."

Then he started talking about the quality problems associated with products sold by Sino's former employer. "They think they can sell us their shit products because we're Chinese," Mr Zheng muttered.

Sino kept quiet. He'd heard that, in the past, the company had tried to dump stuff it couldn't sell in the west on to the Chinese, but now all of its products were made in China, so it was all pretty much the same.

Mr Zheng looked at Sino closely. "The company doesn't care that these agents are trading on the strength of their relationships. Every time something goes wrong, it undermines the agent and makes him look bad."

Mr Zheng was right about that. On frequent occasions, agents had stormed into Sino's office and thrown a fit after their customers had complained about the lousy quality of the company's products. Sino had always brought it to the MD's attention, but he couldn't do anything about it, and the CEO didn't give a damn. "As long as they're selling the stuff, it can't be that bad," he'd once remarked. Sino nodded at Mr Zheng. He'd never dared mention that Mr Zheng's components were frequently implicated in the quality problems. He wasn't going to mention it now.

"I suppose you know these agents rather well?" said Mr Zheng, emptying the last of the wine into Sino's glass.

Lying in bed that night, Sino felt a little uneasy at the thought of co-opting the company's agents to work for Mr Zheng, but why shouldn't he? It wasn't as if he owed the company anything. They'd treated him like dirt. They'd never trusted him and they didn't trust their agents either. They didn't trust the Chinese, period. Westerners never trusted anyone. That was why they always showed up with contracts and lawyers; why they always wrote everything down.

That pretty much summed up the whole history of the west's relationship with China. It was amazing how little had changed; they were still using Chinese agents to sell things to the Chinese. At least they'd moved on from peddling opium.

Sino turned over. Why shouldn't he offer the agents the chance to represent his new employer? It wasn't as if he would be breaking a law or doing anything wrong, and the agents were free to refuse Mr Zheng's offer. Sino rolled over again and concentrated on falling asleep. He knew none of the agents would refuse. Mr Zheng would just be someone else to sell for.

A few days later, they heard that Ms Li had been sentenced to 14 years' hard labour for paying bribes to local officials in exchange for contracts.

"Seems pretty harsh," Sino remarked, showing Mr Zheng the newspaper article.

Mr Zheng shrugged. "Not so long ago they would have executed her," he said.

"How did you manage to stay out of it?" Sino asked.

Mr Zheng looked at him. "She never told me anything. Her job was to get the contracts; mine was to fulfil them. That was how it worked."

Mr Zheng looked out of the window of his little office building. "She didn't do anything wrong, you know. She was just a little boat caught out at sea when the wind changed."

"How did you convince them you weren't involved?" Sino asked.

Mr Zheng shook his head. "I didn't."

Sino frowned.

"You can't convince them," said Mr Zheng. "There's no point in trying. They aren't interested in what you've got to say..." He swallowed and took a breath. "They don't listen. They don't even start to listen until –" he broke off.

Sino kept looking at him, trying not to seem too curious.

"By the time they bring you in, they know pretty much everything already," Mr Zheng continued. "They just keep going until you..." He paused, and swallowed, "Until you tell them what they are waiting to hear."

Sino looked at the floor. "Did they do very bad things to you?" He knew the answer. He remembered what Mr Zheng had looked like the day after he was released.

Mr Zheng started nibbling at his thumbnail.

Sino glanced at him. He wasn't sure he really wanted to know.

Mr Zheng shook his head. "Not to me."

Sino sat up straighter.

"It was the pictures," said Mr Zheng, staring at the table.

"Pictures," said Sino. "What pictures?"

Mr Zheng started shaking. "Photographs of what had been done to people who didn't cooperate. What people looked like when they'd finished with them." The look in his eyes was horrible.

"What?" said Sino. "What did they do? Who did they do it to?"

Mr Zheng shook his head, and wiped his eyes. "I don't know who the people were. I didn't recognise them. Some of them were unrecognisable."

"They said they would do the same to you?" Sino whispered.

Mr Zheng swallowed and shook his head. "Not to me... To my wife, my daughter!" Suddenly, he sat up straight and slammed his fists on the table, then he burst into tears and sank back into his chair.

Sino touched his arm. They sat there in silence for a while. Eventually, Mr Zheng leaned forward and picked up his tea. His hands were still shaking.

"What I never understood," said Sino, "was how you could stand her?"

Mr Zheng smiled sorrowfully. "She was – is – not an easy woman to get along with, and she could be very nasty, but sometimes we have to be nasty to survive."

Sino could still see the odd tear emerging from Mr Zheng's eyes.

"I'm afraid I couldn't understand your relationship," Sino said. "She was just the most obnoxious, terrifying person I've ever known. She seemed hardly human. She was evil."

"No-one is evil," said Mr Zheng. "We are all just products of our past."

"Her past must have been terrible."

Mr Zheng nodded. "It was."

"Where did she come from?"

Mr Zheng shook his head. "I only know that she was abandoned as a baby by her parents, because she was crippled and a girl."

Mr Zheng stopped to compose himself. "She wound up in an

orphanage," he muttered. "In those days, you didn't survive a state orphanage without turning to stone."

"Terrible," said Sino. "But how did you get mixed up with her?"

Mr Zheng started quivering. "My mother told me about her just before she died."

Sino stared at him.

Mr Zheng took a wobbly breath. "So I went to find her."

Sino stared harder.

Mr Zheng nodded. "She is my sister."

Sino stood up and went and looked out of the window. There was nothing here; nothing to China. It was just holes; the worst holes in the world. They thought they'd built a fundament – with all their towers, railways and motorways – but really there was nothing. They were just floating above a vacuum.

Mr Zheng came and stood next to him. After a while, he turned and looked Sino in the face. "It's better than it used to be," he said, putting his hand on Sino's arm.

Sino stared back at him.

Mr Zheng nodded. "Now – most of the time – tomorrow is like today, and the day after is much the same again."

Sino turned back to the window. The view was clouded by the dirty glass and the haze outside, but he could still see the towers of Shanghai in the distance.

"The worst thing would be to throw it all away," said Mr Zheng, "to start over. That never works. We have to keep at it. We have to keep working and building, so that in the end there's something solid and enduring to hold us all, to hold everything, together."

CHAPTER 22

Killing Reg again

For a while, Gideon had been tempted to tell that white policeman the truth about what Reg had done to the man on the street, but how could he explain that he knew it was Reg? He'd have to admit he knew who Reg was and then they might question his mother. She would go to pieces and the whole story would come out.

If they charged Reg, Gideon would have to be a witness and then Reg would know who he was. Even if Reg went to jail – and there was not much chance of that since the police were totally corrupt and incompetent – it wouldn't be for long.

No; the cleanest, simplest solution was still a bullet between Reg's eyes. Gideon had messed it up. He hadn't prepared himself properly – he'd just got a gun and gone looking for Reg. No wonder it had been a disaster. Now he had to get another gun, but he'd learned from the experience. Next time, it would be different, he'd be prepared. He was going to plan and rehearse the whole thing until he had it down pat.

It took a few days to get hold of another gun. This one was a .38 Special – a revolver. It had once been police issue, but on the street it was known as a 'lady's gat', because it had a weak kick and not much penetrating power – at least not compared with the 9 mm or the Magnums. It was a nice little gun. It had a snub-nose, it was easy to hide – you could almost palm it – and because it was a revolver, it never jammed, unlike the 9 mm. Apparently, this one was clean – it had never been used. It was also a 'civilised' gun, the seller assured Gideon. He said that if the bullet came out, it would make the same-sized hole as it had on the way in. A round from a Magnum always made a hell of a mess on the way out, particularly if it was a shot to the head, the man explained.

Gideon had pretended to know all this and had complained that he wanted a big-calibre pistol, but after struggling with the lost

9mm, he was secretly glad to have what looked like a beginner's revolver. It was obvious how to use it and he could see that one could clean it pretty well without taking it apart. Gideon was too embarrassed to ask the seller for a lesson in gun-stripping.

Once he had the gun, he drove out into the veld to do some practising. He had two boxes of 25 rounds each so he had plenty of bullets to play with. He carefully loaded the gun, noticing for the first time that it only took five bullets. He retrieved an empty Coke can from his car and planted it atop some long grass so that it was suspended almost at head height, then moved back till he was about ten metres away. Holding the gun with both hands, he closed one eye and aimed. Then he closed that eye and opened the other one. Now he was off-target, obviously. He realised that he no clue how to aim a gun at something. He turned his head slightly and tried to look at the target with both eyes. He managed it, but had the feeling that he was way off the mark.

There was only one thing for it. He braced himself, and with both eyes open, pulled back the hammer. He aimed again and gently squeezed the trigger as the seller had instructed. The gun kicked back gently. He was surprised at how quiet it was. He'd thought he might have to fire a few shots and then leave, to avoid attracting attention, but out here on the open veld, the sound of the gunshot just dissipated into nothing. The can hadn't moved – it was bobbing very slightly on top of the stems of long grass that he'd stuffed into its opening. Gideon took two steps forward, closed one eye, and tried again. The can didn't register. He moved forward again and tried to position the barrel directly between alternate winks. He fired. The can moved, but the shot didn't dislodge it. Gideon walked up to it. There was no sign of damage; the bullet must have touched the clump of grass underneath it. He moved forward again and this time hit the can. The bullet went directly through it. He was a bit disappointed; he had expected it to be mangled or at least to have been blown off the grass, but it just had a small hole through it and a tiny dent on one side.

It had been incredibly difficult to hit. Gideon had had to get really close. He wouldn't have had a hope of hitting Reg from where he'd been that night, especially in the dark. Thank God he hadn't tried. Reg might have been carrying a gun himself. He would have shot back and probably not missed.

Gideon reloaded the revolver and carried on firing and reloading until he'd emptied one of the boxes. Even though the .38 didn't kick hard, his arm was starting to ache. The can was looking worse for wear, but it was still recognisably a can. More than half of the shots had missed. Reg was a lot bigger than a can, but Gideon would have to get very close before he pulled the gun. Until now, Gideon had assumed that one bullet would be enough to finish Reg off, but now he wasn't so sure. He might need all five.

When he first decided to blow Reg away, it had all seemed so simple. He would walk up to him, say something like: "I've got a message for you from Joseph Mathonsi," and then pull out the gun and – bang – plant a bullet right between Reg's ugly eyes. But Reg's head wasn't that big. Maybe he should shoot him in the chest first. He would probably miss the heart – Gideon wasn't sure exactly how high up in the chest the heart was – but at least a bullet in the chest area would floor him; then Gideon could get really close and finish him off with one to the head.

Gideon looked in the direction in which he had been firing. He realised he had no idea – not the faintest clue – how far bullets travel. For all he knew, the shots he'd fired could have hit something far away. No, the land was uneven. They would have hit earth. What happened when bullets ran out of momentum? Did they gradually sink lower and lower until they eventually skidded into the ground, or did they just stop dead and fall out of the air? Gideon was tempted to fire a bullet up into the air. He'd often wondered what happened to those, especially when he saw revolutionaries on TV driving around in jeeps shooting into the air. At some point, those bullets had to stop going up. What would happen if one landed on your head? He pointed the revolver at the sky, but if he fired it, the bullet might land on his head. There wasn't much chance of that but Gideon wasn't going to risk it. He emptied the spent cartridges out of the gun and walked back to the car. He couldn't believe he'd been stupid enough to go looking for Reg with a pistol that he'd never fired.

Gideon thought about getting a bigger gun; maybe one that

didn't need you to be so accurate. He'd heard that the bullet of a .44 Magnum could go straight through the door of a car, through any passengers that happened to be in the line of fire at the time and out the other side. Presumably, with a gun like that, you didn't need to hit someone between the eyes or in the heart. Presumably, you just needed to hit them somewhere on the head or torso. But that would mean buying a third gun. Gideon had only ever intended to buy one gun; he really didn't want to get in touch with the gun man again, he was almost out of money for the month, and he still had to pay an instalment to the loan shark. He was just going to have to get very close to Reg.

At home that afternoon, Gideon mused over how to proceed. The best way would be to find out where Reg lived; then he could choose his moment. Gideon hadn't been able to learn much more about Reg – no-one was talking – but he'd found out which area was controlled by Reg, so at least he knew where to start.

The doorbell rang. Gideon was surprised. Whoever was ringing it must have access to the complex. He looked through the peephole. It was the white policeman from the other night. For a few seconds, Gideon contemplated not answering the door, but why shouldn't he? Why should he hide from this stupid white policeman? They had nothing on him – he'd done nothing, except save some poor bastard's life. Gideon pulled open the front door.

The policeman smiled at him. "Hello, remember me?"

Gideon nodded, moving his jaw around as if chewing an imaginary piece of gum.

"Mind if I come in?" the policeman asked. He was behind the locked security gate.

"I'm not going to answer any more questions," Gideon said, and immediately surprised himself. He hadn't meant to be so blunt or direct; the words had just come out.

"That's okay, I'm not here to ask you more questions," the cop said. "I just popped by to tell you what I found out."

"Why?" Gideon asked.

"I was passing. I thought you'd want to know."

Gideon didn't believe him for a second, but for some reason, he wasn't worried about this policeman anymore. He unlocked the gate.

The man strolled in.

"Want a beer?" Gideon said, expecting him to refuse.

"Ja, thanks," the cop smiled.

Gideon went into the kitchen. The cop went outside on to the veranda and stood there, looking around the garden. "Nice place you've got here," he said, when Gideon came out with the beers.

Gideon sat down at the table on the veranda and stared at the policeman.

"I checked the files," the policeman said, taking a seat opposite Gideon. "We've had a few attacks in that area in the past few months. No deaths; just people who've had the shit kicked out of them until they need hospitalisation."

"This was a hit-and-run," Gideon said.

The cop shook his head. "Your man was fucked up," he said, with the emphasis very much on 'fucked up'. "The fact that he was hit by a car was simply part of the punishment."

Gideon said nothing.

"We don't usually follow these things up," the cop went on. "No personnel, no time. We're not going to follow yours up either."

Gideon put down his beer. "So why are you spending so much time on it?"

"I'm not really," said the cop. "It's just that I don't see patterns that often. We have lots of cases of mindless violence, especially late at night. Most of it is just random, you know – emotional stuff." The policeman paused and poured some beer down his throat. "So when there's a pattern, I notice it," he said. "It's like the sun's come out."

Gideon looked out into the garden and carried on drinking his beer.

The policeman laughed. "Well, these things make you excited if you're a policeman."

Gideon looked back at the man. It was very odd. The other night, he'd felt very uncomfortable in this man's presence – it wasn't that he'd been afraid. It was just that being close to this big Afrikaner had made Gideon tense and stressed – but today, he didn't mind the man. He didn't like him, he didn't dislike him; he felt completely neutral about him.

Sitting here now, he didn't mind that the cop was on his veranda. He didn't want him here, but he wasn't waiting for the man to leave either. Not long ago, if someone had told him that a big Afrikaans policeman would be sitting on his veranda drinking his beer, Gideon would have laughed them out of the room. Now it didn't seem so strange.

The cop was looking around the garden and at the house. In spite of himself, in spite of not giving a shit what this man thought, Gideon was quite pleased that the cop liked his house. He'd never had a compliment from a white man before. Not a real one. He'd heard tons of patronising, pathetic comments at work, but this man had complimented his house without thinking, just because he liked it. Just because it was probably nicer than his own house. It was the first time Gideon could remember a white man saying something genuine to him.

The cop looked at him and smiled. "You know Reg Gumede?"

Gideon almost reacted as the name went into his ears but he managed to stay absolutely still.

"Who?" he enquired.

"Reg Gumede," the cop said, over-articulating the name.

Gideon looked upwards thoughtfully and put his hand to his chin. "No, doesn't ring any bells," he said, slowly shaking his head.

He looked at the policeman innocently.

"Sorry," the cop said, giving Gideon a knowing look. "I said I wouldn't ask you any more questions."

"That's okay," Gideon replied. "It doesn't feel like I'm being interrogated now."

The policeman took another swig of his beer and wiped his mouth with the back of his hand. "I'm pretty certain Gumede is the man behind those attacks."

"Who is he?" Gideon asked, in the most disinterested tone he could muster.

The man stuck his jaw out to one side. "He runs a protection operation in the south. I reckon the victim was a thief and Gumede was trying to scare him off."

Gideon put his empty beer bottle down on the table. "You want another beer?"

The cop shook his head. "I'm driving."

Gideon grinned at him. "You're a big man; I sure you've got enough blood to dilute a second beer."

The cop laughed and patted his stomach. "Well, if you can throw in something to line the gut."

Gideon went into the kitchen. The cop had given him a shock, but now he'd recovered. He'd spent days trying to find out about Reg Gumede – now he had a man on the veranda who probably knew everything he needed to know. He emptied a big packet of chips into a bowl and took it outside with two more beers.

"Thanks," the cop said, pouncing on the chips.

Gideon stared out into the garden and waited for the cop to start talking again. Normally, whites couldn't handle sitting in silence – it made them uncomfortable – but not this man; he just sat there, chomping chips and washing them down with beer.

Eventually, Gideon decided to take the initiative. "Have you talked to the man who got hit?"

The policeman nodded. "Surprise, surprise: he's not talking. His story is pretty much the same as yours."

Gideon shrugged. "That's what happened."

The cop gave him another look. "I can understand why the man is not talking. If I was in his shoes, I'd keep quiet, too."

Gideon looked at him inquisitively. "Reg Gumede must be a bad man."

The policeman nodded.

"I would have thought you – the police, I mean – would be happy to have someone like this man – Gumede – helping you keep the streets clean," Gideon observed.

The cop shook his head. "The problem is, Gumede is terrorising the neighbourhood. In a situation like that, the police can't be effective. He's undermining the system."

Gideon looked at the ground.

The cop looked at him earnestly. "We're not all corrupt and incompetent, you know." He shifted his position. "In many places, the police and the local community work very well together. Reg

Gumede is a hangover from the past; he's like a bad smell that won't go away."

Gideon carried on staring at the ground. He was starting to feel tense. "You seem to know him very well."

The policeman nodded. His nostrils moved as if he was smelling Reg.

"Tell me about him," Gideon said.

"Why?"

"Why not? What else do you want to talk about?"

The policeman swallowed another handful of chips. "He used to be a police informer, back in the '80s."

Gideon moved in his seat.

"He was one those typical apartheid-era informers," the policeman said, looking up at the umbrella covering the veranda. "A bit of a psycho, you know. Should really have been locked up, but because he was useful to the police, he got away with murder." The policeman looked at Gideon. "And I mean murder!"

Gideon stared at the ground. He was holding very tightly on to the arms of his chair.

"I wasn't in the police then," the man continued, "but I heard all about Reg Gumede after I joined the force. What he used to get up to. I can well imagine that many, many people wanted him dead." The cop shrugged. "That's the problem when the state is a criminal. It criminalises the population. There were lots of Reg Gumedes – white and black – who did pretty much whatever they liked and got away with it." He shook his head. "It's incredible, when you think about it. I knew of one guy – a real psycho – who terrorised a whole neighbourhood for years; kidnapping women, stealing cars, beating people up, a real thug. Every charge laid against him was dropped; every attempt to prosecute the bastard failed." The cop exhaled. "I remember one day, this psycho kidnapped this woman – I don't know why. Anyway, he kept her a prisoner for days on end, and did all sorts of really bad things to her – burnt her with cigarettes, and stuff like that. The cops were probably going to do nothing, as usual, but then it turned out that the woman was somehow connected to the editor of one of the big national newspapers."

He pulled in his chin. "Suddenly, after all those years of getting away with everything, the bastard went to jail." The policeman finished his beer. "She killed herself."

"What?" Gideon said.

"The woman he burned with cigarettes. I heard she committed suicide."

Gideon swallowed. He could feel the tears hovering in his tear ducts. "Why don't you kill him? Reg, I mean."

The cop gave him a quizzical look. "That wouldn't be very professional."

"Well, he's never going to jail."

The policeman stuck out his lower lip. "Probably not – at least not as long as no-one is prepared to give evidence against him." The man tapped his fingers impatiently on the table.

"What would be the point?" Gideon snorted.

"Got to start somewhere," the cop said.

"What are you doing here?" Gideon asked him.

"I wanted to know if you knew Reg Gumede."

Gideon didn't answer.

"Do you?" the policeman said.

"I already told you, no."

The cop looked disappointed. He stood up. "Well, thanks for the drinks and chips."

Gideon felt a bit bad. "You take your job very seriously," he said, "for a policeman."

The cop grinned at him good-naturedly.

"What I meant was that it must be difficult to give a damn when so many criminals are getting away with murder," Gideon said, quickly.

The policeman shrugged. "People think the police are just there to catch bad guys, but that's not how I see my job."

Gideon followed him to the door. "How do you see it?"

The policeman turned around and put out his hand. Gideon shook it.

"My job is to protect the community, to help honest and law-abiding people stay safe in their neighbourhoods. That's what gives me job satisfaction. It's not all about catching bad guys." The cop stepped outside and closed the security gate. "Keep safe," he said, smiling. As he spoke, he waved his index finger in Gideon's direction.

Gideon had the impression the man knew exactly what he was planning.

On Saturday, Gideon went to Reg's part of town. He had the .38 Special on his ankle, in the same place as the 9 mm. He would have preferred the gun to be more accessible, but on his ankle it was hardly noticeable. After driving around for a while, he stopped at a bar for a beer. It was just after lunch and the place was emptying out. Gideon decided to take the bull by the horns. "I'm looking for a man called Reg Gumede," he told the barman. "Know him?"

The man was evasive. Gideon ordered a beer and put a note twenty times the price of the beer on the counter. "I need some help with something," he said. "I was told Reg is the man to talk to."

The barman picked up the money and went away for a few minutes, then told Gideon that Reg would be there in half an hour. Gideon spent the next 30 minutes concocting a story for Reg.

He saw him as soon as he walked in. He was a few minutes earlier than anticipated. The barman pointed at Gideon, who was sitting at a table near the window. Reg walked directly up to him, as if he owned the place. "You looking for me?"

Gideon nodded and stood up. He was almost a head taller than Reg and quite a bit broader.

Reg moved so that the table was between them. "What do you want?"

Gideon sat down and waved vaguely at a chair. Reg didn't sit down.

"I have a problem and I was told you might be able to help me."

Reg just stared at him.

"I'm owed some money and I'm looking for someone to get it back for me."

Reg said nothing.

Gideon looked at him inquisitively. "Is it worth continuing this conversation?"

"How much are you owed?" Reg's voice was completely flat and distant.

"I have a few debts to collect, actually," Gideon said, "but the urgent one is currently around R200,000."

"Where do you live?" Reg asked him. He spoke in a patronising, cynical way, as if he was expecting to be lied to.

"Sandton."

Reg sat down and sucked at his teeth. His head was swaying very slightly on his neck. There was something weird about his movements; it was as if his limbs weren't properly connected to his body. Close up, Gideon could see flashes of gold all over Reg's mouth. Quite often, when he blinked, his eyes stayed closed for long enough for you to see his pupils moving around under his eyelids, like something squirming under a sheet.

The rest of Reg's face wasn't bad – it was really only the eyes and the teeth that gave you the creeps. He had a few deep lines around his mouth and across his forehead, but otherwise the skin was totally smooth and had the appearance of burnished brown steel, especially around the temples. His chin was covered with a very fine layer of greying stubble.

In the darkness of the shebeen, Gideon had thought Reg looked evil, but here, with the sunlight coming through the window of the bar, there was no evil in those eyes. They were just empty. It was like looking into space, or into the eyes of a corpse. It wasn't going to be that difficult to kill Reg after all. All Gideon would have to do was look him in the eyes.

"Well?" said Gideon.

Gideon could see Reg's chest inflate slightly as he inhaled.

Reg titled his head slightly to one side and gazed at Gideon. "Who owes you this money?"

"People," said Gideon.

"Why do they owe you this money?"

"I lent it to them."

Reg looked around the room. "How long have you been lending money?"

Gideon shrugged. "A while."

"Why do you need me to get it back?"

Gideon gave him an impatient look. "Is there somewhere we can go to discuss this?"

Reg stood up. "No," he said, his head wobbling. He turned around and walked out.

Gideon watched him through the window until he was out of sight and then got up. He saw Reg walk down the street and disappear into a shop. Gideon got into his car and waited, keeping his eyes firmly on the shop front. A few minutes later, Reg emerged. Gideon stayed some distance behind him. Reg walked a few blocks and then got into a car. It was probably the one from the other night, but Gideon wasn't sure. Keeping his distance, he drove after him.

Reg got on the motorway, heading south. He drove carefully and predictably as if worried about being stopped by the police. Soon they were out of town, heading south, in the direction of Vereeniging. Gideon wondered where the hell this man was going. A while later, Reg left the main road and headed into the countryside. Soon, the road was virtually deserted and Gideon was forced to drop further and further behind to avoid being spotted.

Eventually, in the distance, he saw Reg's car pull up near a small house on what looked like a farm. Gideon drove past slowly. He could see Reg's car was empty. He continued until he was out of sight and then turned around. He waited a few minutes and then drove past again. Reg's car was still there. The place seemed deserted. Gideon parked behind some trees and got out. Keeping low, he moved quickly towards the house, which was really just a cottage. It was pretty dilapidated and had probably been the servants' quarters. A short distance beyond was the main house. It was much larger and had once been fairly grand. Beyond were buildings that looked like warehouses.

As Gideon closed in, he gave Reg's car a wide berth and approached the cottage from the opposite direction. It was easy to find cover – there were bushes and trees all over the place. He surveyed the cottage slowly from a safe distance. There were windows on three sides, permitting fairly uninterrupted views of the interior. Gideon couldn't see a soul; Reg must have gone over to the main house. Gideon wondered whether to go over there himself or to wait. He looked around. The house wasn't far away but there was a fair bit of exposed ground to cover. He decided to stay put for the moment. Reg had to reappear sometime.

Gideon went around the cottage again. It was definitely empty. He considered trying to get in but he felt more comfortable outside, where he would be able to see Reg coming. He retreated into the bushes nearby and positioned himself so he could see all the access routes.

He hoped Reg would reappear soon; this was the perfect place to shoot him. Gideon was sure he hadn't been seen driving into the area and, because it was Saturday, the people who lived here probably wouldn't be back until the late afternoon. He withdrew the revolver from his ankle holster and opened the chamber cylinder. There was no reason to do this. He knew it was fully loaded.

With the gun in his hands, Gideon suddenly felt uneasy. Until now, he'd been so focused on staying behind Reg without being spotted that he hadn't thought about why he was following him. Now, crouched in the bushes, he was feeling tense and nervous again like the other night. He clenched his teeth. This time, it would be different; this time, he was ready. He'd held this gun in his hands for hours every day for a week. He knew exactly what it felt like to fire it; how it would react, how softly it kicked. At home, he'd spent ages in front of the mirror, pulling back the hammer, squeezing the trigger five times in quick succession.

As he sat there waiting, trying to ward off the tension, Gideon wondered how best to handle the actual moment. It was too risky to try and hit Reg from the bushes – he'd probably miss him completely – but if Reg saw him coming, he might pull a gun himself. The best thing would be to surprise him; to approach him from behind and get close enough so that he could shoot Reg at point-blank range. Then he would say something and, as Reg turned around, he'd shoot him. He would aim low, for Reg's gut, so that he survived the first shot. He wanted to tell Reg why he was going to kill him.

It would be much easier and safer, just to blow the bastard away without warning – to shoot him in the back. But that was a coward's way, and Reg had to know why he was about to die. This was so important that it almost seemed not worth killing him, if it wasn't possible to tell him first why he was about to die. Gideon had to get that message across to Reg before he finished him off.

Suddenly, he caught sight of Reg coming over from the warehouses. Making sure the safety catch of the gun was off, Gideon moved towards the cottage. He used the bushes for cover until he was hidden by the building and then silently sprinted to the wall without windows. He couldn't see him now but it was obvious that he'd been heading towards the cottage rather than towards the car. Gideon edged his way along the wall towards the corner of the building. He would wait there and, as soon as he heard Reg opening the door, he would lean around the corner and shoot him. Gideon waited. After a few moments, he realised he was holding his breath. He gently let some air out of his nostrils. He listened again. There wasn't a sound. He started to breathe again. Where the fuck was Reg? Gideon leaned as close to the corner of the cottage wall as he dared, straining to hear. Maybe Reg had gone back.

It was taking too long; he should have been there by now. Gideon couldn't decide what to do. Should he retreat back to the bushes or look around the corner? What if Reg was standing right there? Angry at himself, Gideon straightened up and looked around the corner. There was no-one there. He moved forward slightly. Reg was nowhere to be seen; he must have gone back to the warehouses. Gideon retreated back into the bushes. He was shaking so much that he squatted down on his haunches and put the gun back in its holster. This was ridiculous. He'd gone over this so many times in his head. He'd imagined so many things: the bullet missing Reg, Reg pulling a gun, Reg running away, Reg writhing in agony on the ground after being shot; but he'd never imagined that the biggest problem was going to be finding the bastard in the first place. He should have killed him on the road that night. It would have been the perfect opportunity.

Gideon heard a sound behind him. He turned around. Reg was standing there, partly hidden by a bush, with a gun in his hand.

"Up!" he said, beckoning Gideon with the gun.

Gideon got up slowly.

Reg stood there motionless. He wasn't pointing the gun at

Gideon, just holding it in front of him, with the barrel pointing in Gideon's general direction. Gideon could see it was a revolver – a big one. Far larger than the .38 on his ankle.

Reg moved the gun, indicating that Gideon should come towards him. At the same time, he was walking backwards very slowly and carefully. Reg kept moving until they were out of the bushes.

"What do you want?" he said. It sounded like he didn't care if he got an answer.

Gideon's mouth was so dry he could hardly breathe. He tried to say something but only a raspy breath came out. He couldn't think of anything to say.

Reg walked right up to Gideon and then seemed to change his mind. He turned as if to move back again. As his body changed position, the side of his gun suddenly smashed against the side of Gideon's face. Gideon didn't even see it coming. The blow sent him sprawling backwards to the ground. For a few seconds, he lay there stunned, not sure what had happened. There was no pain.

Reg stood there looking down at him. Time seemed to be going very slowly. Gideon felt a bit like a spectator, as if he wasn't part of this performance being played out in front of him. After a few moments, he noticed Reg waving the gun at him, beckoning him to get up again. Now he was starting to feel the side of his face. It felt heavy and strange, as if something was glued on to the side of his head. The skin felt sunburnt, the flesh numb, as if he'd being lying on that side and his cheek had fallen asleep. But still there was no pain. He slowly got to his feet.

Reg moved towards him. Instantly, Gideon's arms shot up to protect his face and he dropped into a crouching position. Reg jumped backwards quickly. Gideon was surprised; he hadn't meant to do that, he hadn't even been aware of doing it. It had just happened. His body had acted independently of him.

Gideon looked up into Reg's face. The man's eyes were more alive than before. He was watching Gideon intently. It was like having a snake slithering around you, waiting for the right moment to strike.

Reg moved towards Gideon again. He was moving very carefully, as if he was afraid of something. Slowly, Gideon rose until he was standing upright again. Now he was looking down at Reg, staring into his eyes. He realised the man was afraid – of him. Gideon was surprised.

"Why are you following me?" Reg said. He waved the gun at Gideon. The move was menacing.

Gideon's face was starting to hurt. The skin felt like it was burning and the flesh was throbbing. His skull felt hollow. Reg lifted the gun and pointed it directly at Gideon's face. Slowly, he pulled back the hammer.

Gideon looked into the barrel, then into Reg's eyes. Suddenly, it dawned on him that Reg was about to kill him. Gideon's stomach went cold; it was as if his entire midriff had turned to ice.

He saw the muscles in Reg's arm tighten. His eyes had turned into slits.

Gideon felt his legs starting to wobble. He took a deep breath. "I think you're my father," he said. It came out as a whisper. He said it again, louder.

Reg's head twitched ever so slightly. His eyes opened a fraction.

"Who are you?" Reg demanded, loudly. He was still pointing the cocked gun at Gideon.

Gideon stared into Reg's eyes. "My name is Gideon Mathonsi." He paused, swallowing. "My mother is Grace Mathonsi."

Reg stood slightly more upright and stared at him hard.

Gideon quickly told him the story he'd heard in the shebeen so many years ago. It was easy to tell, easy to be convincing; he'd believed it himself for half his life.

"What does your mother say?" Reg was still holding the cocked gun, but he had lowered his arm; the barrel was pointing at the ground.

"I never told her."

Reg inspected Gideon. "You don't look like me," he said.

They faced each other for a while in silence.

"Why did you come looking for me?" Reg asked.

"I don't know. I just wanted to see you."

Reg's eyes dropped. Standing there, he suddenly looked awkward and uncomfortable; like a man who'd stumbled into the wrong place and just wanted to get away. He stood there for a while longer, then released the hammer of the gun and stuffed the weapon into the back of his trousers.

Gideon could feel the revolver against his ankle. He looked at Reg. He'd disarmed him. He would be able to kill him now. All he had to do was get the gun out of his ankle holster.

Reg was still facing him but he wasn't looking at him. Suddenly, he looked tired and small. He seemed to have turned into a little old man.

"Do you have any family?" Gideon asked him.

Reg shook his head, then he looked at Gideon in the face again, hard.

"I don't think I'm your father," he said, shaking his head.

Gideon shook his head. "No, I don't think so."

Reg turned away. He hesitated for a moment, as if he wanted to say something else, then walked off, back to his car.

Watching Reg, Gideon slowly lifted his foot off the ground and prepared to grab the gun. He stood there on one leg for a moment, but his hand wouldn't move. He didn't want to kill Reg anymore. His face was hurting. He just wanted to go home.

Gideon watched him go. It would be so easy to kill him now; he could shoot him right in the back.

Gideon started walking back to his car. He heard Reg start the vehicle behind him and drive away. Gideon stopped, but he didn't look around. He just stood there waiting for the sound of Reg's car to fade away.

Gideon got behind the wheel and looked across at the passenger seat. Suddenly, it hit him. Rosemary was never coming back. His eyes started to sting.

He clenched his teeth and roughly wiped his sleeve across his eyes. The thought that he was never going to see her again was making him feel sick. He clenched his teeth harder, then harder; so hard that it felt like they might shatter. He started the car.

As he looked into the rear-view mirror, the first thing he saw was Lydia's car seat. The tears came flooding back with a vengeance. Now he was missing his children. Now he wanted to be at home, with his children. It was ridiculous; he'd seen his children that morning. He pushed down hard on the accelerator and dropped the clutch. The car's rear wheels spun in the dust. For a few seconds, he struggled to keep control of the car as it veered wildly towards the road.

He slammed on the brakes as the front wheels hit the Tarmac and stopped. His mother was right; he was a shit father and he'd been a shit husband. He'd never given anything of himself to his wife or his children, and now for Rosemary it was too late. She hadn't deserved him. He'd been so obsessed with killing Reg that he hadn't even realised his wife was dead. He'd hardly noticed the funeral; Belinda had organised everything. Rosemary had deserved someone better; someone like his father.

He banged his forehead against the steering wheel and started crying. Then there was his mother; he'd spent half his life blaming her for being something she wasn't, then he'd been so obsessed with killing her rapist that he'd forgotten to forgive her. Now that he had forgiven her, he hadn't even told her.

For the first time, it was painful to be away from his family; it hurt more than anything, more than his damaged face. He thought back to the children's births, then to Lydia's and Joshua's first day at school. He'd pretended to be happy about those things, pretended he'd given a damn, but he hadn't – not really. Those moments had hardly touched him. He'd missed his children's first years – when they were turning into the people they were – and he'd been there all the time. *He* should have died, not Rosemary. It would have better for his children if he'd been the one who'd died.

For a while, he sat there sobbing like a baby, unable to believe what a shit person he'd turned out to be. His wife had been a good woman and a good mother. His parents had been decent, respectable people. His mother had done everything – given everything – to bring him up properly, despite the best efforts of the rapists and the racists, and he had let them all down.

He stared at Lydia's car seat in the mirror. Maybe it was meant to be this way; his mother always said things happened for a reason. If he had died, Rosemary would have taken the kids back to Europe and they would have grown up into Europeans. Now they would be Africans – half-Africans. It was strange to think that they were half-European; that he was the father of half-whites. If he was honest, it had bothered him, but maybe it didn't matter. They were coloured, that was all. What was wrong with that? Maybe one day, with all the mixing that was going on, everyone would be coloured. Maybe it would be better that way.

He got back on the road.

CHAPTER 23

The whore from the hill

Sam stared out of his wall at Manhattan. It was only lunchtime, but he was going to have a drink – he deserved one. He went to the drinks cabinet and poured a shot of whisky down his throat.

Everything had fallen apart. He'd spent a lifetime holding it all together, and in the space of two lousy weeks, the whole thing had unravelled like a homemade sweater. There was no chance now that Rosemary's kids were ever going to be able to run the business; not with a loser like that as a father. The bastard hadn't done an honest day's work in his entire life. What the hell was wrong with the world? These kids weren't interested in anything anymore. In his day, getting somewhere – doing something with your life – was the whole point. To him and every other able-bodied male of his generation, that had been the point. Now it was different; these youngsters didn't give a shit about anything.

You only had to pick up a newspaper or turn on the TV to see where it was all heading. It was scary. The Chinese were already calling the shots in much of Asia and Africa. What the bastards lacked in creativity they made up for with sheer ruthless persistence.

Sam went back to the wall and stared out at the skyscrapers. Between the wankers on Wall Street, the whores in DC and the bible punchers down south, America's only hope was that the Chinese might still screw things up on their own. It wasn't impossible – they'd screwed it up before – but it wasn't something you wanted to count on. When the hell was America going to wake up? Half the country had their heads up their asses, and the other half were hell-bent on handing the economy over to the whores. It was as if the Cold War had never happened.

Even Mary was losing the plot. Since Rosemary had died, she'd gone all religious, lighting candles and mumbling prayers all the time. It was like living with a neurotic nun. What the hell was the point in praying for a dead person? It was the living who needed help. He supposed Mary would calm down again once the shock had worn off. She was probably over-compensating because her faith in God had been shaken, which wasn't surprising. What kind of God allowed a sweet, innocent little creature like Rosemary to be murdered like that? She'd never harmed a fly. Christ, she wasn't even forty. God – God, schmod! He, It, Whatever, was something else you couldn't count on.

Sam's mother used to say the good die young, but that was only because young people who died hadn't had time to turn bad. The younger they were, the better they were. Why couldn't someone else have died? Someone old, someone who wouldn't be missed – someone like that bastard, George?

Sam downed another shot of whisky. He'd thought George was different, but the swine had turned out to be just like all the other whores on the hill. For years, he'd been happy to collect a pay-check for putting in the odd appearance at board meetings, but as soon as he was needed, as soon as he might have been able to do something vaguely useful the bastard had got cold feet and gone running for the hills.

Sam picked up the whisky bottle and looked at it. What kind of scumbag resigned at a time like this? No explanation, no apology, after all those years. Just fuck you, Sam. The only thing George gave a damn about was his precious little reputation. When it came to saving face, he was worse than the Chinese.

Sam waved the bottle to and fro, watching the liquid slosh around inside. He'd had two on a virtually empty stomach. He wanted another to calm him down, but he was buggered if he was going to let George get the better of him. George owed him. He should have told the bastard that when he resigned. He should have told him a lot of things – like there were worse things to be caught doing than sitting on the board of a company facing bribery charges – but when George dropped his bombshell, Sam had been so stunned he hadn't been able to think of anything to say.

Sam looked at the phone. Maybe he should call the bastard and give him a piece of his mind. No, what he needed to say to George had to be done face-to-face. Sam looked at his watch. He'd better do it now. As much as he hated him, he still needed the bastard. Sam picked up the phone and told his secretary to organise the jet.

Two hours later, he was standing outside George's front door. He hadn't been to George's for a long time. He hadn't been invited for a long time. He rang the bell. A few seconds later, George opened the door.

"Come in," George said cheerfully, shaking Sam's hand warmly. It was like nothing had happened.

Feeling self-conscious, Sam walked into George's study and allowed himself to be ushered to one end of a brown leather sofa. The room made Sam feel claustrophobic. It was like a library; not large, but the walls were covered with bookcases that stretched almost to the ceiling. There were books everywhere; not the leather-bound, expensive editions that rich people normally have decorating their studies, but real books – books that George obviously read and probably re-read. Sam couldn't remember when he'd last read a book. He only ever read summaries of business books, and usually he had trouble concentrating on those.

George put a glass of whisky down on the table in front of Sam and sat down on the same sofa with a drink of his own.

His body was turned sideways so he was facing Sam. He seemed completely composed, as unperturbed as ever. Well, they were about to find out just how imperturbable the old senator really was.

"I really am very sorry about everything that has happened, Sam," George said. His tone was sincere; his face earnest. Sam had seldom seen him so serious. It sounded like he genuinely gave a shit. Sam wasn't sure what it was that George was supposed to be sorry about.

Sam picked up his drink and looked at it. Then he put it down again. "You know why I'm here, George."

He waited a few seconds, but no reply came. He turned his head and looked at the old senator. "I've swallowed my pride to come here, George, and you know that's not easy for me."

George just carried on looking at him, saying nothing.

Sam waited a few seconds more. "We need you, George. The company needs you."

George leant forward and put his glass on the table, then leaned back and looked Sam directly in the face. "I've made my decision, Sam."

He stared at Sam very intently. "If I thought there was something I could do – something that would make a difference – I can assure you I would." George waited a few seconds, then leaned forward again and picked up his drink. "I'm sorry to be so blunt and uncompromising, Sam, but I feel I owe it to you to be honest and direct. There's no point in wasting your time."

Sam looked back at the table. "That's a big disappointment."

George said nothing.

"Do you have any advice?"

The corners of George's mouth dropped and he gave a slight shrug. "I assume you're going to do the sensible thing and pay the fine."

"Would you be willing to testify on the company's behalf?" Sam said, continuing to look at the table.

George quickly put his drink down again. "What on earth for?"

Sam turned his head and looked at him. "To explain that, contrary to what the bastards in the media are saying, the company is in fact a professionally run, ethical organisation that has done everything humanly possible to make sure that bribes are not paid; that the law is respected."

He watched George carefully as if daring him to contradict him.

The old senator didn't bat an eyelid. "Sam, we've known each other for a long time, but I don't know anything about how these issues are handled in your company and that's what the court is interested in."

Sam's patience was almost out. "They want to know if we're fucking crooks, for Christ's sake. I'm sure you have an opinion about that!"

George leaned forward and touched Sam's arm. "Think about the questions they would ask me and the answers I would have to give."

Sam's back stiffened. "What answers would you have to give?"

George stood up and poured himself another drink. Sam hadn't touched his.

Sam didn't take his eyes off him. George returned to the sofa, sat down and again positioned himself so he was facing Sam. One arm was on the back of the sofa, the other at his side.

"You know what lawyers are like," he said, smiling.

Sam didn't respond.

George looked down. "Sam, it's a very difficult political environment at the moment, and this case is about as political as it gets."

Sam took a deep breath. "George, I'm a decent, honest, hard-working American. I've given my life to building the kinds of businesses that have made this country what it is. My companies employ thousands of Americans. I pay a fortune in taxes. I need a break here."

George leaned forward. "I agree with everything you've said, Sam, and I would be happy to say that, but the court isn't interested in that."

Sam stared at the floor. He'd hoped George would be reasonable; he'd hoped he wouldn't have to escalate things, but George was obviously too much of a politician. You could count on him to stand next to you when the sun was shining – and run off with your umbrella as soon as it started raining. It would have been bad enough if he'd just refused to testify, but to resign from the board when the company was bogged down in a bribery investigation…

In truth, Sam wasn't surprised, but he prided himself on always giving people the benefit of the doubt. George had been kicking his heels on the board for a long time.

He gave the old senator a long, hard stare – of the kind that sent his managers into paroxysms of panic. "Thank God I'm not a politician," he said. "If I were, my career would have been over long ago."

George frowned. "I wouldn't underestimate how exposed you might be in your position, Sam."

Sam dropped the corners of his mouth. "Well, at least my wife is the only person who would give a damn if she found out that I was sleeping with a hooker."

George exhaled and tilted his head slightly to one side. "Well, there is that, I suppose."

"I expected more from you, George."

"If there is something useful I can do, Sam, I'll do it."

"Testify."

George shook his head. "I understand that you think it's worth a try, but I promise you, it would do more harm than good."

"To you or me?"

George lifted his eyebrows. A gentle smile appeared on his face. "You know full well that I have the company's best interests at heart."

"I haven't done anything wrong, George."

George nodded, bowing his head slightly.

"I'm going to ask you a direct question now, George," Sam said.

George looked up at him.

"Why won't you testify?"

George looked down again.

"I deserve an answer, George."

The old senator swallowed. "Like I said, Sam, I don't know what's going on in your company." He paused and gave Sam a sharp look. "You never told me."

Sam took a deep breath. "You don't trust me!"

George tried not to breathe too audibly. "Think about it, Sam. All I could say on the witness stand is 'I don't know', and that wouldn't look very good – for either of us." George raised a finger before Sam could interrupt. "I'm thinking about you and the company, Sam, whatever you may think." He leaned back.

"So what am I supposed to do?" Sam said.

"Settle it as quickly and as quietly as possible, Sam. You can't win this."

"I expected more from you, George."

George said nothing. He simply glanced out of the window.

"People are out to get me, George!"

George turned and smiled at him. "Exactly, Sam! You've got it. You're being made an example of."

Sam frowned. "And I should just accept that?"

George felt tired. "You don't have a choice." He regretted it the moment he'd said it.

"For God's sake!" Sam exclaimed. "Someone's got to stand up and defend the values that built this country – to inject some realism into that fantasy land on the hill. For Christ's sake, George, politicians used to live in the real world. It was Churchill who said capitalism was the worst of all possible systems except all the others that had been tried."

"Churchill said that about democracy," George muttered before he could stop himself. He sucked in his cheeks and looked away.

Sam stiffened slightly. George smiled at him.

Sam leaned forward. "You think you're so fucking smart and superior, Mr Senator, but that didn't stop you from sharing a hooker with the likes of me."

George's face dropped. His mouth was slightly open.

"I need some help here, George," said Sam, taking a sip of his drink for the first time.

Slowly, George stood up and went to fill his glass. Sam's wasn't low enough for a refill. He came back to the sofa and sat down.

"Sam, I have an idea," he said cheerfully. "Let's start again. Let's pretend this conversation never happened and that you've just walked into this room. Do you think that would be possible?"

Sam opened his mouth, then closed it again. He picked up his glass and drained the rest of it with one gulp.

"I don't want to waste your time either, George."

George bit his lips together momentarily and then sat down.

"For the last time, George, will you testify on my behalf?" Sam asked.

George shook his head.

Sam stood up. "Well, then there's nothing more to discuss."

George stayed on the sofa. "May I ask what you plan to do now?"

Sam gave him a hard stare. "I'm going to sleep on it!"

George stood up. "Don't do anything you'll regret, Sam."

"What, you mean like screw a hooker?"

George looked slightly amused, as if he'd got the reaction he'd expected. He finished his drink and stood up. "Do you honestly think I would sleep with a prostitute?" His tone was a mixture of incredulity and mirth.

Sam looked at him suspiciously.

George grinned at him. "Don't worry, Sam, it's not about

morality." George moved closer. "I'm an intellectual – as you never failed to point out – and we all know that an intellectual is someone who has discovered something more interesting than sex."

George put his hand on Sam's shoulder. He seemed in a bit of a daze. George eased him forward and gently marched him to the front door.

"Don't lose sleep over the bribery charges," he said, as he took Sam's hand. "The only thing you're going to lose is money and, God knows, you have plenty of that."

He watched Sam walk down the stairs to the car. Businessmen were like dogs: they could feed themselves, but left to their own devices, they soon wound up in the gutter.

George went back inside and shut the door. He chuckled to himself. Sam had really imagined they were sharing that prostitute. He wouldn't have shared a sandwich with him, let alone a woman.

George heard a car door close outside and then footsteps walking up to the front door. It was Mary; he could recognise the sound of her heels.

George walked quickly to his study. He wasn't in the mood for Mary now. He would see her at dinner.

Unusually, she came and found him in his study.

"I just saw Sam leaving," she said, sitting down on the couch. "I haven't seen him for ages and he didn't even wave!"

George handed her a drink and sat down with his own. They were in exactly the same position as he had been in with Sam just minutes before. He was almost surprised that Mary couldn't feel the heat left by Sam's backside.

"What's the matter with him?" she inquired.

"Just business," he said.

Dents appeared in his wife's cheeks. Her lips moved forward into a slightly sulky pout.

"How was your day?" he asked, pleasantly.

She looked down at her lap and inhaled through her nostrils. "Fine." After a few seconds, she looked at George again. "Why haven't we seen Sam for so long?" Now she was smiling, and her tone was inquisitive.

George smiled back. “To be honest, honey, I can’t stand the man.”

“You’ve had an argument,” she said immediately. “What’s wrong?”

George took a sip of his drink. He might as well tell her. Her curiosity was aroused. He would enjoy her disappointment. Women were always disappointed by what men told them. Usually, it was because they didn’t have the juicy details. Today, she would be disappointed because it really was just business.

“I’ve quit his board,” George said. “That’s all.” He stood up and went to refill his glass. He poured the drink and glanced across at her. He’d expected her to change the subject or make her excuses and leave the room, but she just sat there, looking concerned.

“Like I said,” he smiled, “just business.”

“Why?” she asked suddenly. It was a sharp question, as if he’d done something wrong.

He was surprised. Mary had never taken the slightest interest in what he did; she just liked the fact that he was a senator – that he’d been important.

He shrugged. “I’d had enough.”

Her cheeks went in again. “Is his business in trouble?”

“No.”

She looked at the floor. Her face was troubled.

“What is it?” he said. He was still standing at the drinks cabinet.

She didn’t look happy. “I recently bought a lot of shares in Sam’s company,” she said, “on the advice of my financial advisor, who thought you were on the board.”

George couldn’t help being amused. His wife hardly ever took him into her confidence about her financial affairs. She’d never told him how much she was worth, or even where her money was invested. Her secretiveness irritated him slightly; it was as if she didn’t trust him. He didn’t even know how much it cost to run the house. All the finances were handled by people working for her. She knew exactly what his assets were, and where they were. Since the banking crisis, her people had been looking after what was left of his money, too.

Mary was still looking at him.

"It's a perfectly good investment," he said, enjoying himself. "You can have absolute confidence in the opinion of your financial advisor."

She stood up. "I didn't know you were unhappy on Sam's board. Why didn't you tell me?"

"I wasn't sure you even remembered I was on Sam's board."

She looked down. "What am I going to do now?" Her tone was forlorn. She sounded like she'd lost something precious.

He waved a hand at her. "It's better this way, Mary. Now there's no danger of a conflict of interest, and as much as I would like to pretend otherwise, the truth is that my presence on the board didn't make any difference either way."

"How can you say that?" she exclaimed. "You're a senator! There's no-one with anything like your experience and influence on Sam's board."

He smiled at her. "I used to be a senator, Mary. I stepped down from Sam's board because there really is nothing I can do any longer. Staying on would be tantamount to taking the man for a ride."

His wife's mouth mutated into a real pout. She edged closer to him.

George looked down at her. Mary hadn't pouted at him in decades. Once, her pouts had been vaguely cute; now, with her old lips, she just looked grotesque. He'd never understood why women felt the need to pull such faces.

She grasped his upper arm and squeezed it affectionately. "George," she said in a voice that sounded like she might be in the mood for more than talking.

He smiled down at her, wishing she'd go off and do whatever it was she did at this time of day. "What is it, honey?"

"Who's going to look after poor little Mary's investment?" she said. It sounded like she was reading aloud from a children's book.

He grinned at her. "Don't worry about it, honey. Sam might not be that accomplished with a knife and fork, but he's very good with money."

She pushed out her lower lip and stared at him with eyes that were something between seductive and sad. She looked like a labrador.

"Mary's going to lose money and it's all going to be George's fault," she said. Her lips were trying to sustain the pout.

He raised his eyebrows and looked down at her. It was a strain to keep the smile on his face.

"Stay on Sam's board, Georgy. Do it for your little Mary." She was still speaking in that same irritating, childish tone.

George ran his tongue around his teeth. This was unexpected. He'd prepared the ground impeccably, as always, before breaking the news to Sam. He'd never imagined Mary was going to have an opinion about it.

She stood up on her tiptoes and kissed him on the cheek. Her lips stayed there for a second or two, pressed against his face. Her mouth was slightly open and he could feel the wet undersides of her lips touching his skin.

"Please, Georgy," she said. "Mary will be so grateful."

She took a step back but kept holding on to his arm. He could feel her watching him.

"It's only a few meetings a year," she carried on, "and it would mean so much to me." Her lower lip was protruding. He felt like pushing it back into her mouth.

Then she started smiling; that Sid smile, the one he hated. When she smiled like that, he could see her old father, Sid, grinning out of her face.

The 'frozen food king', they'd called him, because he'd made his fortune in frozen fish and vegetables. George would never forget the day Sid died. It had been one of the best days of his life.

"I'll think about it," he said, smiling back at her.

Instantly, Mary jumped as if someone had stuck a welcome finger into the back of her. "Oh, thank you, Georgy!" she squealed. "Thank you."

She leaned forward and kissed him again on the cheek, then she daintily retrieved her handbag from the sofa and glided out of the room.

George stared out of the window at the trees. The glass in his hand was empty. He went and poured himself another drink. He couldn't remember whether this was his third or his fourth. He'd better make it his last.

He'd call Sam tomorrow and tell him he'd had a change of heart. Sam wouldn't believe him, but he'd take him back all the same. He didn't have a choice. None of them did. George drained his glass and reached for the bottle. One more wouldn't hurt.